Confessions

Tattoos and Tears
Book 3
By Amiee Louise

This is a work of fiction. Similarities to real people, places, or events are entirely coincidental.

CONFESSIONS

First edition. October 2, 2025.

ISBN: 978-1968759278

Written by Amiee Louise.

1

Sam

I come around in an all-too-bright room, the dull beep of the machines rings in my ears and my head is pounding.

"Marley, darling, he's awake." My mum's soft, soothing voice breaks through my consciousness, and I look around the room with wide eyes. "Sam, sweetie."

She takes my hand and kisses my knuckles. The tenderness makes my eyes glaze over, and I know I don't deserve an ounce of sympathy.

"Mum?" I rasp.

"I'm here darling, I'm here." She strokes my hair and a solitary tear slips down my cheek. "You gave us all a scare, sweetie, what the hell were you thinking?" She says sharply, and my dad shakes his head.

"Lori, not now, my love."

I am silently grateful for my dad's intervention. The door opens and, a nurse steps into the room. She is a short, plump, older lady with short blonde greying hair and warm kind hazel eyes.

"How are you feeling, Mr. Newbolt?" She says in a West Country accent and, I look at her.

"Please, call me Sam."

She nods and smiles earnestly.

"How are you feeling, Sam?"

I shrug, and I suddenly feel the overwhelming urge to vomit.

"*Shit!* I'm going to be sick." The nurse holds a grey cardboard bowl out for me and, I vomit violently. "*Christ*, I'm sorry."

She smiles.

"No bother, my lovely, it's all perfectly normal," She says brightly. She pours some water into a glass and hands it to me.

"Thank you, I appreciate your kindness, but I don't deserve it."

I take a long drink of water and drain the glass, relishing the cold liquid and soothing my dehydrated throat.

"We all handle grief in different ways, my love, but we're going to keep you in for a few days, just for observation."

I nod.

"You have some very loyal fans, Sam, they're camping out outside. We've had to get in extra security to keep the press out too, bloody vultures."

She rolls her eyes and proceeds to take my blood pressure. My mum kisses me on the forehead.

"We're just going to get some coffees and let the boys know you're awake, sweetie."

I nod. My dad brushes my hand in reassurance, and they both leave the room.

"I'm Kate, by the way," the nurse introduces herself, and I smile.

"Pleased to meet you, Kate."

She smiles brightly.

"My daughters and my nieces are huge fans of your band, Sam."

She finishes checking my blood pressure and writes it down on a clipboard.

"Thank you, I'm flattered, we can sign something for them if you would like?" I ask, and she nods.

"That would be lovely, thank you."

I smile.

"The doctor will be in to see you in a little while, my lovely, I'll be back to check on you."

She winks and exits the room, leaving me to my thoughts. After Kate leaves, I doze off, I am not sure how long I am asleep, but when I wake the rest of the band are all sat around my bed. I can't meet Jax's gaze; he has such a haunted look in his eyes, and I feel responsible for it. The sense of guilt that washes over me is overpowering and the silence in the room palpable. Brody breaks the silence.

"What the fuck were you thinking, soppy bollocks?"

With those words, Jax scrapes the chair across the floor; he gets up and leaves the room.

"He's just upset, dude," Lucas says, and I scrub my hands down my face.

"I can't say I blame him, to be honest, mate," I say softly, and I know I have a lot of making up to do. Jax has seen me at my worst, and I will never be able to apologise enough for him finding me like that.

"The press are having a fucking field day. On the plus side, our album sales are up, and we're back at number one in the rock chart. It's fucking amazing what a suicide attempt can do for our careers," Brody jokes, and we all laugh. I realise that this is the first time in days that I have actually laughed, and it feels pretty fucking good, I'm definitely making progress. The door opens, and Kate walks back into the room.

"It's good to see that smile back on your face, Sam, it suits you, my love."

She smiles warmly, and if I'm not mistaken, she actually swoons on the spot at the presence of the other boys.

"Kate, these are my friends and bandmates, Brody and Lucas. Brody, Lucas, this is Kate."

I introduce them, and Brody stands up. He moves over to Kate and kisses the back of her hand.

"Pleased to meet you, Kate, I've always liked a woman in uniform."

He winks cheekily, and I can't resist bantering back.

"Oh, yeah, what was her name?"

Brody smirks.

"Funny fucker, see you haven't lost your charming wit and sense of humour."

I roll my eyes dramatically, and Kate observes the exchange between us, chuckling softly.

"And here's me thinking it was my dazzling personality and my dashing good looks!"

Brody laughs, and his face turns serious.

"Seriously, though, dude, we're glad to have you back, you scared the living shit out of us all."

My face turns serious too.

"I'm sorry," I say softly.

"You ever pull that shit on us again, and I'll fucking bury you myself."

Brody snarls and I nod. Lucas looks at me.

"Give Jax some time, dude, he'll come 'round."

These boys are like my brothers, and I couldn't bear the fact that my selfish actions could potentially cause a rift between us. They say time can be a healer, I can only hope that they're right.

Two days pass in a blur of well-wishers and hospital staff. I am on suicide watch, monitored twenty-four hours a day, and I'm never left alone, not even to use the bathroom or the toilet. When I take a shower, the door is left ajar, and Kate keeps watch outside, asking if I am OK every couple of minutes. Kate has played a significant role in my stay at the hospital. She keeps track of my mood and writes down what and how much I eat. She has been like a mother hen, and I have been grateful for her company and mindless chatter.

I am wearing a hospital gown because any clothing I own that has strings, laces, or belts attached has been confiscated. I have been seeing a counsellor once a day, which has been helping a lot. On the second day, I wake to find Sophia sat next to my bed.

"Sophia?" I rasp, and she leans back in the chair.

"How could you, Sam? How fucking could you? What the fuck were you thinking trying to take your own life, you selfish bastard!"

She snaps, and I don't think I have heard Sophia swear or curse once since I met her.

"You were the love of Peyton's life, and you tried to take that away from us, you selfish, heartless wanker!"

She shouts.

"What the hell would Peyton say? I'm fucking disgusted at what you've done, how could you do that to your poor mum and dad? To us? To your fans? To those boys?" She spits angrily, and her anger shocks me, but it suddenly hits me with crystal clarity. I am overwhelmed by guilt and shame of what I have put those around me through by trying to take the cowards' way out.

"I-I—" I stutter, and she looks at me with disgust.

"Don't you bloody dare say you're sorry, Sam Newbolt!"

She shouts again, and a tear rolls down my cheek, I am disgusted with myself.

"After all you and Peyton went through, you do this. You're a coward Sam, a weak, pathetic, selfish coward. We have already lost our daughter, isn't that enough? You fucking disgust me."

She narrows her eyes at me.

"I'm a disgusting human being, and I can't bear to think that I've caused you and Max any unnecessary pain. I'm sorry, I'm so fucking sorry, I'm so ashamed," I sob. "*Oh, Christ*, oh fuck, I'm sorry, I'm sorry." I sob harder, and the door opens.

"What the fuck is going on, Mum? I could hear you shouting down the corridor." Dexter comes in and observes the situation unfolding in front of him between his mum and me. "*Jesus Christ*, please tell me you haven't, Mum? You didn't-" he says sternly. The door opens, and as Dexter is about to speak again, Kate steps in.

"I'm sorry, but I'm going to have to ask both of you to leave. I can't have my patient put under any unnecessary distress," she says austerely, and I am thankful for her intervention.

"Sam, mate, I'm so sorry," Dexter says, and Sophia narrows her eyes on him.

"Don't you bloody dare apologise for me, Dexter Harper."

Her and Dexter both leave, Kate picks up her clipboard and takes a seat.

"I'm going to have to jot that down, Sam, I'm sorry."

I shake my head and sniff, wiping my eyes on my sleeve.

"It's fine, *Christ*, I'm so ashamed. Everything she said was right."

Kate looks at me sympathetically and places her hand on mine.

"You're mourning a loss, sweetheart, it's understandable."

She writes something down on her clipboard, and I regard her intently.

"I'm just doing my job, my love," she says softly, and smiles. Her warm, compassionate nature has aided my recovery over the past few days, and I will be forever grateful to her. The door taps and Jax walks in. It is the first time I have seen him since he walked out two days ago. Kate turns, and her mouth drops open as she catches sight of Jax in all his blonde tattooed glory. He reminds me of Thor, with his blonde flowing locks and goatee beard. I smirk at the thought.

"Kate, this is my friend and bandmate Jax. Jax, this is Kate."

Jax salutes.

"Kate, pleasure to meet you, babe."

He shakes Kate's hand and winks as she stands up

"I'll leave you boys to it, I'll come back to check on you in a little while, Sam."

She stands up, smiles brightly and leaves the room. I gesture for Jax to take a seat and he sits down.

"Are you actually going to look at me?"

I break the awkward silence that seems to have settled in the room. He lifts his head, and his eyes lock with mine. The haunted look from two days ago has disappeared and has been replaced with one of concern.

"I'm so sorry, Jax."

He shakes his head.

"Do not ever fucking pull that crap on me again, Sam," he says sharply.

"Finding you like that...*fuck*, it was probably the worst thing I've ever witnessed. Finding you in a pool of your own blood, there was so much blood, Sam."

He closes his eyes briefly at the memory and swallows harshly, as if he is swallowing back a lump in his throat.

"I thought ... I thought you were fucking dead. If you felt so low, you could have fucking talked to me, instead of trying to take your own god damn life!"

His eyes are glazed over, and he runs his hands through his hair.

"It's bad enough that I have to listen to my girlfriend crying herself to sleep every night because she misses Peyton so much. It breaks my heart, Sam, it tears me the fuck apart every single time."

This time a tear escapes and rolls down his cheek. My heart clenches at the thought that I am the one responsible for this.

"I couldn't bear the thought of losing my best friend, *my fucking brother*. We might not be related by blood, but you're my family, Sam."

I look up at the ceiling struggling to rein in the emotions that are threatening to overwhelm me.

Breathe, Newbolt.

"I'll never be able to apologise enough for what I put you through, Jax, but ... but I couldn't see another way out, the pain of losing her... it ... *Fuck* ... it consumes me. It hurts so fucking badly, I just wanted it all to stop."

Jax takes a breath and looks at me.

"Do you think she would have wanted this?"

My heart aches at his words, and the truth is, no, she wouldn't have wanted it. Peyton was so full of life, so beautiful on the inside and on the outside. She made my life worthwhile; she made life bearable again for the first time in years. She made me feel alive and to have her so cruelly ripped away from me like that, was more than I could stand. I like to think that I am a strong person but deep down I know I'm weak. I'm weak for wanting to purposely take my own life when she would have given everything to be here with me right now. It is with that thought that I vow to get my life back on track not just for me but for Peyton too. *My Peyton.*

***

A month passes by, and I have been discharged from hospital. A lot has changed in a month. Brody has been admitted to rehab for his out of control drug addiction; it seems Peyton's death hasn't just taken its toll on me. As a band, with J.D's blessing, we have decided to take a year out of the music industry.

Jax and Ruby have finally taken a leap and have moved in together, taking their relationship to the next level. It is so good to see them both happy. Jax is pursuing some solo projects and collaborating with other artists. After the pain of losing her best friend, Ruby decided that life was too precious to waste time regretting things and she has become a permanent fixture to the Rancid Vengeance family.

Lucas has decided to take some well-earned time out and is spending some time in America to pursue his other passions, which are surfing and photography. He always tells me that there is nothing like the rush you experience when you catch a wave. Before the band made it big, Lucas would sell his photographs to pay the bills. His talent goes way beyond drumming, and some of his photography has been used in our album artwork over the past ten years.

I was discharged from hospital two weeks ago, and during that time, I suffered from constannightmares. I wake up drenched in sweat and screaming as a result, I have hardly slept. Everywhere I go in the apartment I am reminded of Peyton; every room holds a special memory of her. The hole she has left in my life has had a significant effect on my mental state.

I have made the decision to sell the building that houses mine, Jax, Cole, and Lucas' apartments. A billionaire by the name of Nolan Wilder, who is looking for a new place in London has shown more than a keen interest in buying the building. I have looked at a few houses on the outskirts of London and have managed to secure a nine-bedroom mansion in Sawbridgeworth, Hertfordshire. A whole hour and a half away from the hustle and bustle of Central London. It is a world away, and I think it the peace and quiet will be good to help me heal.

I have been told that time can be a healer, even though it has only been a month since Peyton's death, there isn't a day goes by that I don't think about her. I believe that you only ever experience true love once in life and my great love was Peyton. *My Peyton.*

2

Sam

1 Year Later

"Vengeance, Vengeance, Vengeance."

The crowd is going absolutely crazy for us, cheering, clapping, and stomping their feet. The chant is so loud, I'm sure I can feel the walls of the backstage area vibrate and shake. It's an amazing feeling to be waiting backstage hearing a crowd of twenty thousand fans eagerly anticipating our comeback gig. It has been a whole year since we have played a live gig.

Jax is tuning his guitar and getting himself in what he likes to call *'the zone'* before we go on stage. Making sure he keeps himself to himself, he doesn't like to be distracted before a gig, he remains the consummate professional. He, however, lets his hair down after a gig; that boy is the biggest party animal I have ever met. Though not so much these days because he is engaged and loved up with Ruby. She is three months pregnant with his baby, and she travels on the road with us when she can. She is a welcome addition to the madness of Rancid Vengeance and a calming female influence on us all.

Lucas impresses his groupies with his stick spinning trick, living up to his stage name *The Axeman*. They're all hanging on his every word and practically falling at his feet. That boy can have the ladies eating out of the palm of his hand with just a look. A look that he has been perfecting over the years and it always seems to work, one hundred percent fail-proof!

Brody, the most eccentric and most unpredictable member of the band, with his newly-shaven head, is nowhere to be seen. He is probably getting laid on the tour bus with one of his many groupies; he calls it *'Exorcising his nerves'*. Brody never fails to amaze me; he is such a talented rhythm guitarist. He can get away with not practising for a show, which is why he spends so much time getting laid and chasing skirt!

Now me, Sam, I'm a completely different story altogether. My heart is pounding, and I'm feeling a little nervous after being away from the spotlight for a whole year. Actually, *fuck* nervous, I feel like am actually shitting a brick!

The night of this gig...I have been dreading it for the whole year. I have been throwing myself into music, writing and recording our new album. In my opinion, it is our best album to date. However, getting up on stage and performing in front of a twenty thousand strong crowd after a yearlong break, it sets my nerves on edge. I stare absent-mindedly at the floor, and I feel myself start to shake uncontrollably. Jax comes over and rests his hand on my shoulder.

"Sam, are you OK, mate?"

By my silence, I know that he understands what it is taking for me to even be here tonight. Even though we are at Madison Square Garden, which is over two and a half thousand miles away from where she was taken and killed, I feel like I'm reliving it all over again.

Get it together, Newbolt, for fuck's sake.

"If you need me, dude, I'll be just down the corridor."

Jax smiles reassuringly, pats me on the back, and leaves. After all of our years of friendship, there is a silent and mutual understanding between us.

I lean heavily on the dressing room table and look at my reflection in the mirror. My stage persona, Bolt, is staring back at me with full stage make-up, black eyeliner, my tight leather trousers, black vest, and black leather waistcoat with angel wings stitched into the back. I am wearing a leather cuff to hide the deep scars on my wrists, chains, and studs, complete with my newly raven-black shaggy spiky hair and customised cowboy boots.

Deep down I don't feel like Bolt right now. Usually, as soon as I get my stage makeup and my stage outfit on, I am instantly transformed into my alter ego Bolt. But, I just feel like the same old Sam. The Sam that lost the woman he was going to marry and the woman who was carrying his unborn child. I reach into the drawer and take out a pill bottle of my anti-depressants, Seroxat. After all these years, I still need them to even drag myself out of bed in the mornings. I take two and wash them down with a bottle of water.

The dressing room door taps softly.

"Sam, it's Ali, are you OK in there, mate?"

Our new manager Alistair, the owner of our record company, shouts from outside the door. J.D disappeared just over six months ago. One day he was there, the next he was gone, disappeared without a trace. None of us have heard from him or seen him in six whole months. I can't say I'm sorry to see him gone because there was never any love lost between us, not after what happened anyway. I look at my reflection in the mirror and paint the old Bolt smile on. I clear my throat and take a deep breath.

"Yeah, I'm OK, mate, just give us a sec."

There is a pause, and I know there is a mutual understanding between Alistair and me. There is a mutual respect and a growing friendship between us, which was never present when J.D managed us. J.D was just our manager; to him, we were a product that made him a lot of money, generated publicity for him and his record company. Alistair is different. He is young, full of ideas and the most laid back person I have ever come across. I will never forget the day he told me the secret he was keeping.

3

Sam

Past

We are in the studio, having just laid down a few tracks for the new album. The rest of the guys went on to some club a while ago, and I said I would join them as soon as I have finished chatting to Alistair. He is so different from J.D, he actually listens to what we want as a band. He gets us in a way J.D doesn't, and he is refreshing to be around. I send a quick text to Peyton promising her I'll see her soon. As I'm putting my phone in my pocket, Alistair comes out of the recording studio and out into the reception area. He sets a glass of amber liquid down on the glass table and sits on the sofa next to me.

"You deserve it, mate."

I laugh, and my phone chirps a response from Peyton. I pull my phone out.

Can't wait to see you baby

I'm waiting at yours

I'll be the one naked and horny! ;)

Love you

P xx

I smile to myself as I read her words. I fucking love her so much, she satisfies a deep need in me to protect her with every ounce of my being. It's crazy I have been with her for such a short amount of time, and she has already reduced me to a shy, quivering mess every time I'm around her. In contrast, I'm a total wreck, pacing up and down like a caged animal when she is not around. I'm totally smitten.

"So how're things with ... Sorry, mate, I'm shit with names!"

Alistair smiles.

"Peyton."

He nods inquisitively.

"Things are going great right now, I'm smitten with her, mate, first time I clapped eyes on her."

I puff out my cheeks and let out a long breath at the memory of the day we met. Alistair crosses his legs at the ankle and takes a sip of his whiskey.

"Make sure you hold onto her mate, treasure those little moments together however insignificant they are. Definitely be one hundred percent honest and totally up front, don't wait to tell her how you really feel."

I look at him and take a sip of my whiskey.

"I won't."

He lets out a breath.

"My fiancée died, and I left it too late to tell her how I really felt and how sorry I was for the way I behaved."

My eyes widen at his revelation.

"I'm so sorry, mate."

I don't want to push him further because the hurt in his eyes is evident.

"We were in a car accident four years ago. I was driving, and I took my eyes off the road for a split fucking second. That split second caused us to crash head-on into a truck and roll into a ditch. She died on impact. I came round in the hospital, and I asked where she was. Before they told me I knew, I knew she was gone."

Alistair pauses, tears pricking at his eyes as he tells me his story. He clearly is hesitant to continue, but he finally does.

"I...I cheated on her with an ex-girlfriend. It's the biggest regret of my life, and I didn't get the chance to make it up to her. We had a son together, Alfie. He is six now. He is growing every single day, and I couldn't bear to look at him in the beginning because he is so much like his mum. I felt so numb, and I remember thinking after she died why her and not me. I survived, and she didn't get to. They call it survivor's guilt; I escaped with a broken leg, a broken wrist, head injury, and a few minor cuts and bruises. I felt so guilty for being the one that survived. I didn't want to live, and I attempted suicide. I'm not proud of that, definitely not my finest hour, but I saw a counsellor for a year because of the flashbacks. But time is a great healer, or so they say; I have a new life now. Lexi and I, we have twin girls, Autumn and Bella. They're two now. I felt so guilty for moving on, and I thought I was betraying Izzy's memory, but I know she would want me to carry on living my life. I feel like I've got a second chance."

I listen to Alistair tell his story intently. Wow, I couldn't ever imagine losing Peyton, I would lose my mind, and she is already my world. She waltzed into my life with her tattoos and feisty personality. I can't begin to comprehend what Alistair must have gone through, and I vow to protect my Peyton with every fibre in my body.

4

Sam

Present

A gentle tap on the dressing room door catches my attention.

"I said I'll be out in a sec, mate."

There is a pause.

"It's me, sweetie, can I come in?"

I hear Ruby's soft, singsong voice and I open the door. She is standing there with her long black hair flowing around her shoulders, her warm hazel eyes, and tiny pregnant bump.

"Ruby."

She smiles and steps into the dressing room. She brushes my arm.

"How are you feeling?"

I nod, and she cocks her head, giving me a knowing look.

"Really?"

I let out a breath.

"A mixture, really."

I flop down onto the sofa and put my head in my hands.

"*Fuck*, I can't do this, Ruby."

She crouches in front of me and takes my face between her hands.

"Sam, look at me, yes you can. Peyton wouldn't want you to be sitting here miserable and brooding. She would want you to go out there and rock the shit out of this place! You know how much your voice affected her, and she loved hearing you sing, she was your biggest fan!"

She chuckles softly, and I look up at her with tears brimming in my eyes.

"*Jesus Christ*, I miss her so fucking much, Rubes. She was my reason to get up on stage, my good luck charm, and now she is gone. It has been a year since we last played a gig. How the fuck can I get up there and sing, when I don't believe in what I'm singing about?"

My hands start to shake uncontrollably again, and she takes my hands in hers.

"I miss her too, babe, so bloody much. I've still got her number stored in my phone. I sometimes call it just to hear her voice on the answering machine, but it's normal to grieve. It's only been a year, no one would expect you to be over her. It takes time... Time can be a healer. That's what all those self-help books say, right?"

I look her in the eyes, and I can see the hurt. That very same hurt that I'm feeling right now. My heart is thundering in my chest, and I'm still shaking.

"How can I go out there and face the fans, Rubes, I'm a fucking mess without her."

A stray tear rolls down my cheek; she wipes it away with her thumb.

"We're all going to be there, front row centre, me and your family. This gig is for her. You need to go out there and give them a show, give her a show, perform for her, show her that you're still the same Sam Newbolt that she fell so in love with."

I stroke her face and she smiles. She gets to her feet, and I stand up, towering over her slight frame. She cuddles me tightly.

"Knock 'em dead, Bolt." She pulls away and winks. "For Peyton," she whispers, and I smile, grateful for the pep talk and the shoulder to cry on.

Christ, I need to get my shit together.

"Thanks, Ruby."

She brushes my arm and blows me a kiss.

"Anytime, babe."

She leaves the dressing room, and I emerge from behind her.

"Have you been hogging my woman, Sammy boy?"

Jax laughs and slaps me on the back. Ruby cuddles him.

"Just giving Sam a well-needed kick up the arse, babe."

She laughs, and Jax squeezes her. My heart constricts seeing the two of them so loved up. I am happy that Jax is finally happy and settled down, but I take a deep breath to quell the jealousy that's bubbling in the pit of my chest.

That should have been Peyton and me.

"Come on, Bolt, let's go and give them a show."

I walk with Jax and Ruby down the corridor, and I can hear the fans screaming for us, the noise is deafening. Ruby kisses Jax, wishes us luck, and leaves to take her seat. Donovan thrusts a microphone in my trembling hand and hands Jax his signature Schechter Blackjack guitar. Lucas is spinning his drumsticks, psyching himself up, and Brody is tuning his guitar.

"Are we fucking ready, boys?" Brody shouts. "Let's rock."

Jax and I go out first and take our places in the centre of the stage. Jax strums the opening guitar riff, and my adrenaline starts pumping. I notice my hands have stopped shaking as I lift the microphone up to my mouth. Seeing the sea of fans instantly suppresses my nerves, and I take a long calming breath before singing the first line of a classic of ours. As I sing the opening line, I feel as if I have never been away from the spotlight. My adrenaline is pumping, and I feed off the crowd's raw energy. I close my eyes and let the lyrics wash over me until I am consumed by the music. I get to the end of the song and step to the front of the stage, looking out at the sea of fans that have turned out here for us tonight.

"Good evening, Madison Square Garden, how the fuck are we doing tonight? We're Rancid Vengeance; it's so fucking good to be back up on stage in front of you all. Are you ready to rock? Let me hear you scream 'hell yeah.'"

The crowd breaks out into a rapturous *hell yeah*, and a grin spreads across my face.

"Yeahhh! Let's fucking rock this place to the ground, give me a riff, Flash."

I growl, and Jax breaks out into an impressive guitar solo, his flawless guitar skills never fail to impress me. He gives me a wink of encouragement; Brody joins in and moves fluidly across the stage to stand back to back with Jax. Lucas pounds a drum beat, and I start to sing.

"I am lost to the music, lost to the void, lost to my eternal fucking sadness. Somebody, please throw me a lifeline."

I lose myself in the music, closing my eyes, letting the lyrics wash over me. As I hit the chorus Jax's signature guitar riff fills the venue. I open my eyes, looking out at the sea of fans singing back to us and holding banners up for us. That's when I see her, this woman staring intently at me. She has short red hair; she is wearing a red Rancid Vengeance hoodie, leather shorts, and a black beanie hat. She isn't cheering, singing or moving to the music, she is just standing still, her hollow eyes are focussed solely on me. She notices me staring back at her, and she starts to move through the crowd. She moves exactly like Peyton. I freeze on the spot. It can't be, it can't possibly be her. *Can it?*

5

Sam

My heart is thundering in my chest, and I somehow manage to make it to the end of the song, whilst frantically scanning the crowd for another glimpse of her. In my fucked up brain, I actually start to question my own sanity.

Is this the moment where I lose the plot completely? Where I start to see things that aren't really there?

I pull out my earpiece and step away from the microphone towards Jax.

"I think I've just seen, Peyton."

Jax pulls out his earpiece.

"Sam, mate, you're just nervous that's all. The first gig back after a year out...It's just stress, trust me, *please* you have to stop fucking torturing yourself."

He brushes my arm in reassurance. I run my hands through my hair and sprint across the stage, towards where Cole is standing.

"Cole, I think I've just seen Peyton, find her now," I say sternly, and it isn't a request. He looks at me as if I have lost my mind. *Why won't these people fucking believe me?*

"I'm on it, Sam."

He nods curtly, speaking into his earpiece. I stride back onto the stage, resuming my position at my microphone and replacing my earpiece.

"I apologise for the fuck up, we were experiencing a few technical issues. This next song is a new one for us, it's going to be featured on our new album, and it's the first time we have performed it live. It's called *My Private Hell*, and I hope you all like it. Give me a beat Axeman."

Lucas tosses his sticks into the air, catches them effortlessly, and pounds a relentless drum beat. The crowd goes wild, and my adrenaline starts pumping. This is what I have missed. Feeding off the audience's raw energy is what drives me. I soak in their pure elation as I reach deep into their souls with each lyric I sing. We all perform each song as if it will be our last, and as the first half reaches a close, I feel as if we have never been away. As we make our way backstage, a passing stagehand hands me a towel and a bottle of cool water. I take a long pull from the bottle, and Brody rushes to catch up with me.

"What the *fuck* was that all about, dude?"

I look at him.

"It was her, Brody, I fucking know it."

He places his hand on my arm in a gesture of support. He is about to speak when Cole strides towards us and stops in front of us.

"We can't find her, Sam. We've scanned every inch of the venue, are you absolutely sure it was her?"

I scrub my hands down my face, and I start to doubt myself.

Get it the fuck together, Newbolt, you're losing the plot.

"I was so fucking sure it was her," I whisper, more to myself than anyone else.

"Fuck me, dude, you need to get laid!"

Brody laughs, and I start to think that maybe he is right, because right now, I am in serious danger of being carted out of here in a fucking straight jacket. Brody takes his smartphone out of his pocket and swipes the screen with his finger.

"I'll give Amber a call, this sassy little redhead I know. She told me to look her up if we were ever back in the area. She can hook us up with a few hotties."

He winks and strides off down the corridor. *Typical Brody.* His heart's in the right place, fucking shame his brain isn't. As the second half of the show begins, we pull out all the stops. We share some cheeky banter with each other, interact with the audience and pull a few fans out of the crowd to join us on stage.

"Madison Square Garden, you're looking fucking beautiful out there tonight."

The crowd breaks out into frenzied screams, and I grin widely, revelling in their excitement. I step to the front of the stage and put my hand to my ear, they scream louder. Over the past ten years, I have perfected the art of commanding an audience, and it feels pretty fucking good to hold that power over them. As I scan over the sea of fans a girl holding up a banner catches my eye which reads *'I love you Bolt, you inspire me'* I smile at the dedication of our fans.

"Wow, boys that girl back there says I inspire her!"

The rest of the boys chuckle.

"Sweetheart, there isn't a day goes by that we aren't thankful for all your support. Your dedication inspires us, and you're our inspiration to keep coming back and making music for you all. Because if it wasn't for you, we wouldn't be up on this stage in front of you now. You've stuck with us through everything, and we love you all."

The girl with the banner is jumping up and down excitedly and tears are streaming down her cheeks. I blow her a kiss and give her a wink; she practically melts in a puddle at the gesture.

"Now, that's enough of that soppy shit, let's give these guys a show to remember," I growl, and the crowd gets louder as Jax moves across the stage to stand back to back with Brody.

Jax strums a riff, and Brody matches him. Seeing the two of them play so effortlessly together brings a smile to my face. These boys are like my family, and I'm grateful for everything they have done for me over the past eleven years. We are like brothers, and we have seen each other through some of the greatest and worse times of our lives.

It is almost the end of the second half and the finale of our show. We have made every effort to impress and have put one million percent into every performance. We all come alive when we are on stage, and we complement each other musically. As a band, we have perfected our craft over the years, and we fit together like a musical jigsaw. We are all sweating abundantly from jumping around the stage, and I am actually starting to enjoy myself. I have missed being in the spotlight after our year away.

"Madison Square Garden, you've been fucking amazing this evening, you're all beautiful. This is our last song of the night, and this is the song that put us where we are today, so we're going to fucking rock the shit out of it!"

The crowd roars.

"This is *'Corrupted'*, give me a beat, boys."

My heart is pounding, and my adrenaline is coursing through my body. I lift the microphone to my lips, and we rock as we have never rocked before. As the song draws to a close, we all come together at the front of the stage.

"We've been Rancid Vengeance, hope you all enjoyed the show, goodnight and keep fucking rocking."

We all salute and exit the stage. We all remove our earpieces and move down the corridor towards the dressing room. As we enter the dressing room, we are all totally pumped after the show. We all pop open some beers, and we all gather round to make a toast.

"Welcome back, boys!"

Brody shouts, and we all clink our bottles together.

"Let's go out and fucking celebrate."

I take a long pull on my beer.

"I don't know about you fuckers, but I need a shower."

Brody chuckles.

"Aww, I didn't know you felt that way about us, dude!"

We all laugh, and I love the banter we have between us, I wouldn't have it any other way. I consider myself lucky to have these boys in my life, and I'm grateful for their friendship.

The rest of our entourage entering the room followed by my family and Ruby interrupts us. They all congratulate us on an epic show, and as I observe their animated conversations, my phone vibrates, signalling a text message. I pick it up from the table and swipe my finger across the screen. The message is from an unknown number.

The person who kidnapped me is close to you

Meet me at West 110th Street

Near the Blockhouse at Central Park

Come alone

Peyton x

My eyes widen, as I read the message and my blood chills in my veins. *What the fuck?* Willing my legs not to buckle underneath me, I tuck my phone in my pocket, and I make eye contact with Jax, who is looking at me questioningly. I ignore him and stride purposefully out of the dressing room. The text message is really from Peyton, and it was really her in the crowd. She is alive, I know she is. A smile spreads across my face at the thought; I am going to get the opportunity to hold her in my arms once again. As I make my way down the corridor, I see Donovan pushing an equipment case, and I call out to him.

"Donovan."

He spins around.

"Sam, how's it hanging, mate?"

I nod.

"Yeah, all good, thanks, look, dude, I need a favour?"

He smiles and nods enthusiastically.

"'Course, man, go for it."

I clear my throat.

"I need a car."

He nods.

"Here, take the keys to my bike; it's parked in the underground garage."

I am impressed. *We should really make more effort to get to know the people who work for us.*

"I didn't know you were into bikes?"

Donovan grins at my interest.

"Yeah, man, I always hire a bike when we come on tour. I like to ride on my days off."

I nod and smile as he hands me the keys to his motorbike. *Jackpot.*

"Cheers, man, I owe you one."

I wink, and he grins.

"Anytime, dude."

I walk through the corridor and down a flight of stairs into the private underground parking garage. I click the key fob and the lights flash, I use that to locate the bike which is parked in a lone bay. It is a shiny lime green and black Kawasaki Ninja 300. *Nice.* I make my way over to the bike, fasten on Donovan's black skull helmet, put the keys in the ignition and start up the bike. A few moments later I'm roaring out of the underground garage and into the busy New York traffic. I have a loft apartment in Soho, Manhattan so I navigate the New York traffic like a pro and make it to my destination in ten minutes.

My heart is thundering in my chest at the prospect of seeing her again. I have so many questions I want to ask her, so much I want to tell her; most importantly, I just want to hold her in my arms. A part of me is angry that she let me and everyone else think she was dead, but another part of me is relieved and happy that she is really alive. I slow down as I approach my destination and come to a stop at the side of the road. I dismount the bike and kick the kickstand into place. I pull off my helmet, hooking it to the handlebar and I walk slowly down the street, scanning the area cautiously as I go. With every step, my heart beats that bit faster, and I tuck my hands in the pockets of my leather trousers. I make my way to the place where the text message said, and I look around. Every sense I possess is on high alert, and I can't help but feel like something is off. The area is dark and dimly lit, I feel a sharp blow to the back of my head, and everything is plunged into darkness.

6

Peyton

Past

"Please, please just stop."

I sob, but I know it won't do any good. That is all I can think. I have never wanted to die as much as I do right now. *Please, just put me out of my misery, and fucking kill me now.* I am in so much pain, I can't see straight. My vision is blurred, my head is spinning, I can feel the warm trickle of blood running down various parts of my body, and my whole body feels like it is shutting down.

How the fuck did I even get here? How the fuck did we get here, boo? You are the only one who is keeping me going right now, you are the one keeping me sane, and keeping me fighting. I will not give up boo, I promise you. I am imagining your tiny fingers wrapped around mine, your sparkling green eyes like your daddy's, and your sleepy dimpled smile, as you look up at me so helplessly, loving me unconditionally. You are my shining light, my reason not to give up, and my reason to keep breathing. In, out, in, out...that's it. Come on, focus.

"Wake the fuck up, bitch." His sharp slap to my face jolts me back to the here and now. His wide beady eyes come into focus, he is enjoying this. He is enjoying watching me suffer. "Are you ready for some more, bitch?"

His maniacal laugh echoes throughout the room, and I try in vain to struggle against my restraints. I think my wrist is broken, and the cable ties are biting into my skin.

"Stop struggling, whore," he says venomously, as I feel the back of his hand connect with my face. "I'm not done with you, not by a fucking long shot. I want to watch you suffer, I want him to see you take your last breath."

I shake my head, and my stomach roils as I think of Sam. Was anything he ever said to me true, or was it all just a horrible lie?

"No, no, no, please don't do this," I plead. I always plead, but it doesn't seem to get through to him. He is so hell-bent on breaking me, on watching me suffer, all because he is so blinded by jealousy.

"He'll be upset for a while, but he'll get over you, he'll be back to his usual self in no time at all. A leopard never changes its spots, sweetheart, he'll be back to a different girl every night, or he might even end up in my bed. Although he kept you around longer than the others, he never really wanted you, not really. You were just a distraction, something pretty to fill the time," he spits, and I can see him trembling with pure blind rage, on the cusp of losing it completely. This is it; he is going to kill me.

"JUST FUCKING KILL ME NOW," I scream hysterically, and he laughs bitterly.

"Kill you? Oh, sweetheart, you're deluded. Killing you would just be too easy. I planned on having a little fun first. We're going to make a little film, you and me."

He strokes my face, and I shudder as his fingers make contact with my skin. I feel physically ill, and he makes my skin crawl.

Grow some balls; do not under any circumstances show weakness, your mum, and dad bought you up better than that.

"I'm not fucking scared of you." I choke out defiantly, and he is so close to me now, I can feel his warm stale breath on my cheek.

"Oh, I think you're way beyond scared, darlin', you're fucking terrified, just the way I want you," he whispers.

He moves his hand, and I can see the glistening of the blade. *Oh God no.* He runs the back of the blade down my cheek, and I am trembling with such fear now. I can't take it anymore.

"I can smell your fear now, and it's fucking exquisite," he says in an eerie, melodic voice.

I struggle against my restraints again, and I sob hard,

"Please, please, please don't do this."

"God, I love it when you beg, when you plead with me, please, please don't do this," he mocks. He moves over to the camera set up on a tripod in the corner of the room, and a red light appears, as he presses record.

"Showtime, sweetheart." He laughs, with a sadistic glint in his eyes.

I am not going to survive this, not this time. I love you boo. I am so sorry...

7

Sam

Present

I look up, and my whole world comes back into focus. My eyes widen in complete and utter shock, as I recognise the figure in front of me.

"*You?* What the fucking fuck?"

My head is still fuzzy from the bash on the head, but I would recognise that face anywhere. *J fucking D.*

"Surprise!" he says, in a singsong voice and laughs maniacally.

My head is throbbing, and I am tied to a wooden chair, with cable ties. I struggle to get my arms and legs free, but there is no give at all. He circles and stops in front of me, with his hands behind his back. His wide beady eyes regard me with rapt interest. His hair is dishevelled, and he is wearing an off-white shirt with the sleeves rolled up, dirty jeans, and scuffed trainers. He is so close, I can feel his warm, alcohol breath on my cheek. I try to focus on my surroundings and realise I am in some sort of derelict warehouse. There is a wooden table to his right, and the only light in the room comes from the moonlight filtering through the windows.

"What the fuck is going on?" I say in a confused tone, my fuzzy brain still struggling to comprehend the situation I currently find myself in.

He removes his hands from behind his back, revealing a sharp, serrated combat blade, which is at least six inches long, and moves towards the table. Suddenly, he slams the knife violently into the table top. After all the times I watched that DVD repeatedly, as the hooded figure plunged a large menacing combat blade into Peyton's chest, I would recognise that knife anywhere.

"*You!* This was all you! You sick fuck!"

I am totally and completely stunned. *Fuck me, this is not happening.*

"It was me, all of it was me! Don't you see, Sammy? It was me all along!"

He laughs, and suddenly my whole world starts spinning. I am in freefall, and I feel like I need to vacate my guts all over the floor. *Breathe, Newbolt, in through the nose, out through the mouth.*

"It was meant to end this way!"

What the fucking fuck is he talking about?

He dances around me, laughing maniacally, and I think he has finally lost the plot. He taps my cheek, and I flinch away from his touch.

"Come on, Sammy, keep up, son."

I look up at him and inwardly curse the day I laid eyes on this sick, demented, freak.

"You killed her, you motherfucking son of a bitch!" I spit out angrily and struggle vehemently against my restraints. He claps frenziedly.

"Finally, the fucking penny drops! Bra-fucking-vo!"

My heart is beating a frantic tattoo, and I am struggling to rein in my boiling rage.

"I fucking loved her, and you took her away from me, you fucking bastard! You made me think she was fucking alive, you sick twisted cunt!" I snarl, and he smiles smugly. He is smug that he took someone else's life. *Christ, could this bloke be any more mental?*

"Who was she?"

He looks at me, narrowing his eyes.

"Who?"

"The fucking lookalike in the crowd, how did you find someone who looked so much like her? TELL ME, YOU FUCKING COCKSUCKER!" I roar, and his smile fades, as a look of pure bewilderment crosses his face.

"I don't know what you're talking about, what fucking lookalike?" He feigns ignorance, and I narrow my eyes at him. *Is he fucking with me?*

"STOP LYING, AND FUCKING TELL ME WHO THE FUCK SHE WAS, OR SO HELP ME FUCKING GOD, I WILL KILL YOU!" I shout. I am so full of rage, I can feel the vein in my neck pulsing. I struggle and buck violently against the restraints.

"Stop fucking struggling, you definitely need to learn to calm that temper of yours, Sam."

He completely ignores my question and moves lithely over to the table. He pulls out the knife that he stabbed into it. He runs his finger over the blade and examines it, as if it will give him all the answers he seeks. His eyes look wide, agitated and crazy. He moves closer to me and begins dancing crazily around me again, humming a tune, which sounds oddly like *'Bring Me Sunshine'* by Morecambe and Wise. *Fuck me; he really has lost the plot.*

Unexpectedly, he stops in front of me, raises the blade, and stabs it through my right hand. As I see the knife penetrate through my hand, the memory of the same knife plunging through my sweet Peyton's chest and robbing her of life overwhelms me. I scream in agony as the pain rips through me. I look down at the blade protruding from the back of my hand; the pain doesn't immediately register, and there is blood, so much fucking blood. The sight of the dark, glossy, crimson blood triggers a flashback, and I see her face clearly in my mind, pleading with me to help her. My breath comes out in sharp pants.

Fuck me, come on, Newbolt, breathe.

He quickly pulls the knife out of my hand, and I bark out as the pain lances through me. *Breathe.*

"Now look what you made me do, Sammy! I didn't want to hurt you, but you were confusing me, and you were really beginning to piss me off with your incessant fucking questions."

His wipes the blood from the knife, on his shirt and tucks it into his jeans. His expression changes and turns cold.

"You know she was just like all the others don't you?" he says calmly and starts circling me again, as if nothing has happened.

"She was different to all of the others; she was fucking pregnant with my baby, you prick!" I growl, and he looks at me with fire in his eyes.

"She was just like all the others, ten a fucking penny, a gold-digging groupie whore. There's a thousand other girls just like her, more than willing to take her place," he spits out, and I start to struggle against my restraints, to no avail.

"Don't you ever fucking speak about her like that; you're just a fucking sick, twisted man."

I look him in the eyes, and he laughs bitterly.

"I killed her, that knife went through her like warm butter, and it was absolute fucking perfection."

He pinches his fingers together and makes a kissing motion. *All I want to do is to break free from this chair and rip his motherfucking throat out.* I buck so violently against my restraints, it causes the chair to rock backwards onto two legs.

"I watched her take her last breath, and she fucking deserved it, every fucking second of it."

His voice is hard, and his beady eyes burn with something that resembles pride as he speaks. I feel so overcome with rage, I can't focus on anything other than how much I want this sick fuck to die.

"She deserved everything she got, she could never make you happy the way I can. With her out of the way, we can finally be together... That night...all those years ago, we had something special, Sammy, don't you see? IT'S ONLY EVER BEEN ABOUT YOU!"

8

J.D.

Past

"That's a wrap, good job today, boys; the album is sounding pretty amazing so far. Go and celebrate, you all deserve it, have one on me."

I pull out a fifty-pound note and hand it to Lucas. The boys excitedly laugh and hi-five each other. Their childlike enthusiasm lights me from the inside, music is what I live for. I can tell Sam is not like them; he is different. He is shy, sensitive, handsome, and brooding.

"Fancy a few fucking beers, boys?" Brody declares, in his crass, low brow way, and they all rowdily agree.

I can't let him go, not yet. Make your move.

"Sam, I need a quick word, if that's ok? I won't keep you long."

He looks at me and looks quickly away shyly. He nods.

"I'll catch you up, boys."

Jax pats Sam's arm.

"We can wait if you want, mate?"

In my head, all I am thinking is, *please say no, please say no.* He tucks his hands boyishly in his pockets and shakes his head.

"I'll be fine, Jax, I'll catch you up, give me ten minutes tops."

He winks, and I feel my cock harden in my trousers. Jesus Christ. I clear my throat and turn away to hide my painful arousal. Although, what I have planned will take more than ten minutes.

"We'll be in the Black Chicken, down the street. I'll get the drinks in, first rounds on the gaffer. Usual, with a chaser, dude?" Brody asks, and Sam nods as the boys follow him out.

The door shuts behind them, and I am not a religious man, but I thank God for this moment. Alone at last. I go over to my filing cabinet and take out the bottle of Jack Daniels I keep there for emergencies. This being the emergency. I pull out two glasses and set them down on the table.

"Won't you join me for a drink, Sam?"

He bites his lip piercing, and my cock twitches. *Fuck me, easy fella.* He nods, and the gesture makes him look so vulnerable and boyish.

"Sit down, Sam; you're making the place look untidy."

I grin a little too widely, and he sits down awkwardly. He is tall, lean, and his long legs look amazing in those tight jeans he is wearing. This is going to be an extremely long night.

"Is there a reason you asked me to stay behind?" he asks curiously.

We all know what curiosity did to that cat, don't we, Sammy? I think idly as I pour us both drinks and move over to him. I hand him his glass; his fingers briefly brush mine. *Jesus Christ, I must show some fucking restraint.* I sit down next to him.

"All in good time, Sam, drink."

I take a long gulp of my whiskey, and he does the same. I watch as his throat bobs, as he takes a gulp. He even makes a simple gesture like having a drink erotic. He smiles and unleashes his dimples. *Fuck, how is it possible for a man to look so innocent, yet so completely and utterly sinful all at the same time?*

"I can make you very rich; I've proven how my influence can make a star of you and your band, Sam. Recording this album, you can be an overnight success; I can make Rancid Vengeance even bigger than the Lightning Bolts."

Checkmate. I take another sip of my drink, moving closer to him. I place my hand on his leg, and I feel him tense.

"Just relax, Sam."

He downs his drink in one gulp, and I chuckle softly. I am so close to him I can smell the sweet masculine scent of his aftershave and the familiar Newbolt smell I have become accustomed to over the years.

"I've always liked you, Sam. You're handsome, innocent, beautiful on the inside and on the outside."

I stroke his hair, and it feels so soft and silky under my fingers. I lean in and press my mouth to his. The contrast of my clean-shaven face and the scruff of his light stubble make my cock twitch. I introduce my tongue and just for a minute, he kisses me back, until he realises what is going on. He jumps back at the realisation, and his green eyes widen, as if he can't believe what just happened.

"What the fuck?" he curses, and I smile. The look of horror on his face is quite adorable.

"For the briefest moment there, Sam, you wanted this as much as I do, you kissed me back."

He shakes his head and says resolutely, "No."

I reach over and grip his penis through his trousers. He has a semi-erect cock, and I smirk.

"This fella says different."

He angrily shoves my hand away from him, and cups his erection with both hands, trying to hide his obvious arousal. I imagine how big his cock is, and how it would feel in my hands.

"I...I...I'm not fucking gay!" he stutters, and our eyes lock. He has this adorable pink hue to his cheeks; he's blushing and fuck me if it doesn't turn me on even more.

"You don't have to be gay, Sammy, just...a little adventurous. Do you want to...experiment?"

He jumps up off the sofa and moves toward the door.

"I...I should go, the boys will be wondering where I am."

Think, fucking, think.

"You know I can make or break your band, don't you, Sammy?"

He frowns, and I know I am being a bastard, but I just can't help myself. He makes me crazy just thinking about him. He has no idea of the effect he has on me.

"I'm just...gently reminding you who holds the power."

I get up from the sofa and stride towards him. I back him into the wall; we are roughly the same height, and I look him straight in the eyes. Those green eyes of his are so bright and intense. He is so innocent and so...pure.

"You scratch my back, I'll scratch yours, and you'll be an extremely rich man by the time you're twenty-five. You'll have the ladies falling at your feet; you'll have so much money you won't know what to do with it. You'll be famous. The women will want to fuck you, the men will want to be you, everyone will know who Sam Newbolt is. You'll be a household name, don't you want that?"

He swallows, and he nods slowly.

"Good, we understand each other then don't we, Sam?"

I stroke his face, with the back of my hand and his skin feels so soft. I crash my lips feverishly to his, and this time, he kisses me back with all the passion I have been imagining for all those months. His kiss is soft and rough all at the same time. I push my erection against him, and I grab a handful of his hair. He is so awkward; I can feel his heartbeat pounding in his chest. I reluctantly pull away from our kiss, and we are both breathless.

"Breathe, Sammy; you want this just as much as I do, relax," I try to soothe him as I pull the blinds down and flip the lock on the door.

9

Sam

Present

J.D. moves closer to me, and his eyes are crazed. He strokes my cheek, and I feel dirty just from his touch alone. He makes my fucking skin crawl, I buck against my restraints; feeling them bite into my skin. The earlier injury I sustained, from when he stabbed me in the hand, suddenly feels insignificant. I feel helpless and at his mercy, like a fly being caught in a spider's web.

"Get the fuck away from me," I spit out angrily.

"Don't be like that."

He moves closer until he is inches away from me, and he presses his lips against mine. I thrash wildly until he moves away from me and I spit in his face.

"YOU'RE A SICK FUCKING BASTARD!" I shout.

"It's always been you, Sammy, from the moment I first laid eyes on you. I knew we were destined to be together, you were such a sweet, handsome and shy boy. You were so different from all the others, you saw me, not what I could give you. I knew I wanted you, I wanted to feel that body against me."

He is so close to me now, I can feel his breath on my cheek, and my stomach turns at the thought of his hands all over me. He strokes my face with the back of his hand, and I buck against my restraints again in the vain hope that he will just give up. I feel the familiar bite into my skin and feel warm liquid trickling down my wrists. *Shit, I am fucking bleeding.*

"Stop struggling, I would never hurt you intentionally, I love you. I've loved you for years, surely you've worked that out by now?"

I can feel myself trembling with white-hot rage. *Come on, Sam, think. Buy yourself some fucking time, you can do this.*

"If you really truly loved me, you would never have taken the woman I fucking loved away from me! We were fucking happy!" I growl, and he shakes his head.

"I didn't plan on it, not at first, but she was getting too close, *way too fucking close.*" He grits out and takes a breath.

He strokes my face with his fingers, the same fingers he used to kill my Peyton. My stomach roils at the thought, and I feel the overwhelming urge to vomit. He runs his fingers through my hair and presses his mouth to mine for a second time. I bite down savagely on his bottom lip, until I taste the metallic of his blood. I spit on the floor and attempt to awkwardly wipe my mouth on my shoulder.

"GET THE FUCK AWAY FROM ME!" I roar. I can't control it anymore; I vomit all over him and all down the front of my t-shirt.

"Oh dear, oh deary-me."

He laughs maniacally, and his eyes are wide. He's high; I can clearly see the signs. Dilated pupils, wide, crazed eyes, the runny nose, the profuse sweating, and the jittery, agitated movements. All sure signs he's been on the cocaine.

"I think we need to get you cleaned up."

I look up at him, regarding me intently.

"Don't fucking touch me! I don't want anything from you; I don't want you anywhere near me, you disgust me. You couldn't stand to see me happy, could you? I fucking trusted you, and you ruined everything!" I bellow, as he folds his arms and cocks his head to the side. He reminds me of a fucking cockroach, as he narrows his eyes at me.

"No, she ruined everything, how do you think it felt for me to hear you and her...at it night after night. The way she screamed, as you pleasured her, as you shouted her name as you came, it should have been me!" he yells and jabs himself in the chest with his thumbs. "IT SHOULD HAVE BEEN ME!"

10

J.D.
Past

"Strip."

Sam complies and starts to clumsily remove his jeans. He unbuckles his belt, with unsteady hands and kicks off his shoes. I move over to him and place my hands on his.

"Breathe."

I take control, ridding him of his jeans and his boxers. He lifts the hem of his t-shirt and pulls it off. I am taken aback by the sight of his body. He has a lean, muscular frame; his pale creamy skin is a sight to beholden. Jesus, this man is sex on a stick. My eyes move down to his manhood, it is extremely impressive, he is huge, just like I imagined.

"Lie down and let me feel you, Sam," I whisper, and I remove my clothes.

When I turn around, Sam is lying on the sofa, worrying his bottom lip between his teeth. I climb on top of him and straddle his lean hips. I run my fingernails down his chest, and he shivers at my touch. I smirk at his reaction.

"Have you ever been with a man before, Sam?"

He shakes his head, and he blushes. His face turns the most adorable shade of pink.

"Just relax, we'll take it slow."

I kiss from his neck down his chest, and I relish the feel of his body underneath me.

"You feel incredible underneath me, Sam," I breathe.

I am so turned on, and my cock is so hard, it's fucking painful. *Take control, you've waited so long for this moment. Control it.*

"Bend over the sofa and grip the back," I order, and I get up, waiting for him to do as I say. When he doesn't move right away, I clear my throat, and his nervous gaze snaps back up to mine. *God, I could stare into those green eyes forever.*

"I said, bend over the fucking sofa and grip the back, NOW."

My voice is commanding and impatient, as he lifts himself up. He bends over and grips the sofa so hard, his knuckles turn white. His tight arse is exquisite. I move over to my desk and open the drawer, removing what I need. I walk back over to him and whisper in his ear, "I need you totally relaxed for me, Sam."

I lubricate my finger and spread it over his tight arsehole. He flinches at the cool lubricant, as it makes contact with his skin.

"Sh, shh, relax." I soothe, and I linger at his tight hole, wanting to prolong this moment.

I want to bottle this moment and keep it for all eternity. I kiss a trail down his spine, reaching down between his legs, to grasp his impressive erection. His cock twitches in my hand and I can feel every vein throbbing under my touch.

"Christ, your cock feels so good."

I move my hand back to his puckered hole and slowly push my fingers past the tight sphincter. He gasps at the intrusion of my fingers and whimpers with pleasure. I almost come on the spot at his reaction.

"Mmm, does that feel good?"

I move my fingers in and out of his tight hole, loving the way my fingers feel deep inside him. He moans softly and bites his lip piercing, causing my cock to twitch. Suddenly, I can't wait to be inside him. I am almost desperate with want for this exquisite man, who is completely at my sexual mercy. I introduce another finger, and he pushes eagerly back against me. I smirk at the gesture.

"Look at what you've been missing out on all these years, Sam."

He moves his trembling hands from the back of the sofa and grasps his growing erection in his hand. He strokes himself and the little noises he makes have me practically panting like a randy dog. I reach down into the pocket of my jeans and take out a rubber. I tear the foil packet between my teeth and sheath my hardness.

"Are you ready? I can't wait any longer; I need to be inside you."

He worries his bottom lip between his teeth, in the most adorable way and he turns his head, so his eyes lock onto mine.

"Yes," he rasps, and I take that a green light.

I smile and remove my fingers from his puckered back entrance. I grasp my cock in my hand, and as I slowly enter him, I think I've found heaven.

11

Sam

Present

Time to up your game, Newbolt.

"What would your dad have said?" His face contorts, as I mention his dad. "What would Jed have said? He wouldn't want this; he wouldn't want you to do this."

He moves closer to me.

"You know nothing!" he spits harshly. "You know nothing about my relationship with my dad, NOTHING! How fucking dare you even speak his name!" he shouts, and he violently hits himself in the side of the head. *I know I'm getting to him.*

"I know that you worshipped the ground he walked on, you followed him around like a lost fucking puppy for years, desperate to please him. He was proud of you, though, that much was clear, and you looked up to him, any idiot could see that."

He shakes his head, and I can see the tic in his jaw start to pulsate.

"NO! NO! I was a fucking disappointment to him! All he ever did was put me down and belittle me! I was the son who would amount to nothing in his eyes, I wasn't worthy of carrying the family name, he never took me seriously, I WAS A JOKE! A PATHETIC *FUCKING* JOKE!"

I look at him defiantly.

"Diamond Records was his life; how do you think he would react now if he knew you had pissed it all up the wall? His beloved legacy now belongs to someone else, all because you let the power go to your fucking head!"

He is literally trembling with rage now, and he moves closer to me.

"SHUT THE FUCK UP!"

He slaps me with the back of his hand, and I blink a few times, smirking at him.

"Is that all you've got? The great Jed Dalton's son hits like a fucking girl!" I mock and start to laugh hysterically.

Fuck me Newbolt, you're losing the plot.

He grabs my vest and punches me square in the face. He removes the knife from his jeans, and before I know what is happening, he plunges it into my left shoulder. The pain rips through me, like a bolt of lightning and I howl in pure agony. He pulls the knife out as if it has burned him and flings it across the room where it clatters on the concrete floor.

"Why do you make me fucking hurt you, Sammy? WHY?" he bellows and runs his hands frantically through his hair.

I look him square in the eyes, as I feel a warm wetness trickling down my chest.

"How could you ever think I had fucking feelings for you? What happened between us all those years ago, was purely for my career. I did it for the boys, I took one for the fucking team!"

He shakes his head profusely and yells out angrily, "NO! NO! YOU DON'T MEAN THAT! YOU'RE FUCKING LYING!"

I narrow my eyes at him, and I see his nostrils flare at my words.

"I wanted my music career so badly, I fucked my manager, and you know what? It wasn't even that good. You're *disgusting*, you fucking sick, *pathetic* pervert!" I roar, and that's when he moves forward with a look of pure hatred on his face. He moves so close to me that we are nose to nose and his voice is low and menacing.

"You know what? I enjoyed killing Peyton and the little fucking cockroach that was inside of her. I did the world a fucking favour by ending both of their lives. 'The whore and the rock stars child'. That would have made a great title for a novel, don't you think, Sammy? Although, I howled with laughter when I stabbed her in the chest, and then I stabbed her in the stomach, over and over again, just to make sure the little bastard was dead!"

He smirks, and that's when every ounce of my resolve finally snaps. My forehead connects with his nose, spraying blood all over his face; I am running purely on adrenaline, and I'm fuelled by burning, white-hot, molten rage. I throw myself forward with such brute force, I wrench the arms of the chair completely off, and it splinters easily apart. I get to my feet and straighten. I am trembling with such intense anger, I want this man to fucking die, and *I* want to be the one to end him.

The wooden arms of the chair are still attached to my forearms, and I swing my right arm forward until the wood connects with the side of his head. The force is so great, the *cracking* sound echoes throughout the room. He stumbles sideways and collapses on his knees, but he doesn't go down. I see red, and I am blinded by such inconsolable rage, I can't focus on anything other than the fact that I want to smash the life out of this sick, twisted piece of shit. I want him to look into my eyes, as I end his fucking life. I want to watch the light fade from his beady fucking eyes, just like he watched the life fade from my sweet Peyton's eyes.

I am driven by the need to watch as he takes his last breath, just as he watched Peyton take her last breath. I move in front of him and kick him so hard with my boot that he falls flat on his back. I hover over him, and I repeatedly hit him with the piece of wood attached to my right arm. He is screaming and pleading with me to stop.

"NO SAMMY PLEASE! PLEASE STOP! PLEASE!"

The sound of his incessant whining and pleading only fuels me to hit him harder. *I am willing to do prison time, if justice is served.*

"IS THAT WHAT YOU DID TO HER? DID YOU MAKE HER FUCKING BEG FOR HER LIFE, YOU SICK FUCK!" I roar.

The red mist has descended, and I can't stop myself. I am so focused, and hell-bent on vengeance for myself, the woman I loved and my unborn child. It is like the past year of grieving and the intense fucking hatred I feel for this vile excuse for a human being, is rushing to the surface, it is overwhelming. At this moment, I feel like I am the angriest man on the fucking planet.

As I continue to rain down blow after blow on this sorry sack of shit, I remember all those nights I spent lying with Peyton, her scent, and the way her beautiful, svelte body felt against me. I realise that I am crying uncontrollably. He took her from me, and I will never *ever* forgive him for that, but Peyton's sweet nature would not have wanted me to kill him, no matter what he has done. I stop abruptly, and as I look down at his battered and bloody body lying in front of me, I realise that this is what became of the once great Johnnie *fucking* Diamond. I kneel, reaching into his front pocket where I know he always keeps his phone, and call 911.

12

Sam

I come around in an all too bright room with a throbbing head, a throat like Gandhi's sandal and a dull ache in my shoulder. My hand and my wrists are bandaged. *Ouch! That shit fucking stings!* There is an officer of the NYPD standing next to my bed, with his hands behind his back. My mum and dad are on the other side. My mum looks as if she has been crying and my mum almost *never* cries. My dad is silently standing with his arm wrapped around her, being the rock she needs. I turn my head slightly to see Cole stationed outside my room; that's when I see her. *She* is standing awkwardly near the door, and I instantly think, *this can't be fucking happening to me. What the fuck is going on? Am I dreaming? Are my eyes deceiving me?* I feel like Alice in Wonderland, I have fallen down the rabbit hole and entered someone else's life. A parallel universe, where *she* is standing right in front of me, living and breathing.

She is more defined, tanned and so much thinner than I remember. Her eyes are still that sparkling sapphire blue, which haunted my dreams every single night. She is still so impossibly beautiful, and she takes my fucking breath away. Her hair is now pillar-box red and cut into a short, sleek bob, but it is definitely her. *My Peyton.* I look to the tall, muscled, light coffee skinned officer standing next to my bed. He is wearing a grey suit, with a silver pinstripe tie, a detective badge pinned to his belt and a handgun in a brown leather holster, concealed inside his jacket. A look of pure confusion crosses my face, as I struggle to focus on what is going on.

"What the fuck?" I croak, and her eyes are glazed, but she doesn't say a word. "Mum?"

My mum steps forward and clasps my hand in hers.

"I'm here, honey," she says in her soft, familiar American drawl.

She reaches over to pick up the glass of water on the table next to my bed. She hands me the glass, and I suck water through a straw to hydrate my dry throat. I polish off the glass of water in one long pull. The liquid feels like heaven, as it slides down my throat in an ice-cold cascade.

"How long have I been here?" I rasp, as my dad moves forward and pats my uninjured shoulder.

"You've been here for three days, son. The police found you collapsed from blood loss at the side of the road. You were in a bloody awful state, but we had you transferred to a private hospital. They patched you up, so you're good as new, and you're going to be just fine," he says in a tone of quiet concern that only a father would have for his son.

I narrow my eyes at the officer, who is regarding me intently.

"Who are you?" I say frostily.

"I'm Detective Paxton Devin, Mr. Newbolt. My kids are huge fans," he says in a thick, prominent New York accent.

I nod curtly and smile weakly, and as my eyes find hers, I am somewhere between shock and disbelief. The officer sees the exchange between us and looks curiously from her to me.

"We're going to need to ask you both a few questions, but for now I'll leave you to it, Mr. Newbolt, Miss Stonebridge. You look like y'all have a lot to discuss."

He smiles, nods and leaves the room. *Why the fuck is he calling her Miss Stonebridge?* I want to scream at him that that's not her name, but I am pulled from my thoughts by my dad stepping closer to my bed, looking from me to her.

"Do you want me to get Cole to come and remove her?" he says with more than a hint of venom to his voice.

I glance at her, and she looks so tiny, scared and vulnerable as tears roll freely down her cheeks. I shake my head, without breaking our eye contact.

"No," I say gruffly, as my mum squeezes my hand and kisses me softly on the cheek.

"Me and your father are going to find a decent cup of coffee in this God-awful place, are you going to be ok, darling?"

She looks from her to me, with narrow, guarded eyes and I nod in reassurance.

"Yeah, I'll be fine, mum."

My dad smiles, and I know he's dying to say something, but he stays silent, just to keep the peace.

"Love you, sweetie."

My mum blows a kiss to me, and I smile.

"Love you too, mum."

My dad steers my mum out of the room with his hand at the small of her back. The door closes behind them, and it's just her and me. I wince as I sit up, and my shoulder burns in protest while my hand throbs with pain. But it doesn't quite match up to the pain I feel in my heart right now. All I have wanted for this past year is to see her, hold her, and to wake up from the nightmare I have been in without her. I have wished for someone to come and tell me it was all a dream, a bad joke, that she was alive. I was made to think she was alive, only to have my hopes dashed so cruelly by the man who took her from me in the first place. *Fucking J.D.*

"You died; I saw it with my own eyes."

My voice is barely a whisper, and I don't recognise it as my own. She moves back from the bed, distancing herself from me. She sees the look of pure anguish and disbelief on my face. She looks like a rabbit caught in headlights. She takes another step back and hugs herself, as if to protect herself from this, from me. My heart constricts at her obvious skittish behaviour. *Jesus fucking Christ.*

"I know you must be angry and upset, Sam, but you need to understand that what he did to me was...it was...horrific, brutal...torture. This past year hasn't been easy for me."

Her small voice trembles and I can't believe what I am hearing. *Angry? Upset?* That's a fucking understatement. It doesn't even begin to cover what I am feeling right now. A part of me is upset and angry, but I'm also so very relieved that she is alive. Mainly, I feel a sense of hatred towards this woman I once loved, for destroying me and for making me believe she was dead. I tried to take my own life because she was gone, and I couldn't see another way out. I don't think I'll ever be able to truly forgive her for that.

"It wasn't easy for you? *Fuck!* I've spent the past year in absolute hell because you died! I grieved for you! I went to your goddamn memorial when we couldn't find your body, we said goodbye to you, Peyton. I lost you and our baby that day; I lost everything, and it was all because of fucking J.D."

My voice is thick with unshed tears and pent-up anger towards her total disregard for my feelings. A tear rolls down her cheek, and even though I am so fucking angry, all I want to do is hold her in my arms.

"I'm so sorry, Sam, I really am."

She swipes the tears away with the sleeve of her shirt. Her favourite purple and black checked shirt, the one she was wearing the day we met.

13

Sam

The day they met

I can think of a million places that I would rather be right now. I'm hung-over to shit, I'm fucking exhausted, and I can't remember the last time I had a decent night's sleep. We played a gig last night in Hammersmith, and we partied hard, the way rock stars should. The vodka was flowing; the groupies were fast, looser than usual, and they were there on demand to relieve the tension after an all-out, energetic performance. The groupie I ended up with was a tiger, an all-around, kinky bitch and I didn't even bother to lay on the old Bolt charm. She was an easy fuck, just the way I like them. We fucked for hours, and I didn't even get her name. Or if I did, I don't remember it! I kicked her out when I was done, in my typical Newbolt style. Hey, I am under no illusion that I am a perfect gentleman. I am a complete fucking arsehole; I admit it, and I have totally made peace with that.

I would rather be anywhere other than a pokey little tattoo studio in the middle of Islington. Fucking Islington of all places. I could do without this shit because my head is fucking banging like a shit house door. But, apparently, we all insisted we wanted new tattoos after a little too much vodka. After J.D pulled some strings with the owner and manager, Seb Henry, here we are. I step off the tour bus with my aviator sunglasses on to shield my eyes, followed by the rest of the boys, who are equally as hungover. We are greeted by a flock of screaming female fans, and flanked by our security team Cole and Skip, we are led through the crowd and into the shop.

That's when I see her. A five foot nothing, tattooed goddess, and fuck me, I think I'm in love. Her blue eyes lock with mine; I give her a cheeky wink and one of my signature killer dazzling smiles. I can see that she feels it too because neither of us can look away. My heart starts beating faster, and I can't remember the last time I felt...something. I clear my throat, to rid myself of the thought. Come on Newbolt, turn on the charm.

"Hey beautiful," I rasp.

I see the muscles in her slender neck contract. She bites her lip, and her eyes glaze over. *Oh yes, she is so affected by me. If I am correct, she is probably thinking of how my cock is going to feel buried inside her tight, wet...Whoa! Steady on son! Get it together, fuck face.* She shakes her head, as if to rid herself of her previous thought, and takes a deep breath. She has no idea that I was having the same thought, at the same time.

"Hi, and I'm not beautiful, I'm Peyton."

The rest of the boys erupt with laughter. *Feisty and hot...Fuck me, I am in so much trouble.* I can feel my dick harden in my trousers. Fuck, this isn't good. I want to feel the way she feels beneath me, I need her beautiful breasts pressed against my chest; I need to hear her scream my name, and I need to see her look into my eyes as I bring her to orgasm. *Fuck me, where did that come from? Focus, dickhead. Think unsexy thoughts, think unsexy thoughts.*

She extends her hand to me, and I take it in my tattooed one. I feel electricity shoot through my veins, feeling her tiny hand in mine and I can't fucking breathe. I swallow hard and clear my throat before I can speak. *Get your head in the game, Newbolt.*

"I'm Sam."

I reluctantly let go of her hand because I like feeling her soft hand in mine and I can't take my eyes off her. Five feet three inches tall, tattooed, long, shoulder length, dark brown hair with purple streaks and the bluest eyes I have ever seen. They remind me of sparkling sapphires. She has a lip piercing and the most beautiful smile that make those stunning eyes of hers dance. My thoughts are interrupted by Jax.

"You got owned by a girl, Sammy!"

He takes her hand and kisses the back.

"I'm Jax; any girl that can shoot down our Sammy, is definitely the girl of my dreams!"

She laughs, which is the most beautiful sound I have ever heard in all my twenty-nine years. *Back off, Jax. She's mine, fucker. She doesn't know it yet, but she is going to be mine, I will make damn fucking sure of it.*

"I'm Peyton, pleased to meet you, Jax."

She smiles, and I think the ice I had around my heart starts to melt after all these years. Seb moves to stand next to her, as if he is her bodyguard or something. *Is she fucking him? Are they together? Fuck me, I hope not, I clench my fists at my side. Rein it in, Newbolt; she isn't yours...yet.*

"We should get started, babe. You take Jax and Sam, and I'll take Brody and Lucas, is that all good with you?"

She nods, and her eyes lock with mine. Inwardly, I am doing a very manly victory dance at the prospect of having her hands on me, and with that thought, my dick hardens. I hope to fuck she doesn't notice, that would be...extremely fucking embarrassing.

"Yep, that's all good with me Seb. Do you have designs, or do you want me to draw something up?"

I could listen to her voice all day. *Fucking hell, man up, Newbolt. This most definitely isn't one of those soppy romance novels that your mum reads.* I relax my shoulders and saunter forward confidently.

"I've got a rough idea, but I think I need a second opinion."

She smirks, and I begin to wonder what she finds so amusing.

"Ok, that's all good with me, Jax what about you?"

Jax nudges me out of the way, we are always mucking around with each other. I love the boy like a brother, but he should know me well enough by now not to fuck with me where a beautiful woman is concerned. I grab him in a playful headlock and ruffle his precious blonde locks.

"I'll get her to tattoo 'emergency exit' on your arse if you're not careful, Jax."

We both laugh, eager to entertain her. I want her to feel comfortable around me and not tread on eggshells to try and please me just because I'm a rock star.

"Bring it on! It can't be any worse than your lightning bolt."

Jax looks at her and leans in close to her. As he gets closer to her, my blood starts boiling and my famous temper spikes. *Back the hell up, she's mine fucker.*

"That's where he got his band name from; he lost a bet, and he has a lightning bolt tattooed on his arse!"

He winks cheekily at her. *Come on, Newbolt; lay on the charm, with a fucking trowel if you must. Show her you are interested, reel her in.*

"I can show you if you want?" I say in my trademark husky voice, attempting to be flirtatious. I even throw in a cheeky wink. *You charming son of a bitch.*

"In your dreams, rock star."

My mouth drops open, my dick hardens to the point of pain, and I think I might possibly be close to orgasm. No woman has ever been immune to my charms before, that's a first. Usually, I bring out the husky voice and the dimples and then bam, they are swooning at my feet. After that, all it takes is a few choice words, and they're on their backs, legs wide open for me. All the boys erupt with laughter again, and I place my hand on my chest.

"You're wounding my ego, sweetheart."

Bring out the big guns, Newbolt. I smirk, bringing out my infamous dimples

"If you want to follow me."

Wow, she practically ignored me. I'm going to have to step it up a notch and unquestionably try harder with this one. I can't let her slip through my fingers; she will be mine whether it fucking kills me...

14

Sam

Present

"He...he...he told me that you asked him to kidnap me." She swallows a few times and then continues, "J.D made me believe that you never really loved me at all. He got inside my head and convinced me that you masterminded the whole thing. He said...he said you wanted him to hurt me, to make me suffer, that you wanted me dead, so you and he could finally be together."

She closes her eyes as if she's remembering his words and tears are rolling freely down her cheeks. *What the fuck*? I can't believe what I am fucking hearing. *She thought I wanted her dead? That I wanted her gone? How could she believe something so sick and fucking twisted?* I feel like I have been punched in the gut and that my head is going to explode. I feel like I am about to throw up and I can't breathe. *Fuck me.*

"How could you think that? I went through hell because you died; losing you destroyed me. I would have taken a thousand fucking bullets for you, Peyton. I worshipped the ground you walked on. We were having a baby! We were fucking engaged! I wanted you to be my wife, and we were going to get married. We were supposed to fucking have our happily ever after!"

I raise my voice a few decibels louder, I can't help myself. *My head is fucking spinning.*

"So, what? Instead of coming to me and fucking asking me if it was true, you what? You decided what he said must be true? You took his fucking word over mine, and you made me carry on thinking you were fucking dead?"

She scrubs her hands down her face and when she looks up her pained blue eyes lock with mine.

"I was fucking hurt! I felt like my whole world had crashed down around me. You destroyed me! I was heartbroken, and I thought our relationship was based on a fucking lie, Sam. I was totally crushed when I had some fucking lunatic plunge a knife into my chest whilst telling me that you *asked* him to fucking do it! What the fuck was I supposed to think? When I eventually got away from him, I was terrified he would come back for me. So I just ran, and I didn't look back. I wasn't fucking thinking!"

She sobs. As I listen to her words, I feel some of the earlier fire and anger I felt before I heard her explanation, leave me. I will never be able to forget what she did, but I think I understand her reason behind it.

"You have to believe me, I didn't want this for us, and I definitely didn't want our baby to start his life like this, Sam."

She stops, as if she's said too much, and my eyes widen. *Our baby?*

"What? Whoa! Wait, back up a fucking second, *our* baby?"

She nods her head and sobs. *What the fucking fuck?*

"Oh God, Sam, I'm so sorry; I'm sorry, I'm sorry, I didn't have a choice. I had to keep him safe Sam, not just for me but for you."

I go to move, and the pain rips through my shoulder.

"FUCK!" I growl, and she is at my side in a second. She reaches for my hand, but she stops herself, I can't fucking process this. *This is a dream and any second, I am going to wake the fuck up.* "I-we...have a baby?" I stutter, and I can't comprehend what I'm hearing. *What the fuck?* I clear my throat, and I subtly pinch myself. *No, definitely not dreaming.* "You had *my* baby?"

She nods and gives me a watery smile.

"We have a baby boy, Freddie. He's so, so beautiful, Sam; he looks so much like you. He's got your eyes."

Her blue eyes are filled with so much pride and joy when she speaks of our son. *Fuck me, I am someone's dad.*

15

Peyton

Past

Tonight is Rancid Vengeance's comeback gig at Madison Square Garden, New York City. I have made the six-hour journey from Santa Monica with Remy Logan, Ruby's brother, and Freddie. I am currently putting the finishing touches to my outfit. I have styled my sleek red bob poker straight, and I am wearing a black beanie hat. I am also wearing a black vest, leather shorts, black patent Doc Martens, and a bright red Rancid Vengeance hoodie with the band's logo, a skeleton playing a burning guitar on the back of a motorbike, emblazoned across the front. I acquired it while I was on tour with the band all those months ago. I pull it on and roll up the sleeves. Remy has been quiet for the past few days after he reluctantly helped me purchase a ticket for the sold-out show on eBay. We are staying at a hotel close to the venue and Remy is holding Freddie.

"Are you sure this is the right thing to do, beaut?"

The truth is, after everything Sam put me through asking J.D to hurt me, the kidnapping and all the bad things that followed, I want to see him one final time. I want to see him as the rock god I once knew and loved... before I cut him out of my life completely. I have to hear his husky voice over the microphone. I have to watch him while he has the audience eating out of the palm of his hand, and I have to watch the passion in his eyes as he sings to a huge crowd of his adoring fans.

"We spent all that time and all that fucking money getting you a new identity as Louise Stonebridge from Myles, and you're just going to fuck it all to hell by showing your face in the one place you shouldn't be? Which is anywhere near Samson fucking Newbolt. Yeah, real smart move," he says sarcastically.

I run a brush through my hair and spin around to face Remy. The pain in his brown eyes makes my heart slam against my rib cage, and I rub at my chest to rid myself of the ache.

"Babe, I have to do this, I have to lay Sam Newbolt to rest."

He takes a breath and laughs bitterly.

"Just like he fucking laid you to rest?" he spits angrily, and I wince at the cold, harsh tone of his voice.

"I'll let that one go because I can see that you're angry with me, but that was a low fucking blow, Rem, and you damn well know it," I snap, feeling hurt at Remy's cruel words. Remy's never been cruel, not in all the years I have known him.

"I'm not going to apologise for caring, beaut. I'm sorry for speaking out of turn and if I was a prick, but after everything that motherfucker put you through, I get that you still have feelings for him but..."

He stops himself, puffs out his cheeks, and closes his eyes, as if to rid himself of his previous thought.

"No, I don't. Go on, Rem, don't sugar coat it," I say sarcastically.

He gets up from the bed and strides across the room to the window, with Freddie in his arms.

"No, you know what? It doesn't fucking matter."

I move towards him, hating that I'm the one who put that look in sweet Remy's eyes. The man who has taken care of my baby and me for the past year. Even though he's acting like a jealous lover right now, I can totally understand his point. Damn you, devil's advocate.

"It doesn't change what's happened over this past year. I want closure, then I can end that chapter of my life and start a brand new one. Please understand that Rem. I really love living in Santa Monica, and I've kind of gotten used to you being around."

He chuckles softly.

"Is that your way of saying sorry and that you like me, beaut? Just a little tiny bit?" He jokes, and in that moment, our argument is forgotten, reminding me why we are friends in the first place.

Remy can make a joke out of any situation, whether it is serious or not. He is easy to be around, and I do not know what I would have done without him this past year. He hugs me tightly, and I relish being in his strong, safe, arms.

"Stay safe, stay out of sight. Don't draw attention to yourself, don't do anything reckless, and for fuck's sake, be careful."

I smile against him, at his concern and snuggle closer to him.

"I'll be careful, babe, I promise."

He kisses the top of my head and pulls away.

"Call me as soon as you're on your way back, and I'll come and get you. Doesn't matter what time it is, I'll be there."

I go to protest, and he narrows his eyes, pointing his finger in my direction.

"No arguments on this one, I care about you. Me and this little dude just want you back in one piece."

I salute sarcastically, and he cocks his eyebrow.

"Later, beaut."

He winks, and I blow him a kiss. I leave the hotel room with butterflies fluttering around in my stomach and a heavy heart.

I make my way to Madison Square Garden, and the venue is huge. A sea of Rancid Vengeance fans are shouting their familiar chant.

"Vengeance, Vengeance, Vengeance."

I get the familiar pre-gig butterflies, and I feel the buzz around the venue; the atmosphere is electric. I show my ticket at the door and try to keep my face hidden, as much as I can. I can't afford to be recognised. I know I am taking a huge risk by even being here, but I need some sort of closure. I need to say a proper goodbye to Sam, even if it is from a distance.

I follow the flow of fans into the arena, and I am astounded by the sheer size. I start to wonder if the boys are backstage. I imagine them all encouraging each other, drinking a few beers, and going through their pre-show rituals. Jax tuning his guitar, Lucas spinning his sticks, Brody in a world of his own, or on the bus shagging some random groupie. And Sam, ever the professional, silently and coolly keeping his nerves to himself.

I make my way to a spot near to the stage and as I hear the support act, 'The Devil's Henchmen', Draven Michaels' melodic scream fills the arena. I start to remember the time that Sam and I spent together. The familiar glint in his green eyes and the way the light caught his back tattoo and made it look like the wings of his phoenix were moving with each flex of his muscles. I think of his panty-dropping smile, his adorable dimples and the feel of the soft spikes of his hair against my skin. I start to remember the day we met; the first time I saw him on stage and the first time we made love. I remember the first time I told him I loved him; the moment I told him I was pregnant with his baby and the moment when he proposed to me in Las Vegas. All those precious moments showed me the sides of Sam Newbolt that no one else sees: the shy, vulnerable, sweet, kind lover that he was when we were together. At the same time, he was the fierce, protective warrior and the invincible, untouchable rock star... the one that let me in and welcomed me into his world.

I am suddenly snapped out of my reverie, as I hear Sam's familiar growl and my nerves start to kick up a notch. I start to wonder what the fuck I'm doing here.

"Good evening, Madison Square Garden, how the fuck are we doing tonight? We're Rancid Vengeance; it's so fucking good to be back up on stage. Are you ready to rock? Let me hear you scream 'hell yeah.'"

My skin erupts with goosebumps, as I hear Sam's familiar husky voice fill the arena and at that moment, I know without a shadow of a doubt, I have to stay. As the crowd around me erupt with a cheer of 'hell yeah', a panty-dropping grin spreads across his face, and I am mesmerized once again by his stage presence. I read on the internet that Rancid Vengeance have had a year away from the music industry, but seeing him up on stage now, it is like he has never been away. He is a born performer. Up on stage in front of his fans, is where he truly belongs. He is a true showman, and his presence commands attention. He is larger than life, just as I remember.

"Yeahhh! Let's fucking rock this place to the ground, give me a riff, Flash," he growls.

Jax breaks out into his signature guitar solo, and Lucas pounds an impressive drumbeat. Sam begins to sing, and his voice sends chills down my spine. I am transfixed by the music, the lyrics and the man performing in front of me.

"I am lost to the music, lost to the void, lost to my eternal fucking sadness. Somebody, please throw me a lifeline."

As he sings, he loses himself in the music, closing his eyes. As he hits the chorus, Jax's haunting guitar riff fills the venue. He opens his eyes, looking out at the crowd, and despite the other fans surrounding me, our eyes lock, green to blue. I am frozen to the spot, and I can't move. My heart slams against my rib cage as his green eyes seem to recognise me. *Shit, Remy warned me about this, I should never have come here.* It is at that moment that I realise that I am standing completely still, not moving, and not cheering. I am just staring at the man who was once my whole world. His eyes roam my body in recognition. *Does he know it's me? Fuck me; this was such a bad idea.* With that thought, my brain sends a message to the rest of my body, and I begin to push my way through the crowd. I have to get out of here, quickly. My heart is pounding, and I feel an impending panic attack. I manage to get to the exit and desperately try to navigate my way out of the building. I can see an exit up ahead when I hear a sound behind me.

"Yep, all clear down here, I can't see her. I'll do a final sweep of the building, but it's a negative that she's here. I swear that boy is losing the plot."

Bollocks, it's Cole. I pull my hood up to shield my face and slow my pace. *Shit, shit, shit. Think, Harper, think.* I hear footsteps getting closer, and I let out the breath I didn't know I was holding as he walks right past me. I can't get away quick enough.

Fuck. That was way too close. I need to go call Remy and forget this ever happened. I need to go back to Remy, back to Santa Monica, back to my new life, a life without Sam Newbolt in it.

***

I have not been up long, when I am snuggled on the sofa in the hotel room with Remy and my morning cup of coffee. We are watching reruns of Supernatural, getting lost in Sam and Dean's world of monsters and demons. Freddie is still asleep in his travel cot in the bedroom. Today is one of those lazy duvet days, days where I do nothing but veg out on the sofa and watch T.V box sets on Netflix. Pure heaven.

I am reminded every day of Sam and the life I left behind in London. I can't help but feel bitter every time I see his beautiful, stupid, arrogant fucking face smiling back at me from the T.V screen. My head is all over the place right now, and I'm not thinking straight. I shift closer to Remy, and he looks down at me with such a tender look in his eyes. It breaks my heart.

"You ok, beaut?" he whispers.

I don't know what comes over me, but before I realise what I'm doing, I'm crushing my lips eagerly to Remy's. Each stroke of his tongue with mine is a symbol of the past year. It begins to release all the pent-up sexual tension that has been slowly building between us. As Remy crushes his lips even more desperately to mine, I can feel every single one of his emotions, just by the touch of his lips on mine. His tongue wrestles with mine as his kiss becomes more heated. He presses me closer to him until I can feel his steel erection digging in my stomach. His hands are holding me to him, as if he is terrified, I am going to run. I wrap my hand in his long brown hair and a deep growl rumbles from within his throat. He pulls away from our kiss and rests his forehead on mine. My heartbeat starts to quicken, and the look in Remy's brown eyes is smouldering.

"Make me stop, because if you don't, we're both going to do something we'll regret."

We are both breathing heavily, and if an onlooker were to see us, they would see the glazed look in both of our eyes, the mussed tangle of our hair, and the bruising of our lips.

"I don't want you to stop, Remy, I need you."

The husky purr of my voice doesn't sound like my own, but I do need him. I need him to ease the ache between my legs; I need to fuck *him* out of my system, once and for all.

Over the past year, our relationship has been based on friendship and purely platonic. But, somewhere over time, it has become something more, and the lines have become blurred. It's as if Remy is somehow jealous of the amount of time I have spent thinking about Sam and over analysing our relationship. As if, he has been hiding his feelings for me, after all the years we spent apart.

"Don't say things you don't mean, beaut, I couldn't bear it," he says with a pained expression on his beautiful, chiselled face, which is so similar to his sister's.

"Don't make me beg, Rem," I say with determination.

Remy nods curtly and grabs my hand in his, dragging me into the bedroom without waking Freddie. He stalks towards me, like a predator stalking his prey and the look in his eyes tells me all I need to know, he wants me. We start frantically tearing and clawing at each other's clothes, with a desperate want. It doesn't take us long until we are naked. Remy's eyes shamelessly roaming over my body.

"Fuck me, your tits are...fucking perfect."

I chuckle softly as his mouth descends down on my nipple. He sucks my nipple into his mouth and our moment is interrupted as I hear the sound of the T.V in the background. He must have forgotten to switch it off.

"Reports are just coming in that Samson Newbolt, frontman of popular rock band Rancid Vengeance, has just been admitted to the hospital after being kidnapped and falsely imprisoned by former manager John Dalton, also known as Johnnie Diamond, son of late record company mogul, Jed Dalton."

My head snaps up as I hear Sam's name, and the moment is lost. I clamber off Remy, and I turn the volume up on the T.V.

"Dalton, thirty-eight, kidnapped and stabbed Newbolt. Police found him collapsed along FDR Drive, near to the Harlem River, with stab wounds. Bolt, as he is known to his die-hard fans, has been taken to a nearby hospital and his stab wounds are not thought to be serious or life-threatening. The NYPD traced the cell phone, which made the anonymous 911 call, to an abandoned warehouse where Dalton was found."

I watch the screen in shock at the events that are unfolding. *J.D kidnapped Sam?* I see a video of the police dragging J.D out of the warehouse. He is badly beaten and thrashing violently against his handcuffs. His icy cold gaze makes my stomach roil and brings back memories of a time I would rather forget.

"Police reports say that Dalton admitted to murdering Mr. Newbolt's fiancée, Peyton Harper. Harper, twenty-seven and the daughter of former model Sophia Bailey, was three months pregnant with Newbolt's baby. The police have taken Mr. Dalton into custody for further questioning and refuse any further comment."

He laughs maniacally at the camera as the police bundle him into the back of the police car. A cold chill runs down my spine as I remember that terrifying laugh, a laugh that has haunted my nightmares. I am shaken by the news reporter's words. *Is it possible that J.D lied about Sam wanting me dead?*

I watch the pictures from the screen unfolding in front of me. I am shaking and crying uncontrollably now. *Christ, I feel like I want to throw up. Is it possible that this past year has all been for nothing? A terrible mistake on my part?* My head is all over the place, and I feel Remy's strong, corded, comforting arm around my shoulder, supporting me.

"Beaut?" he says with concern in his voice.

I can't comprehend what I have just seen and heard on the T.V. Remy pulls me into his bare chest, softly soothing me just with the sound of his voice.

"Beaut, talk to me."

I am speechless, and my thoughts are racing at a million miles an hour. *Has this past year really all been for nothing?*

"Are you ok?"

I look up at him with glazed eyes.

"What the fuck have I done, Rem?"

I sob, and Remy strokes my hair so softly that it makes me cry harder. Here I am, in a hotel room with the man that has taken care of my baby and me for the past year, about to have sex for the first time in eleven years. Then there's Sam, the man who I spent some of the best days of my life with, the father of my child, and the man who I was tricked into believing he wanted me dead. Instead of returning to him and asking him if it was true, I automatically took the word of a complete psycho over the man I was supposed to be so in love with. It feels like both parts of my life are colliding in a spectacular, disastrous, potentially life-altering fashion.

Fuck, how can I make this right? Will I ever make it right? As Remy comes back into the room, with Freddie in his arms, I get up from the bed with a renewed purpose. I know what I have to do; I have to go to him.

16

Peyton
Present

I must make him understand. I have to make it right, because right now, I can't stand the way he looks at me. His usual sparkling, intense green gaze has been replaced by coldness and indifference. He looks at me as if I am a total stranger, as if I am nothing to him and all those months we spent together never happened. Ever since I arrived, I have been met with nothing but hostility from the Newbolt's. I can't say I blame them, but they have to hear my side.

I have spent so long craving his touch and to feel his strong, safe, warm, arms around me. I have spent every day in conflict with my own thoughts. Part of me hates Sam for what J.D made me believe. Another part of me is desperately wishing things could have been different and is silently praying for things to go back to the way they used to be.

I have been waiting for this moment to arrive, the moment where he can tell me that everything J.D said was a lie. Where I can be back in his arms, where I belong. I ache to feel his lips against mine and the way his hard-muscled body feels pressed into mine. He snaps me out of my reverie, and his intense green eyes lock with mine. He is visibly trembling, and I'm not sure if it's the effects of his medication or the anger he is rightly feeling.

"You kept him from me, this whole fucking time?"

The cold tone of his voice cuts through my thoughts.

"I had no other fucking choice, Sam! It was too dangerous! I couldn't risk J.D finding us, please, you have to understand," I plead.

He holds his finger up and runs his uninjured hand frantically through his hair, my pleas falling on deaf ears.

"No, no, let me try to process this. You not only made me think you were dead, but while I was fucking breaking down and pushing everyone away because I was grieving for you, you had my baby and kept him from me for *six fucking months!* That wasn't your fucking decision to make, Peyton! We created that baby together! Don't you think I deserved to know? What kind of monster are you? You fucking robbed me of the first six months of my son's life!" he roars, and as I listen to his words, the tears start to flow uncontrollably. Everything he is saying is true. *How the fuck am I going to fix this mess?*

"*Jesus fucking Christ*, Peyton. I should have been there! You fucking robbed me of seeing him enter the world, his first breath, his first smile, and his first tears," he says through clenched teeth, as his nostrils flare. He shakes his head and scrubs his hand down his face. "You're a selfish fucking bitch do you know that Peyton?"

My heart constricts at his cruel words and the look in his eyes completely destroys me. *I can't bear the fact that I'm the one that caused this, it's all my fault.*

"JUST GET THE FUCK OUT; I REALLY CAN'T BE AROUND YOU RIGHT NOW!" he shouts, and I run out of the room crying.

I expected him to be angry, and I don't blame him. I am in the corridor at the hospital, suddenly I feel so lost and so alone in this moment, but he *has* to understand. I know it was selfish, but I didn't want this; I never wanted any of it. Not for him, me or our baby boy. I have spent a whole year believing he wanted me gone and looking over my shoulder because I was so terrified J.D would find us.

17

Peyton

Past

Even though I have probably only been here for a couple of hours, it feels like days. I am tied to a chair with cable ties, and no matter how much I cry, I beg, and I plead, it does no good at all. I am helpless, completely fucking helpless.

He is pacing the floor in front of me now, his eyes wide and glossy. He actually looks mental and totally unhinged, like a complete fucking lunatic. I struggle hopelessly against my restraints.

"Stop struggling, bitch, you won't get away from me, I won't fucking let you," he yells, and I sob softly. "Stop fucking snivelling," he spits harshly, and he circles me.

"You're just like all the other girls that have been in his bed, pretty for the first couple of months, then gradually he gets bored and moves onto the next. While he was seeing you, I arranged for some girls to sleep with him. You see, because of his depression, he has an insatiable sexual appetite, and you just weren't enough to satisfy him. You weren't quite doing it for him, you weren't quite hitting the spot for him, and our Sammy has...very specific tastes."

With those words, I feel my heart constrict in my chest. *He's lying, he's playing mind games. He is a manipulative, evil liar. Breathe, Harper.*

"No...No, you're fucking lying; it's not true Sam wouldn't do that, he loves me."

He laughs maniacally.

"Oh please, he's just like the rest of the men in the world, darlin'. Only he's Sam Newbolt, he can do whatever he wants and get away with it, because he fucking can!" he spits and folds his arms as he comes to a stop in front of me.

"You're definitely our Sammy's type though, without a shadow of a doubt. Brunette, check, pretty eyes, check, impressive tits, check and I'll bet you've got a pretty pussy too."

He moves closer to me. I can feel and smell his stale, alcohol breath on my cheek. He strokes my face with his fingers, and I buck violently against the restraints.

"DON'T YOU FUCKING TOUCH ME!" I scream, and he presses his forehead against mine.

"Ah, there's that fire that Sammy kept talking about, I can definitely see why he kept you around longer than the others."

He moves his hand down and roughly gropes my breast in his hand, causing me to wince in pain. He moves down to my stomach and lingers on my small bump. As his hand makes contact with my stomach, my mothering instinct kicks in.

"Don't you dare fucking touch my baby," I say through clenched teeth, and all I want to do is protect my baby from this evil monster.

"I'm just saying hello to Sam's spawn, if it even is Sam's spawn," he accuses.

How fucking dare he.

"This baby is one million percent Sam's, and if you hurt him or her, I swear on my life I will fucking kill you."

He laughs hysterically.

"You'll kill me? Who's the one tied to the chair, sweetheart?"

I buck against the restraints again to no avail, and he laughs maniacally.

"I have to take a dump, feel free to amuse yourself while I'm gone."

He winks and strides off out of the room. I look around taking in my surroundings; I am in some sort of storage facility. There are no windows, but I can make out a large set of storage shelves and a small table to the left side of the room. The darkness is an eerie sort of darkness. I feel my heartbeat start to quicken and that is when the tears start to fall. I am terrified that we are not going to make it out of here.

"I'm sorry, I'm sorry, I'm so sorry boo, I promise I'll protect you with my life, I won't let anyone hurt you. Mummy will get us out of here," I whisper to my baby, wishing I could believe my words and close my eyes.

I picture Sam's sparkling green eyes and his dimples, his hard, inked, muscular body and the way he looked at me, as if I was the only woman in the world. That thought will get me through anything.

***

I'm not sure how much time passes, but I am shaken by the cold chill of J.D's voice.

"Wakey, wakey, bitch. Round fucking two."

I look up, his eyes are wide, glossy and he is sweating profusely. If I am not mistaken, he has been taking cocaine. He goes to retrieve something from the other side of the room and moves back over to me. He crouches down in front of me and pulls the blade he used on me from behind his back. I flinch as it comes into view, and he smirks.

"Say hello to my little friend."

He mimics the famous Scarface line, and I swallow back the lump that has formed in my throat. He holds the knife in front of his face and looks at it in awe. He examines it and runs his finger along the knife-edge.

"Sam says hello, by the way. I called him while I was gone, and he asked me to send his love."

My eyes widen, and my blood runs cold. *Sam knows I'm here.*

"He...he...he knows I'm here?" I ask with disbelief in my voice, and he laughs.

"Of course, he does, sweetheart, he asked me to kidnap you, and he asked me to make sure you didn't make it to the gig. He said he wanted to break up with you, so him and me could finally be together. I knew he would see sense in the end; I told you, you were just a stopgap, something pretty to fill the time. He said I'm welcome to do whatever I want with you, I can kill you if I want, kill you and the demon spawn inside of you. He never wanted you; it's always been me."

As he says those words, my whole world feels like it has crashed down around me. I am truly crushed. *Why would Sam do this? Why? I thought he loved me. All these months he's been stringing me along. Because what? Because he's gay? Because he's in love with J.D?* His grating laugh snaps me out of my thoughts, and he starts clapping.

"Well done! You're finally getting it, sweetheart! All the pieces are at long last falling into place!" he says brightly and claps his hands animatedly.

I shake my head, feeling physically sick.

"NO! NO! YOU'RE FUCKING LYING! IT'S NOT TRUE! SAM LOVES ME!" I scream, as his maniacal laugh echoes around the room.

"Oh, you're so deluded sweetheart, Sam's in love with me; he has been for years, ever since that night we spent together! He uses women because he can't come to terms with his sexuality, but he always comes back to me. Now, after all these years, he's seen that no matter how many women he has in his bed, I'll always be here. I'll be the one who he comes back to in the end. He asked me to punish you, to do with as I please and you know what? He doesn't fucking care!"

He raises his voice and spits out those final four words with such venom, I have no doubt in my mind that he is telling the truth. I am sobbing uncontrollably now, and I feel bile rising in my throat.

"NO!" I yell, and he jumps up from the floor. He moves closer to my face.

"YES!" he mocks, and I violently thrash against my restraints, screaming hysterically.

"HELP! OH GOD PLEASE! SOMEONE HELP! PLEASE HELP ME! PLEASE!"

He slaps me with the back of his hand across my face, and the slap is so harsh it echoes around the room.

"Shut the fuck up, bitch. This will all be over soon, and then I'll take a few pictures, maybe a lock of hair." He twirls my hair around his finger and the feel of his hands on me, makes my skin crawl. "Just as a reminder, a souvenir if you like, to show Sam. He'll be happy that I've done this for him, and I plan on making him show me just how grateful he is," he says menacingly, and I zone out to a place where all this is just a bad dream.

18

Peyton
Present

"Beaut."

Remy's voice is rough, and his face is filled with concern as I see him walking towards me in the hospital corridor. He is wearing jeans, a black t-shirt, and white Converse trainers; his long dark hair is tied up in a ponytail. I have never been so glad to see a friendly face, in this moment, he is my saviour.

Remy Logan is Ruby's older brother, I went to him for help after J.D kidnapped, tortured, and supposedly killed me. Remy is three years older than Ruby and me, at thirty-one years old. He is six feet five inches tall, lean, and muscular with kind, deep brown eyes, with olive skin and long, dark brown, wavy hair. He reminds me of Heath Ledger in the film 10 Things I Hate About You. You can definitely tell him, and Ruby are brother and sister; they look so alike it's scary. I lost my virginity at the age of seventeen to Remy, who was twenty at the time, and we have always had a soft spot for each other. If I am honest, he was my first love. We were inseparable, and I was besotted with him.

Ruby and Remy were once estranged due to their parents, Pearl and Ray, favouring Remy. However, as they grew older, they set their differences aside and kept in touch regularly via phone, letter, email, and Skype. A year after Remy took my virginity, he joined the army and left without a word. I was heartbroken and totally devastated when he left. I really thought he was the one. Remy and I kept in touch by letter while he was stationed in Afghanistan. Six years after he joined the army, he had his left leg blown off below the knee by a roadside bomb in the Helmand Province. Shortly after this, we reconnected and started chatting again, before I got together with Callum. We started to keep in touch regularly via phone, email, and FaceTime, as he did with Ruby.

At twenty-seven, Remy was honourably discharged from the army, due to the injury he sustained. He also received somewhere in the region of one point six million pounds in compensation after a long, drawn-out legal battle. He spent some time in Camp Bastion Field Hospital after his injury before he was flown back to the U.K to undergo a number of operations and extensive rehabilitation. After he had recovered, he moved to America, invested in some properties and he has been there ever since. He has a prosthetic leg and walks with a slight limp. He works in a bar and is a part-time self-defence trainer, not that he needs to. Even though he was once serving for his country, he isn't bitter at all. He is lucky to be alive, and even though he suffers from P.T.S.D, he is happy to live out the rest of his days as a civilian and in relative peace. I will be eternally grateful for everything he has done for me.

I run into his arms and as soon as he wraps his arms around me, I break down. I sob in his arms. I sob for Sam, for the past year of my life I have been without him, for the lies J.D fed me, for putting him through hell, and for Freddie, our innocent, beautiful baby boy.

"Shhh, it's alright, I'm here. I've got you, shhh everything's going to be ok," he soothes and kisses the top of my head, pulling me tighter to him. "Let it all out, beaut, I'm not going anywhere."

His voice is soft, as he runs his hands up and down my back.

"Let me take you back to the hotel. Freddie's missing his mummy, I left him with Marta in the hotel crèche."

I shake my head and pull away from our embrace. Suddenly overcome with the need to go back into Sam's hospital room and make him listen to me.

"I can't...Rem...I can't, Sam...he...he needs to listen, he h...has to understand why," I choke out, and he cups my face in his hands.

"Hey, look at me, beautiful, chances are he's angry, upset, or both, am I right?"

I meet his sympathetic brown gaze, and I nod.

"Then maybe it's for the best, if you leave it until he's at least calmed down a little, you need to trust me on this one."

I know he's right, but I have to make him understand. I have to make him see that I never wanted any of this. All I ever wanted was to keep Freddie safe and protect us both from J.D. I have gone a whole year believing J.Ds twisted, sick lies and I intend to make it right, even if I die trying.

19

Sam

After a restless night's sleep, with all the thoughts of Peyton, our son and the past year running through my mind at a million miles an hour. I wake the next morning to Peyton sitting next to my bed. As my sluggish brain registers the fact I am not dreaming, I take in every inch of her once again. Pillar box red hair in a short, sleek bob secured by a red polka dot headband, a red vest top, tiny, faded, ripped, denim shorts, and red Converse trainers. She is visibly thinner and looks almost too thin. The muscles in her biceps are taut and more defined. Her heavily tattooed skin is sun-kissed and golden; the sun definitely suits her. *God, she is fucking stunning.* Vulnerability and sheer anguish shroud her face, and I can't fucking stand to see that look on her.

The anger I felt yesterday, has somewhat dissipated. I was in shock, I was angry, upset and my feelings overwhelmed me all at once. I needed some time to think, and even though my night was restless, my thoughts are finally clear. I am willing to try, to take things slow. All I know is, I *need* her back in my life, fuck the consequences. I don't think she realises I'm awake, until I reach over to tuck an errant strand of her hair behind her ear. She flinches violently at my touch and my heart slams against my rib cage at her reaction to me. *What the fuck happened to her in the year she was gone?*

"Morning," I rasp, and she looks up at me like a rabbit caught in headlights. "I didn't mean to startle you," I say apologetically, and I notice that her eyes are red, puffy and bloodshot. "You've been crying," I say matter of factly, as she sits up straight and wipes her eyes with the back of her hand.

"It's nothing," she whispers, and I cock my pierced eyebrow.

"I can smell bullshit, angel."

She sniffs, and she goes to get up from her chair.

"You look exhausted."

I regard her intently, and I reach for her hand to stop her from leaving.

"Look, please don't go, sit down and talk to me. I'm so sorry about the way I reacted yesterday, I was angry, upset, shocked, confused. I didn't mean all those things I said. It was said in the heat of the moment. I'm sorry, please forgive me, angel."

Dejectedly, she sits back down in the chair, shaking her head and laughing bitterly.

"Forgive you? I'm the one who should be begging your forgiveness. You were right, what I did was unforgivable, Sam. I let you think I was dead, and I gave birth to your baby without telling you. I should be on my fucking knees pleading with you to forgive me."

I look at her and cock my head, as she angrily swipes at her eyes.

"What the fuck happened to you, Peyton?"

That's when I see it, the pained look in her eyes. Seeing that look in her beautiful blue eyes crushes my soul.

"I...I don't want to talk about it, it's not important."

It is as if the shutters have come down on her emotions and she dismisses me instantly. She stands up and I know I have to think of something to make her stay. *Think Newbolt don't let her leave.*

"Can I see him?"

She looks at me.

"Freddie, can I see our son?"

She smiles and nods. I catch a glimpse of the girl I fell in love with in that moment. The feisty, carefree, woman whose blue eyes dance when she smiles. My heart fills with hope that there still might be a chance for us. Even if it's just a small sliver of a chance, I'll hold onto that.

20

Peyton

"Can I see him?" he blurts out.

His phrase shocks me to the core, and I look up at him, regarding him intently. I am so taken aback by his words, I don't know what to say. His mood seems to have shifted dramatically from our initial encounter yesterday.

"Freddie, can I see our son?"

I smile and nod at the thought of our son Freddie meeting his daddy for the first time. The thought makes my heart swell with pride and love, not just for Freddie, but for Sam too.

"Yeah, of course. It was never my intention to keep him from you, Sam, you have to believe that."

My voice is barely a whisper, I look to the floor, and I'm having trouble maintaining eye contact, because of the hidden hurt I see when I look at him.

"Look at me, angel," he whispers huskily, and I can't help but obey his commanding voice.

I look at him, and he is still that breath-taking man I fell in love with. His raven black hair is longer, shaggy and falling into his eyes. His arms are more sculpted and corded with pure, hard, muscle. He is tanned, and he looks like he has added even more tattoos to his perfect body. Peeking through the top of his hospital gown, I can see he has a chest piece spanning from one collarbone to the other. The words *My Angel* are inked in large, black, gothic script lettering. There isn't an inch of skin on his arms that isn't tattooed, and he looks even more perfect. My eyes skim over his chest tattoo, the elegant flowing script is visually beautiful, and I can't take my eyes off it. He gently runs his long-calloused finger down my arm, and I shiver at his familiar touch; the touch I have missed so much.

"For you, you were...*are* my angel, Peyton. You saved me in so many ways, from myself most of all," he rasps.

I wipe away tears that escape from my eyes, and I hate that I've done this to him. I hate that I'm the one that put that look in his eyes. *Fuck, I really can't do this.* I step back from the hospital bed. My heart is pounding at what feels like a hundred miles a minute. He reaches for me, but I move away before his hand makes contact with mine. If he touches me, I know I'll cave and give in to the feelings threatening to overwhelm me.

"Don't go, please."

His husky voice sounds pained and thick with unshed tears. I shake my head.

"I'm...so s...sorry, I can't, I can't do this," I choke out and rush through the door quickly, feeling a panic attack threatening.

"FUCK!"

I hear him roar, as I leave the room. As I try to make my escape, I collide with a hard wall of muscle, and strong arms catch me before I fall to the ground. I look up to see Remy's kind, friendly, face, full of concern.

"*Whoa!* Where are you going in such a hurry?"

That's when the tears come, and I break down. I sob harder than I have in a long time and it feels good to finally let it all out. Remy pulls me close to him and envelopes me in his arms.

"Let it go, beaut," he soothes in his soft voice, which has become familiar to me in the time I have known him.

I cling to him for dear life, because I have no idea how I'm going to make it right. *It's all such a fucking mess.*

21

Sam

I step out of the hospital room after her, and my shoulder screams in protest. *I feel like such a fucking tit in this hospital gown. I need Cole to arrange a change of clothes for me.* As I step further out of the room, I see a guy with long dark hair, who seems to be a little overly familiar with Peyton. He has his arms around her, and he is whispering softly to her while rubbing his hands up and down her back pacifyingly. She is sobbing, and I know I don't really have a right, but all I can think is that *it should be me.* I need to feel her in my arms again; it's been so fucking long. I am aching to hold her, to let her know that contrary to what she might think, I don't hate her. I'm aching to tell her that there still could be a chance for us. I clench my fists at my side and try to rein in the overwhelming sense of jealousy that's clouding my judgement. I clear my throat, and she jumps back from his embrace, like a deer caught in headlights. Her sad, watery, blue eyes lock with mine and my heart slams against my rib cage.

"Peyton, can we finish our conversation, please? I wasn't done talking," I ask graciously, and she nods reluctantly.

She smiles warmly at the guy, who I am beginning to hate more with every passing fucking second. *Get your hands off my girl, motherfucker.*

"I'm on my mobile if you need me, beaut. I'll go get the little guy, and I'll come pick you up in a little while. Call me if you need anything at all?"

He winks and kisses her forehead. She nods. I gesture for her to go in ahead of me and she steps back into the room. I follow her, close the door behind me and hop carefully back up onto the bed. I nod for her to take a seat in the vacant chair next to my bed; she sits down half-heartedly, and I regard her with narrow eyes.

"So, what's the deal with you and the long-haired lover?" I say a little too abruptly.

He folds her arms defensively and presses her lips into a thin line.

"Are you fucking him?" I blurt out, and she winces at my crass question.

"So, what if I am? It's none of your fucking business, Sam; you don't get to act like the jealous lover because I'm no longer yours. You've made that abundantly fucking clear."

Her tone is harsh, and my heart clenches at her phrase. Her reaction to my question wasn't what I was expecting, and I see the shutters come down on her blue eyes once again.

"You never fucking stopped being mine, angel," I say softly.

She takes a deep, shaky breath and looks up at me.

"Please stop calling me angel."

Her voice is small, and I frown as a tear slips down her cheek. She shakes her head.

"Please, Sam, I don't deserve it. I lost that right when I made you think I was dead, I can't bear to see you look at me like...like."

She sobs softly, and I reach out to tip her chin up.

"Look at me, like what?"

She looks up at me, and that only makes her sob harder. Hearing her sob like that completely tears me apart and I can't fucking bear it.

"Like you hate me...like...you c...can't bear to touch me or even be near me."

She manages to choke out, and I swing my legs off the bed, ignoring the burning sensation ripping through my shoulder. I move closer to her and cup her face in my hands.

"Listen to me, angel, I could *never* hate you. *Jesus fucking Christ,* I'm struggling not to wrap you in my arms and carry you out of here. There hasn't been a day that's gone by that I haven't wished, and even though I'm not remotely religious, I fucking *prayed* for this moment to come. I've dreamt of holding you, kissing you."

I get off the bed, ignoring the pain. I crouch down in front of her, and I softly touch her cheek with my bandaged hand.

"*God*...you're even more fucking beautiful than I remember."

She leans into my touch and closes her eyes.

"I've never stopped loving you, angel, *never*. You were always in here."

I place her hand over my thundering heartbeat. Her tiny, trembling hand feels warm against my chest, and I relish her touch. As silence descends on us, neither of us knows what to say to the other. I hold her gaze and run her silky hair through my fingers, swiftly but subtly changing the subject.

"I like your hair. I love the colour, it really suits you, angel."

I smile; she returns my smile, and somewhere in those beautiful blue eyes, I see a glimpse of the woman I fell in love with.

"In answer to your question, no I'm not fucking him; Remy is Ruby's older brother, and he's...just been a really good friend to me."

I smile a genuine smile, and my shoulders sag with relief at hearing her say those words.

"He was there...when I really needed a friend. I was so alone; all I wanted was to get on a plane back to London, let myself into your apartment and snuggle up in bed next to you."

The truth is after she '*died*' I couldn't bear to be in the apartment without being reminded of her everywhere I went. Every room had a memory of her in it. So, I sold the building to a billionaire CEO called Nolan Wilder, who was looking to set roots down in London. I moved out to Sawbridgeworth in Hertfordshire, just over nine months ago, to get out of the rat race that is London. As a condition of his release from rehab, Brody lives with me too. He has his own wing of the house, and the arrangement suits us both. It has become a sanctuary for us, and it is the epitome of the phrase '*bachelor pad*', with our own cinema room, game room, pool table, swimming pool, and hot tub.

"The bloke who lives there now would have had a shock if you had crawled into bed with him! I don't live in the apartment anymore, angel."

I say with an amused tone to my voice and her eyes widen.

"You loved that place."

I smile at her sentiment and shrug nonchalantly.

"It's just bricks and mortar, babe; just four walls and a roof. I sold up and moved into a nine-bedroom mansion in Hertfordshire with Brody. *Everywhere* I went in that apartment, I saw you: in the bedroom, in the bathroom, in the studio, on the balcony, in the kitchen. *Fuck*, your ghost literally haunted me for months, so I *had* to leave. I had no other choice. I tried so hard, but I couldn't fucking bear it, I had to for my own sanity."

I shake my head to rid myself of the thoughts of the dark place I ended up in after her death. My heartbeat quickens, and she looks at me questioningly.

"I know I don't have the right, but there's something you're not telling me, Sam Newbolt."

She narrows her eyes, and I smile. *My smart girl.*

"No getting anything past you is there?"

Her shy smile reminds me of the day we met, the way she looked at me, the sly glances and the way her hands felt on me as she was tattooing me.

22

Sam

The Day They Met

I've been on the leather bed being tattooed by her for over an hour. Every time her hands make contact with my skin, I feel like I am on fucking fire. She feels it too, I know she does. I know I should just stop fucking about and ask her out. Usually, I wouldn't hesitate, but she's turned me into a fucking pussy within the matter of a couple of hours. The doorbell of the shop chimes to signal someone entering, and I look up. Peyton stops tattooing me, and she looks up at the same time. A tall, leggy, olive-skinned, brunette walks in, her heels clicking across the floor. She has bought coffee, and she comes closer to us as she greets Peyton.

"Hey, sweetie."

She smiles; she's gorgeous, but not as gorgeous as the girl in front of me.

"Hey, babe."

My body feels bereft as she moves her hands away from me. She kisses Peyton on the cheek.

"I bought you some coffee; I thought you could do with a break."

Peyton takes the coffee from her friend, takes off the lid and sips the steaming liquid. Her shoulders visibly relax, but I'm too enamoured by this beautiful creature to notice anything else going on around me. I don't know what the fuck is wrong with me. I swing my leg off the bed and lean down close to her.

"Can I get a sip of that please, darlin'. I'm spitting feathers," I boldly ask her, fully expecting her to say no.

She politely offers me the cup, and I take a long sip of the warm liquid. It is way too sweet for me, but it fits her perfectly.

"Thanks, babe."

I wink and flash her a dimpled grin. *Nicely done, you fucking smoothie you! Go in for the kill, Newbolt, just ask her. What's the worst that can happen?*

"Do you fancy coming out with me when you're done? Maybe I could take you to dinner? I can be very persuasive," I rasp, and she bites her lower lip.

Fuck me, that was easily the most erotic thing I have ever seen, and my cock instantly comes to life. Easy fella!

"Are you fucking with me?"

She lowers her voice, and my face turns deadly serious. *How can she possibly think I'm joking? How can she not know how beautiful she is?*

"I never fuck about when it comes to a beautiful woman, babe."

She seems to think about my answer, and she pauses for a few seconds, giving me time to actually take her in. Her blue eyes are captivating. They say eyes are the windows to the soul, and I can sense that she's been hurt in the past. I've seen that look before.

"Sorry, I don't date arrogant, cocky rockers, it's not my style," she quips, and I smile.

So that's the way she's going to play it? Game on, sweetheart.

"Playing hard to get, ok I can deal with that," I say in my calmest voice.

I get back up on the bed, and she continues tattooing me as if nothing has happened. My body is rejoicing at feeling her hands on me once more. It has been such a long time since I have had a proper relationship, but there is something about this woman that makes me want to try. *Engage her in conversation Newbolt; show her you're just a normal, regular guy.*

"So, how long have you worked here?"

Is that all you've got? Fucking pathetic, totally lame, must try harder.

She sighs.

"Are we really going to do this? The small talk, like you're really interested in a girl like me."

I frown, and I want to physically hurt the guy that hurt her in the past to make her doubt herself so badly.

"Just because you see my life splashed all over the tabloids, doesn't mean you get to judge me. I wouldn't have asked if I wasn't genuinely interested, babe, seriously."

I roll my eyes, and I'm actually hurt. All I want is for her to just give me a chance to show her I'm not the bad boy rocker the newspapers make me out to be.

"I'm sorry, it's just..."

I stop her. *Try again dude, second times a charm.*

"Come out with me, please."

She shakes her head.

"I'm not going to be subjected to fangirls swooning over you, interrupting us for photos and autographs at every available opportunity."

I laugh mischievously, and it seems to disarm her momentarily. *She's actually jealous; keep going you'll break down her defences eventually.*

"Is that jealousy I sense?"

She rolls her eyes, and I smirk wickedly.

"Why would I be jealous, I hardly know you?"

Keep denying it, darlin', I've got all day. I bite my lip piercing seductively, as my eyes lock with hers.

"Green is a colour that definitely suits you, babe," I say in my husky tone and her neck muscles contract. *She's so fucking affected by me.*

"You seem to have forgotten my name again; you keep calling me babe. It's ok, my name is Peyton. Do you need me to spell it for you? It begins with a P."

Whoa! I was definitely not expecting that! I hear snickers from the boys across the shop. *I'm glad my predicament is amusing; you bunch of fuckers.*

"Stop busting his balls, babe and give the guy a chance."

I look across the shop at her friend; she seems to be sticking up for me.

"It seems you've forgotten her name too, sweetheart."

I banter back, and she cocks her perfectly groomed eyebrow at me.

"Oh yeah, silly me, my mistake. I'm sorry Peyton."

She emphasises her name, accentuating the 'P' and narrows her eyes at Peyton. I smile.

"Are you usually like this around other guys, or is it just me?"

I am curious to know, and she seems stunned into silence. I think she might have met her match with me, because the way she's looking at me, tells me she isn't used to being called out on her behaviour.

"Wow, no wonder you're single, assuming you are single. God help the guy if he puts up with you, Miss High Maintenance. He must have the patience of a saint," I say sarcastically, and I didn't mean for that to come out as harsh as it did.

Shit! Nice one Newbolt, dick move. Engage your brain, before you engage your extremely large fucking mouth. She stops tattooing me and slams her tattoo machine down on the table with a clatter. She rips off her gloves, and she can't even bring herself to look at me. *Fucking fuck!*

"I'm taking a break," she snaps and storms to the back of the shop.

I instantly feel bad for making her feel that way. She probably thinks I'm exactly like the rest of the male population and she's never going to agree to go out with me now. I'm such a fucking dickhead. Her friend casually walks over to me, and I feel instantly calmed by the smell of her perfume. How do women do that? She brushes my arm, in an affectionate gesture. Her big brown eyes look up at me, and she smiles warmly. She definitely doesn't make my dick twitch like Peyton does. That's a good thing...I think!

"Don't worry, babe, she's not usually like that. I think it's her way of letting you know she likes you; it's sort of...a defence mechanism."

She explains as I smile and nod.

"She's been hurt badly in the past, it's not you, she's just overly cautious when it comes to men in general, that's all. Don't take it personally, babe."

She beams, and as she says those words, I immediately want to bury the guy who hurt her so badly.

"I'm Ruby, by the way."

She offers me her hand, and I take it. I don't get the electricity as she touches me, Peyton is definitely something special.

"Sam," I introduce myself in an amused tone, and she nods.

"I know who you are, I'm a huge fan."

She giggles nervously, and instead of her giggling being annoying, I find it endearing. I throw my head back and laugh. Her eyes roam to the other end of the shop and stop on Jax. She's definitely hot for him, and by the way, he's eye-fucking her. The feeling is definitely more than reciprocated.

"I could put in a word with Jax, if you like? You did me a favour by trying to stand up for me back there; it's a fair trade I'd say."

She smiles shyly and nods. She leans in, as if she is sharing a secret with me, and whispers in my ear.

"She loves Italian food, and her favourite dish is chicken, bacon, and mushroom Alfredo, hold the parmesan. Just don't tell her I told you."

I laugh and wink cheekily at her.

"Thanks for the tip, sweetheart, I really appreciate it."

I instantly like her, something about her tells me that she is more of a sister to Peyton than a friend.

"I like you, now get after her, hot stuff!"

She winks and struts off across the shop towards Jax. I stand up and walk with purpose to the back of the shop. I have to make it right with her; she makes me feel things I haven't felt in a long time. I hang back, watching her wage an internal war with herself. Even in profile she's beautiful. She's short, but perfectly in proportion. Her button nose, her soft plump lips, her huge breasts, her flat stomach, and her gorgeous arse. I've got it so bad. I move closer to her, and she lowers her head as if she senses my presence. I tower over her small frame and lean casually in the doorway. Don't grovel, be cool.

"Look, I'm really sorry, Peyton; I didn't mean to be such a dick."

She shakes her head, and by the look on her face, she's still mad at me. Ok, now might be a good time to start grovelling.

"I'm not usually like this around people, women in particular, I'm complete and utter mush around you. Ever since I set foot in the shop and laid eyes on you, you do something to me, Peyton. I've never felt like this before, like ever."

See, that wasn't so hard, was it? A bit of honesty and sincerity, that's what women like, right?

She looks up at me, but she cheekily banters back.

"Was that a line?"

God, this woman is going to be the fucking death of me! I laugh.

"You caught me! I think it might have been!"

We both laugh, and I brush her arm, feeling the familiar electricity crackling between us. Our eyes lock, and I can't look away.

"Please tell me it's not my imagination, you feel it, too, don't you?" I whisper, and I notice my hand is still on her arm.

I lean close to her, and my stubble grazes her cheek. I expect her to put some distance between us, but she doesn't. *She wants you, Newbolt. Move in for the kill.*

"I'll ruin you, Peyton."

My voice is gruff, and our eyes lock. Neither of us can look away. My heart starts thundering in my chest, and she bites her lip. Fuck.

"Maybe I want you to."

I smile wickedly, and a growl rumbles from deep within my chest. *Great, she probably thinks I'm going to club her over the head and drag her back to my man cave, by her hair.*

"Is that a challenge?"

She's flirting, just go with it, Newbolt. I raise a pierced eyebrow, and I laugh. *Third time lucky.*

"Please, come out with me," I whisper huskily.

"Ok, I'll come out with you."

I am doing my inner manly victory dance, and I tuck a strand of her soft, dark, hair behind her ear.

"I'll see you at seven then."

A look of satisfaction crosses my face. I have never tried with a woman before, and it feels good. She folds her arms, and her teeth chatter from the afternoon chill. *Make your move, Newbolt.*

"Are you cold?"

She nods, as her teeth chatter.

"Just a little...actually I'm bloody freezing!"

We both laugh, and I silently wrap my arms around her, unable to stop myself. I pull her close to my chest, she feels so good in my arms. Her scent envelopes me, as I run my hands up and down her back. I can feel goose bumps break out across her smooth tattooed skin.

"There's something between us, Peyton."

I know she feels it too, she's desperately trying to deny it, but I can see it clearly. She looks up at me as if she's taking me in.

"You feel it, too, don't you? I know you do, the way your eyes glaze over when I'm near you," I whisper and bury my nose in her hair. She smells so good of strawberries and tropical fruit.

She wraps her arms tighter around me and pulls me closer to her, by the hair at the nape of my neck. She presses her lips greedily to mine and kisses me as if her life depends on it. The contrast of her soft lips on mine and the way her tongue erotically strokes mine instantly arouses me, and I feel my erection press against her thigh. She pulls away, and we're both breathless. *That wasn't what I was expecting. Fuck my life.*

"I'm sorry...I..."

Why is she apologising? That was probably the single best kiss of my life. The way her lips felt, the way her hands subconsciously ran through my hair, the way she gripped onto my biceps and the soft, delicious, erotic moan that escaped her as she stroked my tongue with hers. She runs her fingers across her lips, and I start to imagine what those lips would look like wrapped around my cock as she's taking my length in her beautiful mouth. Her eyes are blazing with arousal, and I don't think I'm able to speak. I clear my throat and find my voice.

"Don't be sorry, I'm not."

She looks at me and shakes her head. She hurries back inside, leaving me standing there, with a satisfied grin plastered across my face.

23

Sam

Present

"We spent almost a year together, why the fuck are you acting like we're strangers, angel?" I question, and she reluctantly looks up at me, from beneath her eyelashes.

"Because everything's changed now, Sam. I've changed; you've changed...*fuck*. We're someone's parents now, don't you get that?"

I still can't get my head around the fact, that while I thought she was dead, she gave birth to my baby. Our baby, *my son*. She takes her phone from her pocket and starts tapping at the screen. She moves closer to the bed and shows me a picture on her phone. As soon as I see the picture, I instantly fall in love with the little boy on the screen, and I can't find my breath. *Jesus fucking Christ*. The little boy on the screen is my double; he has my cheeky dimples, the brightest green sparkling eyes and wild tufts of black hair. I swallow back the golf ball size lump in my throat before I speak and blink back the tears threatening to track their way down my cheeks.

"H...he's...he...*fuck me*...he's beautiful."

She grins with such pride and once again, I see my girl. The girl I fell in love with.

"He's six months old now; he was born on the first of June, he was two weeks overdue, and he was eight pounds four ounces. He reminds me so much of you, he has your mannerisms. Every day he does something new, he learns something new, and he gives me hope, Sam."

Her voice is thick with unshed tears, and I reluctantly hand her phone back to her.

"He's so pure and innocent, Sam. He's my little miracle, and he melts my heart every time he looks into my eyes. It's like he can see straight into my soul."

She tucks her phone away. I hear the awe in her voice, and a small smile ghosts her lips as she speaks of our son.

"I still can't believe it myself; I almost lost him. I'm terrified someone's going to take him away from me, and I find myself getting up in the middle of the night, just to watch him sleep. I have to remind myself that I'm his mum and he's a little person, who is completely dependent on me. The day I gave birth to him, I was fucking terrified, and I'd never felt so alone."

A tear slips down her cheek, and she swipes it away. I regard her intently and take her hand in mine. I expect her to pull her hand away, but she lets me hold it in mine. I softly stroke her knuckles soothingly and she seems to visibly relax, for the first time since she came here.

"I won't apologise for protecting our son, I did what I had to, but I'm so sorry for putting you through that, Sam."

She sobs, and the sound pierces my heart.

"Shhh, it's alright, angel, everything's going to be alright, I promise you."

As I say those words, I am not sure whether I really truly believe them. After a few minutes of letting me hold her, she pulls away, and I am bereft of the loss of her warm body against me. Before I can get my thoughts in check, I tangle my hand in her hair and crush my lips to hers. Fuck, I have missed the feel of her soft lips, the contrast of her softness against my ruggedness. We both lose ourselves in each other, and for that moment, I forget the day I lost her. It is almost as if it never happened. Death stole everything from me that day. It tore her from me and turned my life upside down. Now, suddenly to have a second chance, a decent shot of happiness and I'll do everything in my power to make that dream back into a reality.

24

Peyton

Past

I look like a fucking whale. I'm exhausted, my back aches, I have been experiencing painful cramps, and my baby boy is kicking the shit out of me every time he moves around in my stomach. He's two weeks overdue, and I'm desperate to meet him now. Remy is being a total sweetie, and I'm getting daily visits from my friends Joel, Blaze, and Henley. In the months I have been in Santa Monica, I have made some lifelong friends. I will be forever grateful for their support and for accepting me as one of their own.

"That baby's going to come out wanting Ben and Jerry's instead of milk, you know that don't you, beaut?" Remy says playfully, and I laugh.

"Only the best for my boy, Rem."

He chuckles. I am in the kitchen helping Remy put the shopping away. I have been having pains for a few months, but according to my baby book *What to Expect when you're Expecting* a woman can experience pains in the last three months of pregnancy. 'Braxton Hicks', or so I'm told. I am putting some milk into the fridge when it happens, a sharp tightening cramp in my stomach and a gush of warm liquid trickling down my leg. *Shit. It's happening.* I drop the milk on the floor and clutch my stomach.

"Rem, my water just broke. I think the baby's coming," I say in a panicked voice.

His face goes deathly white. He swallows a few times before he speaks.

"I'll go and get the car, hang in there."

He rushes as fast as he can out of the house. I use the worktop as an aid to make my way out of the kitchen and into the large open plan living room. That's when the pain rips through me, and I thought I had experienced pain, but this is a completely new kind, I scream out in agony.

"REMY!"

I hear the roar of his car's engine in the driveway and the sound of his boots across the floor, as he comes bounding in through the front door.

"I've called ahead, beaut, they're expecting us."

He grabs my hospital bag and puts his arm around my shoulder as another pain tears through me. I cry out, and my legs buckle underneath me. His strong, solid arms stop me from falling.

"I've got ya," he soothes, and he carries me down the steps.

He bundles me in the front of his car and goes around to the driver's side. He pulls out of the driveway at breakneck speed and drives us to the hospital.

"Hang in there little fella. Your mum's been waiting patiently for you, and now suddenly, it seems she's not ready. We need you to hang in there, just a little while longer, mate."

He talks to my stomach as he drives, and I suddenly feel the urge to burst out laughing.

"What's so funny?"

I laugh hysterically.

"He's just like his dad. Once he's got his mind set on something, he doesn't give up until he's got it, and he's got his tiny mind set on coming out right now."

I blink back the threatening tears. I will not think of Sam, not now. Remy cocks his eyebrow at me.

"Is that what the rock star did, beaut? Did he set his mind on you and stalk you into submission, until you relented and agreed to go out with him?" Remy says derisively and smirks wickedly. I narrow my eyes on him.

"Ha ha, very funny, Logan."

I clutch my stomach.

"Mummy's here baby boy, listen to Uncle Remy, just a little bit longer, because I'm not giving birth in this car."

Remy raises his eyebrows.

"Damn fucking straight, you're not giving birth in my car! I'll be sending you the cleaning bill!"

He laughs and another pain tears through me.

"Oh God, Rem, it hurts."

I cry as he reaches over the centre console and holds my hand.

"I know, I know it does, it's going to be alright, I promise," he says softly as he plants a kiss on the back of my hand. "Shush, it's alright, beaut, not too much further, we're nearly there."

After what seems like a lifetime, we pull up outside Cedar Sinai Hospital, which is probably only ten minutes from the house, but it seems like so much longer. Remy helps me out of the car and wraps his tanned, corded, arm around my waist. A nurse is waiting outside the hospital with a wheelchair. Remy sits me down in the wheelchair, and I unexpectedly get this overwhelming feeling of loneliness. *God, I want Sam so badly. I know I hate him right now, but he should be here with me.* I grab Remy's hand and squeeze it tightly.

"Remy, please don't leave me, I need you," I plead with him.

"I'm not going anywhere, I'm right here," he appeases, and we are whisked off into the brightly lit hospital.

As we are taken into the maternity wing, another pain rips through me, and I squeeze Remy's hand.

"Fuck me, you've got some strength in those tiny hands!" Remy jokes, and we both laugh.

My laughter soon turns to gut-wrenching sobs.

"I'm so scared, Rem."

We have stopped inside a private room, and Remy crouches down in front of me, clutching my hand tightly.

"Listen to me, beaut, I'm right here. I'm not going anywhere, I promise you. You and that little boy aren't going to want for anything, I can guarantee you that. Even though he's not my baby, I'll take care of you both and look after you as if you were my own. I will protect you with my fucking life, I swear."

He squeezes my hand tightly again. He says those words with such conviction and passion it makes me sob harder. He is willing to sacrifice the life he's become accustomed to, to take care of my baby and me. *Remy Logan, you never cease to amaze me.*

"Hey, I said that because it's the truth, not to make you cry."

Remy smiles, and as he says those words, another sharp pain overwhelms me.

"Make it stop, Rem," I plead with him, and he chuckles.

"I wish I could, but I think we're a little too late for that, beaut!"

I narrow my eyes at him, and he smirks as he holds his hands up defensively. *Hormones and sarcasm, definitely not a good combination.* Remy helps me to my feet and lifts me onto the bed. A nurse steps into the room and starts hooking me up to machines to monitor the baby's heartbeat. The strong, steady sound of my baby boys' heartbeat, da-dum-da-dum, echoes throughout the room and I can't hold back the sobs, as another contraction rips through my body.

"Rem."

He strokes my knuckles.

"I'm here, beaut," he says through clenched teeth as I squeeze his hand. He looks to the nurse with concerned eyes. "Isn't there anything you can do for her? Please?"

His voice is laced with desperation, and I see his eyes glaze over. The nurse smiles warmly at him.

"The contractions are too far apart at the moment, but you and your wife will both meet your baby soon."

A look passes between Remy and I, but we don't correct her. The truth is, I couldn't wish for a better man to help me bring up my baby. He'll never replace Sam, but Remy is the kindest, most caring, gentlest, most loyal man I know, and I am proud to have him back in my life.

A few hours pass, and the contractions are getting more regular. They are so close together now that the nurse is urging me to push. The pain is being controlled by the intake of gas and air.

"I need you to push for me, Louise. You're doing really well," she soothes, and I do as she says. "I can see the head, honey, good girl, a few more pushes."

I scream and look into Remy's terrified eyes.

"Make it fucking stop, Rem, please," I plead, and he takes my hand in his, kissing my knuckles.

"You're doing so well, beaut, eyes on me, don't take those gorgeous eyes off me."

He smiles warmly, and my eyes lock with his.

"Good girl, that's it, focus on me."

The nurse takes her position and looks up at me.

"When your next contraction comes, I need you to do a really big push for me, honey," she says softly, and as the next contraction comes, I push with everything I have. I am crippled by a burning hot stinging sensation between my legs. It feels like someone is branding me with a red-hot poker, on my very sensitive lady parts. Fuck me. I'm in absolute agony, and I feel exhausted.

"Good girl, you're doing really well, honey. Listen to that handsome husband of yours and stay focused."

The nurse smiles.

"One last push, honey, you're doing perfect."

I push one last time, and the room is filled with the cries of my baby. Remy has the biggest grin on his face, and my jaw aches just watching him. The nurse cleans the baby off, checks him over and places him on my chest.

"Congratulations, both of you, it's a boy."

I look down at my baby boy, and I am rendered breathless by how beautiful he is. Dark tufts of black hair, which remind me so much of Sam, the cutest little button nose and he looks so angelic. He is a tiny human, totally dependent on me. He is something so precious, innocent and pure that Sam and I created. My eyes glaze over at the thought, and I kiss his head softly. I'm instantly in love.

"Hello, beautiful," I whisper, and Remy is gently stroking my hand.

He whispers softly in my ear, "I left you once, I'm not leaving you again I promise you, beaut."

He kisses my forehead, and with those words I cuddle my baby boy closer to me, cherishing the most beautiful moment that will stay in my heart forever.

Freddie Maxwell Stonebridge.

25

Peyton

Present

"Why are you pretending you're immune to my charms, angel?" Sam rasps, and my breathing starts to quicken.

I feel the all too familiar heat between my legs and I know I'm completely and utterly fucking screwed.

"I...Sam...Don't."

I am lost for words as his blazing green eyes lock with mine, and he runs his short nail down my arm. I shiver at the contact, and it feels like every nerve in my body is lit up from the inside out.

"See, even after all this time, I still affect you the way you affect me, angel," he rasps.

I follow his gaze down to his impressive erection, clearly visible through his hospital gown, and I feel my cheeks heat.

"God, I've missed being inside you so fucking badly it hurts, we've got some catching up to do, angel. Don't pretend you haven't thought about it, how I made you come over and over again, how my cock felt buried deep inside you. I'm going to fuck you so hard and so thorough, that everyone within a five-mile fucking radius *will* know my name. You'll be fucking *begging* me to stop."

His voice is rough and gravelly with lust; it practically oozes sex. I know my traitorous body will give in to its needs. I will surrender to Sam Newbolt, and there won't be a thing I can do about it. *Shit.*

Our moment is interrupted by the rowdy arrival of the other three members of Rancid Vengeance stepping into Sam's hospital room. They all look so different from how I remember them. Jax's usually messy dirty blonde hair is now straight down to his shoulders and a lighter honey blonde. He has shaved off his signature goatee beard and is clean-shaven, he reminds me of a tattooed version of Thor! He looks more muscular, defined and extremely handsome. His cheekbones are chiselled, and his smile is dazzling. He could be a model, or in a shampoo advert and I can definitely see what made Ruby fall for him. Jax looks relaxed wearing a pair of loose black combats, motorcycle boots and a tight-fitting dark denim shirt with the sleeves rolled up and the first three buttons undone, revealing his tattooed chest. Finding love with my best friend definitely suits him.

Brody's signature Mohawk has been replaced with a shaved head, and he looks so much better than the last time I saw him. He is healthy, tanned, tattooed, more muscular, and actually looks much younger than his thirty-one years. He is wearing baggy jeans with a chain hanging from one belt loop to another, a white vest with pink and blue paint splashes in an elaborate pattern on the front, a white and black skull scarf around his neck, and black Converse. It is so good to see him back on the straight and narrow. Before this whole thing blew up, Brody and I actually became really good friends after a Jack Daniels induced heart to heart conversation over a game of truth or dare. That night defined our friendship and showed me a side of him he usually keeps well hidden. Behind the public, flamboyant facade lies a deeply complex and lonely man who desperately craves the love of a good woman.

Lucas' usual faux hawk hairstyle has been traded for a light brown, almost blonde shaggy spiky style. His clean-shaven face is now stubbled making him look ruggedly handsome. He is also tanned, visibly leaner, and more muscular. He looks as if he has added more tattoos to his ever-growing collection. He is wearing black skinny jeans, a worn black *'Led Zeppelin'* vest, and black biker boots. I am so happy to see them all, they became like family and like the big brothers I never had.

The chatter stops abruptly, as Jax's mouth drops open and forms a perfect *'O'* shape, and his familiar wide hazel puppy dog eyes settle on me.

"Peyton? What the...*Fuck me.*"

His usually warm brown eyes turn cold. He narrows his eyes, regarding me frostily and he steps away from me.

"Get the fuck out," he says through clenched teeth; the tone of his voice is deadly. My smile fades as I feel tears pricking my eyes at Jax's reaction to me. Sam looks up at him, with a fierce glint in his green eyes.

"Jax, rein it the fuck in," Sam says, in his most authoritative voice.

"No, after what she fucking put you through. She waltzes in here like nothing's changed. Like she can just pick up where she left off? She deserves to know dude, she deserves to know what..."

Sam stops him from carrying on his sentence.

"If you know what's good for you, you won't carry that sentence on, Jax. Just fucking leave it," he says low and menacingly, annunciating the last four words.

Jax runs his hands frustratedly through his blonde hair.

"This is absolute fucking bullshit; Sam and you bloody well know it!" Jax snaps, as Sam narrows his eyes at him.

"If I wanted your opinion, Jax, I would fucking *ask* for it!" Sam roars.

Jax is about to give his reply when Lucas steps forward with his arms folded. His bronzed, tattooed muscles bulging. He shoots a look in Sam and Jax's direction, his eyes full of fire.

"GOD DAMN IT! WILL ALL OF YOU JUST SHUT THE FUCK UP!" he shouts, in his familiar American twang. "Has anyone actually stopped to ask Peyton why?"

Sam and Jax avoid his steely gaze. I observe the exchange between the three of them and notice that Brody is stood in the corner of the room. He is stood quietly, with his hands in his pockets, looking to the floor. I find this odd, as Brody is usually the most vocal out of all the boys.

"No, I didn't fucking think so, you need to stop and use your heads, both of you. I get that you're pissed, and you're hurt, but all of you really need to consider the bigger picture here."

He unfolds his arms and points his finger accusingly at Jax.

"And Jax you need to engage your brain before you engage your god damn mouth. I can guarantee she's probably feeling pretty shitty about it but at least have some fucking consideration for her feelings and let her at least explain, assholes."

He turns and nods, acknowledging that he has said his peace. I smile at him and mouth 'thank you' for jumping to my defence. I am extremely grateful for his intervention, and it is actually a welcome change to have someone in my corner, other than Remy right now. Brody breaks his silence and avoids looking directly at me, which breaks my heart.

"I don't know how the fuck they found out you were here, but this place is crawling with fucking press and paparazzi, man. Cole's drafted in extra men to make sure they don't get in here."

Swift change of subject. Sam shakes his head in exasperation.

"Fucking fuckers," Sam curses and I decide now would be a good time to leave, especially after Jax's reaction to me.

For the first time in a long time, I feel awkward, out of place and unwelcome by the boys I once considered an extension of my own family.

"Erm...I should...leave you to it," I say nervously, and Sam grips my wrist gently, his green eyes silently pleading with me.

"Angel, this *isn't* finished," he says gruffly, and I am suddenly engulfed in his familiar scent.

He smells of Joop, mint, and something typically Sam. *It smells like home.* He moves his hand from my wrist and grips my hand. I instantly feel goosebumps erupt all over my body and the familiar electricity crackling between us. I am left speechless, as his intense, hungry green gaze has me instantly remembering what his hands felt like running over my body and what his mouth felt like on my pussy as he edged me close to orgasm. I bite my lip and swallow harshly at the direction of my wayward thoughts.

I am interrupted by the door slamming as Jax exits the room and our moment is lost. He pulls his hand away from mine, and I feel bereft at the loss. I turn to Sam and cautiously rest my forehead on his.

"I just need some air," I reassure him, and he nods, leaning back in his hospital bed with his arms folded across his wide chest.

I leave the room and Brody casually, but silently, follows me out with his hands tucked in the pockets of his jeans. When he catches up to me, he is quiet for a moment, and I can't help feeling uncomfortable. As we walk down the corridor, he breaks the awkward silence and clears his throat.

"The rest of them might be a bunch of fucking spineless pussies, but I'm not afraid to ask you fucking *why*, Peyton."

His voice is barely a whisper, and with tears welling in my eyes, I shake my head.

"Not yet, you have to understand Sam needs to hear it from me first. Just know that I never meant for any of this to happen, Brody, *none of it*," I choke out, and he nods.

"I know, babe, I understand you can't change it, but you can sure as shit make up for it, sweets. Any fucking idiot with a pair of fucking eyes can see that boy still loves you, it's actually *really* fucking sickening!" Brody says dramatically and smiles devilishly. "If it's any consolation, you're looking good, babe. That invite to share my bed still stands you know?"

We both laugh, and I roll my eyes dramatically. *Typical Brody! Diffusing the situation with humour.*

"In your dreams, rock star, I'm a responsible human being now, I'm someone's mum," I say with pride in my voice, and Brody's eyes widen.

"You've got...a kid? *Fuck me*, is it...?"

I hit him on his arm playfully.

"Yes, he's Sam's."

I take my phone out and show him a picture of Freddie. Brody's face breaks out into a genuine grin.

"*Wow!* He...he's a handsome little fucker! He looks so much like Sam, it's scary! That's...fucking amazing, sweets, I'm so happy for you, both of you, congratulations!"

I laugh and pull him in for a hug.

"You're an uncle now, babe, just like you wanted!"

He chuckles softly, and I remember the night we announced my pregnancy at Sam's thirtieth birthday. I wipe my eyes on the sleeve of my jacket and loop my arm through his.

"You look like you're in desperate need of a coffee, sweets, let's go to the canteen. The coffee in hospitals usually sucks, but it's fucking chaos out there, there's a fuck load of fans and press outside. They got wind of Sam being in here, so Starbucks is totally out of the question, I'm sorry, babe."

I smile at his thoughtfulness. He swings us both left, and we walk, casually chatting along the way.

"So, how have you been then, babe?"

He hangs his head.

"You want the truth? Not so good, sweetheart. We took a much-needed year out of the music industry, and I spent some time in fucking rehab. Not my finest hour, but I've been clean for almost six months now. It's been the hardest six months of my fucking life, but I actually feel the best I've ever fucking felt. My relationship with Sam has been totally rebuilt.

I've apologised and made amends for the way I behaved. We're no longer the toxic duo we once were, and surprisingly enough, we're actually living together now; but it's the music that got me through. It's actually my number one priority and not the drugs for once. It hasn't been that way for such a long, long fucking time and it feels so fucking good."

I am genuinely happy that Brody has finally turned his life around and I find myself grinning with pride for him.

"I'm so happy for you, babe, it's good to see you looking so healthy and...*Hot!*"

We both laugh, as I blatantly check him out. His muscles are bulging, his chest is toned, his hips are lean and narrow, and his t-shirt is stretched over his broad shoulders.

"You think I'm hot and you're *so* fucking checking me out! *Wow!* I always knew you had a soft spot for me, babe!"

He winks and clucks his teeth. I throw my head back and laugh. We both get some coffees and sit down opposite each other. He reaches over the table and takes my hand in his tattooed one.

"Joking aside, darlin', I've missed you. Hell, we've *all* fucking missed you, and now here you are, looking smoking hot."

We both laugh, and I know I can always rely on Brody to make me laugh.

"If we had known what J.D was doing all that time, we would never have allowed that to happen. I can't apologise enough, I'm so fucking sorry, sweets."

His voice sounds pained and so full of emotion.

"I wanted to fucking kill the bastard for laying his hands on you and then kidnapping Sam."

He says through clenched teeth and scrubs his hands down his face.

"*Fuck*, it wasn't just Sam that entered the pits of hell, it was *all* of us. You became my best friend in the time we knew each other, Peyton; I missed you so fucking much. The boys too, Jax, Lucas and Ruby; *fuck me* she's going to pitch a fit when she sees you, she's pregnant with Jax's baby."

My eyes widen. *Wow,* I'm so ecstatic that Ruby and Jax finally found each other. Both of them deserve to be happy, I'm glad they defined their relationship and sorted themselves out.

"*Oh my God!*" I shriek, attracting attention from the neighbouring tables.

"*Jesus!* If that's what you sound like when you come, that's...*fuck*...that's hot!"

He smiles cheekily, and he adjusts himself in his jeans as I hit him playfully. I take a long sip of my coffee and Brody is regarding me intently from across the table.

"Where have you been all this time, babe?"

I put my cup down on the table and hang my head.

"It's not important right now. But know this, if I could have come back, I would have, Brody, in a fucking heartbeat. I had to be strong and protect us both. I had to protect myself and our son from fucking J.D. He thought he had killed both of us, but I managed to get away."

26

Peyton

Past

Oh fuck, fuck, fuck. Where am I? Oh god, oh god. Think Harper, think.

My heartbeat is thundering in my chest, as I slowly start to come around and I gradually start to realise what is going on. J.D is hovering above me and shovelling sand over my body in a shallow grave.

Shit, shit, shit! If he knows I'm alive and he didn't succeed in killing me, he'll finish me off, I know he will. I have to pretend I'm dead.

I stay stock still, terrified he is going to realise any second, and I wait, petrified to even breathe. He continues shovelling sand over my bruised and battered body. I can hear his laboured breaths and muttering to himself how 'the bitch deserved to fucking die'.

Just hang in there boo, mummy will get us out, I promise, I think to myself and continue to wait. After what seems like a lifetime, I feel my whole body covered in sand and hold my breath as he shovels sand over my face.

"Rest in peace, you fucking cunt!"

I hear him spit on me and then there is silence, a deathly kind of silence. The sound of a car engine and a screech of tires breaks the silence. I wait a little longer, until I hear nothing but the sounds of the desert surrounding me, and I begin to claw my way out of the shallow grave. I desperately claw and dig my way out of the sand that is covering my body. I'm not sure how much time passes as I claw the remainder of the sand from my body, and I let out the breath I was holding. It feels so good to breathe fresh air, and I relish the humid air on my skin. I look around in the eerie, inky darkness and I can see nothing but vast desert surrounding me. I pull my knees to my chest, and I sob gut-wrenching, desperate, wailing sobs. I'm trembling with fear, and I have no idea how I am going to survive through the night.

I have no concept of time, but my survival instinct, and the need to protect my baby, suddenly kicks in. *I can sit here sobbing, wallowing in my own self-pity, give up, and potentially die out here. Or I can pull myself together, get up, and at least try.* I manage to get to my feet, and I feel dizzy. Then I remember, J.D stabbed me. I look down and feel the stiffness of dry blood on my clothes where he stabbed me through my left breastplate. *Fuck.* In my foggy brain, I start to remember a scene from the film Romeo and Juliet, where Mercutio is stabbed, and I begin to softly chant, "It's just a scratch; it's just a scratch."

I take a deep breath, pull up my big girl pants, and begin to walk.

My thoughts are racing at a mile a minute, and I realise I need a plan. *What am I going to do when I find a road? How am I going to get help without attracting attention? Is anyone actually out looking for me? Who can I call? Shit. I can't call Sam; I fucking hate him with every fibre of my being right now, for telling J.D to kidnap me. I thought he fucking loved me.*

My heart clenches at the thought, and I try to get my thoughts in check. I need to think straight.

I can't call Ruby because of her connection with Jax, or Seb or my family, at least not yet. Think Harper, think. Remy, Remy Logan, Ruby's brother. He lives out here in America, the last I heard, and he told me to look him up if I was ever over here. He lives in Santa Monica, but I know he also has a house in Henderson, not too far from Las Vegas and I know for certain he would come right away if I needed him.

After what seems like an eternity, I hear the dull sound of traffic. *A road! A fucking road!* My feet are throbbing, but I have to keep going. I can't give up, I just can't. I keep walking until the sound of traffic and civilisation gets louder with each step I take, and I smile to myself.

"We're going to be alright boo, I promise."

I stroke my stomach protectively and I am filled with the hope that everything will be alright. I follow the road for what seems like forever, and I find myself in what looks like a small town. In the pre-dawn light, I see a small motel, the lights indicating its name, The Boulder Dam Hotel. I look around for a pay phone, and I spot one to the right of the entrance, concealed from the reception area. I make my way over to the pay phone and read the instructions indicated on the wall. I press zero for the operator.

"Hello, you have reached the operator, how may I be of assistance?"

I clear my throat and try to suppress the sob I feel threatening to overwhelm every sane thought in my head.

"Hello, Erm...I need a telephone number for Remy Logan, please?"

There is a slight pause, and I start to panic that the call has dropped.

"Yes of course ma'am, do you require the Henderson property or the Santa Monica property?"

I breathe a sigh of relief at the sound of the woman's voice.

"Erm...The Henderson property, please."

She recites the number off to me.

"Is there anything else I can help you with, ma'am?"

"Yes, I need to make a collect call to the number you just gave me, please?"

After a few minutes, the operator informs me that Remy has accepted the charges for the call. The phone begins to ring, and I am so overwhelmed, I start sobbing into the receiver.

"Hello."

Remy's deep voice fills my ears, and I try to get myself together.

"Hello?" he says again, and I swallow.

"Remy."

There is a pause.

"Who's this?"

"Rem, it's Peyton, I need your help."

"Peyton, what the fuck, is this some sort of sick fucking joke?"

He raises his voice, and I start to sob softly.

"Remy, it's really me; please, don't hang up. Please, I need you to help me."

I hear him take a deep breath on the other end of the phone.

"It can't be you; the news says you were murdered."

I suddenly start to feel so angry at him. How could he possibly not recognise my voice?

"You took my virginity, and then a year later you fucked off to the army, without even saying goodbye. Rem, how could you not recognise my god damn voice? I listened to our song 'Here Without You' by 3 Doors Down, on repeat, for three fucking months solid after you left, because I couldn't think of anything else but you. You were my first, and you broke my fucking heart, Remy Jeremiah Logan. How could you ever even doubt it's me?" I snap.

I hear a sharp intake of breath at the use of his full name and the story of our breakup.

"Fuck me, it really is you, Peyton."

A feeling of relief washes over me that he actually believes that it is me.

"Please, please don't tell Ruby, no one can know, Rem, promise me," I plead.

"I won't tell a soul, I promise. Fuck me, are you ok, beaut? Are you hurt?"

His voice laced with concern, and I let out a strangled sob.

"I...I've...b...been stabbed, Rem, and I think my wrist is broken. Please, please I need you to help me."

"Fuck," he curses.

"Look, I'm coming to get you, where are you?"

I look around for any indication of where I am.

"I...I don't know, Rem."

I feel myself start to panic.

"Listen to me, beaut, try not to panic. I know it's difficult, but I need you to take a few deep breaths and keep calm for me. Can you do that? Tell me what you can see from where you are right now?" he soothes softly.

I try to collect myself and look around again, taking in my surroundings.

"Erm...I'm using a payphone outside a hotel, it has a sign outside, The Boulder Dam Hotel?"

"You're in Boulder City, just outside Vegas. Good girl, that's fantastic. I'm twenty minutes away at my house in Henderson. Sit tight, I'll be as quick as I can, I promise you. I'll break every speed limit to get to you, beaut."

I close my eyes and take a deep breath.

"Thank you so much, Remy".

"You haven't got to thank me, I'll always come to your rescue you know that? Regular superhero, that's me. Just give me a phone box and call me Superman, minus the muscles!" he jokes, and I chuckle at his sense of humour. "I need you to stay out of sight for me, hang tight and I'll be there as soon as I can, I promise."

I feel my heartbeat quicken and try to choke back the sobs that are threatening to escape. As if Remy can read my mind.

"Please try not to worry, beaut, everything's going to be alright."

I smile to myself, at his pacifying tone.

"How do you do that, Rem? How do you know exactly what I'm thinking?"

He chuckles softly.

"I'll let you into a little secret, I'm psychic, shhh!" he jokes, and I laugh.

"God, it's so good to hear your voice, beaut, it's been too long. Look, I have to go now. I promise I'll be with you as soon as I can. Stay out of sight, stay out of trouble and please try not to bleed to death," he says drolly.

"Thank you so much, Rem."

He stops me.

"Hey, none of that, everything's going to be alright. I'm hanging up now, sit tight, bye."

He hangs up the phone, and my shoulders sag with relief as I tuck myself in the tight space beneath the phone booth. The pain of my stab wound is apparent now, and I feel a sharp ache under my left shoulder blade. All I can concentrate on is my breathing. *I am going to make it, and I am not going to die, not now, not anytime soon.*

I am not sure how much time passes, but I hear the slamming of a car door nearby and cross my fingers that it is Remy. The sun is just coming up, and I try to focus on my surroundings, but the pain has just become too much. I can't focus on anything else but the pain, and my vision is foggy. In my peripheral vision, I see the outline of a tall, lean figure coming towards me. My heartbeat starts to quicken, and as the figure gets closer, I recognise him. Remy. The sun is coming up behind him, and he looks like an ethereal being, an angel, my angel, my saviour.

"Peyton?"

That is when everything went black.

***

The next thing I remember is just a muffled, distant conversation between two men.

"I didn't know she was pregnant, but I couldn't just leave her out there to die, Colt. She needed my fucking help! We were close once. I took her V plates, and at one point, she was practically family."

There is a pause.

"Don't be a martyr, her face has been all over the god damn news for fuck's sake; she's on the front page of every newspaper! She's a fucking murder victim, Logan. She needs to go to the goddamn police, and if you're not going to do that, then you need to get her the hell out of dodge, as soon as possible. Take her to your place in Santa Monica and keep her out of sight, at least for the time being, until you figure out what to do and the heat dies down."

Remy chuckles softly.

"All that time in the military has made you paranoid, brother. You need to bloody relax and unravel those panties of yours. Peyton came to me for help, and I intend to help her. I couldn't just turn her away. What the fuck was I supposed to do, Colt?"

The other man sighs, and I want to say something; I want to let them know I can hear every word they are saying, but my mouth refuses to co-operate with my foggy brain.

"You know I'll do anything to help you, Remy. You know I have your six, one million fucking per cent. I've stitched you up so many times after all those god damn bar fights you used to get yourself into, but you're such a fucking sucker for a pretty face. Are you really ready to take in a girl you haven't seen for years and be responsible for someone else's kid?"

There is a silence, and I don't hear Remy's answer, as the room plunges into darkness once again.

***

I come around in unfamiliar surroundings. I open my eyes and look around.

"Here she is. How are you feeling, beaut?"

Remy strokes my hand, struggling to take in my surroundings in my disorientated state.

"Remy, w...where am I?" I say with a panicked edge to my voice, and he strokes my knuckles softly, to reassure me.

"You're safe, shhh; you're safe with me, I'm going to take care of you, and I won't let anyone hurt you, I promise."

I go to sit up, but a shooting pain rips through my shoulder, and I cry out in pain.

"Fuck, please try not to make any sudden movements, beaut. You need to rest."

I look wide-eyed and panicked into Remy's deep brown eyes. He takes my hand and strokes my knuckles soothingly.

"Sh, sh, just rest, I'll be right here when you wake up."

With those words, I am a slave to sleep once again, and when I finally come around for a second time, I feel a little more aware of my surroundings. I am in a small cosy, house, which feels and looks like a log cabin. It is warm and inviting, decorated in warm cream and taupe tones. Remy hands me a glass of water and sits next to my bed. I take a long welcome sip of water on my dry, scratchy throat. The cool liquid instantly makes me feel better. As I drain the contents of the glass, Remy begins to explain where I am and what happened.

"You're in my house in Henderson, I called in a favour from a friend, Colton Gray, he's an ex-army medic. We attend a support group for wounded soldiers together. He's a good friend, and I trust him implicitly. I called him as soon as I got off the phone to you and he came as soon as I asked him. No one else knows you're here apart from me and Colt. I'm going to keep you safe, Peyton, you have my word."

The other man in the room steps forward, and I regard him intently. He is average height around five feet nine inches tall. He is lean but heavily built around his shoulders. He has light brown skin, green-grey eyes and black hair styled in a buzz cut. He is wearing khaki trousers, a grey t-shirt, and I can see an army tattoo poking out from the bottom of his sleeve.

"Remy bought you back here a week ago, and I stitched you up. You and your baby, you're both going to be just fine, Peyton. Your wrist is just badly bruised, not broken, and the stab wound was deep, but not life-threatening. You lost a lot of blood, but I did the best I could with the resources I had. I managed to stop the bleeding, and I gave you some pain relief. I also sedated you, so your body had time to properly heal."

I squeeze Remy's hand, and that is when the tears finally start to fall. Remy climbs up on the bed and pulls me into his arms.

"Shhh, I've got you, beaut, you're safe now."

He strokes my hair, and I start to wonder if I ever will truly be safe.

I have been lying with Remy for a while, content to feel the warmth and safety of his body next to me. When the sound of his voice rouses me from my sleepy state.

"Do you want to tell me what happened, beaut? You're all over the news."

I begin to tell him, briefly, what happened, and he gasps as I fill him in on the unbelievable events. He informs me that there was a DVD of me being killed, which was played at a Rancid Vengeance gig in Las Vegas, and the police are looking for my body. I give a sharp intake of breath at his revelation and the recording J.D made seems to make a lot more sense now. Remy resumes his gentle stroking of my hair, instantly relaxing me.

"I have a place in Santa Monica; I'm going to take you there to recover. You can stay with me for as long as you need to in my house, and I'll take care of you, I promise. Money isn't an issue. I know people who can make Peyton Harper disappear; I can pull a few strings and make a few calls. I've got contacts; I can get you a brand-new identity, find you a job, and you can start fresh again... If that's what you want."

As Remy says those words, I start to wonder if all this is possible. A new start somewhere new. I can build a life for my baby and me. I find myself agreeing all too easily to the American dream.

27

Peyton

Present

I feel myself trembling uncontrollably at the unwelcome thoughts of what I endured at the hands of J.D. I start to wonder how things could have turned out so different. *I could have died.*

"*Fuck me,* sweets, you're trembling."

Brody takes both of my hands in both of his, and the warmth of his touch strangely soothes me.

"I'm so fucking sorry, sweets. I shouldn't have asked, it's not my business."

I look up at him with glazed eyes and shake my head.

"No, it's fine. I was fucking terrified that J.D would find us; I *had* to stay hidden, Brody, and I had to keep my baby safe. He had to believe that he had succeeded in killing me, or he would have come back to finish the job, I know he would. You don't understand what he was like, but if I could have done things differently, I would have in a heartbeat."

My trembling voice betrays me, and he squeezes my hands.

"He can't hurt you anymore, prison is too good for that motherfucker, and I hope he fucking dies a painful death. The night...that night...at the gig in Vegas, there was a v..."

His voice is trembling, and I stop him, finishing his sentence for him.

"A video, yeah, I know I've seen it, babe. It was all over the internet for months. I watched that fucking video over and over again."

My voice is small, and Brody moves his hands up to my face.

"Look at me and fucking listen, sweets. *None* of this is your fault. Sam is a stubborn fucker, but even he knows that none of this is down to you. He might be a fucking dick sometimes, but he's definitely not an idiot. You just did what you thought was right. You're not a bad person, babe; surely you have to know that?"

With Brody's words, I can't stop the tears that fall down my cheeks. Brody comes around to my side of the table, and he pulls me into his arms.

"Shhh, you're safe now, sweets, I've got you."

As Brody's hands roam soothingly up and down my back. I sense a presence behind us, and something tells me that it isn't Sam. Brody must sense it too, as I feel him tense.

"Now is not a good fucking time, dude," he says softly against my hair.

"I just need five minutes with Peyton to say my bit, that's all. There's no need to get all protective, man."

I recognise the voice as Jax. *Shit,* Brody pulls away from our embrace and kisses me gently on the forehead.

"Are you going to be ok? Yell if you need me, sweets? I'll be just outside the door."

He winks reassuringly, and I nod as he strides out of the canteen. The earlier crowd seems to have dispersed, leaving Jax and me alone. The only sound is the clanking of plates and cutlery coming from the kitchen. He runs his hand through his long blonde hair and tucks his hands in his pockets.

"Answer me one question, why the fuck did you come back?" he says tersely, and I shiver involuntarily at his frosty tone.

"I had to make sure Sam was all right, I never stopped caring about him, surely you have to know that. I saw what happened on the news. When I heard he had been stabbed, it bought back...terrible memories for me."

I swallow back the lump in my throat, as Jax chuckles bitterly.

"Bought back terrible memories for you? *Fuck me,* Peyton, I found my best friend lying in a pool of his own blood, unconscious after he slashed his own wrists and took a fucking overdose. I thought he was *fucking dead!* So, don't you dare fucking give me that bullshit, I still have nightmares. It terrified the living shit out of me, the blood, the noise he made before I booted the door down, that will stay with me for the rest of my fucking life. And all that? *It's on you,*" he spits harshly.

My stomach drops as I process his words, and I feel my heart slam violently against my rib cage. I feel the colour drain from my cheeks, and I feel like I have been punched in the gut. I can't breathe.

Sam tried to take his own life, because of me. Oh my God, he's right, all this is my fault.

Bile rises in my throat, and I start to sob.

"I'm...I'm..."

He smiles coldly.

"Let me guess, you're sorry? Fucking save it, sorry doesn't make up for the fact you stayed away and hid like a fucking coward. We would have protected you; we could have kept you safe! You were like a Goddamn sister to all of us, and we were like family! Sorry doesn't make up for the fact that my girlfriend, the girl who you called your sister, cried herself to sleep night after night because she'd lost the one person who knew her better than she knew herself."

I swipe my tears away angrily.

"Sam, my best friend, my *fucking brother,* tried to take his own life because you were a cold, heartless, selfish bitch!" he shouts, and it makes me sob harder because everything he says is true.

"I'm sorry, I'm so sorry," I sob.

"The ambulance men said he was so fucking lucky to be alive; he missed severing his main artery by a quarter of an inch, but that doesn't make up for the fact he was so fucking devastated, that instead of talking to us, he shut us all out and tried to take the cowards way out!" he bellows.

As Jax tells me of Sam's suicide attempt, my heart constricts, and I find myself sobbing uncontrollably. *I caused this, it's all my fault. I don't deserve his forgiveness.*

"I should never have come here."

He untucks his hands from his pockets and steps closer to me, jabbing his finger angrily in my direction.

"No, you're right, you fucking shouldn't have, and you need to fucking leave, right now. Make your excuses and go, because he doesn't need you fucking his life up anymore. He's a mess, Peyton, and he's fucking broken. He's changed. He's not sleeping, he's drinking, he's..."

His sentence is stopped abruptly by the sound of Sam's familiar deep, commanding tone.

"Jax, that's enough," he rasps.

"She needs to fucking know, Sam, what she put you through; what she's done. She needs to fucking see first-hand the consequences of her actions," Jax yells, as Sam menacingly steps forward with his fists clenched at his sides.

I retreat into myself, backing a few steps away from both men.

"You need to shut your motherfucking filthy mouth, Jax."

Jax squares up to Sam. Jax's lean frame is eclipsed by Sam's large muscular one as he comes up a few inches shorter than Sam.

"Stop fucking defending her, for Christ's sake, Sam! We were the ones who were there for you; we were the ones who picked up the pieces. I was there through the nightmares; I was the one who listened to you wake up screaming night after night. I watched you break down and turn into a shell of what you used to be. You have to take pills day after day because you can barely manage to drag yourself out of bed and that's not you! So, don't you fucking dare stand there defending her, not when she's the one who did this to you!" Jax shouts.

"STOP TALKING AND SHUT THE FUCK UP JAX, I SWEAR TO GOD!" Sam snarls and grabs him by his t-shirt with his uninjured arm, pinning him to the wall.

I am frozen to the spot. I feel my heartbeat start to quicken, and I know I am going to have a panic attack. *Shit.* My breathing becomes erratic, and I feel my legs start to buckle underneath me. Before I hit the ground, I feel myself being scooped up in a strong familiar arm and my vision is swimming. It is as if everything is in slow motion and my chest starts to tighten. I am struggling to force precious air into my lungs.

"*Fuck.*"

I hear someone curse.

"Breathe, angel, I've got you, stay with me, deep breaths," Sam says gently, and his voice brings me back. "Breathe."

My eyes lock with his concerned green ones, and he grips my hand softly. He is sat back on his haunches in front of me.

"Breathe with me, angel. I need you to focus. In and out. That's it, eyes on me, just keep breathing."

We start to breathe in sync with each other, and I feel my heartbeat return to normal.

"Good girl."

He smiles his familiar dimpled smile, and he strokes my cheek. My gaze drops to the floor; I feel my face start to flush with humiliation and pure embarrassment.

"Hey, look at me, angel."

He cups my face in both of his hands and forces my gaze to his.

"It's just a panic attack, angel, you're going to be ok, I promise," he says softly, and I manage a small smile as he strokes my knuckles softly with his calloused fingers.

"*Shit!*" Jax mutters, running his hands through his normally neatly styled blonde hair. "*Fuck!*" he curses. "*Bollocks!*"

He storms out of the canteen, leaving Sam on his knees in front of me.

"I see he still doesn't quite have a grip on the English language yet," I say drily, and Sam chuckles softly.

He rises to his feet pulling me up with him until I am standing in front of him, and his six-foot-four stature amazes me once again. His hand and his wrists are bandaged, and his shoulder is supported by a dark grey sling. I notice that his hospital gown has been replaced with a pair of ripped, worn and faded jeans, a *Metallica* t-shirt and black cowboy boots. He has at least three days' worth of stubble on his chin. His raven black hair is messy but still manages to look sexy. He has what Ruby, and I used to call *'just fucked hair'*. I involuntarily lick my lips at the sight of him.

"Angel, please don't look at me like that," he rasps, and I look up at him.

"Look at you like what?" I say innocently, and Sam smirks devilishly.

"Like you're fucking starved for me, like you want me to lay you down across that table and fuck you into next week," he says gruffly, and I let my eyes wander down the length of his tall frame.

I take in his bulging biceps that look twice the size of my own, his broad shoulders, his hard-muscular thighs, his large, calloused hands, the hard, perfectly sculpted bumps of his six-pack. I look down to the delicious V of his abdomen, leading down to his thick, nine-inch member.

I imagine his hands roaming all over my body, the way his large hands cupped my breasts, the way his long finger expertly pushed into my wet aching channel and bought me to an earth-shattering orgasm. I hear a soft moan, and then I realise that moan escaped from my own lips. I look up at Sam, he is smirking sinfully and has that wicked glint in his green eyes.

"I bet if I touched your pussy, you would be soaking wet for me, wouldn't you, angel? You were imagining my hands on you, weren't you? You were imagining what it was like to feel my cock inside you, the way you screamed my name and clenched that tight little pussy around me as I bought you to orgasm."

His voice is rough and full of promise, of pure, desperate want. He moves closer to me, and he is so close I can feel his warm breath on my cheek. I bite my lip to stop myself jumping his bones right here in the hospital.

"I have a place in Manhattan. Come back with me, angel; let me show you how much I've missed you. Let me love you."

I look him in his blazing green eyes, and I suddenly feel overwhelmed by the whole situation. I take a step back and shake my head.

"I...I can't," I whisper.

As he continues to step towards me, I take a step back each time, distancing myself from him.

"Angel," he says huskily.

"Sam, please don't. Everything Jax said was true. I broke you, and I don't deserve your forgiveness. I don't deserve a second chance; all of it was my fucking fault."

The tears that threatened earlier are now freely rolling down my cheeks.

"*Fucking Jax*," Sam growls and clenches his fist at his sides. "*Jesus,* angel, please stop crying, you're tearing me apart."

He reaches for me, but I step back. I can't allow him that power. If he lays his hands on me, I'll give in to my body's voracious needs.

"Jax had no fucking right to say those things to you, angel, no right at all. It wasn't his place to tell you; it wasn't his God damn story to tell. I'm so fucking sorry."

His voice is filled with such sadness and regret it makes my heart slam against my rib cage.

"Cole bought me a change of clothes and the doctors have given me the all clear. I need to take it easy, but I can leave. Please come back to my place with me, angel. We need to talk properly, in private, away from prying ears; somewhere where we won't be disturbed."

I swipe away the tears from my eyes and shake my head.

"No, I can't," I whisper.

I turn to leave, but he grabs my wrist and spins me around, pulling me into his hard, warm chest. He envelopes me in his strong arm, and I clutch his t-shirt desperately. It feels so good to be back in his arms, and the feeling is so overwhelming that I break down in gut-wrenching sobs against him.

"*Fuck*, please, stop crying, you're shredding me. Each sob is like a knife to my heart, angel. I can't fucking stand it," he says through clenched teeth, and he pulls me tighter against him with his good arm.

The look of anguish in his eyes is too much for me to bear, as he runs his hands soothingly up and down my back.

"Let me take you away from here, please, we can *just* talk. No funny business, I promise. You can just let me hold you, like I used to, and you can finally let me meet my boy."

My head snaps up in a blind panic at the mention of our son, Freddie. I wrench myself free from his grip and back away from him, shaking my head.

"I...I'm sorry I need to...I have to get back to Freddie."

I turn and rush away from the hospital canteen, ignoring everything around me but the sound of Sam calling my name.

28

Sam

FUCKKK! Why the fuck won't she listen to me? Why is she behaving this way? Jax had no fucking right to tell her those things, it was down to me to tell her and in my own fucking time. This is all such a mess.

"Dude, is everything alright?"

Brody's concerned voice filters through my thoughts. He is standing outside the door of the hospital canteen with one hand in his pocket. I'm running my hand frantically through my hair, and I'm starting to furiously pace the corridor.

"She..."

I stop because I don't know what the fuck to say, or how to describe what just happened. Brody moves closer to me and pats my shoulder, as if he just *gets it.*

"I know mate, I fucking know."

These past few months, Brody has become my ally. He's the person I go to when I need advice, when I need to talk, or just get things off my chest. He is the one who silently listens and tells it like it is when he knows I need it. Since his stint in rehab, Brody has done a three-hundred-and-sixty-degree turn. Gone is the Brody who would wake up with groupies in his bed. Gone is the Brody who would snort cocaine for breakfast and gone is the Brody who can't function without some sort of chemical running through his veins. He has been replaced with a Brody who appreciates life, friendship, and music again. Brody gets out of bed with a renewed purpose and functions just fine with a strong, black coffee, a bowl of Rice Krispies and a few hours in our fully equipped, state of the art home gym.

"I saw her tear through that door like a bat out of fucking hell, dude; did you go bounding in there with your size twelve's?" he says wryly, as I shake my head and run my hand through my hair.

"Not this time, dude. Jax told her about my suicide attempt, *motherfucker,*" I curse.

"*Fuck me,* dude."

I smirk at Brody's droll reply, and I am about to speak again when we are interrupted by a group of four teenage girls.

"OH MY GOD! You're Bolt and Snake from Rancid Vengeance! OH MY GOD! OH MY GOD!"

They all shriek and I inwardly curse our fame to hell right at this moment.

"OH MY GOD! We love you! You're so hot!" the small blonde one squeals in an American twang, and I instantly turn on Sam the showman.

"The very same, sweetheart, and thanks for the compliment, ladies, it means a lot," I say in my signature raspy tone, and they all practically melt at our feet. Brody and I grin at each other.

"OH MY GOD!"

Fuck me; I love our American fans, but really? Is that really the extent of their vocabulary? The group push a small petite dark-haired girl forward, and she looks nervously up at me with big brown innocent eyes.

"Erm...c...could we get a picture with you guys please?"

Her voice is small, and I touch her arm.

"Sure, sweetheart. Don't be so nervous, we don't bite."

I wink and bite my lip piercing. Her friends start screaming again, attracting the attention of a few nurses passing us in the corridor.

"OH MY GOD! Bolt just touched you, Bree!" the over-enthusiastic blonde shrieks and she catches a man walking past by his arm. I recognise him, as the guy who had his arms around Peyton yesterday.

"Excuse me, can you take our picture please?"

She thrusts the camera at him, and he smirks.

"Sure, no problem, love."

So, he's British then? Interesting. He steps forward, and I notice he walks with a slight limp. He takes the camera and the blonde plasters herself to my side.

"Smile!" he says, clearly amused.

I plaster on my best smile for the camera. He takes a few snaps, and they all jump up and down in unison. He hands back the camera with a smirk on his face.

"Thank you so much!"

He nods.

"You're most welcome, ladies."

They all skip off happily, and he turns to leave.

"Wait," I say sharply, and he spins around.

"Are you talking to me, mate?"

I look at him. He has to be an inch or so taller than me, with long dark hair, brown eyes and I can definitely see the resemblance between him and Ruby.

"I saw you with Peyton yesterday."

He nods.

"Ah, the famous Mr Newbolt, I presume?" He regards me intently, sizing me up. "I've heard a lot about you. Remy Logan," he introduces himself, and I nod.

He changes his stance, folding his arms and widening his legs.

"I know exactly who you are, are you fucking my girl?" I ask candidly, and he cocks his eyebrow.

"That, mate, is none of your business. And last I checked, Peyton doesn't *belong* to anyone. I take it you *are* talking about Peyton?"

The fucking cocky son of a bitch. I take a step closer to him, and he doesn't flinch.

"Do *not* fuck with me, Logan, because it's really not a good idea," I spit angrily, and I know I am way past angry. I am boiling with jealous rage.

He got to spend the past year with my Peyton, and he's been able to see my son grow for the past six months.

"I don't plan on fucking with you, mate. I care about that girl more than I should, and I know she's so fucking cut up about you. She's hurting, I can see that quite fucking clearly, but what I don't like, is to see her upset. She hates herself for what she did, and I've witnessed first-hand the effect it's had on her. I've sat through the nightmares, I've sat through the screaming, the tears, and it ripped me the fuck open to witness that while knowing I couldn't do a damn thing about it. She went to the Madison Square Garden gig, against my better judgement might I add, but as soon as she saw the news about you being kidnapped by J.D, she knew she had made a terrible mistake. I couldn't let her come here alone, not with the state she was in. I would have given my right nut sac to protect her from all this, shield her from all this fucking pain, but she's so feisty, strong and independent. So, no, I don't plan on fucking with you, mate. Not if you don't fuck with her. Because believe me when I say I will knock you down and I'll make damn fucking sure you won't be getting back up."

He says it all with such conviction that I don't doubt he would make good on his threat. Brody quietly observes the exchange between us and I hold my hand up in defence.

"You want my advice, mate? Give her some space, time to think and shit. That's what women want, right?"

He smirks, and I smile at his typically male dry sense of humour. *Maybe he's not so bad after all.*

"It's nice to have finally met you, mate, I'll perhaps see you around sometime?"

I nod, and he shakes my hand graciously as he turns to walk away. Brody moves to stand next to me with a bemused look on his face.

"What the fuck just happened?"

That is a good fucking question.

"I'm fucked if I know, dude."

I think I just met another man, who is in love with Peyton.

29

Peyton

Past

We have just closed up the coffee shop for the day, and we are sitting on one of the sofas, having a well-earned cup of hot, refreshing, lemon tea after a long and extremely busy day. *God, I miss my cups of coffee.* My feet are fucking killing me, my back is in bits and all I'm craving, is a hot bubbly bath and a tub of Ben & Jerry's.

"Come on, babe, please? It will be fun, I promise. You've only been here what...three months, give or take? You haven't experienced a night out until you've been with me, Blaze, and Henley," Joel says enthusiastically in his Californian accent and gives me his best puppy dog eyes.

I smile at his attempt to cheer me up. He's right; I came here just over three months ago. I live in Santa Monica with Remy, and I have a job working at a coffee shop called 'Cool Beans', where I met Joel. He has become a really close friend. He is twenty-nine years old and was born and raised in China. His family disowned him when he announced he was gay, saying that he bought shame upon them. He cut all ties with his family eleven years ago, when he had just turned eighteen, and he moved out here and hasn't looked back since.

He has an Italian boyfriend, who is an underwear model, named Valentino or Val as he calls him. He is around five feet eleven inches tall, has platinum blonde hair, and wears it in a sleek side quiff. He has the most unusual golden amber eyes, a bright white grin, and is tall, and lean with a diamond stud in his ear. His personality matches the way he looks. He is flamboyant, bright, and from the moment I met him, he never fails to put a smile on my face. He is the assistant manager and the best coffee barista I have ever seen. He trained me, showed me the ropes, and took me under his wing from the moment I started working here. I am six, almost seven, months pregnant, and every day I am reminded of the life I left behind.

"I'm nearly seven months pregnant, Joel, look at the fucking state of me," I complain, and Joel rolls his eyes dramatically.

"Bullshit! You look fucking beautiful, I'd bet money on it that you're the best-looking mama-to-be Los Angeles has ever seen," he says with an elaborate sweep of his arm, which makes me laugh out loud.

I can always rely on Joel to cheer me up. He has become an extremely close friend; someone I can confide in and turn to. He's not Ruby, but he makes a good substitute.

"Come on, babe, just because you're pregnant doesn't mean you're not allowed to have fun."

He takes my hand and bats his eyelashes.

"Please, for me?"

I roll my eyes and chuckle.

"Alright! You've twisted my arm, I'll come."

He laughs and claps his hands excitedly.

"Yay! Good girl! B and Henley are so looking forward to meeting you, Lulu."

I smile and get to my feet.

"I better go home and make myself look beautiful then, babe."

He blows me a kiss.

"You can't rush perfection, darling. Blaze's boyfriend, Rayne, is driving. We'll pick you up at eight."

I hug Joel and leave the coffee shop after my shift. A few hours pass and I have showered, eaten dinner with Remy, and dressed. When I first came to Santa Monica, Remy suggested I cut and dye my hair, just in case someone recognised me, so I took the plunge and visited a hair salon. I love my new look. I have a short, sleek, pillar-box red bob. It is so different from what I'm used to, but it works. I dress in a white dress with red skulls all over it. It accentuates my boobs and flatters my growing bump. I finish the look with my usual natural makeup, red flat pumps and a red hair band. I feel good.

"Wow, you're looking good, mama!" Remy compliments and I blush.

"Why thank you, kind sir!"

He chuckles, and I hear a car horn beep outside the house. I grab my bag and say goodbye to Remy.

"Have fun, beaut, and if you can't be good, be lucky."

He winks and clucks his teeth as I kiss him on the cheek and make my way outside. I am greeted by Joel sitting on the hood of the car, wearing tight jeans, a pink vest and a white blazer with the sleeves rolled up. His platinum blonde hair is styled into his signature sleek side quiff.

"You bitch! You look fucking amazing!" he shrieks, and I laugh.

He comes over to me and wraps me in his arms. He pulls away and opens the door to allow me into the car. I climb in, and he squeezes in next to me.

"Lulu, these are my friends Blaze Spencer and Henley Marshall. The hottie in the driver's seat is Rayne, Blaze's better half."

Rayne salutes coolly from the driver's seat. I nod and smile.

"Nice to meet you all. Joel's told me a lot about you," I say shyly.

"Doesn't she look stunning, girls?"

Blaze looks at me and beams.

"You could totally be a model, you look gorgeous. I'm Blaze, by the way. My dad was a fireman, hence the name!"

She chuckles and I instantly like her. Henley, the pink haired girl, on the other hand, seems a little hostile. She regards me with cautious, narrow eyes and Joel rolls his eyes.

"FML, Hen, don't be a bitch! Ignore her, I think she must be on her period!" Joel says sardonically, and Henley flushes a shade of pink to match her hair.

She hits Joel on the arm a little harder than intended. Joel rubs his arm and pouts.

"Fuckin' asshole."

Joel blows her a kiss.

"You love me really, Hen."

We make the rest of the journey to downtown Los Angeles in half an hour, and the car is filled with music and animated conversation. Soon we arrive at our destination; an exclusive hotel bar in Los Angeles called the SkyBar. It is situated on the roof of the Mondrian Hotel, overlooking the Sunset Strip. When we enter the bar via a lift, and I am instantly in awe of my surroundings. There are low-slated wooden tables and chairs with plump, white cushions situated around a large swimming pool. The lighting is low, and there are candles on all of the tables. Joel chuckles and wraps his arms around my waist.

"Pick your chin up off the floor, mama!"

I laugh, and he leads me to a table where a group of three muscular, tattooed men are sitting. They all look out of place in such a trendy place, and they stick out like a sore thumb from the rest of the hip, beautiful people. The one man stands up. He has shoulder length brown hair, with streaks of grey, a short beard, and a bandana around his head. I can't help but think that he looks vaguely familiar. He is at least six feet six inches tall; he is huge, has muscles the size of my head and is rather intimidating. He is wearing tight black jeans, a black vest that make his bulging muscles look even bigger than they actually are and black biker boots. If I were to guess his age, I would put him around mid-forties. His steel blue eyes rake over me, and he grins, causing laughter lines to crease around his eyes, which soften his harsh features.

"Who's this sweet thing, Hen? Are you not going to introduce us?" he says in a Boston accent, and Henley steps forward.

"This is Joel's friend, Louise. Louise, this is my pain in the ass best friend and business partner, Jared DeSilva," she introduces him with a cheeky grin, as I nod and smile.

He takes my hand and plants a kiss on the back. I find out that Jared has his own tattoo shop and has a tattoo show on one of the cable channels over here, which is how I recognised him.

"That is some mighty fine ink you have there, sweet thing."

I smile proudly.

"Thank you, you have some amazing ink too, Jared."

He smiles widely.

"Thanks, darlin', make room for the lady, boys."

The other two men who are with him stand up and move from their seats. One is lean and muscular; he is around five feet ten inches tall and has blue-grey eyes. His arms, neck, and the left side of his face are covered in tattoos. He has a white, blonde Mohawk in the centre of his head and two old style pistols tattooed on either side of his head. He is wearing leather trousers, a black shirt and studded cowboy boots. If I were to guess his age, I would say he is around late thirties.

"I'm Axl, pleased to meet you, beautiful."

His voice is deep and baritone. He takes my hand and kisses the back of it. Henley rolls her eyes and slaps his arm. I'm not sure whether she is being serious or if she is just being playful.

"She's off limits, asswipe."

Henley takes me by the hand and leads me to a chair while introducing me to the third man in their party.

"And this handsome motherfucker here is, Clay."

He salutes coolly. He has dark coffee coloured skin, brown-green eyes, a small afro and black-rimmed glasses. He is wearing ripped faded jeans, a grey t-shirt and Reebok trainers. Henley passes me a tall glass of orange juice, and I smile as I take her in. She has short, cropped, bright pink hair, which suits her bronzed and heavily tattooed skin. She is around five feet seven inches tall, with unusual turquoise eyes that remind me of the colour of the ocean, and she has a prominent New York accent. She is wearing a pair of white hot pants, showing off her tattoos, a blue cropped Captain America t-shirt, and blue, knee-high, Converse with white stars all over.

During the night, I find out that Henley Marshall is twenty-nine and she is the business partner of one of Los Angeles' most famous and influential, tattoo artists, Jared DeSilva. Henley and Blaze both attended school and college together. They have known each other since they were nine years old.

Blaze Spencer is also twenty-nine years old, and she is a lap dancer and part-time model. She has dark chocolate, flawless skin with long poker straight black hair tumbling down to her waist. She has green eyes and also has a prominent New York accent. They both moved to Los Angeles after they left high school and have been here ever since.

"So, you know pretty much everything about us, Lou, now it's your turn."

I bite my lip and wonder how much to tell them about my life before I came here.

"Not much to tell really. I'm Louise Stonebridge, my friends call me Lou or Lulu. I'm twenty-eight years old, and I moved here from the U.K. I wanted a fresh start, after a messy break up with my fiancé; I'm pretty boring compared to you and Blaze," I say cheerily, hoping they don't spot the lie, and they both laugh.

"We don't mind boring, honey. In fact, boring is good. So is your ex the father of your baby?"

Henley points to my prominent bump and Blaze elbows her in the ribs, throwing her a knowing look.

"Hen!"

Henley takes a sip of her drinks and shrugs. I brush Blaze's arm reassuringly.

"Blaze, its fine, honestly, I don't mind."

I smile and nod, trying to swallow back the lump forming in my throat.

"He hurt you pretty bad didn't he, honey? I can tell by the look in your eyes," Blaze says sympathetically, and before I get chance to answer, Joel plops himself down on the seat next to me.

"Fuck that, baby girl. What I really want to know is what the deal is with you and Mr Tall, dark and Handsome? The long-haired God who picks you up from the coffee shop. All I know is that he's a close friend of Dax, and he's very mysterious, like one of those brooding heroes. Come on spill it, sister," Joel says dramatically, and I chuckle, thankful for the subject change.

"We're just friends, that's all, babe."

Joel cocks his eyebrow.

"Really? That old chestnut? Friends with benefits? Fuck buddies? Come on Lulu, give me something!"

I throw my head back and laugh.

"No! Me and Remy are just...good friends."

I bite my lip, and he gives me a knowing look.

"Hmm, by the dramatic pause, Aunty Joel senses history between you two? Am I right?"

He regards me intently, and I take a sip of my drink, suddenly feeling my face burning with embarrassment at discussing my sex life with a group of virtual strangers. Henley brushes my arm in a gesture of reassurance.

"Ignore him, honey. You should know by now that he's too God damn nosey for his own good sometimes. You don't have to answer his lame ass questions."

I shake my head.

"No, it's fine, babe, honestly. I...lost my V-card to Remy, when I was seventeen."

They all laugh and whoop at my admission.

"Wow! Mr Tall, Dark and Handsome looks like he has some stamina? Am I right? Marks out of ten? I want all the gory details, babe!"

Joel sucks his drink through a straw and bats his eyelashes wickedly. I laugh and wink.

"Definitely nine and a half!"

Our group erupts with raucous laughter.

"Ha! I knew it!" Joel shrieks. "So, why nine and a half and not the full ten?" Joel inquires, as I take a sip of my drink and smirk at the memory.

"Because he kept his socks on!"

Everyone bursts out laughing, and as the night progresses, I feel myself relax around these strangers. I start to think to myself that maybe life here in America won't be so bad after all.

30

Peyton

I am looking for an exit in the hospital when I hear the sound of heels clicking across the floor of the hospital corridor.

"Peyton?"

I instantly recognise Ruby's familiar singsong voice, and I spin around. She walks towards me, and I take her in. She is still as beautiful as ever; her long dark hair is glossy and falling down her back. She has quite a prominent bump, and she is wearing a navy polka dot dress, with a pair of Gucci sunglasses perched on top of her head. She narrows her eyes at me, and the look in her eyes undoes me. I shake my head as we take each other in.

"Please don't hate me, Rubes, I couldn't bear losing you as well."

A tear slips down her cheek, and she holds a manicured nail up at me.

"I...*Jesus!* You could have fucking talked to me, Peyton! Me, your family, the boys, your brother is a policeman, and Seb is ex SAS, for fuck's sake! We would have protected you from that twisted piece of shit! You're part of my family, you silly bitch! I don't have a memory within the last twenty years that you aren't part of you could have fucking trusted me! I was just a phone call away. But instead, you made everyone think you were dead! How fucking sick and twisted are you?" she shrieks and moves closer to me with her hands on her hips.

She narrows her eyes at me, and I shake my head. *I'm seriously tired of people making assumptions about the reason why I stayed away.*

"You of all people, Ruby! You just don't get it, do you? None of you do! J.D was fucking *dangerous!* He's a complete psychopath, pure fucking evil. He wouldn't have stopped until he had killed us, and I couldn't risk that! You're just looking at it through those perfect rose-coloured glasses of yours; life isn't all fucking unicorns shooting rainbows and glitter out of their arses. Get your god damn head out of the fucking clouds! No one so far has asked me why, apart from Brody! No one gives a fuck what he put *me* through! No one has even bothered asking how *I* feel, Ruby!"

I try to stay calm, but I feel my resolve slipping, and I'm not sure how much longer I can keep up the facade that everything is going to be fine.

"I know it sounds like I'm a selfish bitch, but I *had* to keep us safe, me and my son, Ruby! I had a *baby*! Sam's baby," I shout, and her eyes widen as she moves closer to me.

"O-M-F-G! A baby!" She shrieks and throws her arms around me, bouncing us both up and down.

This is the first time in a long time I have felt like I'm truly home. She encases me in her arms and clings tightly to me.

"Rubes...babe, I can't breathe!"

She pulls away from our embrace.

"Fuck me running, babe, I'm an Aunty!" She whispers, and she takes me in.

"You skinny bitch, you're looking good, babe. I love the hair, it suits you."

She grins widely, and her infectious grin makes me smile too. She makes it impossible to stay mad at her. It feels like I haven't smiled properly in such a long time.

"Thanks, and you look like you've swallowed a melon!"

She narrows her eyes and strokes her stomach.

"*Bitch!*" she quips, and we both laugh.

"God, I've missed you so bloody much, babe."

She crushes me to her, and the familiar scent of her perfume instantly soothes me.

"I've missed you too, like you wouldn't believe."

I hug her tightly, and someone clears their throat behind us.

"Ahem..."

We pull away from each other, and I turn around to see Remy clutching two cups of coffee.

"Sis?"

His voice is rich and deep. Ruby turns to look at Remy, and her mouth hangs open, as if she can't believe he is here.

"Remy?"

He looks her up and down, regarding her intently.

"*Fuck me*, it really is you. My baby sister."

He moves closer to us and hands me a cup of coffee, giving Ruby a one arm squeeze.

"Thanks, babe."

I smile, and Ruby looks from Remy to me.

"Please tell me you two...haven't?"

She gestures between us and Remy chuckles.

"I haven't seen you in over a year! The only contact we've had is phone calls and FaceTime, and all you're worried about is whether I've been slipping Peyton a length? Fuck me, Rubes!"

She places her hands on her hips, narrowing her hazel eyes on both of us.

"So, have you two...?"

She gestures her perfectly manicured finger between Remy and me.

"In answer to your question, no, we haven't," I reply, and a look of relief passes over Ruby's face.

"So, what if we had? Hypothetically speaking?"

Remy smirks while stroking his chin mischievously and I roll my eyes, hitting him playfully. *Remy is such a wind-up merchant!*

"Rem!"

He laughs, and Ruby observes the exchange between us.

"You've been staying with Remy all this time?"

I nod, and I can't help but feel a slight shame. Over this past year, Remy and Ruby have kept in contact via telephone and FaceTime, all the while keeping me hidden.

"Yeah, Rem was there...when I...I needed him the most," I stutter, and she brushes my arm reassuringly.

"You can tell me all about it later, babe."

She winks, and I nod. I am glad of the reprieve and the incessant questions.

"I've just had the pleasure of meeting the delightful, Mr Newbolt."

I look up at him, and he smirks at the worried look that crosses my face. *He just met Sam.*

"Don't look so worried, beaut, we're both still in one piece. Not a drop of blood was spilt, cross my cold dead heart."

He winks and makes a cross over his heart.

"He was being accosted by a bunch of pre-pubescent teens outside the canteen, it really was quite amusing!"

He laughs, as he takes a sip of his coffee and makes a face.

"*Christ*, this coffee...sorry *sludge,* leaves a lot to be bloody desired, beaut."

I chuckle.

"You are such a coffee whore!"

He laughs looking between Ruby and me.

"On that delightful note, I'm going to leave you two to catch up."

He winks and leans in to kiss me on the cheek.

"I'll meet you back at the hotel, beaut; I'll pick Freddie up, and I'm on my mobile if you need anything."

He hugs Ruby tightly.

"It's so good to see you, sis. We'll catch up later, I promise."

He turns around and leaves. Ruby looks at me and narrows her eyes.

"*Beaut?* Seriously? What the fuck is that all about?"

We both laugh, and I can't help blushing.

"I can't believe you've been with my big brother this entire time, babe. Fucking hell, that boy has still got it so bad for you."

She fans herself with her hand dramatically, and I roll my eyes. *I can't understand why people keep saying that.*

"Sooo, before I got here you looked like you were deep in thought back there, something you want to get off your chest?"

I smile. *God, I've missed my best friend so much.*

"Jax and I had a bit of a run in, that's all, no big deal. Nothing I can't handle."

She frowns and gestures nonchalantly.

"Don't you worry about him, you just leave Jax to me, babe."

She winks conspiratorially. We are interrupted by the roar of Jax's voice and the sound of his motorcycle boots stomping across the floor.

"I THOUGHT I FUCKING TOLD YOU TO LEAVE!" he yells, and Ruby spins around to reprimand him, shoving him backwards with her hands.

"Jax, don't you dare speak to her like that, what the fuck?" she shouts, and it is at that exact moment when something inside me snaps.

I am not that weak, pathetic, timid girl, who is scared-of-her-own-shadow, cries all the time and jumps every time someone comes near her. I am Peyton Leigh Harper, balls of steel, one of the lads, tells it like it is, doesn't take any bullshit from anyone and definitely doesn't cry all the time. *It's time to pull up those big girl pants, Harper. I AM WOMAN HEAR ME ROAR!* I spin around and stride with purpose towards Jax until I am toe to toe with him. I glare at him and, I jab my finger into his chest.

"You've got no fucking right to speak to me like that! I'm sorry for what I put Sam through, I truly am, but what about what I've been through? No one has bothered to fucking ask me how I feel, or what I went through! I endured hours of J.D playing sick, psychotic, mind games with me. He beat me senseless, he cut me, and he fucking *stabbed* me! He told me that Sam *asked* him to kidnap me and hurt me. I've spent a year believing that the man I loved was nothing but a manipulative liar, playing on the fact that I fell in love with him! I believed J.D over the man I was going to spend the rest of my life with the father of my fucking baby! What sort of a person does that make me? I kept my son from him, all because J.D lied and because I couldn't pick up the bloody phone and ask him! I know Sam's hurt, because I'm fucking hurting too, every damn day. I look at my son and every day I'm reminded of the life I left behind, just to keep us both safe."

Ruby is sobbing softly in the background, and Jax's eyes widen at my admission. He runs his hand through his hair and puffs out his cheeks.

"*Fuck me*, I had no idea, babe, I swear. I'm so sorry," he says sincerely, and I jab my finger into Jax's chest. *I am so fucking angry right now.*

"No, fuck you and your god damn apologies, Jackson Chase! You've got no bloody idea what I've been through, so don't stand there and pretend like you do. I'm not the same person I was a year ago. I'm fucking damaged, and it's all because of that sick, twisted bastard. He ruined *everything,* and I fucking *despise* him. I hate that he's done this to me, to Sam, and to our *son.* Sam's missed six months with his son, all because I was so stupid and naive enough to believe a lie over the man I was in love with. I don't expect any of you to forgive me, but at least fucking understand the reasons *why* I did it," I spit angrily, and Jax hangs his head in shame.

Ruby rushes towards me, pulling me in for a hug and she sobs softly into my shoulder.

"I'm so sorry, babe, I'm sorry I wasn't there for you."

I pull away from her and cup her face in my hands.

"Look at me, Rubes, you've got nothing to apologise for. I wasn't alone, Remy was there, and it's ok. I'm ok, I promise you, I'm a survivor remember?"

I smile and wipe away her tears with the pad of my thumb.

"No, it isn't. How can you say that Peyton? You gave birth to your son without the people you love around you. No woman should have to endure that."

I am about to speak when I hear someone clear their throat behind me and Sam is standing there awkwardly with his hand tucked into the pocket of his jeans. He must have heard everything.

Fuck, fuck, fuck.

"Angel," he rasps, and Ruby kisses my forehead.

"You look like you've got a lot to talk about. I'll leave you and Sam to it, babe. Unless you want me to stay?"

I shake my head.

"I'll be fine thanks, Rubes. Love you."

She winks and blows me a kiss, as I smile weakly.

"Right back at ya, Harper! Good to have you back, babe."

She jabs her finger at Sam.

"You, be gentle with her, I know what your mood swings have been like for this past year, Newbolt."

She warns, and Sam nods curtly.

"I'll see you soon. I'll get your number from Remy, and I'll call you. We can have a proper catch up before we head back to London, yeah?"

I nod, and she smiles widely as she turns and leaves with Jax. Sam steps forward, and I take a wary step back from him.

"You heard everything?"

My voice is barely a whisper. He nods and steps closer to me.

"Every single word, angel, I had no fucking idea."

His gruff voice sounds pained.

"I don't need your fucking pity, Sam," I say defensively, and he shakes his head.

"Fuck me, *no*; no, it's not pity, not at all. This wasn't supposed to fucking happen, angel, none of it!"

His voice almost cracks, thick with unshed tears.

"You don't understand! I was supposed to fucking protect you, but instead, I let him take you. I let him lay his filthy fucking hands on you; I let him hurt you! I might not have been the one holding the knife, but I'm the one responsible, this is all my fucking fault. I failed you, angel, I'm so sorry."

He can't stop the tears from falling, and he swipes his eyes angrily. Even though the man I am still madly in love with is breaking down in front of me, I can't hug him or offer him any words of comfort. *I am truly broken.*

31

Sam

What the fuck is wrong with me? I never cry.

I spent six months grieving for her and then I dealt with the overwhelming loss the only way I knew how. With sex, lots and lots of hot nasty sex. Groupies, fans and any woman with tits and a heartbeat. The truth is, reverting back to my old ways was the only way I knew how to deal with the shit that life threw at me. The pressure of fame, losing Peyton, taking a year out of the music industry and starting the next chapter of my life without her in it, all led to my downfall. For six months, I had been on a downward spiral, and I can't make any excuses for it.

Sam

Past

I wake up on the sofa with the hangover from hell, and Amy throws the curtains open.

"Look alive, sunshine!" she says cheerily.

When I fully open my eyes, she is standing over me, with her hands on her hips. Her cheery demeanour from a few seconds ago is replaced by one of disgust.

"For fuck's sake, Sam, how many times do I have to walk in here and find you like this?" Amy snaps.

I shield my eyes from the sunlight coming in through the windows and look up at her. She is frowning, her curly brown hair framing her face.

"You know you carry on frowning like that, babe, you're going to need Botox before you're thirty-five!"

I smirk, and she punches me on the arm.

"Samson Newbolt, get your sorry arse off that fucking sofa now!" she shouts, and I clutch my head, trying to find some relief against the dull pounding in my head.

"I can get you some Botox injections for Christmas if you would like me to? You only have to ask, Aims!"

I smirk, and I know I'm pushing my luck, but I can't help it. She slaps me again, and I look down at myself. I am wearing a dark blue Superdry hoodie unzipped. I am bare-chested and wearing just a pair of black and yellow Batman boxers.

"Get some fucking clothes on, Sam!" She reprimands, and I hear the familiar sound of tiny footsteps running into my living room. I zip my hoodie up and ruffle my already sleep-mussed hair.

"Uncle Sammy!" Addison shouts.

Fuck me, backwards. As much as I love her, I really can't deal with hyperactive, screaming four-year-olds, when it feels like there is a marching band in my head.

"Uncle Sammy, you stink."

Addison scrunches up her nose, and Amy tries to stifle her laughter by biting her lip. I sniff my armpit and find myself scrunching my own nose, trying desperately to remember the last time I showered.

"Yes, I do, Princess. Uncle Sammy is going to get a shower."

She stands with her tiny hands on her hips and pouts. She is adorable. Her cute curls and big brown eyes melt me every time. She is wearing short jeans, a pink Rancid Vengeance t-shirt, which we got specially made for her with her name on the back, and a pair of bright pink Converse trainers.

"I might be almost five now, Uncle Sammy, but I still want to be your princess."

I get up into a sitting position on the sofa, and she climbs on my lap, throwing her tiny arms around me.

"You'll always be my princess, baby girl."

I squeeze her, and she grins.

"Do you cross your heart, Uncle Sammy?"

I smile and make a cross over my heart.

"Cross my heart, princess."

I wink, and she squeezes me tighter.

"I need a date for my party, will you be my date, Uncle Sammy."

I look at Amy, and she holds her hands up defensively.

"Don't look at me, it's nothing to do with me, sugar."

She shrugs, and we are interrupted by Addison tugging on the hair at the nape of my neck.

"Pleeeeeeeeease, Uncle Sammy?"

She pouts and gives me those puppy dog eyes she knows I can't resist.

"Ok, you've twisted my arm baby girl, and you know I can't resist those adorable puppy eyes! I would be honoured to be your date."

She claps excitedly and plants a wet kiss on my cheek.

"Yaaaaay! All the girls in my class are going to be soooooo jealous!"

Amy laughs, and I smirk at her dramatic eye roll.

"But you need to shower first, Uncle Sammy," she says matter of factly, and I nod.

"Ok, you win, baby girl, I'll go and grab a shower."

I set her on the ground and get up off the sofa.

"I'll make you some coffee and tidy up; seeing as you can't be bothered, and you sacked yet another housekeeper. I'm not your bloody mother, Sam," Amy says sharply, and I salute as I make my way to the bathroom.

An hour passes, I feel almost normal and human again. The pounding in my head has somewhat dissipated, and I no longer smell like I slept in a skip. I am freshly showered and dressed in loose jeans, which hang low on my hips and a black vest. My hair is spiky and still damp from my shower. I pad barefoot through the house, and it looks spotless. I'm impressed.

"I should start bloody charging you by the hour for cleaning! I'm not your slave, Sam; I do actually have a real job at the magazine, which I get paid substantially for, and it doesn't involve tidying up after your sorry arse!" she rants, and I smirk.

She must be on her period! She narrows her eyes on me as she passes me a cup of steaming black coffee. I take a welcome sip, and the door opens. Brody strolls in; he is fresh from rehab, and he looks so much healthier. His freshly shaven head, black jeans, biker boots and a crisp V-neck white t-shirt.

"Morning dude, you look like shit," he says, and I cock my pierced eyebrow at him.

"Thanks, and a bloody good morning to you too, prick."

He laughs, as Amy pours him a cup of coffee and she hands it to him.

"Thanks, hot stuff."

He winks, and she rolls her eyes. He perches himself on a bar stool at the breakfast counter and leans on his elbows.

"I'll leave you two to it; I'll let you know the details of Addison's party. Do not let her down, Sam, I mean it," she says sternly.

"Bye Uncle Sammy! Love yooooou!"

Addison blows a kiss to me, and I pretend to catch it.

"Bye Princess, right back at ya, baby girl."

Amy picks Addison up and leaves. Brody takes a sip of his coffee.

"Fuck me, that woman is seriously fit!"

We both laugh.

"Just don't let Cole hear you say that."

Brody rolls his eyes.

"Cole's a pussycat. He knows we bust his balls; he's worked for us long enough."

I take a sip of my coffee. As the hot black liquid slides down my throat, I feel revitalised and ready to face the day.

"So, it's been what six months? You need to get the fuck back out there, dude."

I shake my head.

"I can't."

He cocks his eyebrow.

"Seriously, Sam, six fucking months. I'm surprised your dick hasn't fucking shrivelled up from lack of use. You're coming with me and the boys tonight, we're going to hit Len's strip club, have a few drinks, and get ourselves some pussy. Jax excluded. He's pussy whipped, Ruby made him agree to some date night, and like a love-struck fucking sap, he couldn't say no."

He rolls his eyes, and I chuckle at Brody's bluntness.

"Is that really a good idea, dude, for you to be going to bars?" I say, concerned for my friends' health. He's fresh out of rehab, I would hate for him to go back to the drugs.

"I was only addicted to drugs, Sam, the booze was never the problem. A few drinks aren't going to kill me, dude. I'm a big fucking boy, I can handle the temptation, seriously."

He rolls his eyes, and as I am about to speak, he stops me.

"No more fucking excuses, Sam, you're coming, no arguments."

I salute.

"Yes, boss!" I say sarcastically, and he laughs.

"Bring your condoms tonight, dude, because we are getting fucked!" He says in a singsong voice, and I throw my head back laughing at Brody's joke.

For the first time in a long time, I am actually looking forward to something.

Brody, Lucas and I are pulling up outside a strip club in Shoreditch, in a black limo driven by Cole. Jax decided to sit this one out because Ruby made him agree to a date night. Two words, pussy whipped. I have actually been looking forward to tonight, ever since Brody suggested it earlier. If I'm honest, I need this. I need to kick back, have a few drinks and relax. We all step out of the limo to bright flashes of cameras. *Fucking paparazzi scumbags. How the fuck did they know we would be here?* I run my hand through my hair and turn on Sam, the showman. I give them a dazzling smile and a cheeky wink.

"Good evening, fella's."

I nod and salute as Brody leads us into the club called 'Lust and Redemption'. The door is black leather, and the name of the club is emblazoned in classic black script lettering. The large doorman nods to us and shakes Brody's hand, as he drops the black and gold velvet rope to allow us entry. We step into a narrow corridor and Brody's sober sponsor, Lenny, greets us. He is average height, grey slicked back hair, pale blue eyes, wearing a black suit with a dark grey shirt with the buttons open revealing a smattering of white chest hair. He hugs Brody tightly.

"Good to see you, my son, fuck me you smell like a tart's handbag!" he says in a thick, gruff East London accent, and they both laugh easily.

"Lenny, good to see you too, old man!"

The man cocks his eyebrow.

"I'll give you old man, you cheeky little fucker!"

Brody laughs.

"Len, you've met my bandmates, Sam and Luke before, boys, you remember Lenny?" he says.

Lenny Nicholas has been Brody's sponsor for ten years on and off, after his many stints in rehab. He is like a father figure to him, and Brody has always spoken so highly of Lenny. On the few occasions we've met him, Lenny seems to ground Brody and keeps him on the straight and narrow.

"Boys."

Lenny nods and shakes my hand in a firm grip.

"Ah, Lenny, good to see you again."

I smile, and Lenny regards me intently.

"Leave off, I'm not the press, boy, you don't have to pretend here. This is my gaff, mi casa, su casa. Anything you want, just let me or one of my girls know; they can be extremely accommodating."

He winks and laughs throatily.

"First drinks are on me, boys."

He nods, and Brody hangs back to chat to Lenny.

"I'll be there in a few boys; I just need a quick word with Len."

Brody winks and a tall, tanned, blonde girl joins us. She is carrying a black tray, and she is wearing a purple diamante thong and no bra. Her heels make her legs look like they go on forever. She has light blue eyes and long blonde hair framing her face like a blonde halo.

"Boys, I'm Heidi, I'll be your waitress for the evening, if you would like to follow me?"

She winks at me, and I cock my eyebrow at Lucas. He chuckles and clears his throat.

"Jesus fucking Christ," he mutters, and I laugh, as we follow Heidi down the mirrored corridor.

She leads us into the main hub of the club, and it is decorated in black geometric wall coverings. Along the walls are a set of black and white prints that depict different body parts; the splashes of colour in the images makes them look that bit more erotic. There are black round tables, with low black leather chairs around them, scattered throughout the club and the floor is covered in dark grey slate.

There are around ten or more girls walking around in various stages of undress, ranging from tall, to short, from thin to curvy, black, to white and everything in between. It is nothing if not diverse. The back of the club houses the well-stocked bar, which is black leather on the outside and has a white marble top. There is a grand staircase off to the right side of the club, which has LED lit stairs leading up to the section which states 'V.I.P's only'. Heidi sidles up next to me and grips my bicep suggestively.

"This way, gentlemen," she purrs, and she starts up the stairs.

I raise my eyebrows at Lucas, and he smirks. I follow her up the stairs, as she swings her hips from side to side. I drop my gaze to the floor, actually more than a little embarrassed that my cock hasn't stirred once since stepping into the club.

"Seriously, wouldn't you tap that, dude?" Lucas drawls, and I shake my head.

"I'm not one for blondes these days, man," I lie. What I really want to say is 'I'm not really one for women who aren't Peyton these days.'

I swallow back the lump in my throat and shake that thought away. We get to the top of the stairs, and it is decorated in the same style as downstairs. But instead of tables and chairs scattered around, there is a series of booths running down both sides of the club and an area in the middle where there are a set of podiums and naked women dancing atop them. Heidi leads us into a booth with black Chesterfield couches either side and a marble top table in between the two. I sit down on the one side, and Lucas sits opposite me.

"What can I get for you, gentlemen?"

I look to Lucas, and he rolls his eyes as my eyes start to wander, taking in my surroundings. There are five podiums, and my eyes lock on a stunning brunette who is gyrating against a pole. She is naked apart from a black lacy thong, and she has a tattoo across her chest. She catches me staring at her, and she winks at me. I quickly turn back to face Lucas. *What the fucking fuck is wrong with you, Newbolt?*

"Bottle of Jack and three glasses please, sweetheart. Could we get two bottles of Cristal champagne too, please? Three glasses."

She smiles at him and flashes him a cheeky wink.

"Coming up, handsome."

She sashays off across the club and Brody joins us. He dives into the booth next to me, and we all laugh at his outlandish behaviour.

"Chin up, you miserable fucker, you're my wingman tonight, Sammy, I need you on top form."

He laughs.

"So, what are you fuckers in the mood for tonight, blonde, brunette, redhead or something...a little bit more exotic?"

Brody swipes his split tongue across his bottom lip and wiggles it suggestively, causing Lucas and me to laugh out loud at his over the top behaviour, which is typically Brody.

"Dude, I think our Sammy needs a little pick me up, say a few tequila shots? He refused Miss-Come-Fuck-Me-Now over there. She was showing all the signs, man, the cheeky wink, the subtle bicep brush, dude, she even shook her tight, peachy little ass in his face on the way up the stairs and nothing from our boy here," Lucas explains, and Brody looks at me with disgust.

"Fuck me, man, what the fuck? She's gorgeous, I would be more than happy to take her to heaven, dude; I'm not picky when it comes to your sloppy seconds, it's been too fucking long!"

He laughs, and Heidi comes back over to the table with the bottle of Jack, three glasses, two bottles of champagne in two ice buckets and three champagne flutes. She sets them down on the table, giving me a blatant peek at her perky breasts. I glance and then look away; Brody notices and clears his throat, smiling wickedly.

"Heidi."

Brody winks at her, and she drapes herself over his lap.

"How are you doing this evening, gorgeous?"

He nods, and she runs her perfectly manicured fingernails down his chest. He brings her hand up to his mouth and plants a kiss on the back.

"I'm all good, look, darling, you see we've got a little fucking problem. My man Sammy here is feeling...a little fucking lonely, and he needs a playmate. Do you think you could help him out, sweetheart?"

She giggles and nods as Lucas starts pouring us all a drink.

"Of course, anything for you, B. You're Lenny's boy, he likes to keep you happy, and that includes keeping your handsome friends happy too."

He nods.

"Good girl."

Heidi looks at me as if she is undressing me with her eyes and I look shyly away. *Fuck my life, what is wrong with me? I never act this way, not when it comes to women. Pull yourself together, dick.*

"Any preference, Sam?"

Brody's voice cuts through my thoughts. I am silent, as I pick up my glass with a trembling hand. Brody notices, and he clears his throat to avert Heidi's attention away from me.

"He's really not fussy, sweets."

He winks, and I smile, grateful for his intervention. Heidi cups his face in both of her hands and kisses him on the lips.

"I'll take care of it personally, gorgeous."

She winks and whispers seductively in his ear.

"Oh, could you get us some tequila shots and few slices of lime please, darlin'? And keep 'em coming? Put it on my tab."

He winks, and she nods, as she lifts herself off his lap. She walks across the club, swinging her hips from side to side seductively, as if she can sense

Brody's eyes on her. Brody adjusts himself in his jeans, wipes his lips with the back of his hand, and puffs out his cheeks.

"Fuck me, that girl is hotter than Hades. I'm skipping heaven, dude, and I'm going straight to hell, seriously."

I chuckle softly, and he hits me playfully.

"Snap out of it, for fuck's sake, dude. You need to get laid, and if my girl Heidi has anything to do with it, you'll get your dick wet, and you'll be drowning in fucking pussy for the rest of the night. That's an ideal way to go out from this mortal fucking coil, wouldn't you agree?"

I down my whiskey and I welcome the burn, as it slides down my throat.

"You need to show the world that infamous ladies' man. Bolt is well and truly back on the fucking market."

Lucas beckons a tall, leggy, small-breasted redhead, with deep jade green eyes who is dressed in a green thong and a pale green lacy garter over to us, and she struts over to our table. She leans down, and Lucas whispers in her ear, tucking a wad of notes in the garter, as she brushes her naked breasts against his chest. He grabs her hand, gets up, and gives us a thumbs up, as he leads her off to a private room. That leaves just Brody and me sitting in the booth. Brody pours us both more whiskey, and he looks at me.

"What the fuck, dude? You need to get your fucking head back in the game; do you think we came here just to get you out of your man cave? No, we came here to get you knee-deep in pussy."

I knock back my whiskey and grimace at the burn in my throat.

"I can't do this, Brody, I've still got that gaping hole in my chest. It's been six fucking months, and everywhere I go I see her. She's in my dreams, she's in every memory, she's in every lyric I sing, she's..."

Brody stops me and pours more whiskey into my glass.

"Stop! I get that, dude, I really fucking do, but you need to stop thinking, just for a little while. Stop thinking with your big head and think with the little head in your pants. Pick yourself a playmate and bury your dick so far inside her snatch that you're tickling her fucking tonsils."

I shoot back my drink, run my hand through my spiky hair, and glance over to the podium where the brunette's eyes roam hungrily over my body. Brody nudges me and urges me forward.

"You're up, dude, she's giving you the eyes, give her the Sam Newbolt experience. Show her a good time. Jobs a good 'un, rinse and fucking repeat."

He winks and clucks his teeth at me.

"Come on, Sam, for fuck's sake, you've never needed this much persuading before. Get your head out of your fucking arse, you cocksucker!"

I stand up and twist my head from side to side. Deep down, I know Brody is right. *Come on, Newbolt, get it the fuck together.* I plaster a smile on my face, and Brody slaps me on the back in encouragement.

"That's my boy; go fuckin' get 'em, tiger."

I go to walk away, but Brody stops me. He takes out a strip of condoms from his pocket and hands them to me.

"You might need these, dude; your little gentleman needs a fucking suit."

He winks, and I saunter casually over to the brunette, who has stepped down from the podium, with my hands tucked into my pockets, trying to halt the slight tremble that is still clearly visible. She walks slowly towards me, and I take her in, she is medium height, brunette. She is stunning, has amber coloured eyes, long brown wavy hair tied up in a high ponytail, and she has a slight tan and curves in all the right places. She has a tattoo across her naked chest of two brightly coloured swallows and a large birdcage in the centre of her sternum. She has quite large breasts, with a piercing in her left nipple, and is wearing a black lacy thong with a pair of fuck me heels. She smiles brightly as she stops in front of me, the scent of her perfume invading my nostrils. I run my finger down her arm.

"Hey, gorgeous," I rasp.

"Hey yourself, handsome," she purrs and moves closer to me as she swipes her pierced tongue across her bottom lip.

"Can I help you with something, hot stuff?"

She places her hand on my chest, and I chuckle softly.

"Yeah, you could say that beautiful."

I cock my pierced eyebrow, and she nods as I flash her my famous Newbolt grin.

"Follow me; we'll go somewhere more...private. Special clients get special privileges."

She winks, grabs my hand and leads me to a dimly lit corridor.

"So, you're the famous, Bolt?"

I nod coolly, as she sashays in front of me.

"The very same, gorgeous," I say gruffly, as she leads me into a private room.

She whispers to the bouncer and closes the door behind us. There is a white curved booth in the middle of the room; the walls and the ceiling are mirrored. The lighting is soft and tinged with pink. She pushes me down in the booth and climbs on my lap. She gyrates her hips and grinds herself onto me, giving me a lap dance.

"Do you have a name, sweetheart?"

She laughs, and as she licks her bottom lip, I feel my cock stir in my pants as if he has just woken up from a six-month slumber. *Fucking traitor.*

"Cherry."

I nod, and I'm about to speak when she silences me by putting her finger to my lips.

"I know who you are, no real names in here, honey. I'm Cherry, and you're Bolt."

I raise my eyebrows and smirk. If that's the way she wants to play this, then bring it the fuck on. I suck her finger seductively into my mouth, and she lets out a small whimper.

"That works for me, Cherry."

I practically fuck her name, and she seems to relax as she continues her lap dance. I look at her and take in her curves as she lowers herself down onto my lap, brushing my growing erection with every swing of her hips, making her intentions clear.

"God, you're so fucking fit!"

I laugh at her compliment and spread my arms out across the back of the booth.

"Thanks, you're not so bad yourself, sweetheart," I say smoothly, and she smiles shyly.

"I usually get landed with the old, fat mingers."

I reach up and pull her hair loose; it falls down in a chocolate brown cascade around her shoulders.

"Well, it's lucky I'm neither old, fat, nor a minger. Last time I checked, I was quite the opposite, sweetheart."

I pull her closer to me and nip her neck until she is writhing on my lap. She slides her hand into my shirt and lazily roams over my chest. I cup her breast in my other hand and gently knead it. *Definitely all natural, no silicone here. Thank fuck for small mercies.*

"Mmmm," she moans softly as I nuzzle my face into her neck and nip her earlobe between my teeth.

"You like that, sweetheart?" I rasp, and she shivers in my arms.

"I've seen you in interviews, but the girls weren't lying when they said your voice..." she whispers, and I silence her by crushing my lips to hers, gently stroking my tongue along hers. I pull away and look up into her innocent, golden eyes.

"Ah, ah, I thought we weren't doing real names. That includes talking about who I am, what I do, who I have, or haven't, slept with and how much is in my bank account. In here, I'm just ordinary, regular Bolt."

She giggles, and I lean down, taking her nipple into my mouth. She gasps aloud and writhes in my lap, causing my erection to grow painfully stiff. She reaches back and rubs my erection through my trousers. I growl, and in an instant, I lift her up, lay her down across the booth and undo my belt. I take it off and grasp her wrists, holding them prisoner above her head. I loop the belt around them and tighten it, suddenly feeling a little unsure of myself. *What the fuck am I doing?*

"Is...Is this ok?"

She bites her lip and nods.

"You're a kinky one."

I wink cheekily, but the truth of it is, I can't bear for another woman to touch me the way Peyton did.

"Oh, sweetheart, I haven't even gotten started yet."

I unzip my trousers, reach into my boxers, and fist my erection in my hand.

"Fuck, your...your muscles are...huge!" she blurts out, and her cheeks stain an adorable shade of dark pink.

I smile and bite my lip piercing suggestively.

"Are you sure it's just my muscles, sweetheart?" I rasp, and she shakes her head.

"You've got the whole fucking package, honey, now get over here and fuck me hot stuff."

I move back over to her, and my hands dance over her slim frame, causing her body to erupt with goosebumps.

"All in good time, sweetheart. Good things come to those who wait; come being the operative word, babe," I say suggestively.

I sit back on my haunches and move her black lacy thong to the side, giving me full access to her glistening pink slit. I swipe my finger up her wetness, and she arches her back. *Fuck me, she's soaking.*

"Oh God!" she moans.

"You like that?"

She nods, and I push my finger deep inside her, expertly twisting it to stroke her inner walls.

"Oh, Jesus!"

I chuckle softly pulling my fingers free of her slickness. I wink, and she smiles a genuine smile. As she smiles, her face morphs into Peyton's, and I jump off her as if she has burned me. *Not now, fuck me, not now.*

"What's wrong, hot stuff? Did I do something wrong?"

I sink to the floor and run my hands through my hair. *Fuck, fuck, fuck, fuck.*

"Fuck, this was a mistake, I'm sorry."

My voice is barely a whisper, and she manages to sit up.

"Untie me, please?"

I quickly untie her hands from the confines of my belt, and she sits down on the floor next to me with a concerned look on her face.

"Did I do something wrong?"

She places her hand on my bicep, and I flinch away from her. I scramble across the floor like a scared animal and get to my feet. I pace the floor, and she sits on the edge of the booth, straightening her thong.

"Look, I don't know what I did wrong, honey. I know we weren't doing real names, but if it makes it easier for you, I'm Angelique, but you can call me Angel."

As she says her name, I feel all the colour drain from my face. *Angel. The name I used to call Peyton.* My stomach roils, and I feel bile rising in my throat. *Fuck me, I think I'm going to throw up. Breathe Newbolt, breathe.*

"FUCK!" I curse loudly, and she stands up.

"I've never had that reaction to hearing my real name before; throw a girl a rope, honey."

I appreciate her attempt at humour, but the thoughts in my head are warring with my heart. My head is telling me to forget her and move on, just bury my cock to bury the pain inside me. My heart is telling me that I'm betraying her and defiling her memory by using other women to get over her. The truth is, I'll never be over her, but can I really go through life wondering what if and living in the past, wondering what could have been? My head is swimming with unwanted thoughts, and I have to get out of here. I haphazardly zip up my trousers and the tremor in my hands returning with a vengeance. She stands there watching me, and as she sees me trembling, she moves closer. She brushes my hand.

"Breathe, honey," she says softly, trying to calm me. She strokes my knuckles reassuringly, and I let her.

"Just give me a fucking minute, babe," I say a little more harshly than I intend, and she flinches back, dropping my hand and eyeing me warily.

"Look, I'm sorry, babe, I...I've got fucking issues, ok?"

I laugh bitterly, and the concern in her eyes breaks my heart. I can't allow a near stranger to see me like this. I move past her and drop down onto the chair. I lean forward and scrub my hands down my face.

"You don't need to see me like this, babe, I...I should go."

She crouches down in front of me and looks up at me.

"It's fine, honestly, don't go. I told the bouncer to turn the cameras off, so if you just want to talk, no one has to know."

I smile weakly, grateful for her discretion.

"I understand, you know, I saw...on the news...what happ..."

I cut her off and cover my face to rid myself of the image of my Peyton.

"Please, do not carry on that fucking sentence," I say, with a hint of warning in my voice.

"I'm sorry, Sam."

I uncover my face and look at her, regarding her intently. She gasps and looks visibly shocked that she said my real name out loud. But instead of being mad, I oddly like it and feel comforted by it.

"Do you mind me calling you, Sam?"

I smile and shake my head.

"Oddly enough, no."

Her face transforms into a bright grin, and her face turns into Peyton yet again. I stand up, and she moves backwards out of my way, allowing me to continue my pacing. Fuck, what's wrong with me? *You've got a nearly naked woman, ready and willing for you to fuck her senseless right in front of you, and you're being a goddamn pussy.*

'Stop thinking with your big head and think with the little head in your pants.'

Brody's voice echoes clear in my mind, and I spin around finding her watching me with those innocent golden eyes. In that moment, everything stops, and I see everything with crystal clarity. The voice in my head quiets. The swimming in my brain stills. The trembling in my hands stops, and for the first time in six months, I am thinking clearly. I stalk across the room like a predator ensnaring its prey, and I push her down across the sofa, crushing my lips against hers. I cup her breast roughly in my hand.

"Do you want it slow and gentle or hard and fast? Because right now, I'm not sure I'm capable of gentle. It's been too fucking long," I say huskily, and she grasps my erection.

"What do you think? I'm not the slow and gentle sort of girl, Sam."

The corners of my mouth quirk up into a smile, and that's all the consent I need. *Game on.* I unzip my trousers and free my steel erection. Her eyes widen as she sees it. I smirk cockily and reach into my pocket for a condom. I tear the foil packet open with my teeth, and her eyes lock with mine. She reaches down and starts to play with herself. I growl at the sight of a nearly naked woman beneath me and quickly roll on the condom. The head of my cock finds her slick opening, and I shove forward, burying myself deep inside her to the hilt. She gasps as I hit her g-spot, and I quicken my pace.

"Oh God, Sam! Fuck me harder."

I look down at her, and her face morphs into Peyton's. I blink my eyes and shake myself. *Fucking focus.* I lean down to pick her up, and she wraps her legs around my waist. I move lithely across the room, still buried inside her. Her back hits the wall, and I pull her closer to me, burying her head in my neck so I can focus on my end game. I nip her neck, and I start to quicken my pace, pistoning in and out of her wet heat, each stroke becoming harder and more frantic. I lift her up and impale her on my cock as she moans softly. Suddenly, I hear Peyton's voice in my ear.

"Is she worth it, baby? Does she compare to what we had together?"

I try desperately to shake the voice away by slamming her against the wall. I know I'm being rough, but it's the only way I can take back the control I urgently crave.

"What does her pussy feel like wrapped around your cock, Sam? Is she really worth it? You're mine, Sam, and I'll always be yours."

I shout out in frustration and squeeze my eyes shut, trying to block out the sound of her voice.

"Does that feel good, baby? Do you like it rough?" I rasp, and I slam her against the wall, driving her higher.

"OH FUCK! Give it to me, Sam, harder, oh God harder!"

Angel screams, and she lifts her head up, looking me straight in the eye. As her eyes lock onto mine, they morph into the blue of Peyton's eyes and any semblance of control I maintained completely fucking snaps. I ram my cock deep inside her, and she gasps audibly. I move my hand from underneath her bum and cover her mouth. Her eyes cloud with obvious arousal, and I slam so hard into her that her eyes begin to water.

"You like it hard, Angel? Do you like feeling my cock deep inside you? Fucking beg me for it, beg me."

I move my hand from her mouth and lay her down on the floor.

"Please, please, please, Sam, fuck me like an animal. I fucking need it. I need you to make me come, and I want to come all over your big, hard cock."

I quicken my already frantic pace, and she reaches down to play with her clit, writhing and moaning beneath my large frame.

"That's it, fucking come for me," I growl, and I feel her walls tighten around my cock.

"Oh Christ, Sam, I'm coming."

Her orgasm crests over her like a tidal wave of pleasure. As she starts to cry out, riding out her release, I find mine and growling incoherently as we both come down from our orgasms. She is panting on the floor beneath me, and as I pull out of her, I feel nothing. I don't feel the usual post-sex feeling of warm contentment, I just feel numb. I pull off the condom, knot it and dispose of it in the black bin in the corner of the room. I tuck myself back into my boxers, zip up my trousers, and straighten out my clothes. I button up my shirt and my waistcoat as I run my hands haphazardly through my hair in silence. She is standing in front of the booth, regarding me intently. She smiles warmly, but as I turn around and as she sees the expression on my face, her smile fades.

"Are you ok? That was...incredible, did I...?"

I pull out a wad of notes from my pocket, not allowing her to finish her sentence. I tuck the wad of notes into the waistband of her thong and avoid her gaze. I clear my throat.

"Thanks for the...thanks for the fuck, babe, it was...fun"

I wink cockily. The expression on her face is priceless, and as I turn to leave, she takes the wad of notes I tucked into her thong and launches it at my head.

"I'm not a fucking whore!" she shrieks, and I roll my eyes.

"If the cap fits, babe, you sure as hell acted like one."

Fuck my life; I need to get out of here.

She goes to grab my hand, but I snatch it away, open the door and leave the room.

Fuck, fuck, fuck. I'm a goddamn mess. Will the real Sam Newbolt please stand up?

Sam

Present

"Look, I have to go, Sam; I really need to get back to Freddie," she says softly, and I reach for her wrist.

"Angel, please don't go. Don't run from me again, I can't bear it. I'll get down on my knees and fucking beg you if I have to. I'll do anything, please, just don't go. I've spent the past year in hell because I thought I had lost you. But you coming back to me, it's fate. We've got a second chance. *Fuck,* we're someone's parents now; we have a child together. Surely that must mean something to you."

I look deep into her blue eyes and see a years' worth of pain.

"Of course, it fucking does!" she chokes out.

She opens her mouth to speak again, but her words seem to get trapped in her throat, and she doesn't say another word. Her silence echoes off the walls of the hospital corridor we are standing in.

"Talk to me, angel, please, your silence is fucking killing me."

My voice is barely a whisper, and she looks up at me, shaking her head as she turns and runs out on me.

Fuck my life.

32

Peyton

I am back at the hotel with Remy and Freddie after leaving Sam standing speechless in the hospital corridor. Even though I have ached to hear his voice for this past year, his words shredded me. The fragile truth of it is that I can't be with him, no matter how much I love him. He doesn't deserve this broken version of me. It might look like I'm making excuses, but I know deep down in my heart that Sam fell for the feisty, no-nonsense version of me. Now, I feel all the fight has literally been knocked out of me. A whole year has passed, and I have totally rebuilt my life under a brand-new identity and consigned myself to the fact that my relationship with Sam was just a distant memory.

My thoughts are interrupted by my Samsung Flip 6 ringing. I pick it up from the low coffee table in front of the grey sofa, I am sat on, and I don't recognise the number. I connect the call apprehensively, my heart beating a frantic tattoo.

"Hello?" I say cautiously.

"Angel," he rasps, and I involuntarily shudder at the sound of his familiar voice.

Sam. How did he get this number? Only a handful of people know the number to this phone.

"How did you get this number, Sam?" I say through gritted teeth, and I can't help but sound irritable. *Infuriating fucking man!*

"I told you when we first met, I can get any information I require, within reason. I have access to the best people money can buy, you can't hide from me anymore, angel."

I hear the amusement in his voice, and I get up from the sofa. I start to pace the hotel room. I go over to the window and look out at the New York City skyline.

"You could have just asked me for my number, or does that not fit in with your stalkerish tendencies?"

I smirk to myself at the familiar, easy banter between us, and he chuckles softly.

"Fair point well made, babe, but I had to get you to talk to me somehow, angel. You're so intent on fucking constantly running from me. I'm a desperate man, what can I say? I'm nothing if not inventive," he rasps, and we both laugh.

In that moment, I feel exactly the same way as I did a year ago, caught up in the whirlwind that is Sam Newbolt.

"Come to me, angel, I'll send a car for you and Freddie, just say the word. Please let me meet my son."

I lean my forehead against the window, contemplating his request for a second, and I realise that his request isn't unreasonable. I've punished him enough by keeping his son from him for six whole months. *Freddie deserves to know his daddy.*

"Ok, I'll come over; we're at The New Yorker Hotel on Eighth Avenue."

He clears his throat and replies cautiously as if he was expecting me to say no.

"*Wow,* ok...I'll send Cole for you, angel. Wait in the lobby for him. I would come and get you myself, but I'm kind of on our fans radar here, especially after everything that's happened. We're front-page news."

I take a deep breath, and my heartbeat starts to quicken at the prospect of being with alone with Sam again after all this time.

"Cole can be with you in ten minutes, angel. My place isn't far away."

I clear my throat and continue to pace again.

"Ok, I need to grab a shower and get changed. Give me an hour, and I'll be waiting."

He pauses for a moment.

"Ok...yeah, an hour...that's...cool. I'll see you in a little while, angel, bye."

He hangs up the phone and doesn't wait for me to say goodbye. I put my phone down on the bed, wondering what the fuck I just agreed to. Remy comes out of the bathroom with a towel around his waist, his long dark hair damp from his shower. He goes over to his bed, which is next to mine, and starts to pull some clean clothes out of his bag.

"You look a little green around the gills there, beaut. What's up? Did Freddie do one of those massive shits that stinks like sprouts?"

I laugh at his joke and shake my head.

"I wish it was something that simple and trivial, babe. That was Sam on the phone."

He cocks his eyebrow.

"Oh ok, how did he get your number?"

Curiosity getting the better of him. I get to my feet and start pacing the room.

"He's Sam Newbolt, Rem. Everything has a price."

He shakes his head, and a frown line jumps into place in between his eyebrows.

"There are fucking laws against that sort of thing. It's an invasion of your privacy," he grits out and brushes my arm.

"He's sending a car for Freddie and me."

He nods and puffs out his cheeks in exasperation.

"Oh, right ok, and you just agreed like the dutiful little woman? I thought you were stronger than that, beaut."

My eyes widen at his obvious and unnecessary possessiveness.

"How fucking dare you, Rem! He's Freddie's dad, I've punished him enough!"

I get up and storm past him, but he grabs my arm.

"*Punished him?* Unbelievable! You stayed away because you were protecting you and your son, Peyton. You didn't stay away because you *wanted* to; it was because you had *no other* fucking choice!" he grits out. "When are you going to tell him the fucking truth?" he snaps and runs his hands through his long damp hair as I scrub my hand down my face.

I know he's one thousand per cent right. He has a right to know what I've been hiding from him all this time. All of a sudden, the fight is drained from me.

"Just don't, Rem. I can't, not now; it's not the right time. I'll tell him soon."

He sighs and let's go of my arm, holding his hands up defensively. I step past him, grab some clean clothes, and go into the bathroom, closing the door behind me. I strip off my clothes and step into the walk-in shower cubicle. I turn on the shower and let the scalding hot water sting my skin as I sink down to the floor of the cubicle. I pull my knees up to my chest, and I let myself get lost in the thoughts of what has been, what could have been, and what the future could be. I can't stop myself from thinking how different this past year would have been if only I would have allowed myself to pick up the phone and let Sam explain. I was so in love with him; I *should* have believed his word over J.D's.

I finish my shower, and I wipe the condensation from the mirror to look at my reflection. I don't recognise the young, skittish, vulnerable, woman with the haunted, hollow blue eyes staring back at me. My appearance is so different. I decide then and there that I am going back to my natural hair colour, maybe then I'll start to feel more like Peyton Leigh Harper, the girl I left behind a year ago.

I step out of the bathroom with my short red hair styled in short, tousled waves, my usual natural makeup applied, and I am dressed in a red and white striped racer back vest, a pair of black skinny jeans, and black Converse trainers. I finish my look off with a black cardigan and a pair of simple silver hoop earrings. I emerge from the bathroom, and Remy greets me with a warm smile.

"Looking good as always, beaut."

He hands Freddie to me, freshly changed and dressed in a pair of jeans, black Converse trainers and a Batman t-shirt. He looks adorable, and his face lights up as he sees me. I can't help myself from smiling at how much he looks like Sam. I take him and cuddle him.

"Are you ready to meet your daddy, baby boy?" I coo, and he giggles.

I sit down on the bed next to Remy and check my phone. I have a text message from Sam.

Cole's outside the hotel, angel

Whenever you're ready, he's waiting

See you soon

S x

I put my phone down, and Remy looks at me with a worried look on his face. His eyes are sad and pained.

"Are you sure you want to do this, beaut?"

I stroke Remy's cheek and smile softly at him. I know this is hard for him, after all, he has been the one who has looked after us both for the past year. He took care of us, gave us a home, found me a job, and was my rock through the times I needed him the most.

"It's going to be alright, Rem, I promise."

His eyes glaze over, and he scrubs his hands down his face.

"I should be the one reassuring you, but the selfish part of me is telling me that I *can't* lose you, beaut. You and this little superstar here have made me feel whole and alive again."

I shake my head.

"You're not going to lose us, Rem, I'll take him to meet Sam, and I'll be back later, I promise. We can veg out in front of the T.V and take advantage of trashy American sitcoms. We can even think about packing up and going back home; New York kind of sucks!"

He chuckles softly.

"Sounds like a plan. I did warn you New York smelled badly and was full of rude people, but no one ever listens to the cripple!"

He laughs, and I roll my eyes at his bad taste joke. We both stand up, and he kisses me on my forehead; I strap Freddie into his carrycot, grab his changing bag, my bag, and my phone. When I'm satisfied, I have everything I need, Remy pulls me in for a hug.

"I'll be back later, love ya, Rem."

I blow him a kiss, and he winks.

"Right back at ya, beautiful."

As I leave the hotel room with Freddie in his carrycot, I start to think of the enormity of this moment and what life would have been like if none of this would have happened. I can't allow myself to dwell on what could have been and focus on what could be in the not-so-distant future. That will have to be enough. *For now.*

I make my way to the opulent lobby of the hotel, with its red and gold decor, high ceilings and decadent marble floor. As I look up, I see Cole standing to the side of the hotel's glass entrance with his hands behind his back. He looks professional as ever, wearing a black suit, black shirt, black tie, black shoes, and a black trilby hat. He nods as he sees me.

"Peyton."

His deep rumbling voice greets me with no emotion at all. He gestures for me to step outside ahead of him and he follows. He opens the door of a black Mercedes CLK with tinted windows, which is parked at the kerb. I climb into the back with Freddie in his carrycot and manoeuvre the seatbelt to strap him securely in the back seat. Cole climbs into the driver's seat and pulls into the New York City traffic like a pro.

"He's a little cutie," he says in his familiar baritone voice.

"His name is Freddie."

Cole's eyes find mine in the interior mirror of the car, and he smiles softly.

"I don't condone what you did, but I totally understand, sugar. I couldn't imagine my life without Amy and Addison. I would kill for them. I would lay down my life and sacrifice myself for them. There's nothing I wouldn't do to protect my girls. I get that that's what you did to protect your son. I'm not going to pretend I know what you went through, what that loathsome, warped man did to you, but I don't hate you, far from it. I get that everyone's angry with you, but they have to accept it and move on, sugar."

My eyes glaze over at Cole's words. He's never been this open and candid with me before. He's a dad too, so it warms my heart and gives me hope that in the future there could be a happy ending for us.

"You gave birth to your kid, probably alone, and I can't even begin to imagine how hard that's been on you, sugar. I admire you; no woman should give birth without the man they love by their side. I would have moved mountains to get to Amy when she was in labour. Sam made sure I got there in time, and I'll be forever grateful to him for that, but he needs to cut you some slack. He can be stubborn and pig-headed, as you know. But if it helps, sugar, I'll talk to him. He usually listens to me."

He catches my eye in the interior mirror again and winks. I smile softly at him, swallowing back the lump that is forming in my throat.

"Thank you so much, Cole."

He moves his focus back to the road.

"I'm a father, I understand more than most. If you ever need to chat, anytime at all, sugar, I'm here. You'll get no judgement from me."

I am humbled and shocked at his kind words. I settle back in my seat, and we are silent for the rest of the journey. I am staring out of the window, and I suddenly feel nervous at seeing Sam again.

"We're here, sugar."

Cole's deep baritone voice cuts through my thoughts, and I look out of the window at our surroundings as we pull up to the kerb. From the outside, the building is a low rise, with only seven or eight floors and surrounded by trees. It looks like a little piece of heaven amongst the hustle and bustle of New York City. Cole comes around to my side of the car and opens the door. I get out of the car and Cole reaches in to unstrap Freddie's carrycot. He lifts him easily out of the car, and I follow him into the building. The lobby is a large, open space, with light marble floors. On the walk inside, Cole explains that the building is manned by a twenty-four-hour concierge. The man on the concierge desk is a tall, thin gentleman with grey hair, a greying beard and black-rimmed glasses. He looks up from his newspaper as Cole and I enter the lobby. Cole tips his hat and the man smiles brightly.

"Good evening, Mr. Benedict," he says in an upper-crust English accent and Cole nods.

"Evening, Mr Grayson. This is Miss Harper, she's Mr Newbolt's guest. If you could add her to the list of people authorised to enter the building and have unlimited access to Mr. Newbolt's penthouse, that would be very much appreciated."

Mr. Grayson nods in response and starts tapping on his computer keyboard.

"Certainly, Mr. Benedict, I'll take care of that right away. I hope you both enjoy your evening."

Cole presses the call button for the lift, and we step in. Cole presses the button marked 'PH. *Typical Sam opting for the penthouse.* The lift stops as we reach Sam's floor, and I step out into the bright foyer. It has a large oval window and an exotic potted plant in the corner of the light grey marble floor. Cole scans his fingerprint and opens the large white oak door with a key card. He winks reassuringly and hands Freddie to me.

"Good luck, sugar."

I smile at his encouragement.

"Thanks, Cole."

I step into the penthouse loft, and it looks like something out of an episode of *MTV Cribs*. The living area is an expansive open space, with floor to ceiling windows that showcase the impressive New York skyline. It is decorated in a nautical theme, its signature colours red, white and blue, which is a stark contrast to his penthouse in Greenwich. The carpet is navy blue, and the white leather U shaped sofa dominates the space. In front of the sofa is a large flat screen TV mounted above the white marble fireplace, which is where Sam is standing, with his back to the room. His broad shoulders make him look huge. He is wearing a white dress shirt with the sleeves rolled up to showcase his tattoos, and a pair of loose ripped jeans, which hang low on his hips. His feet are bare, and his black hair is perfectly mussed. He is leaning on the fireplace, which has an assortment of various award statuettes adorning the mantelpiece. He has a glass of dark amber liquid in front of him. I am not sure whether he knows I am here, so I clear my throat to get his attention.

"Angel," he rasps, as he turns around.

His eyes lock with his son for the first time. *Freddie meet your daddy.*

33

Sam

I drop to my knees as I set eyes on the little boy in the carrycot she is holding, and I can't find my breath. He has tufts of thick black hair, wide, inquisitive green eyes... *my eyes*. He has Peyton's button nose, but he is my double, from the deep dimples in his chubby cheeks, to the infamous Newbolt grin.

Fuck me.

I can't take my eyes off him; he is the most beautiful boy I have ever seen. I am in awe of him as Peyton moves closer to me and sinks down to the floor next to me. She unstraps him from his carrycot as I remove my sling. She takes him out and hands my son to me. As I take him in my arms, I am instantly in love. Suddenly, my heart feels almost too big for my chest, I'm so overwhelmed by this tiny human and the feelings he has evoked in me. I swallow back the lump in my throat before I can speak.

"Hey Freddie, I'm your daddy," I say gruffly, and he giggles, the sound warming my heart.

Peyton softly grips my bicep and, I turn to look at her; I can't stop smiling. The smile she gives in return is genuine, and my heart slams against my ribcage. This extraordinary woman in front of me brings me to my fucking knees. She unmans me with those beautiful baby blue eyes. She cripples me, by just being her. Peyton Leigh Harper. *My Peyton*. She has the ability to see into my soul, she sees the real me. She sees the real Samson Newbolt. She reaches to the depths of my very core. She fucking owns me, even after all this time. I'm reduced to a whimpering, love-struck sap every time she is within touching distance. As I'm sat on the floor of my New York loft, with my baby son in my arms, I am instantly transported back to the day Peyton told me she was pregnant.

Sam

Past

I have been on tour with the boys for the past three months, and I have missed Peyton so much. We have been on a European tour, and I came back ahead of the boys to surprise her. I showed up outside her flat on my Harley Davidson Sportster Iron 883, and in the two months since I last saw her, she looks even more beautiful. Her long, dark hair cascades down her back, and she is wearing a purple polka dot dress, which accentuates her luscious curves. She looks stunning, and the look in her eyes is one of love. If I wasn't already in love with her, I would have fallen right there in that moment.

She goes back to my place with Cole, and I follow on my bike. I can't wait to get her alone and naked; I have missed the feel of her pressed against me. The long, lonely nights spent on the bus with Mrs. Palmer and her five daughters doing the five-knuckle shuffle is no match for the feel of the soft flesh of the woman I love more than life itself. I arrive back to the apartment, and instead of waiting for the lift, I take the stairs two at a time, because I am so eager to be with my girl after all this time. I throw open the door, and I instantly know something is wrong as Cole is sat on his haunches in front of her with a look of apprehension on his face. I stride across the apartment purposefully, and Cole moves out of the way. I take his place in front of her. She looks pale and exhausted.

"Angel, is everything ok?"

She sighs, and goes to rise from the sofa, but falls back down.

"Jesus, angel."

She looks at me, and her blue eyes look troubled. I can't help but be curious as to what made her look that way.

"I'm just exhausted, babe, that's all. It's been nonstop at the shop lately."

She smiles to reassure me, but something in the tone of her voice makes me think she's lying to me.

"I'm taking you to our room, babe; you look like you could use a lie-down."

She cups my face in her hands, and I lean into her touch.

162

"I'm fine, babe, I promise, I just need you to hold me for a while. I've missed you."

I smile and nod as I pick her up and carry her into the bedroom. I set her down on her feet, and I move her so I can look at her properly. My green eyes meet her tired blue ones.

"God, you're beautiful."

My voice is barely a whisper as I stroke her face and tuck an errant strand of her hair behind her ear.

"I have a surprise for you, angel."

She raises her eyebrows, and I smirk mischievously. I have been waiting almost two months to show her the lasting mark I got on my chest. We both stand facing each other, and I strip off my t-shirt. She licks her lips as I reveal my naked torso, and I chuckle at her reaction.

"Don't get any ideas, angel," I rasp and throw my t-shirt on the bed and look at her. "Do you see that?"

I point to a spot above my right pectoral and there, in bold, flowing script, is a tattoo of her name, 'Peyton', with two elaborate black and grey angel wings either side. The day we flew out to Europe I made a last-minute stop to Saint Sinner Ink, to get Seb to tattoo me, as a surprise for her upon my return.

"That's how much I love you, angel. There's nothing I wouldn't do for you. You're my good luck charm, my angel; you're my life, my whole world. You own me."

Her eyes glaze over at my words, and she traces over the lines of my tattoo before she loses it completely, collapsing in floods of tears in my arms. I start to wonder what has made her cry, and I fear the worst.

"Hey, what's with the tears, babe?"

I attempt to soothe her.

"Shhh."

I kiss her forehead, and she snuggles closer to my chest.

"I'll never let anyone hurt you, angel."

We spend the rest of the day catching up and spending some quality time together. I have missed being with my girl and being a normal couple. By the time the evening rolls around, we order takeaway and snuggle on the sofa.

After we finish eating, she falls asleep in my lap, and I lift her from the sofa. I carry her to my bedroom, and she wakes up as I lay her down on the bed.

"I've got you, angel."

She sleepily shakes her head.

"It's fine, baby."

She smiles the smile I have missed, and I kiss her gently on the lips. She gets up and strides to the walk-in wardrobe, taking out one of my oversized Rancid Vengeance t-shirt's. I love seeing her in my clothes. She goes into the bathroom and closes the door. I frown at the oddness of her closing the door. She never closes the door, and I start to think of all the reasons why she doesn't want me to see her naked. I don't knock; I just swing the door open as she pulls on my t-shirt.

"Hey, what's with the closed-door, angel? You're not normally so shy about getting undressed in front of me. Is something wrong? Have I done something?"

My face is filled with worry, and she strokes my cheek softly with the back of her hand.

"Everything's perfect, babe, I've just put on a little weight since you've been away. Too many late nights at work, too many takeaways, and too much Ben and Jerry's. I should think about getting back to the gym."

She tries to dismiss it with a smile, but I don't believe her for a second. I would love her whatever she looked like. She's hiding something from me, I know she is. She comes back into the bedroom with her hair in a loose knot, and I pat the space on the bed next to me.

"I'll stay with you until you fall asleep. I've got some unpacking to do, and I've got some stuff that needs taking care of, but I'll be in soon."

I lie next to her, and she falls asleep in my arms. I lay watching her sleeping form for a few minutes, trying to figure out what is wrong with her. The dark circles around her eyes are a clear indication to me that it is more than just too many late nights spent at the shop.

Has she cheated on me? Has she suddenly realised that our lives are poles apart? Has she fallen out of love with me? My mind is racing at a hundred miles per hour, and I can't keep up with the constant inconsequential doubts. I get up from the bed and scrub my hands across my stubbled jaw. I walk out of the bedroom, leaving my sleeping angel to rest.

I go into my office, pour myself a large glass of whiskey, and drop down into my leather chair, kicking my long legs up on the desk. I fire up my computer, run my hands through my hair, and prepare myself to deal with fan mail, post-tour admin, and requests from various charities regarding personal appearances and donations. The only thought that dominates my brain at that moment is, *Jesus Christ, we need to hire a new personal assistant.*

After I finish dealing with band stuff, I go to join Peyton in bed. I strip off my clothes and curl up beside her. I take in her scent, the warmth of her soft skin against mine, the look of absolute serenity as she sleeps, the way her hair haphazardly spreads out across the pillow, all the things I have missed after almost two months apart. I spoon her, and the feel of her pressed against me is enough to send me into a deep sleep.

I am not sure how long I have been asleep, but I am roused from my sleep by Peyton screaming, which scares the living shit out of me, and I softly call out her name.

"Peyton, wake up, you're having a nightmare."

I softly stroke her hair; her breathing is laboured, and she has a thin sheen of sweat forming on her forehead.

"Jesus, angel, I'm here. Are you ok? You scared the shit out of me," I say quietly, and I go to pull her into me to comfort her.

She looks stricken, and she flinches as if I have burned her. Fuck. She jumps out of bed and runs into the bathroom, slamming the door and locking it behind her. I get up from the bed and run my hands through my hair. *What the fuck is going on with her?* I stride over to the locked bathroom and hear her sobbing hysterically; the sound shreds me. I rattle the doorknob, desperate for her to let me in so I can comfort her.

"Angel, fuck! Open the door, please talk to me."

I try to sound calm but fail miserably. She sobs hard, and I shake the doorknob again.

"The door's coming down if you don't open it, angel."

I soften my voice and lean my head against the door. *Fuck, why is she doing this?*

"I'm not going anywhere until you talk to me, babe."

I sit down outside the door in my boxers.

"Please, just go away," she chokes out, and I lean my head back against the wall.

"Not happening, baby. I'll sit out here all night if I have to."

A few minutes of silence pass.

"Do you want to tell me what your nightmare was about, angel?"

My voice is barely a whisper, as I try desperately to get her to open up and tell me what the fuck she was dreaming about. She unlocks the door, and as she opens the door, I reach my hand out to her. She regards my hand intently and starts to push past me. She runs into the living room, and I follow her.

"Fuck, where are you going, angel?"

My voice is panicked, but she doesn't answer me. Her silence is really freaking me out, and she frantically starts throwing her stuff into her overnight bag.

"Peyton, will you just fucking stop for one god damn second!"

I try to stop her, and I tilt her chin up to face me. Her blue eyes look so sad and troubled, the remnants of her nightmare still visible in the expression on her beautiful face.

"Don't leave me, angel," I plead, and she shakes her head.

"I can't do this anymore Sam, being with you is...unpredictable. Every time I'm near you, I lose myself."

What the fucking fuck? Where is all this coming from? I can't help thinking that it is a lame cop out on her behalf to mask something more serious. She swipes a stray tear from her eye as I move closer to her.

"Why are you doing this? What have I done? Tell me what I've done, and I'll fix it; I'll make it right."

She hangs her head.

"I thought we were ok, please stop and fucking talk to me. Please don't run from me, tell me you'll stay."

The truth is, I can't bear the thought of her leaving me; she's all I've thought about for the past few months. She moves closer to me, and I reach for her hand. She lets me take it and I stroke her knuckles softly.

"What's wrong? Please talk to me. I can't fucking stand you shutting me out like this, angel."

She releases my hand and puts her hands up to her face. She sobs, and as the tears begin, I clench my jaw. *Fuck, my heart feels like it's being ripped apart and it fucking shreds me.*

"Jesus, please don't cry, what can I do? Tell me what I can do, angel," I plead anxiously.

She tries desperately to get herself together, and when she finally does, she chokes out.

"This is all such a fucking mess, Sam, and it's all my fault."

What the fuck? I shake my head.

"Everything's going to be ok, as long we have each other; I'm not going anywhere, I promise you, angel."

I move towards her and pull her to my chest. She clings to me as she sobs, and I hold her close to me, silently begging her to tell me what's wrong.

"Tell me what's going on in that beautiful mind of yours, angel."

My voice is a gruff whisper, and my heart beat starts to quicken as I wait patiently for her to continue. She takes a deep breath, and our eyes lock.

"I...I'm pregnant," she chokes out.

I've never really contemplated wanting kids, but suddenly, now that she's told me she's pregnant, I am instantly on board and thrilled at the prospect of becoming a dad for the first time. I don't say anything at first, I'm still processing the news. She starts to tremble violently in my arms.

"Hey, shush, I've got you, angel."

I try to soothe her and then I find my voice.

"You're pregnant, wow!"

The biggest grin spreads across my face. I cup her face in my hands, and I press my lips eagerly to hers.

"Angel, you have just made me the happiest fucking man to walk this earth! I'm going to be a dad!" I say excitedly as I see the look of relief wash over her face, and she sags in my arms.

I release her and hold her at arm's length away from me. I might not be a mind reader, but I know as soon as I look at her exactly what was wrong. She actually thought I was going to leave her just like her scumbag ex Callum did.

"You thought I was going to leave didn't you, angel?" I say softly, waiting for an answer from her. "Look at me, Peyton."

She looks up at me and nods, her eyes brimming with tears. My heart slams against my ribcage. *How the fuck could she think I would do that to her?*

"How could you think that angel? After everything we've been through?"

She shakes her head.

"I don't know I just panicked...I was...terrified."

I stroke her face softly with the back of my hand.

"I'm nothing like that cock sucker. I'm not going anywhere; you're stuck with me," I say vehemently, as I grin widely.

I lift up my t-shirt that she is wearing to look more closely at her now visible bump.

"How far gone are you?"

I trace her small bump with my fingers, and my smile couldn't get any bigger. She is carrying our baby, a piece of her and a piece of me moulded into one tiny person. She places her hand over mine and smiles.

"Twelve weeks."

She worries her lip between her teeth as I take in a sharp breath.

Three fucking months. She kept it to herself for three whole months. What the actual fuck? I do the maths in my head, and that means she knew she was pregnant before we left for the European leg of our tour. *Why the fuck would she do that?* I curse to myself and walk over to the balcony. I pull open the doors and drop down on the lounger. I run my fingers through my hair so harshly that it is almost painful. I can't believe she kept it from me for so long and I can feel myself trembling with anger. She follows me out onto the balcony and leans in the doorway.

"Why the fuck didn't you tell me, angel? That night you told me about Callum, I promised you if that ever happened to us, I'd stand by you."

I scrub my hand down my face, desperately trying to keep my anger leashed. She bursts into tears again, and I wrap her in my arms, trying to comfort her as she clings to me tightly.

"Shhh, it's going to be alright, angel, I promise. We'll be a family. The three of us: you, me and our little rock star!"

I laugh, and she cocks her eyebrow at me.

"What if it's a girl?"

I cup her cheek and kiss her gently on the end of her nose.

"Then she's not leaving our house until she's at least thirty-five, and I'm not letting any boys anywhere near her!"

We both laugh, and she lets out a yawn.

"Tired, angel?"

She nods, and I pick her up, carrying her into the bedroom.

"I can walk you know, I do have legs!"

I laugh out loud.

"I know, but you're carrying precious cargo now!"

She chuckles softly, and I set her down gently on the bed and lie down next to her. I pull her back to my chest and wrap my arms around her. I gently rest my hand on her stomach and snuggle into her back. At that moment, I feel so happy, jubilant and content with my life. I fall into a dreamless sleep with the woman I love in my arms and my unborn child in her stomach.

Sam

Present

Freddie squirms in my arms, and I get up from the floor and move over to the window. I hold him close to me as I look out across the New York City skyline.

"See, this is where daddy lives sometimes, rock star. Isn't it beautiful?" I say softly. "Look, there's the Empire State building, that's the third tallest building in all of New York."

I chatter idly and smile as his chubby fingers cling onto my shirt. Peyton chuckles softly.

"You're a natural. I think that's his way of telling you he likes you."

I turn around, and she still takes my breath away. Her innocence, her natural beauty, and the way she has the ability to calm my racings thoughts... by just being her. I hold our son close to me, and I am struck dumb by the little miracle in my arms.

"I'm speechless, angel; he's the most beautiful kid I've ever seen. He's a little person that looks like us."

She smirks and cocks her eyebrow.

"Since when did you start getting sentimental, Newbolt?" she says sassily, and I chuckle softly.

"Since I started reading some of those sappy, erotic romance novels Ruby reads!"

She raises her eyebrows and smirks. *I can't believe I just fucking admitted that out loud!*

"Hey, don't judge me, we had a year off. I've had time on my hands, babe!" I joke, and she cocks her eyebrow, silently asking me to elaborate.

"You know the ones? Billionaire alpha male meets innocent young beauty, young beauty tries her hardest to stay away from said billionaire alpha male, but his pull is just too strong for her to resist, blah, blah, blah...you could write the plot on the head of a fucking pin!"

I dramatically make a vomiting motion, and we both laugh. I am comfortable with the easy conversation between us; it is almost like the past year never happened.

"*Wow!* Sam Newbolt in sappy romance novel shocker, that's front-page news right there, babe!"

She cheekily sticks her tongue out at me; I throw my head back and laugh. *There's my girl.*

"Shhh! I've got my rock star reputation to keep up, angel. Let's keep that one just between us."

I put my index finger to my lips and wink cheekily. She visibly shivers, and even after all this time, my presence still affects her. That one single reaction gives me hope that we can move forward.

"Freddie's due his nap; can I put him down in one of your bedrooms, please?"

I nod, disappointed that my time with my son is cut short, but I would agree to almost anything she asked if it meant that I get her to stay. *Christ, I sound like such a pussy.*

"Yeah of course, whatever you need, angel."

I am still trying to process the fact that my Peyton is back, and we have a child together.

"I would offer you some wine, or something stronger, but it's not very responsible, is it? I'll put the coffee machine on; there are two spare bedrooms just through there, angel. As soon as you agreed to let me see him, I got Cole to order a cot and some bedding."

I point along the far end of the apartment, and she smiles. *Amazing what having money can do to get things done.*

"You've thought of everything, thank you," she says softly and reaches up on her tiptoes to kiss me on the cheek.

She turns to take Freddie with her, leaving me alone with my thoughts. I step into my kitchen and turn on the coffee machine, the aroma of fresh coffee beans filling my nostrils. I lean on the worktop and contemplate how I never really knew how much I wanted kids until Peyton told me she was pregnant. As soon as she told me, I knew instantly that I wasn't going to be like that cocksucker, Callum, and bail on her when she needed me the most. I was prepared to stand by her and do the right thing. I was brought up believing that it takes two people to make a baby and I was prepared to support her both emotionally and financially.

When the band first started, I didn't see a future with a girlfriend or a wife with two point four kids. I saw me being a world-famous rock star, an eternal bachelor destined for the single life, moving from one groupie to the next, and touring around the globe without a care in the world.

Seeing Cole, Amy and Addison as a family in the year Peyton was gone, it cut me deep. I have never been envious of anyone in my life, because for years I had it all: the money, the fame, the rock and roll lifestyle, and the women. Yet in that year, I felt like I had *nothing*. I felt resentful towards Cole and Amy for having something that I felt I would never find again. A child created out of love between two people, a family of my own, a legacy, someone to pass on my words of wisdom to, and someone to carry on the Newbolt name.

Cole and Amy's daughter, Addison Rose Benedict, is my goddaughter. The day they asked me to do the honour of being her godfather was up there in the top five moments of my life. It's an honour to have someone entrusting you to look after their child in event of their death and to be someone for that child to look up to.

The night of her birth Cole was doing security for us at a gig; he wasn't supposed to be working that night, but all his guys were out doing various jobs, and Trey, the guy who was meant to be standing in for him, called in sick. He reluctantly agreed to work the gig, and halfway through, he got a call from Milo that Amy was in labour. He gave me a look from the pit in front of the stage, and I instantly knew something had happened. I made an executive decision to cut the show short that night; much to J.D's disgust, but I explained family comes first, *always*. I pulled a few strings, and I personally drove Cole to the hospital, breaking a few major speed limits along the way, but we got there just in time for him to see his daughter being born. It was a beautiful moment for us to see and welcome a new addition to the Rancid Vengeance family. I held Addison when she was just a few hours old, and I instantly fell in love with her. Now, at five years old, she is a little firecracker. She worships the ground I walk on, and that is why, six months ago, I reluctantly agreed to be her '*date*' for her fifth birthday party.

34

Sam

Past

"Uncle Sammy!"

Addison comes bounding into my bedroom, with her black curly hair in pigtails. She is wearing a neon pink tutu, black tights with silver glittery guitar shapes all over them, her beloved pink Converse, and a black Rancid Vengeance t-shirt with our band logo on the front and the number five and 'Team Bolt' on the back. She looks like a tiny rocker, and she is adorable. The glum face I had sported previously disappeared as soon as I saw her. I am getting ready to accompany her to her fifth birthday party, and six months after Peyton's death, it is becoming easier to paint on a smile and pretend everything is ok. I am dressed in jeans, black Doc Martens, a black v-neck t-shirt, and black blazer with the sleeves rolled up. I am styling my hair into soft spikes in the mirror as she stands in front of me with her hands on her hips.

"Uncle Sammy, are you ready yet?"

She sighs dramatically, and I chuckle softly.

"Give me five more minutes, princess."

She rolls her eyes.

"My mummy says you take longer than a girl to get ready!"

I cock my pierced eyebrow and try to suppress my smirk.

"Did she now?"

She giggles cheekily, and I continue to spike my hair. She moves slowly to my left and stands on her tiptoes. She reaches out for my collection of aftershaves on my dresser and points to my Joop aftershave, my personal favourite.

"Uncle Sammy, I think you should wear this one, you have to smell nice if you're going to be my date for my party," she says animatedly.

I finish spiking my hair, wipe the excess gel on a black towel, which is slung over the back of my black leather chaise lounge, and I pick up the bottle she has chosen. Joop, my favourite and Peyton's favourite.

"Good choice, baby girl, that one happens to be my favourite."

I wink and splash on some aftershave while she watches me like I'm the most fascinating person she's ever seen.

"Do you miss Aunty Peyton, Uncle Sammy?" She asks curiously.

My smile fades, and I screw the lid on my aftershave bottle.

"Every day, baby girl, but I know that she's in heaven looking down on us right now."

I pick her up. She clings to my neck, and she wraps her little legs around my waist. Even though it is the middle of the afternoon, I go to the window of my bedroom and point to the sky.

"You see at night when the stars come out, princess?"

She looks at me and nods. I'm not sure I can find the right words to say to her, to make her understand, so I go with my heart's instinct.

"Well, one of those stars is Aunty Peyton. When we're lost, she'll guide us. When we're sad, she'll comfort us, and when we're lonely or confused, she'll put us back on the right track."

She grins at me and points out of the window.

"I think she's definitely the brightest star in the sky, Uncle Sammy."

I swallow back the lump in my throat and nod.

"Yes, she is. Come on then tiger, let's get the birthday girl to her party."

We arrive at Cole and Amy's house, which is a converted barn next door to my place, where the party is taking place. It is a bright, open space with floor to ceiling windows that showcase the miles and miles of rolling green hills behind the property. The house looks like every little girls' fantasy. There is pink glittery shit everywhere, and it looks like someone vomited a Disney film. Addison clings to me tighter as we enter the room, and everyone applauds as they see the birthday girl. But I can't help but hear the audible gasps of her friends' mums as they see who has entered the room with her.

"I'm going to put you down now, princess. Uncle Sammy is going to chat with your daddy, but I'll be right over there, I promise."

I wink, and she giggles girlishly. The sound makes my heart slam against my rib cage. She plants a wet kiss on my cheek, and I set her down on her feet.

She runs over to her friends, and I saunter over to Cole. He is wearing dark jeans, a navy v-neck jumper, black shoes, and a dark grey flat cap. He cocks his eyebrow as he hands me a bottle of beer.

"You do realise that you've just made all of the women in this room cream their knickers? There's going to be a rush for the bathroom any second, they're all going to be checking their makeup, sorting out their hair, and doing all that girly shit."

He chuckles, and I smirk cheekily.

"I can't help the effect I have on women, can I, mate? It must be my devilish good looks and my dazzling charm."

Cole lets out a deep rumbling laugh.

"Yeah, that and the contents of your bank account," he says drily as I take a sip of my beer and roll my eyes.

"So cynical, dude. It has to be my dimples and the size of my cock too!"

Cole punches me in the arm playfully.

"I see that ego of yours hasn't deflated!"

I shrug, and a look of amusement crosses my face.

"I promised Amy I would be on my best behaviour today."

Cole almost chokes on his beer.

"Fuck off! You, on your best behaviour? Is that some kind of joke? I didn't think you knew how to behave, Newbolt!"

I shrug nonchalantly, and we both laugh as Amy joins us. She looks stunning as ever. Her dark, inky hair is pulled up into a bun, and she is wearing black skinny jeans, black heels, and a red off the shoulder top. She is tall and slender compared to Cole's large muscular frame. She and Cole complement each other as a couple.

"Hey, Sam."

She kisses me on the cheek and the fruity scent of her perfume envelopes me as I hug her.

"Hey honey, looking stunning as always."

She rolls her eyes.

"Your charm doesn't work on me, sugar, but thanks anyway! You don't look so bad yourself, handsome!"

She laughs.

"Thanks for bringing Addy to the party. She's been so excited, and she hasn't stopped going on about you all week."

I smile, and that is the moment I look around the large, light area that is the living room and find that all eyes are on me. *Lock up your daughters, it's time to channel Bolt, my alter-ego and inner showman.* I plaster on my famous dimpled smile, and I see at least ten women, some clearly with partners, visibly swoon on the spot. It does wonders for my ego, but it can be incredibly annoying and boring. Especially when I just want to be a normal guy, celebrating my god daughter's birthday. I feel almost out of my depth without the boys with me.

I scan the room, and my eyes settle on a gorgeous, flaming redhead, with mid-length wavy hair, light green eyes, pale complexion, a rocking bod, and huge tits. She is wearing a black pencil skirt, a pale green camisole that compliments her eyes, and a pair of sky-high heels that make her porcelain legs look like they go on forever. I notice her because she is the only woman in the room, apart from Amy, that doesn't seem to be checking me out. She catches my gaze for a split second then looks away, and Cole nudges me.

"The woman you're quite blatantly eye fucking; her name is Fiona Sheehan. She's a therapist, and she's Addison's friend India's mum, just in case you were wondering. I know it's a miracle if you know, or even remember, their names these days."

He takes a sip of his beer.

"Give me some fucking credit, man, I'll be making her scream my name by the end of the day," I say shamelessly, and Cole almost chokes on his beer again.

"Not at my daughters' party, you fucking animal!"

We both laugh.

"Please wait until the party is over at least, mate. Amy will have your balls on a platter if you do that at our daughters' party. But I can tell you now, she's not going to fall for your moves. She's extremely hard to please...or so I've heard."

I cock my eyebrow, and he shrugs nonchalantly.

"What? Us dad's talk!"

I chuckle, and Cole slaps me on the back.

"Go for it, Casanova, but I bet you fifty quid she turns you down!"

I finish my beer and shake his hand.

"Make it a ton, and you've got yourself a deal, Benedict."

He nods, and I grab another bottle as I saunter coolly over to her. She looks up at me.

"Can I help you with something?" she says in a soft Southern Irish lilt.

Instant boner, easiest hundred quid I've ever made.

"I don't believe we've met, I would definitely remember someone as beautiful as you," I rasp, and she laughs melodically.

"Wow, aren't you quite the charmer?"

I smile, bringing my famous dimples out, and she looks at me like I'm from another planet.

"So, I've been told, sweetheart."

She raises her eyebrows.

"Cocky as well? Must be my lucky day."

I smirk. Christ, it's never usually this hard to chat women up.

"So, am I going to get your name before we fuck?" I say boldly, and she widens her eyes.

"How many sexual harassment charges have you had against you since you've been famous? Just out of curiosity."

Strange question, but I'll go with it.

"None, sweetheart."

She looks defiantly up at me.

"Well, I'm going to be your first, if you don't get the fuck away from me," she hisses and storms off, leaving me in a stunned silence.

Cole joins me laughing loudly.

"Take it that it didn't go as planned, Romeo!"

I take a sip of my beer and process what just happened. *A woman actually turning me down, I never thought I would see the day.* My thoughts are interrupted by Cole's deep baritone voice, which is laced with amusement.

"You must be losing your touch; Sam and you owe me a ton!"

I shrug casually and take out my wallet. I hand him one hundred pounds, and he pockets it.

"You win some, you lose some, dude. There's plenty more willing participants."

I wink, and he smirks as I put my wallet back in the inside pocket of my jacket.

"Yeah, you keep telling yourself that, mate!"

He slaps me on the back and Addison comes bounding over to me.

"Uncle Sammy!"

She tugs on my jacket.

"That's my name, sweetie, don't wear it out," I joke, and she giggles.

"You're funny, Uncle Sammy; will you come and dance with me, pleeeeeeeeeease?"

Cole snorts, and he slaps me on the back.

"Good luck with that one, mate."

I chug on my beer and put the empty bottle down. *Fuck me, how can I say no to someone as sweet as Addison? She uses those deep brown puppy dog eyes as a weapon against me, I'm sure of it.*

"Uncle Sammy, please?"

Her bottom lip starts to quiver, and I scoop her up in my arms.

"Come on then, baby girl, show me those moves."

She giggles and plants a wet sloppy kiss on my cheek.

"Yaaaayy! India! India!"

She calls out to her friend, who is a tiny blonde-haired girl with wide green eyes. She smiles a toothy grin, and I start to question my decision in agreeing to come here in the first place. That is until Fiona's pale green eyes lock onto mine. She immediately looks away, and I try to hide my smirk.

I set Addison down on her feet, and the pumping beat of Beyoncé's 'Single Ladies' comes through the speakers. Cole is doubled over laughing, and that's when I see the Jax, Ruby, Brody and Lucas arrive. Just in time for the ultimate humiliation, fucking great.

"You're just in time for Sam's big moment, boys!" Cole booms and Jax starts wolf whistling.

Addison is standing in front of me tapping her foot impatiently with her hands on her hips.

"Uncle Sammy!" She reprimands, and I take off my jacket.

Fuck me, I wish I'd had more alcohol.

"Yeah, Uncle Sammy, do as you're told," Ruby mocks.

Ok, here goes nothing. This is going to be the longest five minutes of my life. I can't dance for shit; I actually look like I'm having a seizure, which is why I stick to singing. I twist my large frame awkwardly around, and Addison dances animatedly around me. I clap my hands and pop my head to the left, then back to the right. I can hear the boys cheering and laughing loudly. Addison moves and shakes her bum to the music in the style of Beyoncé. *Fuck me, this kid watches way too much MTV!* She circles me and points her finger at me. Everyone in the room is watching, and even though I've been in the media spotlight for over ten years, I feel more exposed here than I do when a camera is thrust in my face. *Come on Newbolt, time to bring the showman out to play. Let Bolt take the reins.*

I spin around and move my feet from side to side, popping my head and shaking my hips. Ruby is whooping, and there is a circle of around fifteen kids gathered around me. A few parents are filming me with their camera phones. *Great, I'm going to be a YouTube sensation, for all the wrong fucking reasons.* I circle my shoulders and bust out my best moves, whilst trying not to look like I'm being electrocuted. Addison is copying me and giggling girlishly. We continue this way until the song finishes. As the song ends, the whole room erupts in a rapturous round of applause. I grin widely and take a dramatic bow. *May as well milk it for all it's worth!* I sweep my hand out to the side and Addison takes a bow too. She holds up her arms, and I scoop her up in my arms. She plants a sloppy kiss on my cheek, and I walk over to Cole.

"Well done, baby girl, you got the moves. I can't say the same for Uncle Sammy though!"

He kisses his daughter on the forehead and pats me on the shoulder.

"Please stick to the day job, man!"

He laughs, and I cock my pierced eyebrow.

"Very funny, you fucker."

Addison widens her eyes, and her mouth forms a perfect 'O' shape.

"Uncle Sammy said a bad word, daddy."

Cole narrows his eyes at me.

"Language in front of my daughter, man," Cole reprimands me, and I set Addison down on her feet.

"I'm sorry for using bad words, baby girl."

She stands with her hands on her hips and looks up at me.

"How can I make it up to you, tiger?"

A mischievous look crosses her sweet face, and I start to regret my decision at saying those words.

"Can I have a puppy, Uncle Sammy? Pleeeeeeeeease."

Fuck my life. Cole chuckles throatily.

"You're on your own on that one, man."

I crouch down to Addison's level, and we are interrupted by an average height blonde with stunning, deep, azure, blue eyes. She is wearing a floral printed maxi dress, and her hair is tumbling down her shoulders. She clears her throat.

"I'm so sorry to interrupt," she says timidly as I stand up and my tall frame eclipses her slight one.

"How can I help, sweetheart?" I rasp, and she visibly swoons on the spot.

"Erm...me and my friend Tanya over there."

She points to a short, woman with long black hair and dark chocolate skin. The woman waves in my direction. I wave back, and she smiles widely.

"We were debating on whether your muscles are as big as they look from over there."

I try to hide my smirk, and she giggles flirtily as I hear Ruby mutter something along the lines of 'Oh please!'

"Why don't you see for yourself, sweetheart?"

I flex my muscle, and she wraps her tiny hand around my bicep. She squeezes, and I see the flush creeping up her slender neck. My mind starts to wander to what it would be like if she was beneath me and I had my tattooed hands around her pale neck, slightly squeezing, while I'm balls deep...*Whoa! Fuck me, I seriously need to get laid!* Her throat bobs as she swallows harshly before she allows herself to speak. Her eyes are glazed with obvious arousal.

"Wow! Your muscles are huge...and so solid."

Her cheeks start to turn a dark shade of pink, and as I take a step closer to her, Addison tugs on my t-shirt.

"Uncle Sammy, does that lady want to get in your pants?" Addison blurts out, and I try to stifle my laughter as the woman who was hanging onto my every word rushes off, burning with embarrassment.

Cole swings her up in his arms and places her on his shoulders.

"Come on, my little troublemaker, let's go and find mummy so we can cut your cake, yeah?"

She nods and giggles at me, blowing a kiss as Cole takes her off out into the garden. I pretend to catch her kiss and Brody joins me. He hands me a beer, and I accept it. I catch Fiona's gaze from across the room, and she actually rolls her eyes at me. Brody follows my eyes and chuckles softly as he slaps me on the back.

"Back the fuck away from the MILF, dude!"

I smile and take a long pull on my bottle of beer.

"To obtain the unobtainable, I like your style, but from what Cole said, she sounds like a fucking crazy bitch. If you ask me, move onto the next, dude. Although, asking who you haven't been with is like sticking a pin in the fucking phone book!"

I roll my eyes and punch Brody's arm playfully at his blatant dig at my womanising. I admit that ever since the night at the strip club, I have been putting it about a lot more than I have in a long time, but I'm just blowing off steam. Well, that's what I've been telling myself anyway.

"Ok, I admit I was a whore...once upon a time."

Brody cocks his eyebrow and snorts.

"Was? Are you sure about that? You've been doing a fucking good enough job lately of convincing yourself otherwise, mate?"

I take a long pull of my beer and shrug.

"I learnt from the best, dude!"

I wink at Brody and make my way over to Fiona, who is sitting out in the garden. *Round two.*

"What's a beautiful girl like you doing out here alone?"

She rolls her eyes.

"Don't you ever give up?"

I take a seat next to her.

"What can I say, I'm a glutton for punishment and a total sucker for a pretty face, sweetheart?" I rasp, and she narrows her pale green eyes at me.

"Do your bullshit lines work with all the women you sleep with?"

I bite my lip piercing seductively and smirk cockily.

"Let's get one thing straight, I don't sleep with women, sweetheart; I fuck like a rock star. And in answer to your question, generally my bullshit lines work just fine. Do you want to want to test that theory, babe?" I rasp, and she looks defiantly up at me.

She's about to speak again when we are interrupted by Addison shrieking my name.

"Uncle Sammy! Uncle Sammy! Come and cut my cake!"

I look at Fiona and salute.

"Duty calls, beautiful."

I wink and make my way over to Addison. Brody, Jax and Lucas are standing around the table where Addison's bright pink fairy castle cake is sitting loud and proud. Amy asked me and the boys if we would mind playing an acoustic happy birthday for Addison, and we all agreed whole-heartedly. Amy hands Jax his acoustic guitar, and he starts to effortlessly pluck the strings. Cole picks Addison up, and we all gather around. I clear my throat and start to sing happy birthday, with the boys and everyone else joining in. As I sing, I lose myself in the music, even though it's just a simple happy birthday song. I notice Fiona's curiosity start to pique; she is definitely beginning to pay more attention to me. I flash her my dimpled smile as we watch Addison blow out her five candles.

"Make a wish, baby girl!" Cole says.

Addison blows out her candles and giggles girlishly. It is the most adorable sound I have ever heard and my heart slams against my rib cage as my mind wanders to a fleeting image of a radiant, smiling Peyton holding our baby. I suddenly stop singing. I swallow hard and stand stock-still. All eyes of the people gathered around are on me. I feel claustrophobic all of a sudden, and my heart starts pounding in my chest. *Fuck me; I need to get out of here.*

"Uncle Sammy? Uncle Sammy?"

Addison's tiny voice cuts through my swimming thoughts. Jax continues playing his guitar, but he is regarding me intently with a narrow, cautious stare. I am shaken from my thoughts by Addison tugging on my t-shirt.

"Just give me a minute baby girl, I...I'll be right back, I promise."

I rush out of the room and up to the bathroom. *Fuck, I need to get it together.* Leaving the door slightly ajar, I pull down the toilet seat and sit down. I put my head between my legs. My heart is pounding, and my blood is roaring in my ears.

"Come on, not here. Breathe, Newbolt," I mutter to myself, and the door squeaks open as a soft female voice interrupts me.

"Talking to yourself is the first sign of madness, you know?"

I recognise the voice as Fiona.

"Is that sexual harassment suit still on the table, Red?" I say sarcastically, and she chuckles softly.

"Only if you promise not to dance, because frankly, that was actually quite disturbing!" she says drily, and I laugh.

I get to my feet, and she looks up at me.

"And just for the record my names Fiona, not Red," she says in her soft Irish lilt.

She offers me her hand, and I shake it, holding her hand in mine a little longer than necessary.

"I'm Sam. You don't look like the type of woman who picks up womanising rock stars at kids' birthday parties, Fiona."

She cocks her eyebrow.

"There's that chip on your shoulder again, therein lies the problem. I don't give a shit that you're a rock star; I don't go in for all that. You might have women falling over themselves to have sex with you, but that's not me, and it never will be. I had your card marked as soon as I clapped eyes on you, but in there, when you were singing happy birthday, I saw something change in you, Sam. You showed your vulnerable side."

I nod.

"Fair observation, sweetheart. But a word of advice, don't try to figure me out. I'm not a puzzle you can solve, and I'm definitely not a broken toy that needs fixing."

I take a long pull of my beer, and she narrows her eyes, regarding me intently.

"I've met men like you before."

I smirk.

"I very much doubt that babe."

She frowns.

"Why do you do that? Deflect the subject and make a joke of everything?"

I tuck one hand in my pocket.

"Do you really want an answer to that?" I say coolly.

She turns around, closes the door and flips the lock.

"Not really. I thought you were an arrogant, cocky prick when I first laid eyes on you, but I know now that I made an assumption and judged you before I gave you a chance. What I originally thought was definitely not an accurate observation."

She stalks towards me and pushes me as forcefully as her small frame can manage against the wall, pressing her pert breasts against my chest.

"I want you," she purrs, and I raise my eyebrows.

"I don't do refunds, sweetheart," I say gruffly.

She cups my growing erection in her hand and begins to stroke me through my jeans. I growl.

"I don't want a refund; I just want you to fuck me," she says with a hint of pleading in her voice.

I smile, bringing out my infamous dimples and I reach under her skirt, casually sliding her damp knickers to the side to give me access to her dripping wet pussy. I push my finger inside her and start to slowly finger fuck her. She moans softly.

"Just so we're clear, this is going to be hard sex, no romance, no hearts or flowers, just sex," I rasp, and she grips my erection harder.

"Just shut up and fuck me, rock star," she says breathlessly as she reaches forward to unzip my jeans. I lean forward to free my hard cock from the confines of my boxers and pull my fingers out of her.

"Do you have a condom?"

I pull a condom out of my wallet and tear the foil packet open with my teeth. I wink cheekily, as I roll the rubber onto my rock-hard length. I lift her up effortlessly, as she wraps her legs around me and impale her onto my waiting stiffness. She gasps aloud, and I growl my appreciation.

"God, you're so fucking tight."

She buries her head against my neck to stifle her moans of pleasure as I lift her up and bring her down on my cock again. I find my rhythm and begin to quicken my pace.

"Oh God!" she cries out, and I silence her by pressing my lips against hers.

I suck her bottom lip, and she digs her nails into my biceps as the intense pleasure rolls through us both. I increase my expert thrusts and spin us both around, so she is pressed against the wall. I shove her up the wall with each drive, until I find a delicious rhythm that allows me to plunge deeper inside her. She moans softly and bites her lip, as if she is holding back.

"Don't hold back on me, sweetheart, let it go," I say huskily as I continue my vigorous pace.

I reach into her bra and roll her nipple between my thumb and forefinger.

"Oh fuck, your cock feels so good," she says desperately.

"How long has it been since you've had a cock in you, sweetheart?" I say gruffly as I roughly shove forward, and she gasps.

"Oh, oh God, too fucking long. Oh fuck, Sam, harder. Fuck me harder, don't you dare stop."

I pump tirelessly in and out of her slick, aching channel, and I feel her inner walls grip my cock.

"You're close. I can feel you, sweetheart, the way you're gripping my cock," I say throatily, and she wraps her arms around my neck.

"I want you screaming my fucking name as you come, sweetheart."

She nods, as she tugs the hair at the nape of my neck.

"I'm close, so close. Christ, Sam, I'm going to come."

I swivel my hips as I push into her forcefully and that's all it takes for her to detonate around me as her orgasm sweeps over her. She throws her head back and lets out a strangled cry of pure ecstasy.

"AHH! SAM! OH, OH, OH, SAM! OH.MY.GOD! SAM!"

Moments later, I find my release with a garbled, low growl of satisfaction from deep within my chest. She leans her head back against the wall while she finds her breath as we both come down from our orgasms. I pull out of her and set her down on wobbly legs. I don't feel the usual blissed-out gratification after blowing my load. I feel nothing. I pull off the condom, knot it, wrap it in tissue and flush it down the toilet. I tuck myself back into my boxers, zip up my jeans, and straighten my clothes in a relatively awkward silence. Fiona is combing her hair with her fingers in the mirror, and she catches my lifeless gaze.

"So, aren't you going to say anything?" she says spikily, and I tuck my hands into the pockets of my jeans.

"What can I say, sweetheart? We fucked, and if I'm totally honest, the earth didn't really move for me." I say coldly, and she widens her eyes.

"Wow! You really are a fucking selfish bastard."

I shrug nonchalantly, and she lashes her hand across my face. I smirk cockily and raise my eyebrows. *What is it with fucking women and slapping?*

"There were at least ten women in that room downstairs who would have killed for me to bury my cock inside them and fuck them so hard that they would still feel me the next day. But in my sick, twisted fucking mind, I decided to go for the one who wasn't in the least bit interested in me."

I move closer to her, like a predator stalking its prey, and I drop my voice.

"You see I love a challenge, Red. It's what drives me, it's what makes me tick, and it's what makes my cock hard," I say gruffly and adjust my cock in my jeans. "Thanks for the fuck, babe, you were exquisite."

I wink cockily, spin round and leave, as I hear the distinct sound of a shoe hitting the door.

35

Peyton

I steps closer to him, and I reach out to smooth the frown line between his eyebrows. Just by touching him, I still have the ability to affect him, like I did while we were together. He takes my hand in his and strokes my knuckles softly. He places a kiss on the back of my hand, and I smile shyly. That simple gesture, has my heartbeat quickening and for the first time in over a year, I feel some semblance of happiness. I smile a genuine smile to myself, as he continues to make the coffee and hands me a cup.

"Milk, two sugars, right?"

I nod and smiles shyly, as I take the cup from him, he brushes my fingers as I takes it from him. *Some things never change.* He smirks, as he gestures for me to step into the living room, ahead of him. I catch him checking me out over my shoulder.

"Are you checking me out, Newbolt?"

He chuckles softly, as I look over my shoulder at him.

"That would be telling, wouldn't it, angel?"

He winks, and I visibly shudder. He subtly presses his hard body into my back. We both sit down on the sofa, and he sits close to me, with his arm spread out across the back of the sofa. We sit in silence for a few minutes.

"I wanted to apologise for Jax at the hospital earlier, you didn't deserve that, and he was way out of line."

I shake my head.

"He was right, he was angry, and I don't blame him, Sam."

He places his hand on mine and regards me intently.

"Are you ever going to tell me what happened, angel?"

That is the moment I take a deep breath and begin to speak.

Here goes nothing. I don't particularly want to tell Sam what I endured at the hands of J.D, but part of me knows I have to tell him, for the sake of our relationship, or lack thereof, to move forward. No more secrets, no lies, just pure honesty, from here on out.

"You have to understand, it's hard for me to relive what I went through, Sam. The truth is, there were a few moments where I thought I wasn't going to survive. I thought so many times of just giving up, letting him do what the fuck he wanted to me, to just stop fighting and accept the fact that he was going to kill me... kill both of us. I was so resigned to the fact, that I didn't even have a plan of what I was going to do when I eventually escaped, if I escaped at all. After he stabbed me, I was surprised I had actually survived and grateful he was such an incompetent fucking idiot that he couldn't even manage to kill me properly. As I clawed my way out of that hole, he buried me in, I made a split-second decision to protect my baby, and I didn't hesitate. I couldn't give a shit that I'd been stabbed, and I was bleeding. All I wanted was for our baby to be safe. I was fucking *terrified*. He scared me, Sam. Everything about him: his demeanour, his eyes, his voice, the not knowing what he was going to do next."

I squeeze my eyes shut at the memories threatening to surface and overwhelm me from every angle. He seems to realise and entwines his fingers with mine. His thumb is softly stroking reassuringly across my knuckles.

"He did unspeakable things to me, Sam. He cut me, he stabbed me, he beat me senseless, and he played clever mind games. I fucking *hate* him so much for what he did to me, to you, to us; I wish he had never been born."

Even though my voice is filled with fire and intense hatred, it still trembles. Sam moves closer until we are inches apart on his sofa. I can feel the warmth radiating from his large frame, and I breathe in the scent of him. The smell of Joop, mint, and pure Sam Newbolt.

"I know I should have picked up the phone and called you, to tell you I was alive, but I was so fucking hurt. My world had literally crashed down around me. He told me you asked him to do those sick, depraved things and you knew he had taken me. I was in that fucking room for hours, Sam, listening to him spill those evil, poisonous, vile things."

A tear slips down my cheek, and Sam wipes it away with the pad of his thumb. I shiver as his finger makes contact with my skin, and he chuckles softly. I look at him questioningly, and he shakes his head.

"You shiver every time I touch you, angel."

My lips quirk at the corners into a smile. I take his hand in mine and trace the calluses on his fingers. The contrast of the roughness of his fingers and the softness of mine. I continue my exploration of his hand, and he watches me closely; he doesn't take his eyes off me.

"Having fun, angel?"

I look up at him, and my eyes lock with his.

"Hmm."

He stops my finger tracing his.

"Ah, ah, ah angel, you don't get to zone out on me now. We agreed you would let me meet Freddie, and you agreed we could talk properly."

I drop my gaze, and he tips my chin up to face him.

"Talk to me, angel; make me understand. You're safe now. He's in prison, J.D can't hurt you anymore."

I shudder at the mention of that man's name and at the memories that haunt my every waking thought. A part of me still doesn't believe that Sam didn't tell J.D to do those despicable things to me.

"Believe me, no one wants to fucking kill J.D more than I do, angel; I was so close to ending him when he kidnapped me," he says through clenched teeth.

"It was you that stopped me. He stabbed me twice and his words were, and I quote, 'I enjoyed killing Peyton and the little fucking cockroach that was inside of her, I did the world a fucking favour by ending both of their lives. I actually howled with laughter when I stabbed her in the chest, and then I stabbed in the stomach her over and over again just to make sure the little bastard was dead.' That completely fucking floored me. I was so angry; in fact, anger doesn't even fucking cover it."

As he quotes those words, I feel all the colour drain from my cheeks. *How cold and callous can one person be?* Sam is visibly trembling with anger, and his fists are clenched so tight; his knuckles are white.

"I completely lost it, and I fucking saw red. In a pure rush of adrenaline, I wrenched the arms off the chair he had tied me to. The pain didn't even register, until I saw blood dripping down my wrists. I was so desperate to break free, because I was hell-bent on revenge. I wanted to watch him fucking suffer, the way he made you suffer. I wanted to be the one to end his pathetic, miserable fucking life," he says with a clenched jaw.

He holds out his wrists, and both of his wrists are still heavily wrapped from the hospital. It is at that moment, where I don't doubt for a second that Sam is telling the truth, one million per cent. He really *was* completely oblivious to J.D's actions.

"I swung for him, and I just kept on hitting him, over and over and over again. He was pleading for me to stop, snivelling and fucking begging me. But I couldn't stop myself, it was fucking pathetic. I was so close to ending him, but I saw you, so clearly in my mind, telling me to stop and this strange wave of peace washed over me. That's when I stopped, called the police, and I walked away, leaving him lying in a pool of his own blood."

My mind is reeling at the information he is telling me. I am struck with a wave of such guilt and shame that I let out a strangled sob. Sam pinches my chin between his thumb and forefinger, forcing me to the look into his pained green eyes.

"Hey, look at me, I fucking swear to you, angel. I *never* asked him to kidnap you. We were so happy. I had just asked you to marry me, for fuck's sake. We were going to start our forever together. You said you would be five minutes, you had to get your bag, but you never came out of Lucas' house. I got a text from your phone telling me to go without you and that you would meet me there. I was so close to putting the show on hold, just so I could go back for you. I tried calling you, left you messages. I fucking *waited* for you, but you never came."

His jaw is tight, and I can tell this is as hard for him as it is for me.

"What would I have found if I had gone back for you, angel?"

I close my eyes, and I am instantly transported back to the day my life changed forever.

Peyton

Past

I'm admiring my engagement ring: a platinum band with a large princess cut diamond that is surrounded by small light purple diamonds. It looks exquisite, expensive yet simple, and understated. I can't help the ear-splitting grin that spreads across my face. I'm getting married to Sam Newbolt, my gorgeous, handsome rock star. We're finally going to get our happily ever after. Sam watches me from across the room and chuckles softly.

"God, that smile melts me every time, angel. You're so beautiful, soon-to-be Mrs Peyton Leigh Newbolt," he says huskily.

Sam stalks towards me, pulling me out to the balcony of our room in Lucas' house in North Las Vegas. The sun is just setting, and it is breathtaking. The orange and pink hues on the horizon make it look like something from a picture postcard. My back is to his warm, hard chest; Sam wraps his arms around my waist and settles his hands on my stomach.

"This is the best day of my life so far, angel. You agreeing to be my wife, you carrying our child. I'm so happy right now I could shout from the fucking rooftops. Today is the first day of the rest of our lives."

We both laugh, and he is right, I have never been happier. Our perfect moment is interrupted as someone clears their throat behind us.

"Just give us a sec."

Sam spins me around and presses his lips to mine in a kiss that claims me as his.

"Remember this moment always, angel."

This moment will be forever seared into my memory for as long as I live. This will be a fairy tale I will tell our baby and our grandchildren in years from now. He pulls away, and we walk back inside.

"The car's downstairs, Sam," J.D says in a clipped tone, and Sam nods curtly.

I suddenly realise I have forgotten my bag and my phone.

"I'll catch you up, baby; I need to grab my bag."

He smiles his dazzling dimpled smile.

"Hurry, angel, I need my good luck charm."

He winks and leaves the room. I grab my phone and my bag, and as I go to leave the room, J.D grabs my arm so roughly I know there is going to be a bruise. He leans in so close I can smell the stench of alcohol on his breath.

"This ain't Mills and Boon with guitars, darling. Girls like you don't get happy endings, pregnant or not." He sneers, and the cold tone of his voice makes me shudder. "Remember that sweetheart."

He winks and let's go of me. There is something off about him, and I can't quite put my finger on it; just his sheer presence unnerves me. I push that thought to the back of my head and go to head downstairs to join the rest of the boys. For the first time in my life, I am so happy, and this moment is the first day of the rest of my happy ever after with Sam. I am smiling so wide my jaw aches, and I feel our baby kick as I go to walk down the stairs.

"I know baby, mummy feels you, boo."

I giggle at the unfamiliar feeling of our baby kicking. It never fails to amaze me after the first time I felt it earlier on today in the car on the way back from the best day of my life: Sam proposing to me in the Aquarium at the Mandalay Bay. I am in such a world of my own that I don't feel the strong hand that clamps over my mouth. I rear my elbow back weakly in a reflex reaction, and I hear the 'hummpfh' from a male voice as my elbow connects with his gut. He laughs maniacally as I start to sag in his iron grip. He has a white handkerchief over my mouth, and I am helpless in his arms.

"That's it, don't fight me."

J.D's familiar, evil voice fills my ears, and I limply try to fight him.

"Relax for me. This will all be over in a few hours, and you'll be out of Sam's life, for good this time."

My limbs feel like lead, and my vision is blurry. *What the fuck is happening?*

"Sam," I slur.

"Sammy isn't coming to your rescue this time, bitch; do you fucking get that now?" He spits, and my limbs give out underneath me.

I feel him dragging me along the floor. That's when I succumb to the darkness, and everything went black.

Peyton

Present

I am jolted back to the present by the rasp of Sam's voice.

"Angel, where did you go?"

I shake myself from my previous thought, and his worried green gaze locks onto mine.

"You were remembering, weren't you?" he says gruffly, and I nod slowly as I try to rid myself of the memories that haunt my every thought.

"What would I have found if I had gone back for you, angel? I have to know if I could have saved you... if I could have stopped all this from happening."

The pained look in his eyes breaks my heart, and a lone tear tracks its way down my cheek.

"Sam, don't. There's no point torturing yourself on what if, babe. There's nothing you could have done."

He squeezes my hand.

"Let me be the judge of that, angel, please just fucking tell me," He pleads.

I turn my head away from him, desperately trying to forget the events that happened.

"Look at me, angel," he says in his commanding tone and my eyes meet his.

"He cornered me at the top of the stairs, grabbed me, drugged me and proceeded to tell me how you weren't coming to my rescue this time. He dragged me into one of Lucas' spare rooms and left me there. The next thing I remember is coming around, tied to a chair in a derelict warehouse."

I close my eyes at the memory, wishing I could forget those hours and erase them from my mind. I hear Sam growl and when I open my eyes to look at him; his eyes are full of fire and fierce rage.

"*Motherfucking cock sucker,*" he curses.

"He had his fucking hands on you, angel, and I could have fucking stopped him!"

I shake my head as he unexpectedly lunges forward and crashes his lips to mine in a bruising, pant-melting, heart-stopping, searing kiss. I feel his desperation as I moan softly into his mouth, his tongue seductively dancing with mine. I feel his hand snake down my ribs, as I urgently grab and claw at his shirt. I'm wanting and silently pleading with him, to take me right there on his sofa. Our breathing is ragged, and I can feel his heart pounding in his hard, warm chest.

He moves his hand from my ribs and cups my breast. I gasp as his thumb finds and strokes my pierced nipple into a hard-erect bud. I wrap my arms around his neck and gently tug the hair at the nape of his neck, earning me a deep primal growl from within his chest. I can feel the slick heat pooling between my legs and a fierce, deep ache within my womb. I need him to ease the ache; I want him to take me, carnally and animalistically. Like a lion claiming its mate, like a predator claiming its prey. I climb onto his lap and straddle him, my thighs trapping him between them. I run my fingers through his soft raven black hair and gently tug. I have missed every inch of this magnificent Adonis, who consumes my every waking thought and the man who still holds that vital missing puzzle piece from my heart.

He pushes my cardigan down my shoulder to expose my skin, and his teeth latch onto the flesh between my neck and shoulder. I moan loudly as he bites and nips at me, then soothes the bite with a swift lick of his expert tongue. I start to unbutton his shirt, and I lean in to lick his exposed and heavily tattooed pec. I continue to unbutton his shirt to reveal his hard chest and ripped abs. His body never fails to bring me to my knees, but his perfection is marred by the heavily dressed wound on his shoulder. He chuckles throatily as he catches me ogling his body.

"I need you, angel," he rasps as he pushes my cardigan off my other shoulder and lets it drop to the floor behind us.

He reaches into my vest top and lowers the cup of my bra to allow him access to my full breast. The feel of his warm, calloused fingers against my breast has me pushing myself further into his hand. I reach back and cup his steel erection straining in his loose jeans. He moans loudly as I pop the button on his jeans.

"*Jesus,* what the fuck are you doing to me, angel? You're unmanning me right here."

His voice is barely a whisper, and I love how I still have the power to completely unravel him. I reach into his boxers and grasp his erection in my hand. He takes a sharp intake of breath as he suddenly grabs my hips. In a swift movement, I find myself pinned beneath him. His large wide frame eclipses my tiny one.

"Hey."

He smiles his wicked smile that screams trouble with a capital *T*. His green eyes are sparkling with pure lust and complete sin.

"Hey yourself."

He chuckles softly and pulls off his shirt. He is so smooth and sculpted. The defined, corded lines of his muscles remind me that he is powerful, dominant and has an element of danger lurking beneath his hard, perfect exterior. I lean up, pulling my top off, until I am lying in my bra beneath him.

"God, look at you. You're so fucking perfect, angel," he says huskily, and I cock my eyebrow.

"Have you seen yourself in the mirror lately? You're pretty fucking perfect."

He laughs.

"Perfect, huh? I'll have to remember that one, angel. I've had a lot of time on my hands; in between reading those trashy erotic romance books, I managed to fit in a few work out sessions."

I laugh, as he flexes his muscles. *He really is absolute male fucking perfection.*

He reaches into his boxers to fist his growing hard-on.

"Now where were we, angel? I should put you over my knee for interrupting such an important moment," he coolly threatens, and I press my thighs together to create a delicious, friction, easing the ache between my legs.

"Every orgasm you have from here on out is mine, angel. Do I make myself clear?" he says with a hint of warning, and I try to suppress my smirk as a reply.

"Crystal clear," I say innocently, and he growls.

"You test my fucking patience at every turn, angel. I'm trying to control myself, but you're slowly shredding it, piece-by-piece," he says through a clenched jaw.

Boldly, I reach back to unfasten my bra and pull it off, so I am topless beneath him.

"Sam, I need you," I say huskily.

I am so overcome by lust; I pull him down until he crushes his weight against me and I wrap my legs around his waist. He pulls his boxers down, exposing his nine-inch member, which is now pierced, and I lick my lips at the sight.

"You got your cock pierced?"

He smirks and shrugs his shoulders.

"Story for another time, angel. Let's just say I lost another bet."

He winks mischievously, and I shimmy my jeans down my thighs. As he goes to shove forward to enter me, I hear Freddie's cry on the baby monitor.

I sit bolt upright and lean back on my elbows, suddenly questioning what the fuck I am doing. I look up at Sam and shake my head.

"I can't do this Sam. I'm sorry, I'm so sorry."

In silence, he lets me up from underneath him, and I grab my bra. I quickly start re-dressing, and Sam drops shirtless down onto the sofa, running his fingers through his already mussed hair. I pull on my top and rush quickly to the spare bedroom to Freddie. I push open the door, and Freddie's wide watery green eyes find mine, instantly quieting him.

"Hey baby boy, mummy's here."

I reach down into his cot and pick him up.

"Did you just want a cuddle? You just wanted a cuddle didn't you, my gorgeous boy?"

I coo and cuddle him closer to me.

"Mummy is very silly, yes, she is, she's very, very *fudging* silly. Shall we go back to Uncle Remy now? Shall we?"

He gurgles and clutches my top in his tiny fist. Unexpectedly, Sam appears in the doorway.

"Just for the record, you're not silly, angel; we both wanted that, no matter how much you fucking deny it."

Shit. The fucking baby monitor. He must have heard every word I said to Freddie.

"I'm sorry, it shouldn't have happened. I don't know what came over me."

He leans his large frame against the doorjamb. He is still shirtless; his jeans are hanging open and riding low on his narrow hips. I lick my lips at the sight of him, and he smirks at my hormone-fuelled reaction to him.

"Bullshit, angel. You forget how I know your body, and I also know when you're lying," he says huskily.

"Look, don't go, stay, at least for a little while longer."

He steps forward into the room and moves closer to me.

"Logan isn't going anywhere, please, just let me get to know my son."

He strokes Freddie's cheek and Freddie giggles.

"Hey, how's daddy's little rock star doing?"

I hand Freddie to Sam, and his eyes grow heavy, as he snuggles his chubby face into Sam's bare chest.

"Is someone sleepy, buddy?"

He perches on the edge of the bed, and I sit down on the blue and white striped chaise lounge that is in the corner of the room, observing the bond between father and son. A few minutes of awkward silence passes before his mesmerizing emerald eyes find mine and neither of us can look away. He breaks our stare as he looks down at Freddie, he is fast to sleep in Sam's arms.

"Must have the magic touch, angel."

He gets up slowly, goes over to Freddie's cot, and lays him gently back down. He moves over to me and crouches down in front of me.

"I was lost without you, angel, so fucking lost. I was devastated. All I felt was pure fucking rage at the person who did this to you, to *us*. That fucking person was right under my god damn nose the entire time, and I didn't even know! How could I not have fucking known!" he grits out and squeezes his eyes shut, as if to rid himself of a terrible memory.

He takes my hand in his.

"We have a second chance, angel; please don't write that off, don't run from me again. You made me a promise once, that you wouldn't run."

His voice sounds so tortured, it crushes me to hear him so full of anguish and regret.

"We were...happy, blissfully so. It was...all consuming. I loved you so much. I felt like I couldn't fucking breathe without you, Sam. I've never been that dependent on a man *ever*, not until you."

I let out a shaky breath as I remember what we once had, and my eyes lock with his. There is that familiar electricity between us, it never went away.

"There were times where I...I would think how lucky I was to have such an amazing man in my life. I would get the butterflies in my stomach every time I was within touching distance of you, and I counted down the hours until I could see you again. I was...fucking *addicted* to you...you were like a drug I couldn't get enough of. I was just waiting for the other shoe to drop. Do you know what that felt like? What we had...it was a once in a lifetime thing, and I'm not sure we can ever get back to that, Sam."

I swipe the tears angrily from my eyes.

"You fucking intoxicate me, angel. From the first moment I met you. I can't breathe without you either. I'm a mess, I can't sleep, and I can barely drag myself out of bed in the morning. This past year has been my own personal fucking hell. I've just been going through the motions, pretending to live and I let my alter ego take the reins on my sorry life. My life sucks without you, angel."

I bite my lip to stifle the laugh bubbling up in my chest. He cocks his pierced eyebrow and flashes that adorable, dimpled smirk I have missed so much.

"Yeah, so I'm quoting Kelly Clarkson. I'm officially a fucking pussy."

He smirks wickedly, gets to his feet and offers me his large, tattooed hand.

"Dance with me, angel. Let me prove to you that what happened back there wasn't a mistake."

He pulls me up, and soft strains of music start to play in the background. He leads me out of the room, closing the door gently behind us, until we are back in the living room. I recognise the song as 'Slow Dancing in a Burning Room' by John Mayer. The slow sensual beat of the song begins, and he pulls me close to him, until I am pinned to his hard chest. He starts to move until we are slowly and silently swaying on the spot, with my hand in his and his other hand on my hip. My heartbeat starts to quicken, and the look in his eyes is smouldering. He leans down and kisses me passionately on the lips. The feel of his soft lips on mine coaxes my mouth open, and his tongue strokes mine. His kiss is so tender and so gentle that it makes me want to weep. He pulls me tighter to him, and I deepen the kiss, not wanting it to end. John croons in the background as Sam pulls away from our kiss. His breathing is ragged, and his green eyes are blazing.

"Stay with me, angel," he says gruffly. "Just give me tonight; I can have Cole take you both back to the hotel first thing in the morning."

I snuggle closer to his hard chest, and he squeezes me tighter.

"You don't have to answer now, please just think about it. Stay and let me show you how much I need you. Let me love you, angel."

I sigh deeply, feeling so relaxed and content in his arms that I don't realise what I have said until I feel Sam tense in my arms.

"I never realised how much I missed this. I spoke to my mum, and I told her I made a huge mistake. I was so wrong; I never should have stayed away, Sam."

He audibly gasps. *Fuck.*

"What did you just say?" he grits out. "Did your family know you were alive?"

He pulls away from me, as if I have burned him, and I suddenly feel as if there is a whole ocean between us once again.

"TELL ME THE FUCKING TRUTH, PEYTON, OR SO HELP ME FUCKING GOD!"

He bawls, and I flinch at his sharp tone.

"TELL ME!" he roars.

I nod slowly, trying to hold back the tears.

"I...I was hurt Sam, so fucking hurt. You crushed me, and you broke my heart. I needed my family to know I was alive; I couldn't do it to them."

Shit. His green eyes are fierce and so full of fire.

"You couldn't do it to them, but you could do it to me! I tried to commit fucking suicide because I couldn't go on without you! How do you think I felt? I woke up screaming, night after night. I drank just so I could feel numb. I was fucking broken, Peyton! *You* broke me! My best friend found me in a pool of my own fucking blood because I was too God damn weak to see a life without you in it!"

He runs his hands frantically through his hair and starts to pace the room.

"FUCK!" he curses, as he picks up his glass and launches it at the wall.

The glass shatters everywhere, spraying the room in glistening shards. A tear slips down my cheek as I hear the sound of Sam's footsteps across the wooden floor of his penthouse apartment.

"As far as I was concerned, you had committed the ultimate betrayal by asking some fucking twisted psychopath to kidnap and torture me. He fucking stabbed me; I was terrified, and I thought I was going to die! Don't you get that? He tortured me physically and mentally. I hated you with every bone in my body for making me fall so deeply in love with you and then ripping my heart out like I fucking meant nothing, Sam!" I screech.

He scrubs his hands across his lightly stubbled jaw and walks over to the floor to ceiling windows that look out on the New York City skyline by night.

"Your family knew you were alive; don't you think I fucking deserved to be clued into that fact?"

His voice is barely a whisper, as I shake my head.

"You really don't fucking get it, do you, Sam? I *despised* you for crushing my very being. I wanted you to fucking suffer for what you did. I wanted you and J.D to rot in the fucking ground," I spit harshly, and Sam rears back at my cold, unforgiving tone.

"How could you ever think that angel? I fucking *worshipped* you; we were going to get married, and you were pregnant with *my* baby! Wasn't that a clear indication of how I felt about you? I would have killed for you! I would have willingly done prison time, just to fucking protect you!" he says with such determined conviction in his voice and runs his hand through his raven strands.

He catches my gaze in the reflection of the glass.

"This is all such a fucking mess, and I'm not sure how we can fix it, angel; how we can fix us. Losing you fucking *destroyed* me, Peyton. It wasn't just you that died that day; you took a part of me with you. Nothing else mattered to me anymore. My life was pointless. The fame, the money, the band, the music... *none* of it fucking mattered. Don't you get that? I almost gave up my career because of you."

He turns around slowly, as he says those words and our eyes lock.

"I'm sorry. I'm sorry. I'm so sorry, Sam," I whisper, and he shakes his head.

"The pain of losing you cut so deep, I thought I would never get over you, angel. I tortured myself every single fucking day because I blamed myself. I thought I was responsible for failing the only woman I've ever really loved! The day we met, I told you I would ruin you, but you were the one who ended up fucking ruining me, Peyton! You ruined me for all other women!"

His husky voice sounds so pained, it makes my heat slam against my rib cage.

"Your mum and Dexter came to see me after I tried to kill myself. *Jesus*, your mum was *so* fucking pissed at me, shouting and screaming at me, cursing like a fucking sailor on shore leave. Tell me one thing, Peyton, I have to know. Did they already know then? Was it all just one big act?"

I look up at him and shake my head.

"No, no not at all. Don't *ever* think that for a second. I called them just after I gave birth to Freddie; I was so fucking scared and so lonely, Sam. I had just given birth, and I needed my mum and dad. I needed hope, and I needed some semblance of my old life back again. I know I was taking a big risk, but I needed something to cling on to. I haven't been Peyton Harper this past year. Remy knew people who could make her disappear for good, and I've been living as Louise Stonebridge. I've been residing in Santa Monica, California, under a new identity and working as a barista at Cool Beans Coffee Shop. *A fucking coffee shop.* For the first time in twenty-eight fucking years, Sam, I don't know who I am anymore!"

I run my hands through my hair, and I squeeze my eyes shut, trying to push back the floods of tears that are threatening to spill from my eyes.

36

Peyton

Past

I have been in Santa Monica for over two months now. After recovering from the initial trauma of being tied up and tortured by J.D, I have realised there is only so much Netflix a girl can handle before I start to go stir crazy. There are only so many TV shows a girl can watch. Endless episodes of Vampire Diaries, Sons of Anarchy, Strike Back, The Blacklist, White Collar and Dexter have caused the cabin fever to set in. The boredom is making me feel like I want to climb the walls. I am opening and closing the cupboards like a mad woman, desperate for something to do. I'm searching for something to occupy my otherwise active mind when I hear Remy come in from his morning run.

"Right, that's it, beaut, I've had it with watching you climb the walls. I'm going to grab a shower then I'm taking you out for breakfast, no bloody arguments. You've been cooped up for way too long, and it's about time you started to make some friends other than me. You're starting to turn into a hermit!"

I salute him sarcastically, and he cocks his eyebrow.

"Fucking women," he mutters as he strides off into the bathroom, leaving me curious as to where he is taking me.

I am brushing my newly dyed, short red hair in the mirror as Remy hops out of the bathroom with a towel wrapped loosely around his hips. The towel hanging so low I can see the 'V' cut below his abs. Remy used to be the awkward, gangly, nerdy boy next door all those years ago. He had a side parting, wore glasses and had absolutely no definition to his straight up, straight down body. As I take him in, I am reminded of the significant difference of how he was then, to how he is now as he is standing gloriously in front of me. His body is all muscle and definition. Instead of the traditional six-pack, I swear he has an eight-pack. His olive skin is sun-kissed, and his arms are corded with pure, thick sinew.

"When you've quite finished. I actually feel violated, do I look like a piece of meat to you?" he says with more than a hint of amusement in his voice, and I feel my face flush with embarrassment at being caught ogling him.

"Relax, I'm just fucking with you. Ogle away, it's good for my ego!"

We both laugh as he kisses his muscles on his arms. He drops down on the bed and begins to secure his prosthetic onto his stump.

"It's good to finally hear you laugh, beaut. When I lost my leg, I was so low I thought I would never laugh again. I thought all people were going to see was some injured soldier. I saw the pity in their eyes, and I was resigned to the fact that life wasn't ever going to go back to the way it used to be. I was fucking terrified that people were going to treat me differently. Part of me didn't want to care, but deep down, I knew I did. I met this guy while I was in hospital in the U.K, his name was Dave. We nicknamed him Disco Dave because he lost both legs, an arm and his left eye in Afghanistan. What I admired the most about Dave, was he never lost his sense of humour. He was always laughing, always smiling, always cracking jokes, and he would have the doctors and nurses in stitches. One day, I was feeling particularly sorry for myself. I was so frustrated, and I was in a sort of 'I-hate-the-world-and-everyone-in-it' kind of mood. Dave came into my room, and he poked me in the ribs. And do you know what he said? He said, 'man up and quit bitchin', soldier boy', all the nurses and the doctors, who were in the room at the time, were bracing themselves for World War three to break out right there in the hospital. That was the moment I started laughing, and I was full out belly laughing. It felt so good to feel something, and I'll be forever grateful to Dave for that. What I'm trying to say is, life might not be the same ever again, but us human beings, we're adaptable creatures. We learn to make the best of a bad situation, beaut, so that's why I'm taking you for coffee and to meet Dax. He's a good buddy of mine, and he owns a coffee shop just a few blocks away."

I cock my eyebrow at him, not sure where this is going.

"Hear me out. I know it's not ideal, but Dax owes me a favour, so this is me cashing it in. I'm going to ask him to give you a job."

My eyes widen. *Me, working in a coffee shop?* I can't imagine doing anything other than tattooing, and that breaks my heart.

"I know you're a tattoo artist, but it's not practical, beaut. We can't take the risk. You need to fly under the radar. What if someone recognises your work? What if someone posts pictures online? Your cover as Louise Stonebridge will be blown, and that's a whole new can of worms I don't want to open up."

He limps into his bedroom to dry off, leaving me in the living room to contemplate what he has just told me. *Could I really pull off working in a coffee shop? Am I even capable of doing something other than tattooing?* For the first time in forever, I'm all sorts of confused. I am shaken from my thoughts, by the sound of Remy's soft chuckle.

"Don't shoot it down, just stop over thinking, beaut. I know it's a big step but have faith; I have absolute faith in you. It's going to be fine. Dax is a good guy; he's one of the best. Please do this, if not for me, then for you and your son. Being a lady of leisure doesn't suit you."

Deep down, I know that everything Remy has said is true. I just have to trust my instinct and hope he's right. By the end of that day, I had been hired by Dax, and I was well on the way to completing my fresh start.

37

Peyton
Present

Sam is standing, quietly cursing to himself after the revelation that my family knew I was alive. I'm torn apart at having hurt him, yet again.

"I can't fucking do this, Sam. I have to go."

I take a deep breath and open my eyes. Sam avoids my gaze and nods curtly.

"Cole will take you back to your hotel," he says flatly, and I make my way to the spare room to get Freddie.

Remy was right, I should never have agreed so easily to this meeting. I find myself all too eagerly grabbing Freddie, strapping him in his carrycot, and gathering the rest of my things ready to leave.

Ten minutes pass, and as I make my way back into the living space, I hear the sound of raised voices. One is distinctly female, and my heart slams against my rib cage at the sight in front of me: Lyla, in all her willowy, leggy blonde glory. She is wearing a red trench coat, open, revealing her lacy black lingerie, complete with thigh high stockings, suspenders and six-inch spiked black heels. She smirks as she catches me taking her in.

"Ah, I see Lazarus is back from the dead," she says, with venom in her voice and I try to maintain my poker face, as if her hurtful comment didn't affect me.

"Sammy, baby, you didn't tell me we would be having company," she croons, and for the first time since I re-entered the room, I notice him.

Sam is wearing a black baseball vest, which clings to his muscles and showcases his *'My Angel'* tattoo across his chest. He is also wearing a pair of black silk pyjama bottoms, which hang low on his hips. He must have changed while I was getting mine and Freddie's stuff together. His hair is perfectly mussed, and he is standing barefoot, drinking a fresh glass of amber liquid. He runs his hand haphazardly through his hair and shakes his head.

"Don't go. Look, I'm sorry I overreacted. This conversation is far from finished, Peyton," Sam says gruffly, as he looks between Lyla and me.

I can't help but compare myself to the blonde goddess in front of me. Her tall, lightly bronzed, slim perfect figure, her wavy, platinum blonde hair, dip dyed with blue streaks, her large almond-shaped blue eyes, and her small nose stud that glints in the soft light of the room. Her bow-shaped mouth, her flawless skin and her large breasts make me feel so fucking inadequate. I don't stand a chance against this beautiful, model-like creature in front of me. I swallow back the lump that has formed in my throat and stand taller. *Come on Harper, chin up, tits out.*

"Don't apologise, you're welcome to each other; don't mind me. Me and my *son* were just leaving. I'll be in touch."

I try to sound nonchalant, but there is an edge of malice to my voice, even though inside my heart is breaking all over again. *Has he really missed me, or has he expertly fooled me into thinking he's missed me? Has he been with Lyla all this time? How many other women have there been?* I brush past her, with a little more force than necessary, and leave Sam's apartment as fast as my legs can carry me. I'm desperate to get back to Remy and return to our simple life in Santa Monica.

I take the lift down to the lobby and am alone with my thoughts. As I step out of the lift, I catch sight of Cole quietly sitting in one of the black overstuffed armchairs in the corner, playing with his phone. He stands as soon as he catches my eye and tucks his phone in his jacket pocket. A look of concern marring his features.

"What did he do this time, sugar?"

I shake my head, as my eyes glaze over.

"Take me back to the hotel please, Cole. I need to leave now, I can't be here," I anxiously choke out, and he nods curtly.

He takes Freddie's sleeping form in his carrycot out to the Mercedes, which is parked idly at the kerb. He opens the door, leans in, and straps Freddie securely in the back seat. I climb shakily in the back seat, next to Freddie, and let the tears I was holding back in the confines of Sam's apartment fall down my cheeks. Cole climbs into the driver's seat, and he regards me intently.

"Look, sugar, it's none of my business, but you look like you could do with a friend. Do you want to tell me about it?"

He hands me a handkerchief, and I wipe my eyes.

"Fucking Lyla showed up. I can't compete with her, Cole. I never could." I sob as Cole scrubs his free hand down his face.

"*Fucking Lyla,*" he growls, and I shake my head.

"Please take me back to the hotel, Cole," I plead, and he nods, catching my watery gaze in the interior mirror.

He smiles softly, starts the engine, flicks the indicator, and pulls fluidly out into the night-time New York traffic. I quickly fire off a text to Remy.

On my way back to the hotel now, babe

P xx

Throughout the remainder of the journey, I am silent and lost in my own thoughts. I want nothing more than to pack up our stuff and return to the place I now call home: Santa Monica. Soon we are pulling to a halt outside the hotel and Cole comes around to the passenger door to let me out of the car. He looks sympathetically at me and smiles warmly.

"I've got it, sugar."

He helps me out of the car and unstraps Freddie from the back seat. He carries him to the affluent, glass-fronted hotel entrance and hands him to me.

"Take care, sugar. If you need anything at all, call me."

He passes me a business card, brushes my arm reassuringly and winks. I manage a smile, but I know it doesn't reach my eyes. I enter the hotel and make my way quickly to the lift, carefully trying not to jar a sleeping Freddie awake. I frantically stab the call button, trying my best not to break down in front of the rest of the hotel's patrons. The lift arrives, and I step inside, secretly hoping that I am the sole occupant all the way up to the twelfth floor. The door starts to close, and a large, tanned hand slides between the doors to stop the doors from fully closing.

"Hold the elevator, sweetheart."

I look up into the greenest eyes I have ever seen, they would give Sam's a run for their money. His grin is swoon-worthy, and he is wearing a bright yellow hoodie, emblazoned with the words *'Starr Inc.'* in bright red lettering.

He has his hood pulled up, which covers his light brown hair. He punches the penthouse floor button, and I feel my face flush. The doors close, and the lift starts to move. I try to hide my face, but I can see his smirk out of the corner of my eye.

"You know, where I'm from, it isn't considered a crime to find me attractive, honey."

His American accent is deep and playful; I look up to meet his amused eyes.

"Hey."

He salutes, and I smile.

"Hi," I say softly, suddenly feeling shy as he reaches his hand out to me.

"I'm Jensen, Jensen Starr."

I nod, take his offered hand, and he envelopes my hand in his large, soft, warm one.

"Peyton. Pleased to meet you, Jensen."

He nods, mirroring my body language and he keeps his hand in mine a little longer than is acceptable. Oddly, I don't mind this handsome strangers grip on my hand.

"You look like you could use a drink, beautiful."

His rich, all-American voice washes over me and strangely comforts me like a warm hug.

"It's been a bad week, unfortunately."

Fucking understatement. He regards me intently, maintaining eye contact and cocking his head to the side.

"Ditto. Want to share, sweetheart? I'm an extremely good listener, maybe we could cheer each other up?"

I look shyly away at his flirty tone, and he steps closer to me.

"I don't bite...well unless you want me to."

He smirks, and I shiver as I remember those are the exact words that Sam used when he first came into Saint Sinner Ink on that fateful day. It seems like a lifetime ago now. I drop his hand as if he is on fire and take a step away from him as the lift comes to a halt at my floor.

"I...I'm sorry, this is me."

I sidestep him, and he winks as I step out of the lift.

"I'm in the penthouse suite, just in case you were wondering, beautiful," he calls out, as the lift doors close.

Jensen winks cheekily, and the lift begins its ascent.

I let out the breath I didn't know I was holding and rush down the corridor to our room. Freddie's carrycot is in my hand, and I'm trying desperately not to wake him. I quickly use the key card to gain entry to our room and step inside, closing the door behind me. I lean my head on the door and gulp in precious air. *Fuck me.* In those seconds, I make the snap decision to just pack up and go home. Back to my new life in Santa Monica. Back to my job at Cool Beans, and back to my friends Joel, Henley, Blaze, Rayne and Dax.

I place Freddie's carrycot gently on the hotel room floor and catch Remy's warm gaze. As soon as his eyes lock with mine, I let out a strangled sob.

"Take me home, Rem, this was all a big fucking mistake. I should have listened when you said it was a bad idea. Please, take us home."

I go to move into the bedroom, and Remy stops me by gently taking my hand in his.

"Beaut, the police are here to ask you a few questions."

It isn't until he says those words, that I look up and register the presence of two police officers.

Shit.

38

Sam

As I watch Peyton leave my apartment, I rake my hand furiously through my already unkempt hair.

"What the fuck, Lyla? Do you see what you've fucking done! You can't just randomly show up here when you fucking feel like it! What the fuck are you even doing in New York?" I reprimand her, trying to keep my temper in check and she shrugs nonchalantly.

"Does it matter? It looks like I turned up just at the right time. Besides, I'm here now, baby; why not take advantage of that? I can make you feel good, Sammy."

She moves closer to me and runs her nails down my abs. I recoil from her touch, as if I can't bear her hands on me.

"You need to get the fuck out, Lyla, and don't you *ever* fucking call me Sammy!" I say, in an exasperated tone.

"Say it with a little more conviction, babe, and then maybe, just maybe, I'll do as you say."

Jesus fucking Christ.

She smirks, and I grab her wrist roughly.

"I'm quickly losing my fucking patience, Lyla. You need to leave now; I won't tell you again," I say with a clenched jaw, and I can feel the tic begin in my neck. "I'm fucking done, Lyla. You and me? It's fucking *over*. Whatever we had or whatever you think we had, is *over*," I spit harshly.

She reaches for me, but before her hand can make contact with me, I back as far away from her as I can.

"Sammy, please, it's only ever been you. *I love you!*" she says petulantly, and I half expect her to stomp her foot for effect.

I scrub my hands down my face, fast losing any semblance of self-control. I pick my phone up from on top of the mantelpiece and dial the number I need.

"Cole, it's me."

His deep, rumbling timbre fills my ears.

"I'm driving, you're on hands-free. What can I do for you, mate?"

I watch Lyla cautiously as she regards me intently from across the room.

"Yeah, I've got an unwanted guest in my apartment."

He clears his throat.

"That wouldn't be Lyla would it, by any chance, mate?"

How would he know that? Then I think back. *Peyton. Fuck.*

"Yeah, it's Lyla; look it's a long story, I'll explain later. Could you come and get rid of her, please?"

He pauses for a few seconds.

"I've kept quiet for long enough, Sam. What the hell is wrong with you? What about the woman I just took back to her hotel in floods of tears? Everyone seems to be treading on eggshells around you and not addressing the issue, but I'm not afraid to call you out on your bullshit. I'm your friend *before* I'm your employee. She's the mother of your son, for fuck's sake! Just fucking cut the girl some slack and stop being a stubborn dick for once in your god damn life!" he snaps in his deep, rich voice, which he uses when he's really pissed.

"Spare me the lecture, Cole. You've got no fucking idea, have you? What about what I've been through? I thought she was dead, and it turns out that her parents knew she was alive. They knew, and they said *nothing!*"

I raise my voice, and Lyla's attention piques at the snippet of information.

"It's all you, you, you! *Fuck me,* Sam. You are such a selfish prick. What about all she's been through? Have you considered that? It's obvious she's jealous and hurting at seeing you with another woman. Fucking *Lyla!* Of all the women in the world, it had to be her! Peyton still cares about you, you complete dick! So, I suggest you man the fuck up!"

Cole raises his voice, and I begin to pace the floor of my apartment, feeling more than a little agitated.

"Look, can you come and remove her or not? Because I don't fucking want her here," I bark, feeling all the strings that are holding me together slowly start to tear and sever around me.

Cole sighs.

"Fuck me. Alright, I'm just running an errand. I'll be as quick as I can," he says indifferently, and I hang up without saying goodbye.

I make my way back into the living space to find Lyla sprawled out on my sofa, completely naked and I try to look anywhere but at her breasts.

"What the fuck? Didn't I make myself clear that I didn't fucking want you here?" I shout, and she rolls over onto her stomach.

She rests her chin on her hand, showing off her perfectly manicured, blood red fingernails.

"We all know you're going to fuck me, Sam. It's always a sure thing when it comes to us. We may as well get it out of the way. You want me as much as I want you, admit it. Peyton was just an inconvenience, a stop gap while you figured out it was me you really wanted."

I take a deep breath. *What the fuck? Is she being serious right now or is she fucking with me?*

"You're actually beginning to sound like fucking J.D! When are you going to get it through your thick, pathetic skull that it's just sex! All it's ever been between us is hot nasty sex. Nothing more, nothing less. We're toxic together Lyla; you ended up in fucking rehab because of me, because that's who I am and what I do! I'm Sam fucking Newbolt! I'm every woman's fucking fantasy! I break people, I hurt them, and then I move onto the fucking next, with no regard for the consequences!" I roar and pick up her coat.

"Get your fucking clothes on now and get out of my house," I say coolly.

I throw her clothes at her, and she gets up from the sofa. She moves closer to me, until we are toe to toe, and she grabs my cock through my silk pyjama pants. I swallow harshly.

"Your cock tells me differently, Sam; he wants to come out to play," she purrs seductively, and I will my cock not to react.

Come on you fucking traitor, do me a favour, just this once. I take a step back from her, not trusting myself to be near her.

"Sammy, baby," she croons, as she follows me into the kitchen.

I look up, and she is stood in the doorway in her underwear, twirling her hair around her finger.

Fuck.

"Lyla," I say, with a hint of warning to my voice.

She struts with confidence into the kitchen and stops in front of me. She walks two fingers down my chest and stops at the waistband of my pyjama bottoms. I regard her intently, and my resolve snaps as I let her stroke my growing erection.

What the fuck are you doing, Newbolt?

"Just relax. Let me make you feel good, baby," Lyla purrs and drops to her knees in front of me.

She tugs my pyjama bottoms down until I am totally naked from the waist down in front of her. She takes my cock in her hand and strokes it up and down, but all I can think of is Peyton. She takes me deep in her throat, and I grunt at the feel of her wet mouth around me.

"Stand up, darlin', this isn't working for me."

I drag her to her feet, and she looks at me with those blue eyes of hers, which look almost too big for her face. She runs her finger down the centre of my chest, trying to entice me to continue. I pull up my pyjama bottoms and run my hands through my hair. *This is a mistake, Newbolt.*

"Is something wrong, baby?" she pouts.

It isn't adorable like she thinks it is it's extremely fucking annoying. She presses her already bare, and silicone enhanced breasts against me.

"Why won't you just admit it, Sam? You feel something for me. There's always been a spark between us."

I make my way around the kitchen island, pick up my glass, and fill it liberally with *Macallan* whiskey. As I pour my drink, she moves lithely around the island and slides her hands under my t-shirt. She nips my earlobe and rakes her blood red fingernails across my abs. I growl at the feeling and grip both of her wrists in one of mine. I spin her around and trap her beneath me.

You're going to regret this once it's over.

I try desperately to block out the voice in my head, which tells me it's wrong, and clear my throat before I begin to speak.

"This doesn't mean we're back together, Lyla. This is going to be *just* sex. We were toxic together, and all it ever will be with us is mindless sex."

She looks up at me with those eyes I was once in love with, and all I see is a hole to empty my cock into.

"You don't mean that, Sammy. We were good together, baby."

The way she whines grates on every last nerve in my body, and just to shut her up, I grab her roughly by the shoulders and push her to her knees. She lightly licks the head of my cock and grins up at me. *Fuck me, I hate this woman.* I can't stop this thought dominating my brain as I grab the blonde hair at the back of her head. I push my cock deep into her throat, and I hear her start to gag. Her eyes start to water, but I don't give a fuck as I start to pump back and forth between her soft pink lips. She pulls away with a loud retching sound.

"Sammy, calm down, lover," she manages to say, before I ram my cock back into her mouth.

She pulls away again, her eyes wide and glossy as she coughs and splutters.

"So, that's how you want it is it?" she asks, trying desperately to sound seductive and failing miserably.

"Shut up and keep your mouth busy, you fucking whore," I say, as I force my cock in her mouth again.

As I thrust back and forth, I can feel my balls slapping off her chin, and I realise how thoroughly disgusted with myself I am. With this at the forefront of my mind, I feel my climax building. As if Lyla can sense it as well, she pulls back.

"Not in my mouth, Sammy. You know I don't like it," she says.

I forgot how much she used to hate it when I shot my load in her mouth. I smirk at the thought and grunt as I push as far into her throat as I can. I hold her head firmly in place with both hands as I come down her throat. Her eyes widen, and she tries to pull away, but I hold her head where it is until my release subsides.

"I said not in my mouth, you prick!" she says, as she spits what's left of my come into the sink.

"It wasn't in your mouth, sweetheart. You didn't say anything about your throat," I say, with a wicked laugh and she narrows her eyes at me.

"You're a fucking bastard, Sam. You know that don't you?" she complains.

I take an elaborate, cocky bow and laugh again.

"We're not done yet, babe. Get on your fucking knees and make me hard again," I say, with a commanding tone to my voice.

She looks like she is going to say something, but I grab her shoulders again and push her down.

"Good girl," I say gruffly, as she starts to suck on my limp member.

I'm not even sure I want to carry on, but I know I need to focus this seething anger I feel somewhere. *Why not at this fucking horrendous woman?* As my cock starts to get hard again, she smiles up at me.

"Aren't we in a randy mood, tonight?" She purrs, but instead of it sounding sexy, she makes my fucking skin crawl.

I place my hands under her arms and raise her to her feet. I lead her into the living area and bend her over the sofa. I roughly push her legs apart with mine, and she pants breathily. Everything about this moment feels all kinds of wrong, but it's what I need. At least that's what I tell myself as my cock enters her slick channel.

"OH SAMMY!" she screams like a fucking porn star as my cock moves in and out of her.

I begin to pound in and out of her slick folds. I suck my index finger, and when I take it out, I start to rub it gently over Lyla's anus. She purrs and looks over her shoulder at me. At that moment, I'm glad she is facing away from me, so I don't have to look at her fucking face. I know this isn't what I want, but after the revelation that Peyton's family knew she was alive, I am in desperate need of a release. She looks slightly stunned as I push my finger in her tight hole up to the knuckle. I work my finger gently in and out of her arse while she starts to pant loudly with lust.

"Oh, Sam!" she screams in a pitch that only dogs can hear.

I growl animalistically as I hammer harder into her.

"Harder! You know I like it rough, Sam!" she shrieks, as I quicken my pace.

I want this moment to be over as fast as it began. I thrust so deep I can feel my cock bump her cervix. All the while, I'm pushing my finger in and out of her arse.

"IS THAT HARD ENOUGH FOR YOU?" I bark, as my free hand finds her slender throat.

"CHOKE ME SAM! CHOKE ME LIKE YOU USED TO! SHOW ME WHO'S IN CHARGE!" she yells.

I grip her throat tighter and increase my deep thrusts, fucking her harder each time.

"DON'T STOP, SAMMY, DON'T YOU FUCKING DARE STOP!" she pleads desperately, as my pace becomes relentless and almost brutal.

"Is this how you like to be fucked, Lyla? Treated like a cheap whore?" I say gruffly, as I feel her orgasm ripple through her.

"SAM! SAMMY! OH! OH! OH! SAMMY! OHHHHHHHHH!"

She comes loudly around my cock. I look down at her in the throes of passion, and I feel nothing. I know I should feel bad, but I don't. She looks back at me all doe-eyed and satiated.

"Aren't you going to come for me, Sammy?" she says sweetly and bats her fake eyelashes.

I remove my finger from her arse, pull my cock from her pussy and push the tip of my cock against her tight back entrance. I drive forward firmly, and as the tip of my cock disappears inside her, she squeals.

"Sammy! No one's ever fucked me there before," she says with uncertainty in her voice, and she tries to move away.

I look coldly into her eyes, I grip her firmly by the hips, and reply, "Do you see anyone who gives a fuck?"

I push further into her, and she gasps loudly. *Fuck me she's so tight. I think she might have been telling the truth about not doing it before.*

"Sammy, be gentle. Please, baby," she whimpers.

As I start to push in and out, I can feel my anger starting to subside.

"Slow down, Sammy!" she says in a baby voice, and I clench my jaw at how fucking infuriating it sounds.

In a few more cruel and unrelenting thrusts, I find my release with a deep rumble from within my throat.

"FUCK ME!" I bellow as I empty my cock inside her anus.

I don't give her the chance to say anything, or try to cuddle me, as I pull out of her, pull up my boxers, and my pyjama pants.

"That was incredible, Sammy, darling," she says, with a sigh.

I need her to go, and I need her to go right the fuck now.

"Get your clothes on, Lyla, and fuck off," I spit angrily.

She gathers her clothes and pulls them on haphazardly. She narrows her eyes at me.

"I made it clear from the start that this was just sex, nothing more," I say flatly, and she sits up, her mouth forming a perfect *'O'* shape.

"You know, like a fucking fool, I thought things were going to be different this time, Sam. I thought after we fucked, you'd see that it's not her you want," she whines, as I roll my eyes and shake my head.

"All you've ever been is an easy lay, Lyla."

She has the audacity to look offended, and she goes to slap me across the face, but I grab her wrist before her hand can connect with my cheek.

"Get the fuck out of my house," I say roughly, and I pick up my glass of Macallan.

I take a long pull, enjoying the warmth as it settles in my stomach. A few moments pass, and I look up to see Lyla fully dressed in her red trench coat and heels. She looks thoroughly fucked. She twirls her mussed blonde hair around her finger suggestively, and as she moves closer to me, I smell the sickly-sweet scent of her perfume. I take another long sip of my whiskey and take a few steps away from her. *Give me fucking strength; I could do without this shit.*

"The only spark that has ever been between us was in the bedroom, babe, and it was average at best," I say unenthusiastically, and this time, she manages to lash her hand across my cheek.

"How fucking dare you, Sam Newbolt!" she shrieks dramatically as I hear the door to my apartment close.

"Sam? It's me."

Cole's voice echoes through my apartment.

"I'm in the kitchen, mate," I shout, and he leans in the doorway.

"Everything ok?"

I nod as I take a long gulp of my whiskey, and Cole rounds the kitchen island until he comes to a stop in front of Lyla. He looks from her to me and observes the exchange between us. Her dishevelled hair, her smudged lipstick, my mussed hair. *Shit! He fucking knows I shagged her.*

"Come on, Miss Hudson, you've had your fun. I think it's time for you to go home."

Cole takes her by the wrist, and she struggles against him.

"Get your filthy fucking hands off me, Cole! Sam, are you going to let him manhandle me like this?" she screeches.

Cole rolls his eyes at me, waiting for the signal from me.

"If I ever fucking see you here again, I will have you escorted from the building, no questions asked. I'll also personally see to it that you're issued with a fucking restraining order. That's not a threat, Lyla. It's a fucking *promise,* and I *never* go back on my promises. Remember that sweetheart. Don't fucking test me."

I leave her with one last warning, and I nod curtly to Cole. He lifts her up, as if she weighs nothing, throwing her over his shoulder. She is pounding on his back for him to let her go, but it doesn't faze him as he strides out of my apartment with a screaming Lyla hanging off his shoulder.

As the door slams shut, I am overwhelmed by the silence that greets me. I pick up the almost full bottle of whiskey and stride into the living room. *What the fuck have I done?* I sit down on the floor and close to the window of my apartment, which overlooks the breath-taking New York skyline by night. That's when I break down; gut-wrenching sobs wrack my whole body, until I'm trembling with absolute and utter fucking desolation. I unscrew the lid from the whiskey bottle and swallow it down, as if it is going out of fashion. I need to be numb to deal with this; I need to be totally obliterated to stop this constant, crippling ache in my chest and to quiet the overwhelming sense of guilt I feel.

The events of the past week have crept up on me, completely overwhelmed me, and hit me head on like a ten-tonne fucking truck. My fiancée is alive, we have a son, and my ex-manager, the man I trusted for almost my entire life, the man I trusted to take care of me and my band's interests, the man I considered a friend... he turned out to be a complete psychopath. He is currently locked up in prison for attempted murder and false imprisonment. *What kind of sick, twisted person does that?* On top of all that, I shagged my ex-girlfriend, and I find out that after all this time Peyton's family knew she was alive and didn't think to tell me. *No wonder they weren't at our comeback gig.*

I take another large guzzle of whiskey, enjoying the burn as it slides down my throat and warms my stomach. I put the bottle down beside me and sob hard. It feels like a whole years' worth of tears are breaking free and pouring their way out of me. As I think of my beautiful Peyton and my son, a pain lances through my chest. I let out a distressed scream, and I don't hold back.

I scream until my lungs feel like they are burning, and I feel like I have lost every ounce of control I had over my feelings. The dam has well and truly collapsed, and I'm drowning in sheer sorrow. *Oh fuck, fuck, fuck.* I pick up the whiskey bottle and knock back the fiery liquid. *I am halfway to feeling comfortably numb.*

I catch my reflection in the glass, and I don't recognise the man staring back at me. My eyes are red, bloodshot, and puffy from the tears; the green is a dull, sludgy green and not the usual emerald sparkle that usually stares back at me. My hair is dishevelled and unkempt, and my clothes have the sickly stench of Lyla's perfume clinging to them. The man staring back at me isn't Sam Newbolt; he is a version of me with subtle differences. This version is broken and so full of agony that it's debilitating.

A loud bang on the door pulls me out of my head and back to the here and now.

"Sam, sweetheart, it's me."

My mum's soft, soothing voice fills my ears, and that makes me sob harder.

"Sam, let us in, son. We're all worried about you."

My dad's concerned voice is muffled through the apartment door, yet I make no effort to get up and open the door. I want to be alone. I need to be on my own to deal with all this shit.

"Sam, open the fucking door, you prick."

I hear Brody's brash, loud voice. *Tactful as ever.*

"So help me God, I'll break this motherfucking door down, with my bare hands if you don't fucking open it right now!"

He rattles the door handle as my mum softly berates him.

"Mrs N, no disrespect, but your son is a selfish dick that needs to get his head out of his fucking arse!" Brody shouts and continues to bang on the door.

The *thud-thud-thud* causing a dull throb in my alcohol-soaked head.

"Are you fucking Lyla in there? Because if you are, I swear to God, I'll kick your arse so high you're going to have to take your shirt off to have a shit!"

If only you knew. I gulp down another large mouthful of whiskey. My mind is swimming, and I feel like I'm floating. I hear the sound of the door handle rattling vigorously.

"Sam, let us in sweetie, please," my mum says tenderly.

I manage to clamber to my feet, in a way that I would describe as *'Bambi on the ice'*. I stagger drunkenly to the door and pull it open, stumbling as the door opens. I sway on the spot as I lock eyes with my mum. The look on her face breaks my heart and starts my hysterical sobbing off again. *Fuck me, I'm losing it.*

"Oh, my darling boy," my mum soothes, and I practically fall into her arms.

I am instantly transported back to when I was a kid, being comforted and soothed by my mum. She rubs her hands up and down my back, in a gesture of reassurance.

"Hate to break up the pity party, but you need to sober the fuck up, Sam. Peyton's been taken in for questioning."

Brody's chastising voice breaks through my despair, and I look up, trying to process what Brody has just said.

"*What?*"

He folds his muscular arms across his chest.

"She's been taken in for questioning. I've had that Remy geezer on the phone, and he's freaking the fuck out, man."

A perplexed look crosses my face, and his words are struggling to break through my hazy, inebriated brain.

"Fuck me backwards, dude."

He hauls me from my mum's arms and pulls me into the apartment, closing the door behind him. He pushes me down on the sofa and stands in front of me with his arms folded.

"Are you hearing me, fuck face, or are you completely retarded? Do you need me to speak slower? Peyton has been taken in for questioning. She fucking needs us, dude."

I look up at him, and I'm faced with two Brody's standing over me. *Fuck me, I must be drunk.*

"Did she tell you? Her fucking family knew she was alive and didn't bother to share that delightful snippet of information with me!"

I laugh bitterly. *Pity party for one, anyone?*

"Fine, maybe this will fucking explain it better for you."

Brody snatches up the remote control for the T.V, and the news is on.

"Breaking news just coming in, Peyton Harper, tattoo artist and former fiancée of Rancid Vengeance front man, Samson Newbolt, has been found alive and well after being allegedly murdered by the band's then manager John Dalton, a.k.a Johnnie Diamond. Police are questioning Miss Harper, following up on their line of enquiry. Nevertheless, the question on everyone's lips is, was this a genuine incident, or a cruel publicity trick to fool Newbolt and the world into thinking she was dead? Only time will tell. Harper's family refused comment, and we are eagerly awaiting a statement from Rancid Vengeance."

Brody switches off the T.V and folds his arms impatiently in front of me.

"Now do you fucking get it? She's front-page news, dude. The press are going to eat her the fuck alive, Sam. She's terrified, and she's alone. No matter what shit went down with you two tonight, she loves you and she fucking *needs* you. *Jesus*, your fucking kid needs you too," Brody says, through clenched teeth.

What the fuck is he talking about again?

"Are you fucking her?" I suddenly blurt out, and the look on Brody's face says it all. It is a look of pure shock and bewilderment. I know he's telling the truth, but my drunken mind is working overtime.

Fuck me, I'm going to regret this in the morning.

"What the fuck, dude? Are you actually being serious right now? You know I wouldn't touch her, she's yours. She's been yours from the very fucking beginning, we all knew that. I fucking love her like a sister. She's beautiful on the inside and on the outside, but I don't think of her that way. Fuck me, Sam. I thought you knew that at least, or are you a complete fucking dick?"

I know I am being a complete prick, but I can't help myself.

"You fucked her that night on the bus, didn't you, you cocksucker!" I accuse, and he squares his shoulders as if he is about to attack me.

"Get your fucking head out of your arse, Sam, for fuck's sake!" Brody growls, and I can clearly hear the grinding of his teeth. "You have to know I don't fucking see her that way, we're just friends. I've told you so many times, nothing happened on the fucking bus. We talked, we drank, and we bonded, end of."

The truth is, deep down, I know Brody, or any of the boys, wouldn't do that. I stand up until I am toe to toe with him and I sway on the spot.

Fuck me, how much whiskey did I have again?

My dad steps forward and tries to steady me.

"Sam, son, sit. Let's all calm down, and I'll go and put the kettle on."

I scrub my hands across my stubble and shake my head.

"I don't need you to put the fucking kettle on, dad!" I slur.

Brody moves closer to me, putting a barrier between me and my dad.

"None of this is your dad's fault, Sam. You're being a complete fucking dick. You need to sober the fuck up, and then we're going to the police station to get Peyton. I called Alistair, and he called our solicitor, Vance. He's on the way there to be her legal representative. She's not fucking dealing with this alone, not anymore. She fucking *needs* us, and she's part of our family, whether you refuse to admit it or not."

Deep down in my drunken foggy brain, I know every word Brody has said is the truth. But I'm not sure I can look past the fact that her family knew she was alive. Over the past eighteen months, I have transformed from a cocky, arrogant, egotistical, womanising arsehole into a monogamous, loving, dad-to-be and back again. This past year I have reverted to my debauched, old ways and her parents are responsible for it. I lost everything: my fiancée, my baby, my reason to live, and they could have prevented it all. I pick up the bottle of whiskey and lock eyes with Brody; I knock back the fiery liquid with a look of defiance on my face.

"Are you being fucking serious? I swear to the *baby fucking Jesus*, I am going to cock drop you!" Brody roars and my mum tries to placate him by brushing his arm gently.

"Sweetie, he's in shock. Maybe we should leave him for tonight, let it all sink in, let him sober up. Let him sleep it off, and we'll come back tomorrow."

He shakes her off, and I have to physically stop myself from telling him not to treat my mum that way.

"No, I'm not going to let him do this, Mrs N! She's the mother of your child you fucking cock sucker!"

Brody runs his hand over his head in sheer frustration and moves closer to me, until he is standing over me.

"You're Sam Newbolt! Fucking suck it up and stop being a little bitch!" he snaps.

As I go to take another swig from the whiskey bottle, he snatches it from me. He slams the bottle down on the table and his nostrils flare.

"What the fuck, dude?" I slur, as he clenches and unclenches his fists.

"You know what? I'm fucking done, Sam. Do what you want, but I'm not leaving her. I'm fighting in her corner, whether you fucking like it or not!"

My drunken brain tries to focus on anything but the searing pain in my chest at the thought of *my* Peyton locked up in a police cell, terrified and all alone. However, the bitter side of me wins out again and hopes they lock her up so that she rots in prison. I attempt to stagger to my feet, and my legs feel wobbly, but I manage to stand up straight. I jab my finger in Brody's direction. I know deep down it isn't wise to goad him, but I can't help myself.

"That's right; you go to her. You comfort her, wrap her in your arms and tell her you're there for her... right before you bury your cock inside her and make her scream your *fucking* name!" I say spitefully, and as I say those words, I see Brody visibly tense.

His eyes flash with anger, and before I can say another word, I feel Brody's fist connect with my cheek. *I totally fucking deserved that.*

"I FUCKING WARNED YOU; YOU PRICK!" he roars, and I fall backwards onto the sofa.

My head is spinning, and my nose is bleeding, but I can just about make out the muffled conversation, going on around me.

"It's done, Brody, but you ever lay a hand on my son like that again, and I promise you; I will be the one to knock you down, next time."

My mum's usually soft, placating tone is replaced with an unforgiving austere one.

"I would listen to mama bear if I were you, son. She's fiercely protective of her cubs," my dad says diplomatically.

I make out the broad outline of Brody's large, muscular body and he holds his hands up defensively.

"I...I'm so sorry," he says softly, and I hear the door click shut as I give in to a drunken sleep.

***

I'm not sure how long I have been asleep, but I wake to my dad tapping my cheek and flicking cold water in my face.

"Come on, wake up, soppy bollocks."

He throws a pack of peas at me, and I look sleepily up at him. As I go to sit up, I am struck with a blinding pain in my head, and the room is spinning. *Fuck me; I had way too much whiskey.*

"*Fuck me,* what time is it?" I say gruffly, and my dad looks at his watch.

"Just after one a.m. You were only asleep for an hour or so," my dad says flatly. "You've got some apologising to do, son."

As I attempt to sit up, my dad sits down on the sofa next to me. He puts the peas on my face, and I wince in pain.

"What the fuck happened?"

He sighs.

"You got drunk, accused Brody, bloody Brody of all people, of sleeping with Peyton, and he hit you. I can't say I blame him to be honest, but your mother was extremely pissed off, to say the least."

I groan at my idiotic drunken behaviour, and then it all suddenly starts to come back to me. Peyton, meeting my son for the first time, almost having sex with Peyton, Peyton leaving, having sex with Lyla, the whiskey. *Fuck me, the whiskey.* I remember my mum, dad and Brody showing up and then rest is a blur, to say the least.

"Where's mum?"

My dad checks my injuries.

"She's asleep in the spare room; you might want to give her a wide berth for the time being son. It's going to take a lot more than chocolates and diamonds this time."

I scrub my hands down my face. *Shit, I hate seeing my mum so upset. I hate it even more that I'm the fucking cause.*

"You're going to have a bloody impressive shiner, but you'll live. You can't carry on behaving like this, son. Are you off your medication again? Is that why you're acting like a complete fucking arsehole?"

I shake my head, as he berates me.

"Not now, dad, please."

He hands me a glass of water.

"You're going to drink this, get yourself in the shower, then you're going to make amends with Brody. After that, you're going to do the right thing and go and see Peyton. Are we clear? You're a father now, Sam. You have to be the responsible one, for once."

I go to protest, and he holds his finger up. *Fuck me, my head is banging.*

"Ah, ah, this isn't up for discussion, Sam. Not this time."

As my dad says those words, there is a soft tap on the door. My dad gets up to answer the door in silence, and I hear the dulcet tones of my big brother, Brandon.

"What trouble has my little brother gotten himself into this time?" he says in an amused tone.

His dark hair is pulled back into a ponytail, and he is wearing a black bandana, black skinny jeans, a white vest, a dark grey chunky knit cardigan and black Converse trainers.

"Brand, keep it down, yeah?" I groan and clutch my throbbing head as he chuckles softly.

"You look like shit, little brother. Go grab a shower then you can tell me all about your epic fuck up."

He strides into the kitchen, and I start to feel intense shame wash over me. I am officially the world's biggest fucking idiot, and I don't blame Brody one bit for hitting me. I scrub my hands down my face and make my way into the bathroom. I close the door behind me and look in the mirror. Brandon is right, I do look like shit. I have dark circles underneath my eyes, and the green of my eyes isn't the usual emerald green. My face is pale, I have the beginnings of a huge black eye, and my hair is a state of disarray. I can't help thinking that even a shower won't fix this mess.

I emerge from the bathroom feeling a little better. My hair is still damp, and I am wearing a loose-fitting pair of grey jogging bottoms, which hang low on my hips. My chest is bare, and I have a black towel around my neck.

"*Fuck me,* don't you own a shirt?" Brandon says drily.

He is sitting on my sofa with his one arm slung over the back. His feet up on the coffee table, and he is drinking a bottle of Budweiser. I step further into the living area and drop down onto the sofa next to Brandon.

"Dad told me to tell you he's gone to smooth things over with Brody, although I can't say I blame him. I would have done exactly the fucking same."

He takes a swig of his beer.

"Thanks for being on my side, bro. Really appreciate it," I say sarcastically, and he cocks his eyebrow.

"You really thought I would take your side after that? *Fuck me*, how hard did he hit you again?"

I run my hand through my hair, and I forgot how well Brandon knows me. I also forgot how much he fucking winds me up. Brandon is thirty-five, just four years older than I am. And even though he is older, we have always been close. I find him the easiest person in my family to talk to because he doesn't judge. He is extremely laid back, and he tells it like it is.

"What's this, get at Sam day?"

He chuckles softly and hands me a beer.

"Did I teach you nothing, little brother?"

I crack the bottle open and take a long pull, enjoying the cool liquid as it slides down my throat. *It's true what they say, hair of the dog really works!*

"I'm someone's fucking dad now, Brand. When did that happen? When did life get so complicated?"

He smirks.

"Didn't mum and dad have the birds and the bee's conversation with you? That's what happens when you don't wrap your Johnson, Sammy! First lesson in sex-ed 101!"

I narrow my eyes.

"Very fucking funny, Brand, dick."

He laughs throatily

"In answer to your question, I'm surprised it's taken you this long to knock someone up. You're giving me a run for my money on how many notches are on your bedpost!"

I hit him playfully on the arm, a little harder than I intended.

"So, I'm an uncle? Who knew! Congrats, boy or girl?"

I smile as I think of my son Freddie, the adorable green-eyed boy, who is my double.

"Boy. His name's Freddie, and he's six months old now. He's the most beautiful thing I've ever seen, and I *never* get sappy about babies."

I show him a picture on my phone that I took while he was here, and Brandon nods.

"*Wow!* He's definitely a Newbolt; he's got good genes! How do you feel about it?"

I lean back on the sofa and start to wonder how I feel about having a son, being a father, and being responsible for another human being... a human being that's half me and half Peyton.

"The truth? I'm fucking terrified; I'm terrified of fucking up. What if he hates me when he's older? What if I can't be what he needs, Brand?"

He leans back and looks at me, with a look of sympathy in his eyes.

"Look, you can't go through life wondering what if, Sammy. There isn't a guide that tells you how to be a parent. *Fuck me*, mum and dad raised five of us and do you think that was perfect? *Hell no!* For the first three years of my life, me and Sav spent it sleeping on a tour bus around America, listening to the sound of Milo and Seth's bunks squeaking and the sound of female sex noises. It was far from a walk in the park. I remember mum and dad arguing a lot, her mostly begging him to give up his career. By the time she was pregnant with you, it was much more settled. We had moved into a house, and it was much more stable. Dad was on the road for six months of the year and it just...*worked.*"

For the first time in a few years, I am enjoying my heart to heart with my big brother. Even though he doesn't have kids himself, he just seems to *get it*.

"What I'm trying to say is, he's not asking for perfect, Sam. He's just asking you to be there for him, to guide him, nurture him, take care of him, and be his dad. It doesn't matter that you and Peyton aren't together, you put your animosity aside, for his sake."

I sigh and take another a pull on my beer.

"I take that isn't a good sigh. Come on little brother, out with it. Did something happen with Peyton?"

At that particular moment, I sort of hate the fact that he knows me so well.

"We kissed; we...sort of, almost had sex on this sofa."

He almost chokes on his beer.

"*Gross!* You dirty dog! I did not need that image of my little brother almost having sex in my head, dude!"

We both laugh.

"We got interrupted by Freddie crying on the baby monitor. I can already tell the little dude is going to be a massive cock blocker! Then she freaked out and kept saying it was a mistake. I almost talked her round, when she let slip that her family knew she was alive. If she lied about that, how many other things has she lied about, Brandon? My mind felt like it was about to explode. Then my psycho ex shows up! I swear I'm expecting her next move to be bunnies boiling in pots; she's one crazy bitch! Even though I was so fucking angry at Peyton, the look in her eyes when she saw Lyla broke my god damn heart all over again. She couldn't even look at me, and she just left, taking my boy with her. That's when I lost it."

I scrub my hands down my face, deciding to leave out the fact that I shagged Lyla in the exact same spot.

"*Fuck me;* we need something stronger than beer, brother. Where do you keep your whiskey?"

I puff out my cheeks, and my stomach roils at the thought of more alcohol.

"I've had enough whiskey to last a fucking lifetime. Whiskey makes me turn into a complete dick. I accused one of my best friends of fucking Peyton, and then he punched me."

I point to the black eye, and Brandon shakes his head.

"You never could handle your liquor!"

He smirks.

"I'm surprised it's taken someone this long to knock some god damn sense into you."

I cock my eyebrow.

"Thanks for the support, *brother,*" I say with a hint of venom in my voice.

"Put those claws away, I'm not trying to start a fight. I'm on your side. I am. I've never been against you, Sammy. I'm always in your corner, but..."

I hold up my hand to stop him.

"Brand, just stop, please. I don't want to hear it. I know I'm a disappointment, I do dumb shit, and I'm reckless..."

As I say those words, he rolls his eyes and cuts me off mid-sentence.

"*Please,* spare me the fucking pity party, little brother. Seriously, it doesn't suit you. If you're looking for sympathy look in the dictionary between shit and syphilis," he says wryly, and I smirk.

"Where the fuck do you come up with that shit, dude?"

He smiles and shrugs, as he takes a sip of his beer.

"It's a gift."

With those words, the phone starts ringing. I look at the name on the screen. It's Brody; I swipe my finger across the screen and answer.

"Hello?" I say cautiously, expecting one of his famous Brody style rants.

"Sam, it's me. Look, I wanted to apologise for punching you, dude, I'm really sorry. I shouldn't have hit you like that."

I pause, surprised that he's still actually talking to me.

"I'm sorry too, man, I deserved it. I can't apologise enough. I shouldn't have said that. I was drunk, and I was angry... not a good combination, you know that. Is she ok?" I enquire.

"She's fine. Vance worked his magic, and she went back to the hotel with Remy. She's upset and a bit shaken, which is understandable, but she seems fine on the whole. She's made of strong stuff."

A feeling of relief washes over me at hearing that she really is ok.

"She fucking needs you, Sam, even if she won't admit it. You know what fucking women are like. Call her, go to the hotel, and let her know you're there for her and your son."

At that moment, I decide I have to let her know I'm there for her, despite what she might think of me, and despite everything that has happened between us. Whether she will listen to me, is an entirely different story.

39

Peyton

"I'll ask you one more time, Miss Harper, or is it, Miss Stonebridge?" Detective Price says forcefully.

Exasperated, I rest my head on top of my folded forearms, and I feel like I want to cry. I have been here for a few hours, but it feels like longer. *This can't be happening.*

"We had a report that something had been posted on a social media site informing us of your return."

A look of pure confusion crosses my face. *Who the fuck could have posted about me being alive?* I am about to speak, when the door to the drab, grey interview room, swings open. The tall, dark-skinned detective, who is conducting my interview, gets up from his chair.

"Excuse me for one moment, Miss Harper."

He nods and goes over to the door. He whispers to the short, balding uniformed officer in the doorway and turns around to regard me intently with narrow, guarded eyes.

"A lawyer has been sent to represent you, Ma'am."

I look puzzled, and a figure emerges from behind the officers. He is average height, dark hair with a receding hairline and balding on top. He is average build, with dark hazel eyes. He smiles, and I can't help but think it makes him look like a shark. He is wearing an expensive suit, Armani if I'm not mistaken, and it looks as if it has been tailor-made to fit his height and build perfectly.

"Miss Harper, I presume?" he says in a typically British accent, and I nod. "Ah, good. I'm here to help you get out of this sticky little situation you seem to have found yourself in. May I have a minute with my client, please?"

Detective Price nods curtly and closes the door, leaving me and the mysterious lawyer alone. I get up from my chair, and he looks me up and down.

"Definitely Sam's type, although nothing like Brody described. Allow me to formally introduce myself; I'm Vance Stryker, legal representative of those darling boys, Rancid Vengeance."

I shake his hand in a firm grip.

"Peyton Harper, but I don't understand why Sam would send you here," I say, confused as to why Sam would bail me out when he seemingly hates my guts at this present moment.

"Sorry to disappoint you, darling, but Sam didn't send me, Brody did. I know that one just can't resist a damsel in distress."

My heart plummets at the thought that Sam didn't send him. Vance places his briefcase on the table and looks at me.

"Now, are there any little secrets I need to know about before we proceed? I can't say I'm partial to skeletons in closets, Miss Harper."

He looks at his expensive Rolex watch.

"I have a very expensive scotch with my name on it, and I plan on drinking it in the next thirty minutes, darling. Times-a-ticking."

He smiles his shark-like smile and taps his watch. I start to pace the room, suddenly feeling like a caged animal.

"I just need you to get me out of here."

I feel my breath coming in short, sharp bursts, and I feel my chest start to tighten, the sure symptoms of a threatening panic attack. *Fuck me! Please, not here.* Vance seems to realise what's happening and he pulls out a chair from the desk. He guides me by the shoulders and drops me down onto it.

"Head between your legs, sweetheart. Deep breaths. Good girl. Look, I'm going to do everything I can to get you out of here, but you need to tell me the facts."

He crouches down in front of me, and I take deep breaths. A few minutes of awkward silence passes and my breathing returns to normal. I look at him and cock my head to the side curiously.

"How did you know what to do just then?"

He smirks.

"My delightful ex-wife used to suffer from panic attacks, anxiety, blah, blah, blah. I'm quite the expert, darling. You're in good hands."

He gets to his feet and once he's satisfied that I'm ok and claps his hands twice.

"Now, to the matter at hand, Miss Harper, the facts. I know the basics, but Brody was brief, to say the least. So, you're going to have to fill in the blanks."

He takes a Dictaphone out of his briefcase, presses the record button, and lays it down on the table. I spend the next ten minutes filling him on the events of the past year, up until the moment I returned. His eyes widen, and he nods, taking in the information I have given him. He stops the recording and places the Dictaphone back in his briefcase.

"That's quite a tall tale, Miss Harper; allow me to work my magic."

He winks and strides over to the door, filled with determination; he opens it and calls out to the detective.

"Detective Price, we're ready for you now."

A few moments pass, and the detective enters the room. We both resume our seats at the worn grey desk, and Vance takes the chair next to mine.

"Detective Price, are you going to charge my client?"

The detective regards Vance with a scowl.

"From what Miss Harper has told me, no crime has been committed in this instance, so you can either charge her or let her go. Your choice, Detective," he says smugly.

"Miss Harper was presumed dead. A thorough police investigation took place, and a year later, she turns up alive. I can charge her with wasting police time and falsifying legal documents, which are very serious offences," he says sharply.

"I understand the implications, Detective; also, Miss Harper has filled you in on her version of events, is that correct?"

Detective Price nods curtly.

"Detective, no crime has actually taken place. She didn't do it for tax purposes, or illegal reasons. Therefore, you have no reason to hold my client."

He is about to argue, when Vance holds his finger up. I can see Detective Price silently seething, which makes me smile inwardly.

"I'm good at my job, Detective Price; my employers pay me substantially for my services."

Vance opens his briefcase and takes out a piece of paper.

"I think you'll find all you need in this document, Detective. It states my client's rights and grants her immunity from being prosecuted. Now if you would excuse us, I think we're done here."

He gets up from his seat, gesturing in my direction.

"Miss Harper."

He nods, and I follow suit, getting up from my seat too. I walk out of the interview room, letting out the breath I didn't realise I was holding.

"What the fuck was that, Vance?"

He smiles a genuine smile that doesn't make him look like a shark this time.

"That's why they pay me the big bucks, darling."

He winks.

"Thank you, so much."

He nods curtly, and as he turns around, I spot Remy and Brody. I can't hold back the sob that escapes from me. I am so overwhelmed by the support of the people that mean the most. The only person that isn't here is Sam. I stride up to Brody first and throw my arms around him, he squeezes me tightly.

"Thank you," I breathe into his ear, and he buries his face in my hair.

"Anytime, sweets."

I pull away from our embrace and see that Brody's knuckles are raw and bleeding.

"What happened?"

He shakes his head.

"Don't worry about me, babe, let's just say he had it coming."

He winks, and I can't help but wonder if he means Sam.

"I had to come and see if you were ok. I was so fucking worried, but you don't need me now, so I'll be going."

He smiles, but it doesn't reach his eyes. *Something is definitely wrong*. He turns to leave, but I stop him by grabbing his wrist.

"Don't go."

My voice is barely a whisper, and he strokes my knuckles, pulling me in for a Brody style hug.

"Be with Remy, sweets, he'll take care of you. I...I'll see you soon, I promise."

He smiles, pulls away from our embrace, and before I can protest, he leaves. I am left dumbstruck in the middle of the police station, but Remy pulls me from my thoughts as he wraps me in his strong arms. That's when the tears come, the gut-wrenching sobs that have been threatening spill down my cheeks.

"Shhh, I've got you, beaut," Remy soothes.

At that moment, wrapped in Remy's arms, I start to think of the life I have built for Freddie and me in Santa Monica. I think of the past year with Remy, living my life as Louise Stonebridge, someone I don't even recognise. I hope sometime in the not-so-distant future, I can move back to London, resume my life as Peyton Harper and finally begin my life again as a mother to Freddie Newbolt. I want to make up for lost time, with everyone I left behind.

40

Sam

A week passes and today, after police questioning and helping them with their enquiries and building a case against J.D, it is finally time to head back home to London. After the initial shock at seeing Peyton alive, I have come to terms with the fact that she really is here, and we are now officially parents to our son, Freddie Maxwell Newbolt.

The rest of the boys and me are ready to leave for the airport. After a gig at Nikon at Jones Beach Theatre, we stayed in the penthouse suite at the New Yorker Hotel, which happened to be the same hotel Peyton is staying in, as per my request. I cross the hotel lobby, and that's when I see her. *My Peyton.* Even though the lobby is littered with people, all I see is her. Remy Logan is standing close to her, and he is tucking a strand of her hair behind her ear in an intimate gesture. I start to wonder if something happened between them in the year she was gone, and I feel that familiar boiling jealousy running through my veins. *Get your filthy fucking hands off her, Logan.*

"Are you ready to go, Sam?"

Cole's deep rumbling voice cuts through my thoughts, and I hold my finger up.

"Yeah, just I'll just be a second, mate."

He nods, and I continue to watch the scene unfolding in front of me. Remy wipes a tear from her eye with the pad of his thumb as he pulls her into his chest. I growl involuntarily.

"Sam," Jax says with a hint of warning in his voice. He puts his hand on my shoulder in a silent gesture of reassurance.

"I'm ok honestly; I just need a minute. That's all, dude," I say softly, and I'm not sure if it's for his benefit or my own.

I stride across the marble-floored lobby, until I am face to face with her, ignoring the small crowd of fans who instantly recognise us. She looks so pale and fragile that it makes my heart clench. I clear my throat.

"Hey, can we talk for a second please, Peyton?"

She looks up, and her tired blue eyes lock with mine as she nods. My heart slams against my ribcage as she looks into my eyes.

"Give us a minute, Rem?"

He smiles and kisses her forehead, nodding curtly in my direction.

"Of course, take your time. I'll take Freddie outside, beaut."

He winks and takes my son in his pram outside before I can protest. *Beaut? So, he's got his own pet name for her? Fucking cocksucker.*

"So, you're coming back home to London, then?" I say hopefully, and she shakes her head.

"I need to go back to Santa Monica to tie up some loose ends, and then I'm going back to London."

I try to hide my disappointment and pull the keys to her old flat in Camden from my pocket.

"These belong to you, the keys to your flat; I kept them. I own the building now, but I couldn't bear to rent the flat out, so the keys are all yours... if you still want them? It's your home, you can stay there for as long as you want, rent free of course. It's the least I can do for you and my boy, angel."

She manages a vague smile and takes the keys from me, brushing my fingers as she takes them. The look in her eyes tells me that the familiar spark of electricity is still there as my skin makes contact with hers.

"Thank you," she whispers as her gaze drops to the floor.

I step closer to her and tilt her chin up until her eyes find mine.

"I can't fucking bear to see that look in your eyes, angel," I say gruffly, and she shakes her head.

"I'm so fucking sorry."

I reach for her hand, and she takes a cautious step back from me, to put some distance between us.

"I'm going to miss my flight."

She turns to walk away, and I grab her wrist, not giving her an opportunity to back away. She flinches as my hand makes contact with her, and I rein in my growing temper. *What else did fucking J.D do to her that she isn't telling me? What is making her react that way?*

"Then I'll book you on another god damn flight!" I say through clenched teeth, and she looks up at me. "Please, don't fucking walk away from me, angel."

She looks down at where my hand is gripping her, and I instantly see the fear in her eyes. I feel a pain lance through my chest as I realise my mistake and I let go.

"Please, I have to go, Sam."

I nod and fold my arms to stop myself from pulling her into my arms.

"Yeah, that seems to be the general fucking consensus every time you're around me these days, angel," I say a little more harshly than I intend and laugh bitterly. "You're always so eager to fucking run from me, why?"

She looks up at the ceiling, as if she is asking for answers from the man upstairs.

"Don't you get it? This past week, all I've wanted to do is fucking be with you, Sam. I want to wake up in your arms each morning; I want you to make love to me like it's the first and the last time. I want to laugh with you; I want to spend every waking hour fucking loving you, proving to you that I'm worth a second chance. But everything's different now, and I know that can never happen, not now. I've spent the past year believing that you masterminded the whole kidnapping with J.D, and I can't just forget that. It isn't that fucking easy, not for me. I wish it fucking was... my head is all over the place right now, Sam."

Finally, a little bit of honesty.

Her voice cracks as she says those last few words and she swipes away a stray tear that has tracked its way down her cheek. My heart slams violently against my ribcage. My tall frame towers over her slight one, and it is taking everything I have not to sweep her into my arms. After a whole year of wanting her, wishing that she was with me... she's now standing in front of me, a living, breathing human being, who gave birth to our son. *A beautiful vision. My angel. The other half of my heart.*

Her voice cuts through my thoughts, and the words that come next hit me like a freight train.

"I'm sorry, but I really can't be in a relationship with you right now. I wish I didn't feel that way, but I just can't."

Her lip quivers and her voice shakes.

"So, what? You're saying it's over between us? That there's no hope for us?"

I scrub my hands down my face, hoping that this is a dream and that any moment now, I'm going to wake up.

"That's exactly what I'm saying, Sam. I'm sorry," she says softly but doesn't meet my gaze.

"*FUCCKKKKK!*" I growl, attracting the attention of the patrons in the hotel lobby.

"Don't you think we've both allowed fucking J.D to take enough from us? He's robbed us of so much, Peyton; he took your identity from you, for fuck's sake! He robbed me of the first six months of my son's life. I get that now; it wasn't your fault, and I'm so sorry that I placed all the blame on you. Please forgive me, angel, I fucking *love* you, isn't that enough?"

There is a hint of pleading in my voice, as I take her hand gently and cautiously in mine.

"Angel," I rasp and as she looks up at me. I see conflict in her stormy blue eyes.

"Sam, we've both been through enough, this isn't fair."

I shake my head. *Fucking stubborn women.*

"You're not hearing me, angel. I forgive you. I want to give us another shot. Let me be a good boyfriend, let me be a father to my son; let's start again. You, me and Freddie, we can be a family. I can take care of you both. We can go as slow as you need. Please, I just want you to let me prove to you that I can be what you need. You know I'm not a man who begs, angel, but please, give us a second chance."

I know it sounds like I'm begging, but I just can't help myself. She brings out a side of me that no one else ever sees: the vulnerable, shy, insecure side. The man who craves to be loved, the private side the fans don't get to see. She sees beneath the bravado. She sees the man who hides behind the stage persona. She sees the real me, on and off stage.

I shake my head and stroke my calloused finger over her knuckles softly.

"Please, don't do this, angel."

She squeezes her eyes shut briefly and looks back up at me with conflict in her clear blue eyes.

"My head is all over the place, and I can't think straight right now. You make me lose myself, Sam. I can't, I just can't, and it's not just me anymore; I have to think of Freddie. Everything's different now, I have to be responsible."

Her voice cracks, and she averts her gaze so that she is looking anywhere but in my eyes.

"You could at least look at me when you're breaking my heart."

My voice wavers and I swallow back the lump in my throat as her blue eyes lock with mine.

"I...I'm so sorry Sam. I-it's over."

Those words pull me from my thoughts, and I feel my heart shatter into a million tiny fucking pieces all over again. I can't find my fucking breath. I swallow hard, trying to hold back the threatening tears. I don't know how, but I manage to pull out an advance copy of our new album *'Hurricane Vengeance'* from my backpack with a trembling hand. We recorded it after she died and the lyrics I wrote sum up the way I felt back then. She deserves to hear it, and if I can't get through to her with words, then maybe I can get through to her through my music. *A guy can hope, right?* I hand it to her, and she takes it, carefully trying to avoid skin on skin contact with me.

"Please, just do one last thing for me, listen to this, angel; it says it better than I ever could."

A tear slips down her cheek, and all I want to do is reach out and wipe it away. I want to carry her out of here and onto a plane so we can finally start our forever together. Me, Peyton and Freddie, but I know now that can never happen. *There is no us.*

41

Peyton

The look in Sam's eyes as I told him we were over is playing on a loop repeatedly in my mind, like a car crash that I can't tear my eyes from.

"I...I'm so sorry Sam. I-it's over."

That simple, but heart-wrenching sentence lodged in my throat and threatened to choke me as I said the words aloud. I knew I couldn't take it back, but I regretted those six words as soon as they passed my lips. When I saw the look in Sam's eyes, the look of pure heartbreak, regret, sadness, and the soul-destroying love he feels for me, I felt my heart breaking right along with his.

I boarded my flight back to Santa Monica robotically and in virtual silence. I was stuck in my own head. I have to pretend that my heart isn't broken into a million tiny pieces. I have no other choice; I have to be strong for Freddie. *Our son.* I stare out of the oval window, wishing I could take back every single one of those words, wishing the past year hadn't happened, wishing it was all a bad fucking dream.

"Beaut?"

Remy's soft voice breaks me from my thoughts. I look over at him, his warm, concerned brown eyes lock with mine. He reaches for my hand and strokes my knuckles gently.

"It's going to be alright, I promise."

I smile at Remy's optimism and snuggle closer to him, inhaling his musky masculine scent with a hint of spice, which is typically Remy. He wraps his lean, muscular corded arm around me and I rest my head on his shoulder.

"A tub of Ben and Jerry's, you get to pick the flavour, a weepy film of the ladies' choice, pyjamas and duvet on the sofa. How does that sound, beaut? I might even stretch to a bottle of that pink wine you like."

I smile and nod at his attempt to make me feel better.

"There's my favourite smile."

He kisses me affectionately on top of my head.

"Sounds perfect, babe."

He nods and looks over at Freddie, who is sleeping in the seat next to him in his carrycot.

"He's out for the count."

As I look over at my son, the tears I have held in since the hotel lobby with Sam start to freely flow down my cheeks. I can't stop the endless torrent of tears that escape. Remy rubs his hands up and down my back and pulls me as close to him as I can get, despite the armrests of the aeroplane seats. In that moment, I am content to let him hold me, and the feeling is enough to send me into a dreamless slumber, thirty thousand feet up in the air.

***

That feeling when you return home from a trip or a holiday and everything is exactly the same as you left it, but you feel totally different. That is exactly how I feel as soon as Remy opens the door to our house in Santa Monica.

"It's so good to be home, beaut."

Remy sighs and strides in ahead of me with Freddie in his carrycot. He stirs and giggles loudly, and Remy sets him down on the sofa while I unbuckle him from the confines of his carrycot. His large, inquisitive, green eyes cause my heart to stutter; they remind me so much of Sam. I pick him up and hold him close, inhaling his sweet scent of baby lotion.

"Hey baby boy, we're home."

Remy switches on the T.V, and the news is on.

"Worldwide rock phenomenon Rancid Vengeance have released a statement concerning tattoo artist and former fiancée of lead singer and frontman, Samson Newbolt. Peyton Harper, now twenty-eight, has been found alive and well after being allegedly murdered by the band's then manager, John Dalton, a.k.a Johnnie Diamond. Police have questioned Miss Harper, and no further charges have been bought forward. The band have released a statement regarding recent developments."

My head snaps up at the mention of mine and Sam's name. I still find it strange and I can't get my head around the fact that the press deems me newsworthy. As I look up at the screen, I am greeted by the sight of Sam and the band's lawyer, Vance Stryker. Sam is still a sight to beholden. He towers over Vance, wearing black skinny jeans, a black hoodie, with the words '*#TeamVengeance*' emblazoned in large white letters across the front and the sleeves rolled up to reveal his tattoos and his bandaged wrists. To complete his look, he wears a black beanie hat and black biker boots. His face looks pale. He has dark circles underneath his eyes, and his expression is so sombre that it breaks my heart a little more. Cameras are flashing wildly, and as the rowdy chatter of the press and news reporters dies down, Sam clears his throat and begins to speak.

"We feel nothing but great relief to know that Peyton has been found alive and well. The year that followed her apparent murder and disappearance took its toll on us as a band. However, we have come through the other side, stronger and closer than before. The music will always remain our number one priority. Nevertheless, my relationship with Peyton is at present, complicated, due to current circumstances. Our relationship will continue to remain amicable, for the sake of our son, who was born in her absence. We do not blame Peyton, nor do we hold any grudges towards her, for her actions. The blame lies solely at our former manager, John Dalton's door, and any further questions will go through our lawyer, Mr Stryker. Thank you."

Sam nods curtly as the cameras continue to flash wildly. He handles the press with professionalism and quiet control. I stare at the screen in shock at Sam's words. His green eyes look as though they are staring straight into my soul and I can't comprehend what I have just heard. Even though, just hours ago, I tore his heart out, he still found it in his heart to stand up and speak out for me, letting everyone know the truth. Despite what has happened between us, he doesn't blame me. Remy sits down next to me and brushes my hand.

"Are you ok, beaut?"

I swallow back the lump in my throat, willing myself not to cry, and I nod while plastering a smile on my face.

"Yeah, I'm fine. Thanks, babe."

Remy narrows his eyes.

"Do you want to say that again? Maybe a little more convincingly? Because I don't believe that bullshit for one second," he says drolly.

I look up at him, his deep brown eyes saying more than words ever could. "I'm so fucking confused, Rem."

I cuddle Freddie closer to me, and he wriggles restlessly in my arms.

"What's there to be confused about? You're not the same girl who I found collapsed and practically unconscious in a hotel parking lot a year ago. You've turned into a strong, brave, beautiful, and independent woman. You're a fantastic mum to Freddie; that kid adores you. You've come through the worse year of your life, and you're still standing; you're a survivor. I think you're fucking amazing, and I admire you for not letting what you went through destroy you."

My eyes glaze over at Remy's words, and he softly strokes my knuckles with his thumb.

"The biggest mistake I ever made was running away from the best thing that happened to me. I was a fucking coward for walking away from the girl I loved, and I can't apologise enough for that, beaut. I was young and stupid. I had my chance at happiness, but like a complete dick, I fucking blew it."

He laughs bitterly, and I am taken aback by his words. He says them with such passion and sincerity, that I almost wish I reciprocated his feelings. He kisses my forehead and gets to his feet, leaving me dumbstruck on the sofa to process his words.

***

I don't see Remy until the next morning; I am sitting on the deck at the back of the house, overlooking the calm ocean and our pool. The early morning sunshine is blazing down, and I'm wearing my pyjamas consisting of a grey skull vest top, black shorts and a pair of UGG slippers. I am clutching a cup of coffee and am enjoying the peace and quiet calm before Freddie wakes up. The neighbourhood is so serene, and the only sounds are the birds singing their early morning melody. I lean back with my legs tucked underneath me and look up at the clear blue sky, wondering how things became so complicated in the space of a few weeks. Both of my lives, my life as Peyton Harper and my life as Louise Stonebridge, have collided in an epic fashion. I no longer know who I am anymore, and I am craving the simple, anonymity from two weeks ago.

"Penny for your thoughts, beaut."

Remy's soft, soothing voice interrupts my thoughts, and I look up, greeted by the caring brown eyes of Remy Logan. The man, who for the past year has been my rock, and has taken care of me and my son when we've needed him the most. This morning, Remy's long brown hair is pulled into a low ponytail. He is wearing blue and white checked pyjama bottoms and a tight white vest that clings to his lean frame and showcases his hard muscles. His olive skin is sun-kissed, which emphasises the smattering of freckles on his sharp, angular nose.

"I can hear you over thinking, you know it's not good for you," he says, with a hint of amusement to his voice.

He takes a sip of his coffee and sits down on the padded wicker sofa next to me.

"Have you decided what you're going to do yet, beautiful?"

I lean back and sigh audibly.

"I have no fucking idea, Rem; I'm torn. Being here with you, I've had some of the best times of my life. Moving here was a fresh start for me, but the past few weeks and having Sam back in my life... it's made me question everything. I don't know who the fuck I am anymore. Am I Peyton Harper, or am I Louise Stonebridge? All I know is that I'm not a coffee barista, Remy. I'm a tattoo artist, it's all I've known for ten years. Taking my tattoo machine away from me is like removing a limb. Becoming something I'm not and never will be...it's been so fucking hard for me to adjust to life under someone else's name, under someone else's rules, in a country I don't know."

He takes a sip of his coffee, which I poured for him, and regards me tentatively.

"I think you've just answered your own question."

He cocks his eyebrow and takes a sip of his coffee.

"Things have been so fucking crazy over the past few weeks; hell, this year has been crazy. There have been times when all I've wanted to do is curl up in a ball and hide away. There have been nights where I've closed my eyes and I've dreamt so clearly of the life I could have had. J.D safely locked up behind bars, me, Sam and Freddie living our happily ever after in his castle in the sky, touring with the boys. I've woken up and reached out for him, but all I've found is cold sheets and an empty space."

My voice shakes, and Remy reaches for my hand. He softly strokes my knuckles and clutches my hand, in a gesture of reassurance.

"I think you've already made up your mind."

He smiles warmly, but it doesn't reach his eyes.

"Remy," I say softly, and he lets go of my hand, as if I've burned him.

He swallows harshly and clears his throat before he begins to speak.

"I think it's best for both of us that you go back home to London, beaut. I'm sorry, but it hurts so fucking much knowing that nothing will ever come of you and me. After spending the past year with me, you know I love you. I've always loved you; I never stopped. I love you completely. You were *it* for me. I can't compete with Mr Fucking Perfect. Go back home and forget about me."

His words render me speechless. He gets to his feet and looks at his watch, avoiding my gaze. *I guess the saying is true, if you love someone enough, you have to let them go.*

"I'm going to be late; I need to get to the bar for a delivery," he says in a clipped tone, and before I can speak, he limps back into the house.

Looks like I'm going back home to London. *Fuck.*

***

Tomorrow is the day I return to the life I left behind a year ago. As I begin to fold and pack our stuff together, the door to my bedroom taps softly.

"Beaut?" Remy says cautiously.

His words from earlier echoing in my ears, *"I think it's best for both of us that you go back home to London, beaut. I'm sorry, but it hurts so fucking much knowing that nothing will ever come of you and me. After spending the past year with me, you know I love you, I've always loved you, I never stopped. I love you completely, you were it for me. I can't compete with Mr Fucking Perfect. Go back home and forget about me."*

"Can I come in?" he questions.

This is a new side of Remy that I haven't seen before. The vulnerable, cautious, shy side of him. It is almost as if I am faced with the twenty-year-old Remy from all those years ago, before life happened and took us down different paths, away from each other. My blue eyes lock with his russet ones, and I nod. He steps in the room and tucks his hands in his pockets.

"I wanted to apologise for earlier, beaut. I was angry, and I didn't mean those things I said, none of them. I was a complete dick, and I'm so sorry. If I could take back those words, I would, in a heartbeat. *Jesus,* I don't want you to go, Peyton; I've felt more alive in this past year than I have in a long fucking time. I meant it when I said I loved you; I've been in love with you ever since Ruby bought you back to our house for tea that day, with your pigtails and your infectious giggle."

I smile at the memory, and he steps closer to me.

"What can I do to make you stay, Peyton?" he says gruffly, as he stalks forward until I can feel his warm breath on my cheek. "Tell me what I can do, beautiful girl," he says desperately, taking me in his arms and pulling me to his chest.

I'm helpless to resist, and I know I should walk away, but as soon as his lips touch mine, I'm lost. With each stroke of his tongue, I feel a tiny part of my soul die. This is a goodbye kiss, the kind of kiss that destroys me, the kind of kiss that rips and tears at my insides and ravages my heart, piece by piece. It's slow, sensual and tells me everything he hasn't been able to say for the past year. That he loves me. *Remy Logan is in love with me.*

He is the first to pull away, and we are both breathless. His face is flushed, and his russet brown eyes are almost black and hazy with desire. I am inwardly warring with myself, debating whether this is a good idea, when his gruff commanding voice interrupts my thoughts.

"Decide, beaut. Yes or no?"

I look at him, and everything about him is screaming at me to say yes. I make a split-second decision and throw caution to the wind. I crash my lips to his and fumble with his belt. He growls animalistically and our lips briefly part, allowing him to pull my top off with ease. I pull his belt loose and unzip his trousers. It is a rush who can get naked first as his jeans drop to the floor and he steps out of them, kicking them to the side. It is only then that I notice he has gone commando, and his bare erection presses into me as I turn around. My back is to his chest, and his lips find my neck. He is kissing and nipping softly at me while I reach around to undo my bra. I shrug out of my bra and his soft hand cups my breasts.

"So perfect, beaut, so fucking perfect," he whispers hoarsely as his other hand snakes down and into my jeans.

His long finger finds my clit, and he circles it, softly at first, then increases his pace. I moan softly as he takes my nipple between his thumb and forefinger. The rhythm matching the one he has on my clit.

"Remy."

His name is like a plea on my lips, and he chuckles softly against my neck.

"I won't leave you hanging. I'll make you feel good, I promise."

He pulls his fingers out of my trousers, spins me around, and lifts me up, depositing me in the middle of the bed. He pulls my jeans off, along with my knickers, until I'm completely naked and lying wantonly, waiting for his next move. He strips his black t-shirt off, and I lick my lips at the sight of his tight abs, the clean lines of his muscles, and the perfect ripple of his eight pack. He looks like he could model Calvin Klein underwear with his narrow hips, defined muscular thighs and the light dusting of hair underneath his belly button. Only if you look hard enough, can you see that he has a prosthetic leg, even though the skin tone is a near perfect match.

He fists his cock in his hand as I stare at him, taking every inch of him in and committing his perfect form to memory, as if I'll never see him again.

"I'll get a complex if you keep looking at me like that, beaut."

He smirks wickedly, and I bite my lip nervously. He stalks forward, until he is hovering above me on the bed.

"Don't be nervous, I'll show you how long I've waited for this moment."
He reaches down and strokes my hair.

"I'm going to make love to you, the way I should have all those years ago."

He moves forward until he is straddling me, and I reach for his fully erect cock. I stroke it in my hand and he growls.

"*Fuckkk!* That feels good."

I smile, and he throws his head back in pure ecstasy.

"*Oh, Jesus fucking Christ,* stop, I'm not going to last if you carry on."

I pull my hand free and reach over into my drawer to take out a condom. Remy cocks his eyebrow.

"Always prepared?"

He smirks, and I nod.

"You never know when a hot guy might drop by!" I say sassily, and we both laugh.

"Let me know when this hot guy drops by, I'd love to meet him."

He winks cheekily, and he takes the condom from me, tearing the foil wrapper with his teeth. He rolls it down onto his erection, and I lick my lips at the sight of his length. He is at least seven inches and the thick, angry veins running down his shaft make it a thing of beauty. He settles between my legs, and he pushes forward to enter me. As I adjust to his length, I moan softly as he moves gently in and out. The truth is, I haven't had sex for a whole year. The last time I had sex was with Sam, before Freddie was born and before my life was turned upside down. I will myself not to think of the last time and enjoy the moment, here and now, with Remy. My childhood sweetheart, my rock, my saviour, my guardian angel.

"Oh God, beaut, you feel amazing," he growls.

I mewl softly as he moves in and out at a painfully slow pace. *This isn't fucking, this is making love.* With every thrust, he drives me higher and higher towards my orgasm.

"Rem," I whimper, and he increases his thrusts, expertly swivelling his narrow hips. I am moaning and panting, as his pace quickens with every slow, deep drive. "*Oh fuck,* Remy."

With one brisk move of his cock, I feel my orgasm explode from me.

"*Fuck,* Remy...Oh shit, I'm going to come!"

He pushes his cock into me to the hilt as I scream out. My orgasm floods through my whole body, making me quiver as he explodes into me at the same time.

"Let go, come with me, beaut."

As he finds his release, he whispers *"I love you."* I tangle my fingers in his long brown tresses and pull him closer to me, unable to say the three words he desperately needs to hear. I press my lips to his, and as I relish the feel of his soft lips on mine, he coaxes my mouth open and his tongue strokes mine. His kiss is so tender and so gentle it makes me want to weep. The last time he kissed me it didn't feel this good, this...right. *I need this.* I need him to take away the heartbreak, the feeling of loss, the sad, miserable truth of my pathetic life. I'm returning to London after a whole year of living with this kind, beautiful, caring man in a place where the sun shines all year round. I'm trading that for the dull, cold, wet weather of Camden, London, England. The place that should be and has always been home to me. The American dream was good while it lasted, but I'll always be a London girl at heart. *Home is where the heart is, right?*

42

Peyton

When I wake the next morning, Remy is still sleeping next to me, and his soft snores filling the otherwise silent room. I swing my legs out of bed and pad to Freddie's nursery as quietly as I can, trying not to wake him. I don't do goodbyes, not after last night. I can't, and I don't want to taint what we shared with the threat of goodbye.

I check on Freddie, and he is still sleeping too. I take advantage of the silence, and I use the en-suite bathroom. I shower quickly, brush my teeth, and leave my hair to dry naturally. I wrap a towel around myself and walk quietly through the house into my room. I dry off and pull on some clothes, opting for a black, white and red skull print strapless sundress. I pull my red Converse on and reach for my phone. I dial the number I need and walk out onto the deck, taking in the glorious ocean view for one last time. The early morning sun is reflecting off the turquoise ocean, creating an ethereal shimmer, as if the ocean's surface were covered in millions of diamonds.

"This better be good, honey, I was just about to be ravished by Channing Tatum!"

I laugh as Joel's voice, thick with sleep, fills my ears.

"Good morning to you too, babe. I'm sure you can put Mr. Tatum on ice, because I need a favour, please?"

He chuckles softly.

"What can I do for you on this fine morning, honey?"

I pause before I begin to ask him.

"I need you to take me to the airport, please, Joel," I ask him nervously, and he sighs.

"Are we losing you to London, sweet cheeks?" he says in his soft, American twang that has become familiar to me.

"I'm afraid so, babe. I'm sorry. Look, something happened between Remy and me last night. I'll explain when I see you, but I can't do goodbyes, Joel. I just can't. I need you to take me and Freddie to the airport."

I hear the creak of his bed.

"Of course. Anything for you and the little guy. Did you do the nasty with Mr. Tall, Dark and Brooding?"

Joel chuckles wickedly, and I giggle girlishly at his question.

"A lady never kisses and tells!"

He snorts.

"I'll have you singing like a fucking budgie by the time Aunty Joel is finished with you!" he says dramatically and we both laugh. "Right, honey, I'll grab a shower, and I'll come get you. You bet your fine ass the coffees on you though. Be ready, hugs."

I hear the phone click off before I say goodbye, and I start to think how much I will miss the life I have become accustomed to, here in Santa Monica, and the friends I am about to leave behind. I think of the man, who is currently sound asleep in my bed, unaware that the woman he is madly, deeply in love with is about to leave him without saying goodbye. *Fuck me, I'm such a bitch.* It has to be this way, I can't allow him to see me before I leave. There are too many reasons why I should stay and continue my life here. However, there are also equal reasons why I should go. One being the fact that Remy told me he loves me. I wish to God I could say it back to him, but I don't love him the way he loves me.

I have that to explain to him, but I can't do it in person because I'm a fucking coward. I can't write it a letter because there's too much I have to say. While I am inwardly warring with myself, I hear the sound of Joel's car pull into the driveway. I rush into the nursery to grab a sleeping Freddie and our luggage. I strap him into his carrycot, trying desperately not to wake him up. I take Freddie outside and see Joel in his electric pink *Chevy Camaro SS* convertible. Every time I see him driving it, it makes me miss my car desperately. He is in the driver seat, wearing a white vest, sunglasses and his blonde hair is perfectly styled.

"Beep, beep bitch!" He laughs. "Your carriage awaits! If I had a hat, I'd be sure to tip it!"

He winks animatedly, and he steps out of the car to give me a hand. He takes Freddie, and I go back for the rest of my luggage. As I grab the handle of my suitcase, I look up to see Remy's tall, looming figure, standing in the doorway. *Fuck.*

He is wearing only a pair of grey Calvin Klein boxer shorts, the light grey of the boxers contrasting with the bronze of his skin. He has his hands on his hips, and the look in his eyes all but breaks my heart.

"You were just going to leave, without saying goodbye?" he asks incredulously, and I shake my head.

"I'm not good with goodbyes, Rem," I say, with a slight waver to my voice.

He hangs his head and laughs bitterly.

"And you think I am? *Fuck me!* I know last night was a one-time thing, I was under no illusion that we were going to walk off into the sunset together, but I at least deserved some sort of fucking goodbye."

A tear slips free from my eye, and I angrily swipe it away.

"This is exactly why I don't do goodbyes, Remy."

He stalks forward, still wearing just his boxers and he stops in front of me. He tucks a strand of my hair behind my ear and pulls me to him, enveloping me in his arms. It takes everything I have to hold it together at the feel of his strong, familiar arms around me.

"I'm not pissed, beaut; I'm hurt, *so fucking hurt*. If you're going to go, just go," he whispers flatly in my ear.

Remy releases me from his warm embrace, and I feel bereft as the torrent of tears I've been holding back, burst free. He kisses my forehead tenderly, turns around, and walks away.

The twenty-minute drive to the airport is filled with my quiet, inconsolable sobs and Joel's whispered words of sympathy and reassurance. He pulls up outside LAX, and he helps me with our luggage and Freddie, who is now wide awake and smiling his cheeky dimpled grin, reminding me so much of Sam. Joel towers over me and looks into my eyes.

"It's been an adventure, sweet cheeks, even though you weren't who I thought you were. You've been such a good friend to me, to us all."

His voice shakes, and I swallow back the lump that has formed in my throat. I'll never forget the friends I made over this past year, and I hope we'll always stay in touch. He pulls me into his arms, and I hug him tightly.

"Don't you dare cry, you'll set me off. We won't say goodbye, just...see ya later alligator. And you bet your lily-white ass, that if I'm ever in London, I'll be sure to look you up."

He pulls away and winks, with tears in his eyes.

"You'll always be welcome, babe, and thank you, for everything."

He takes my hand and squeezes it reassuringly.

"It's been a pleasure, Peyton. I know if you could have told me you would have, and I'm sure B and Henley will understand."

He plants a kiss on the back of my hand.

"And I'll be damn sure to keep Mr Tall, Dark and Brooding warm for you!"

He winks, and we both laugh.

"Now go, before I start sobbing like a big girl! Don't be a stranger, sweet cheeks."

He kisses me gently on the lips; I pick Freddie's carrycot up and pull my luggage behind me.

"Love ya, Joel."

I blow him a kiss, and he sobs softly.

"Right back at ya, sweet stuff. Now go and don't you dare look back."

I smile to myself and walk into the airport, away from the life I've built for myself for the past year. I'm going back to the life I left behind, diving in at the deep end and back into the unknown.

I am settled in my seat in economy bound for Heathrow airport, London. After take-off, Freddie fell asleep, and I am sitting here contemplating what the fuck I'm going to do when I get back to London. *Will I get my job back at Saint Sinner? Will the people I left behind be different with me? Will the press be waiting for me when we land in London?* Those are the thoughts that linger in my already crowded mind as I drift off into a fitful sleep somewhere in the middle of the Atlantic Ocean. I am woken by a flight attendant, just as we're landing at Heathrow. My stomach somersaults at the thought of being back in the U.K. I grab my hand luggage, Freddie's carrycot, and wait until the plane is virtually empty before I start to make my way down the aisle. As I step off the plane and back onto British soil, the thought that dominates my overactive brain is, *welcome back to London, Peyton. It's been a while.*

43

Peyton

I hail a local taxi outside Heathrow to take me back to my old flat in Camden. The journey takes an hour, due to the rush hour traffic. As we pull up outside my flat, I pay the driver and jerk the keys that Sam gave me the last time I saw him out of my pocket. I make my way apprehensively into the building that houses my old flat. Jimmy, the doorman from Sam's old building in Greenwich, is on the concierge desk. He tips his hat, and I nod as I head for the lift. I drag my luggage and Freddie's carrycot inside. The lift stops at my floor, and I can't help thinking that something is familiar, yet so different. I walk to the door and unlock the large white reinforced door to my flat. *Home.* The place where I felt safe, my sanctuary, looks so... different. I push open the door; it looks as if it has been knocked into the flat next door too.

The living room is larger; the kitchen is filled with brand new state of the art appliances, including a cooker, microwave, kettle and a coffee machine. It looks so much more open and lighter. As I take in the large, empty space that was once my old flat, I break down. I let the tears that have been building up inside of me fall down my cheeks in large rivers of sorrow. I slide down the wall and onto the floor, unable to bear the weight of the sadness I feel crushing me any longer. I put my head in my hands, and I sob. I sob harder than I've sobbed in a long time, gut-wrenching wails of utter despair. My life as I once knew it, is gone. The clean, bare walls and the empty space that I once called home is just another shell. A cold, stark shell.

I hear a soft tap on the open door, and I look up into the shocked eyes of my neighbour, Danny Debonair, as his alter ego, Debs. He is dressed in full drag, wearing a short, red, sequinned dress, which makes his long, smooth, tanned legs look amazing and put mine to absolute shame. He has thick makeup on, smoky eyes, red lipstick, a long, thick, dark brown curly wig, perfectly manicured, blood red nails and six-inch, red glittery stilettos. He looks like a million dollars, and if I didn't know he was a man dressed as a woman, I would genuinely think he was a real woman. His pouty red lips form a perfect *'O'* shape, as he takes me in.

"*Fuck me backwards*, baby girl."

His high pitched but soft voice, only makes me cry harder.

"Oh, come here."

He sinks down to the floor next to me and pulls me into his lean arms.

"Shhh, I've got you. It's going to be alright," he soothes and strokes my hair gently.

He looks at Freddie's carrycot on the floor next to me and cocks his perfectly plucked eyebrow.

"*Fuck me,* we've got some catching up to do."

I look up at him and offer him a watery smile.

"I've missed you, Debs." I choke out, and he cups my face in his manicured hands.

When he is in drag, he likes people to call him by his drag name.

"I've missed you too, so much. Now, are you going to fill Aunty Debs in on what the fuck is going on and why you look like you've lost a tenner and found a pound?"

He smiles softly.

"Why are you not mad, Debs?"

He strokes my hair with his hand and kisses me on the forehead.

"Because a certain little gossip whore called me and told me that you were alive! Must be those pregnancy hormones, but she couldn't wait to fill me in on *all* the gory details."

He winks, and I smile. *I might have known Ruby would have called him.*

"It's all such a huge fucking mess, Debs. I've messed up so epically, and I don't know how I'll *ever* make it right."

I sob softly, and he shakes his head.

"I think we're going to need something strong for this conversation, baby girl."

He reaches into his red patent clutch bag and pulls out a bottle of vodka. He unscrews the lid and winks, offering me a sip.

"I never go anywhere without this, babe, liquid courage. It's five-o clock somewhere in the world!"

He smiles warmly as I take a long pull on the vodka, and I relish the burn of the smooth fiery liquid as it slides down my throat, instantly warming my stomach. I offer the bottle back to Debs, and he takes it, screwing the lid back on.

"Good girl. Now come on spill, tell Aunty Debs *everything*. And don't you dare bloody miss anything out."

He winks, and I lean back against the wall. He slings his arm around me in a gesture of comfort, and I begin to fill him in on the past year. Leaving nothing out, I start to tell him about J.D, the fucking evil, despicable things he did to me, getting away from him to protect me and my son, Remy, rebuilding my life in Santa Monica under a new identity, giving birth to Freddie, and everything that happened in between, up until I was temporarily reunited with Sam. I choose to leave out sex with Remy. *That's a story for another time.*

"*Wow!* Fuck me."

He puffs out his cheeks, lets out a breath, and wipes a stray tear from his overly made up eye.

"You've definitely been through the wringer and then some."

He sniffles as he hands me back the bottle of vodka.

"Take the fucking bottle, you need it more than me, babe!"

He chuckles, and I manage to laugh right along with him.

"It sounds like the plot to one of those trashy erotic fiction books that Ruby reads!"

I sigh.

"Something tells me this story isn't going to have a happy ending, Debs. I broke his heart by telling him I couldn't be with him. I don't deserve his forgiveness."

Danny sighs. He throws his arm around my shoulder, and I snuggle into him.

"From the moment I met that boy, he had heartbreaker written all over him. It's good you got there first. It might be the old queen in me, but he's got nothing to forgive you for. You were doing what was right for you and your son, who by the way, is *the* cutest little human I've ever seen!"

I lay down and curl up on the floor, with my head resting in his lap. He strokes my hair softly, and I suddenly feel exhausted, mentally and emotionally.

"He would show up here every day without fail. The first few months were the worst. He would show up here with a bottle of vodka every time I left for work, and he was an absolute mess. I would get back from the club, usually in the early hours of the morning, and I would hear him crying; I mean like proper sobbing, it was fucking awful. A few times, I thought about knocking on the door, but I didn't know how he would react to a six-foot bloke in a dress!"

We both laugh, and he continues to stroke my hair gently.

"Things have a habit of working themselves out, baby girl. He wouldn't have knocked into the flat next door if you didn't mean anything to him. He turned up with a team of workmen around a week ago, and they worked all hours of the day, just to get it finished. Besides, if things don't work out, the way to get over one man is to get under another!"

He winks, and I sit up. *If only he knew.* He wipes a tear from my eye with the pad of his thumb.

"Look, I'm not comfortable leaving you alone, right now. How about I call in sick, and we can catch up some more?"

I nod, happy he suggested it, because I really don't want to be alone right now.

"I'd really like that, thanks, Debs."

He pulls me in for a hug and kisses my cheek. He pulls me to my feet.

"You're welcome. Give me five minutes, and I'm all yours."

He blows me a kiss and leaves the flat. Twenty minutes pass, and he's back clutching two bottles of white wine, two glasses, and a corkscrew. He has changed into a purple velour tracksuit, UGG boots, and he is still wearing his full makeup. His dark hair is flat and unstyled after removing his wig. He closes the door with his foot and places the bottle, along with the glasses, down on the floor. He sits down on the floor, in the middle of the bare living room, with his legs crossed and gestures for me to sit down with him. I sit down with Freddie in my lap.

"I've called in sick at work, after an Oscar-worthy performance!"

He fakes a cough, and I chuckle.

"I've ordered a meat feast pizza with extra mushrooms, cheesy garlic bread, and BBQ chicken wings, your favourite, baby girl."

I smile at his thoughtfulness. *He knows me so well.* We spend the next couple of hours catching up on the past year, filling in the gaps. By the time I have finished, it's like I was never away. We are both suitably tipsy, and Freddie is asleep in his carrycot. I yawn, and Danny laughs.

"Fucking lightweight," he mocks, and I childishly stick my tongue out.

"Jet lag is a bitch, babe. I think I might head to bed, if that's ok?"

He nods, as he finishes his wine.

"Yeah, of course, baby girl. You look cream crackered. Get some sleep, and I'll pop back in the morning to check on you; take care."

He winks, and I hug him tightly. *I have missed him so much.*

"Good to have you back, gorgeous."

He turns around, blows me a kiss and leaves. I leave the glasses and the pizza box on the floor. I'm so exhausted; all I want to do is go to sleep. I change Freddie's nappy and I navigate my way around my flat. I open the door to one of the bedrooms and find it completely furnished. There is even a cot for Freddie, with a guitar-shaped mobile above it next to a king size bed. I have no doubt in my mind that this is Sam's doing. He really has thought of everything. The mountain of pillows on the bed looks so inviting, that I almost dive headfirst into them. I open the second door and step into the bathroom. I am overwhelmed by the white, black and silver decor, a corner Jacuzzi bath, a large glass, walk-in shower, with what looks like a built-in surround sound system, a glass sink and a large gilded mirror over the counter. The floor has light grey floor tiles, and the walls are adorned with silver, black and white mosaic tiles. I splash some cold water on my face and look at my reflection in the mirror. I have dark circles underneath my eyes, and I look like I feel tired, so fucking tired. I make my way into the bedroom and pick Freddie's sleeping form up, laying him gently down in the cot. I pull the blackout blind down and collapse fully clothed on the bed. Soon, I am a slave to sleep.

***

I wake the next morning feeling refreshed, and I'm ready to face the day with renewed purpose. I leave Freddie sleeping as I make my way into the bathroom. The flat seems so quiet without Ruby. I take off last night's clothes and step into the spacious walk-in shower. I let the water sting as it rains down on my body. After I finish my shower, I dry off and check on Freddie. He is wide awake and smiling.

"Good morning, my handsome boy," I coo and pick him up, taking him into the kitchen, to explore our newly spacious flat.

I open the frosted glass cupboards, and I find cups. In the next cupboard, I find bags of coffee and sugar. I open the under counter fridge and find a fresh pint of milk. *Thank you, Sam.* I take out a cup and a bag of coffee then load up the coffee machine. It takes me a few attempts, but I manage to get it working, and the aroma of fresh coffee, soon fills the flat. *My favourite smell in the world.* I sit Freddie in his carrycot and set about unpacking some of my stuff from my suitcase. With at least some of my stuff around the place, it starts to feel like home again.

I style my hair, apply natural makeup, and get dressed. Today I opt for a pair of dark denim cropped jeans, a black t-shirt with the slogan *'This is my zombie killing shirt'* in white lettering, with red blood splatters all over it. I am just pulling on my black Converse trainers when there is a knock at the door. I open the door apprehensively, and I take in the man mountain that is standing in my doorway, with his hands casually tucked into the pockets of his dress trousers.

"Cole Benedict sent me, darlin," he says, in a soft Texan drawl.

"Who are you?"

I try to sound confident, but the tremor in my voice betrays me.

"Like I said, Cole sent me, doll. My name is Kai Hunter, friends call me K," he says casually, and I shake my head.

"I don't believe you."

I regard him intently and take him in. He has blonde hair shaved close to his head, deep, piercing indigo eyes, and at least three days' worth of rough, blonde stubble on his chin. He is at least six feet seven inches tall with broad shoulders, narrow hips, and he is extremely muscular. *I think his muscles might have muscles!* He is wearing an expensive black suit, tailored perfectly to fit his large frame, consisting of a white shirt, black tie, black trousers and a black jacket that stretches across his impressive ample shoulders.

"Can I at least come in?"

I narrow my eyes, and I move warily away from the door to allow him to step inside. He looks around as he coolly takes in his surroundings.

"I don't need you here; I can look after myself just fine," I say flatly and fold my arms defensively across my chest, without taking my eyes off him.

He untucks his hands from his pockets, and as he does, my heart beat starts to quicken. I suddenly feel a panic attack start to threaten. *Shit.*

"Please, leave," I say as calmly as I can manage. *Deep breaths, Harper.*

"Look, I'm here under Cole Benedict's orders, darlin'. It's more than my job's worth, and I'm afraid I'm not going anywhere unless Cole tells me to," he says sedately.

I silently count back from ten in my head, and by the time I get to one, I feel a little calmer.

"Please, just go. I don't need you here."

I scrub my hands down my face, quickly losing my patience at this man, who is built like a brick shit house.

"No can do, doll."

I feel intense anger at this man, who is standing in my flat, intimidating the fuck out of me.

"PLEASE JUST FUCKING LEAVE!" I scream, and his eyes widen.

"Calm down, darlin'. I'm not going to hurt you."

He holds his hands up defensively.

"Alright, fine! I'll get Cole on the phone, he can tell you himself."

He takes out his mobile phone, and I swear I hear him mutter *"crazy bitch"* as he dials a number, putting the phone on speaker so I can hear Cole.

"Hey, boss, it's K. I'm at Miss Harper's, as requested. She doesn't believe that you sent me."

I hear Cole curse.

"Hey K, thanks for letting me know. I'll deal with it from here, mate. Sugar, are you there? It's Cole. Look, he isn't lying. I sent him to help. Sam asked me to arrange some protection for you and Freddie upon your return. He's the best at what he does. Kai comes highly recommended, and he's a trusted member of my team. I wouldn't just have anyone working for me; you should know that, sugar. I only hire the best, and I trust him implicitly."

Cole's deep, rumbling timbre fills my ears, and I instantly feel a little calmer after my almost mini-meltdown.

"Sugar, I need you to talk to me."

Kai looks at me, prompting me to speak. *He must think I'm a complete idiot.*

"I'm here," I say softly.

"Please tell me you'll let Kai look after you, sugar. Sam and I need to know you and Freddie are safe. It will put his mind at ease and make my job easier, you know what Sam's like. At least while Sam's not there. The boys are doing promotion for their new album and tour, but he'll be back in London soon. The safety of his son is his number one priority," he says gruffly.

"Ok, but I'm doing this for Sam and Freddie," I say reluctantly, and he chuckles softly.

"Ok, sugar, thank you," he says, distracted by a voice in the background.

"Sugar, Sam wants to talk to you."

I hear rustling, and Sam's husky voice fills my ears.

"Hey angel, how are you and my little rock star?"

I smile at his nickname for Freddie, and he sounds as if our harsh words from a week ago never happened.

"We're good, thanks. How are you?"

He chuckles softly.

"All good, angel, all good. I just wanted to say I hope you don't mind that I knocked into the flat next door, you've got two extra bedrooms. It's bigger for you and Freddie. All of your stuff is in storage at your parents' house in Brighton, and your car is my garage; none of us could bear to get rid of it, so it's all still there. I could arrange for it to be picked up and delivered to the flat today, just say the word, babe and it's done."

My heart warms at his thoughtfulness.

"That would be great, thank you."

He chuckles softly.

"Anytime, angel. Consider it done, I'll make some calls. Kai's there to look after you. His speciality is close protection, so if you need anything at all, let him know, and he'll take care of it. That includes driving you anywhere you need to go."

I look at Kai, and he is casually leaning against the wall with his arms folded, listening intently to our conversation.

"I have to go, but I'll be in touch, angel. Give Freddie a big kiss from daddy...bye."

He doesn't give me a chance to say goodbye before he hangs up. I fold my arms and regard Kai intently as I hand his phone back to him. He tucks his phone into his pocket.

"I'm sorry; I didn't mean to act like a complete psycho bitch, I don't make a habit of it," I say as he throws his head back and laughs.

"I've dealt with worse, believe me, doll."

He shrugs nonchalantly, as if he deals with neurotic, screaming women every day of his life.

"Should we start again?"

He smiles and nods as he straightens his jacket, offering me his hand.

"Kai Hunter, pleasure to meet you, darlin'."

I laugh and shake his hand.

"Peyton Harper, pleased to meet you too, Kai."

I let go of his hand, and we stand in an awkward silence for a few moments.

"Do you want some coffee?"

He nods.

"That would be great, darlin', thanks."

He pulls his phone back out of his pocket. He takes off his suit jacket and hangs it up, on the coat hook that's to the left of the doorway and begins to roll up his sleeves, revealing thick, muscular, corded arms.

"So, Cole tells me this used to be your place?" he asks curiously, and I nod.

"Yeah, I used to live here with my best friend, Ruby."

He smiles.

"Ah, the little piranha fish. She's a force to be reckoned with!"

We both laugh at his nickname for Ruby, and he sits down on the floor. He pats the space next to him.

"We may as well make ourselves comfortable, darlin'. I would run out to get you breakfast, but I've been specifically instructed not to leave you alone, under any circumstances."

I sit down next to him and pull Freddie's carrycot closer, so I can take him out. I unbuckle the straps and pick him up, cradling him close to me.

"Hey handsome boy, mummy's here."

He turns his head and his inquisitive green gaze locks onto Kai.

"Hey, little buddy."

I stroke Freddie's cheek.

"This is Kai; he's going to look after us until daddy gets home," I croon, as Kai starts tapping on his phone.

"So, tell me about you, Kai Hunter," I ask inquisitively.

"I'm Kai Hunter, like I said, and my friends call me K. I'm thirty-seven, and I've worked for Cole for...eight or nine years, give or take. Before that, I was in the United States Marine Corps."

I nod. *Wow, the Marines? That explains the size of him!*

"Are you married?" I ask out of curiosity, and he smirks.

"Yes, I have a wife, Gabriella. We got together in our junior year, been together ever since. We have a daughter, Brooke, she's almost six years old now."

He takes out his wallet and shows me a picture of a beautiful brunette woman, with long waist length, poker straight hair and a little girl, who looks like she inherited the best of both parents. I smile.

"Wow, they're both beautiful. You're a very lucky man."

I feel inwardly jealous of their happiness. I've lost a whole year with Sam, and he's missed six months of his son's life. I'll never be able to take that back, and that thought causes a lump to form in my throat. He chuckles softly.

"That I am, doll."

I hold Freddie close to me, taking in his familiar, unique baby smell. I get up from the floor and go into the kitchen to prepare the coffees. The sound of Kai clearing his throat makes me jump, and I let out a strangled gasp.

"*Shit,* I'm sorry. I didn't mean to scare you, doll," he says apologetically as I spin round to regard him.

His sleeves are rolled up, showcasing his thick, bulging muscles and showing his United States Marine Corps tattoo on his left bicep. The top button of his shirt is undone, and his tie is loose around his neck. He has a small silver stud in his ear, and his eyes are piercing blue, complimenting his blonde hair and tanned complexion. I lean against the worktop with Freddie in my arms, waiting for the coffee machine to finish.

"So, why exactly are you here, Kai Hunter?" I ask, and he smirks at the use of his full name.

He tucks his hands in his pockets and leans back casually against the breakfast bar.

"Like I said, darlin', just doing my job, following orders."

With those words, the coffee machine finishes, and I prepare both cups. "Sugar? Milk?"

He shakes his head.

"Black's good, thanks, darlin'."

I make him a cup and push it across the worktop. He takes it, nodding his thanks, and I make my own. I put in sugar and milk, stir it, and take a welcome sip of the hot liquid as I take in all six feet seven inches of Kai Hunter. I start to think to myself that maybe having a bodyguard won't be that bad.

Half an hour later, I grab my bag, pull on my khaki green Parka, pick Freddie up and leave the flat, closely followed by Kai. I walk down the plush, carpeted corridor and push the button for the lift down to the lobby. The lift arrives, and we step into the lift in silence. A few moments pass, and the lift stops at the lobby. I step out and walk across the foyer, nodding to Jimmy, who salutes and winks. I smile warmly as we exit the building. Parked at the kerb is a large, black 4x4 Land Rover with blacked out windows. Kai opens the passenger door for me, and he straps Freddie in the back seat, in a specially fitted car seat. He puts his carrycot in the boot and comes back round to the driver's side. He started the engine and pulls smoothly away from the kerb.

"Where to, darlin'?" Kai says in his American drawl.

"Saint Sinner Ink, in Islington, please?"

He smiles and nods curtly. I lean back and spend the journey wondering what the fuck I'm going to say to Seb when I get there.

When Kai pulls up outside the shop, I let him exit the car first. He then comes around to my side to open the door. I step out onto the pavement, and as I look up at the shops exterior, my heartbeat starts to quicken. I notice that everything still looks the same as it did a year ago. The shop sign, in its signature yellow and black, reminds me that I'm home. Kai unbuckles Freddie from the backseat and hands him to me.

"I'll wait here, doll," Kai says, and I'm grateful that he chooses to let me do this my way.

I hold Freddie in one arm and push the door open with the other. The bell rings, signalling someone entering the shop, and his eyes snap up from tattooing his client. *Seb.* He instantly stops what he's doing. He gets up from his workstation and walks slowly over to me, as if he can't believe what he's seeing. He looks exactly the same as he did a year ago. Seb is six feet six inches tall, well-built and very muscular from his short time in the S.A.S and work as a doorman. He has tattoos on every inch of his body, except for his face, head and hands. He has dark, intense, electric blue eyes, and dark hair, which he always used to keep shaved bald, but now it has grown out into a short faux hawk. He has added a tattoo of a black and grey rose on the left side of his neck, and a small diamond stud in his ear.

"Peyton."

His voice is gruff with emotion, and I see him swallow hard. He tears his gloves off and throws them into the metal bin next to his workstation. I walk towards him, and he walks forward at the same time. He crushes me to him and almost lifts me off the floor.

"*Fuck me,* babe."

His voice is shaky, and I don't think I have ever seen Seb cry in all the years I have known him. He pulls away and looks at Freddie, then back at me.

"He's Sam's," I answer his unspoken question as Seb's eyes widen and curses softly.

I feel everyone's eyes in the shop focused solely on us. Seb frowns, and he realises I'm feeling more than a little exposed.

"Babe, do you and the little dude want to go into the back? Stick the kettle on, and I'll be right there, as soon as I'm done."

I nod, and I make my way into the back of the shop. It all looks the same as when I left it. The back of the shop is cosy, homely and inviting. It has a comfortable black and zebra print sofa that seems to swallow you when you sink into it, a few beanbags scattered on the black carpeted floor, framed movie posters adorning the walls, a storage area where we store our personal stuff, a desk in the corner where we used to deal with the paperwork, a Bluetooth speaker, and a small kitchen area in the back with a kettle and a microwave. I look around and point to some of the tattoo art on the walls.

"Look, Freddie, this is what mummy's job used to be. Isn't it pretty?" I coo, and he giggles.

I arrange the cushions on the sofa and lay Freddie down. I busy myself making two cups of coffee while keeping a vigilant eye on Freddie. I smile to myself that all the cups are in the same place they have always been. I'm not sure how much time passes, but I am startled by Seb's deep voice.

"For the record, I'm not angry with you, babe. I could *never* be angry with you. I'm just disappointed, and I'm so fucking hurt that you thought you couldn't come to me and tell me that you were ok. I lost my best friend, my fucking little sister that day, and it hurt like you would not believe. I've known you since you were that innocent, vibrant, fresh-faced, persistent as hell eighteen-year-old, with the kick-ass portfolio, and the personality and the attitude to match."

I hang my head in pure shame at the look in Seb's eyes. I can't stand the look of hurt, mixed with such intense disappointment. I think my already broken heart broke that little bit more as his gaze drops to the floor. He swallows and promptly changes the subject when he begins to speak again.

"The shops doing really well right now. We have back-to-back bookings, and we're fully booked for the next six months. I've tried to make exceptions for the odd walk in, but it's just not possible right now. The cable channel has picked the TV show up for a new series, *Inked @ Saint Sinner* and I want you on board. The shop hasn't been the same without you, Peyton. Harley and Parker have been working for me, and I've had the odd guest spotter to pick up the slack when we've been busy, but I need my best girl back where she belongs. The jobs yours if you want it?"

I smile and nod my acceptance, pushing his cup towards him. He picks it up and regards me intently.

"Thank you, thank you so much."

My voice is barely a whisper and thick with emotion.

"You haven't got to thank me, babe."

He folds his thick, corded, heavily tattooed arms across his chest and looks into my watery blue eyes. I hate myself for putting that look in Seb's eyes.

"I am so sorry, Seb."

He shakes his head, puts his cup down and opens his arms.

"Come here."

His deep voice is oddly comforting me. I step into his embrace and he envelopes me in his strong arms. I cling to him, as if I'm using him as a lifeline. I breathe in the musky, intoxicating scent that is pure masculine Seb Henry. It smells familiar; it smells like home and all things safe.

"I would have kept you safe, babe. I was in the SAS for fuck's sake, how could you have doubted that I would have protected you with my fucking life? I would lie down in traffic for you. *Jesus,* you mean the absolute world to me, Peyton. This past year without you has been absolute fucking hell."

He holds me tighter, and I start to sob. I'm clinging to him with everything I have, taking comfort from this six-foot-six gentle tattooed giant who has me wrapped in his arms.

"It's going to be alright, I promise you. They're going to have to come through me first. You're safe now. No one's going to hurt you, *ever.* Not while I'm around, and not while I've got breath left in my lungs."

He squeezes me tighter and strokes my back soothingly.

"I guess I've got another person to take care of now too."

He chuckles. I smile against his chest and nod.

"His name is Freddie. He's almost seven months old, and he's Sam's son. I *had* to protect him, Seb."

He pulls away and looks at Freddie.

"*Fuck me,* he's definitely Sam's kid. He's beautiful, just like his mum."

I smile shyly and hit Seb playfully on his arm.

"Flattery gets you everywhere, Henry! Anyway, how's your love life? You were quite smitten with a certain Miss Newbolt, if I remember rightly?"

I cock my eyebrow knowingly, and I swear I see Seb blush. *That is a sight I've never seen before, and it suits him.*

"*Wow!* Seb Henry blushing! I thought I'd never see the day!"

He chuckles softly and nods thoughtfully.

"Yeah, Willow and I are still together, casually dating and doing the grown-up thing. You know how it is! I met her family, and she's met my mum."

My eyes widen, and I smile warmly. Seb would never take anyone to meet his mum if he wasn't serious about her. He's fiercely protective of his mum, Tracy, who he affectionately calls 'The Duchess'.

"I love her, Peyton, she's...Willow. She's crazy, feisty and funny. She's...*everything* I never knew I was looking for; she gets me. We're on the same level, and she was my rock after..."

He stops himself, and I see the pain evident in Seb's eyes. My heart shatters all over again, and my gaze drops to the floor.

"I was in a dark place for a while, but she got me through. I don't blame you, babe. You did what you had to, for you and your son. You're a survivor, and you look like you've been through hell and managed to claw your way back through the other side...because you're strong, and you're...you. What I'm trying to say is, if you ever need to talk about anything, day or night, no questions or judgement, I'm here for you, babe."

He squeezes my hand in his and smiles tenderly. We both finish our coffees, put our cups in the sink, and I pick Freddie up, cuddling him close to me.

"Congratulations, being a mum suits you."

I smile softly, and I follow him back out into the shop.

"The place looks different, love what you've done with the décor," I say sarcastically, and Seb chuckles throatily.

"Funny! God, it's so good to have you back, babe."

He kisses me gently on the forehead. The truth is, the shop looks exactly as it did a year ago. The shop is a fairly large and open space, decorated in a simple black and white, with black and white floor tiles throughout. There is a large work area, split into three sections for Seb, Parker and Harley. Each station has a leather chair which folds down into beds, a small desk for drawing up designs, a sterilising machine, each has a large shelf with various inks and a drawer section, which holds spare needles, tubes, grips, tips, machines and latex gloves. At the front of the shop, there is a reception booth with a large desk and a comfortable leather office chair. The only difference I notice is, an iPad on the desk, which has replaced the iMac computer, printer and telephone. There is a small waiting area with a small leather sofa and a coffee table in front of it, with various tattoo magazines and design books neatly piled up. The walls are adorned with various tattoo designs, which customers can choose from. I look up towards my old workstation and my eyes widen at what I see. My tattoo machine, which Seb gave me the day I started as his apprentice, is in a large black box frame on the wall. It's a deep purple personalised *Micky Sharpz Iron Hybrid* machine, with silver tribal patterns and my initials '*P.H*' on the top encrusted in Swarovski crystals. Underneath the machine is a picture of me, smiling as I'm tattooing a client. As I move closer, I notice my name, date of birth and date of death. My heart slams against my rib cage. I'm aghast at the extent of what I put those close to me through when I chose to stay away.

"I couldn't bear to get rid of anything that reminded me of you, so Willow suggested framing it as a tribute to you."

Seb's deep rumble snaps me from my thoughts as a tear slips free and tracks it way down my cheek. Seb catches it and wipes it away with his thumb.

"Don't cry."

He pulls me in for one of his famous Seb Henry bear hugs, trying not to crush Freddie.

"I'm so fucking sorry, Seb. Please, forgive me."

He squeezes me tighter and takes Freddie from me. Freddie looks tiny in Seb's large, muscular arms. He holds him close and smiles softly.

"Hey, less of that. You've got nothing to be sorry for. You're safe now, babe... you and this little guy are going to be the most protected people in London. I promise I'll guard you both with my life."

With those words, I know Seb would do everything in his power to protect me and Freddie. I don't doubt those words for a second, and I know he will make good on his promise.

44

Peyton

I have been back in London for almost a month now, and a lot has happened in the month of my return. The press found out about my return and follow me around constantly, taking my picture, and desperate for a story, like a pack of hungry wolves. There is always a crowd of them camped outside my building, which is why Kai is currently residing in one of my spare rooms. He has become a permanent fixture in my life, under the strict orders of Cole.

Also, this past month has been filled with sleepless nights thanks to both Freddie teething and the constant vivid nightmares of the ordeal I suffered at the hands of J.D. I see J.D's face shrouded in darkness, his maniacal laugh, and his wide crazy eyes. In my nightmares, I see Sam behind J.D, willing him to do the things he did. Even though I know it isn't real, I can't help but feel hatred towards Sam for it, to some extent. I wake up in a sweat, gasping for breath and pleading for my life. It is affecting my life in such a big way, that I don't feel in control of my own life anymore. I feel so helpless, and I almost wish I had stayed in Santa Monica.

I have gone back to my old hair colour, in a vain attempt to find the girl I left behind a year ago. I have all my stuff out of storage and back where it belongs. I have the flat decorated and looking like a proper home again, thanks to the help of my parents, Dexter, Eden, Danny, Grace and Ruby. The living room is royal blue with a feature wall, consisting of a navy background, vivid blue parrots and silver gilded cages. The carpet is navy, and I have a navy suede sectional sofa, which you sink into when you sit down. It also has various cushions scattered across it. Often, for the past few weeks, I have found myself falling asleep on it after enduring several crippling nightmares. I have a flat screen TV mounted above the white fireplace, a glass coffee table and a media unit which houses my extensive DVD and C.D collection. The room is kitted out with various matching blue accessories, including a selection of blue and white photo frames and a selection of large beanbags.

The kitchen is red, black and white, modelled like a nineteen fifties style diner. The main feature wall is a red, black and white London scene, with the red phone boxes standing out from the stark black and white of the black London cabs, Big Ben and the London Eye. The state of the art appliances match the decor of the kitchen, including a red chrome kettle, a black coffee machine, a red microwave, black and chrome built-in cooker, a black American style fridge with alphabet magnets scattered across the front, and red tea, coffee, and sugar canisters. Over the cooker are black splash back tiles, and the floor consists of black and white tiles. At the black marble breakfast bar, sits black and red stools and to complete the look is a red and black striped blind at the window.

My bedroom has a zebra print feature wall above my California King bed, which Remy generously shipped over from Santa Monica, along with some other things that I accumulated from my time there. Next to the bed are two black lacquered bedside tables, with a picture of me and Freddie in a frame. The rest of the walls are dark aubergine and are covered with a series of arty tattoo prints that my dad took, pictures of me and Ruby, Freddie, and my family and friends hanging in black frames on the walls. The window has a wind chime hanging in the centre and blackout blinds. I have a zebra print chaise in the corner of the room, and a dark purple carpet completes my sanctuary from the world outside.

Freddie's nursery is next to my bedroom, and his large white cot takes up a section of the back wall. Next to his cot is a changing station with a grey changing mat on the top. Underneath are various drawers, which house baby wipes, nappies, clothes, nappy rash cream and everything I need to change his nappy. The walls are painted in a light blue with a grey border and sports different musical notes and instruments. Above his cot is the guitar-shaped mobile Sam left, his name spelt out in colourful letters, and a picture of us posing on the bonnet of Remy's Shelby GT while looking carefree and happy. It is my favourite picture so far.

Seb has given me back my old job, as a tattoo artist and shop manager at Saint Sinner Ink, and I am settling back into my role, as if I was never really away. I have been throwing myself into work, tattooing clients and doing what I do best, not allowing myself time to think. I am trying so hard to make amends for disappearing as well as adjusting to life back in London as a single working mum. Ruby looks after Freddie during the day while I am at work, and I will be forever grateful to her for allowing me to do what I love and to provide for me and my son, even though Sam is more than willing to support us financially. Freddie is my whole world. He is so pure and innocent, my angel. Just as I was Sam's angel. *Sam.* I can't stop thinking about him, but I know I made the right decision to end it between us. It was for the best, for all of us.

Tonight, Ruby is babysitting Freddie at her insistence that I need some time to myself to let my hair down. The truth is, she's right. I need to forget. I need to drown my sorrows in the bottom of a large glass of vodka. *Neat.* I enjoy the burn as it slides down my throat. It offers me a rare moment of calm where my mind is completely numb. I don't want to think, I don't want to feel. I just want some...peace. Peace from the cacophony of noise that is my fucked-up mind.

I am sat in a bar called JJ's Inferno. I am perched on a bar stool while wearing a short black leather skirt, which makes my tanned legs look amazing. I also have on a black and white, polka dot, halter neck, corset top, which hugs my slim figure and emphasises my boobs, along with my black Christian Louboutin heels. My short, dark brown hair is secured by a black polka dot headscarf, and I am knocking back vodka. The barman doesn't say a word; he just waits for me to shoot my drink and replaces my empty glass with a new one. He doesn't ask questions, he just quietly observes me in a silent understanding. He probably thinks I am some desperate drunk woman, hoping to get laid; but he couldn't be further from the truth. I'm damaged goods now, and J.D's words echo in my ears.

'Sam doesn't do damaged goods.'

A lone tear slips down my cheek, and I quickly swipe it away. The barman replaces my drink and leans over the bar. He is extremely good-looking, with sculpted, chiselled cheekbones. He is tall, muscular, and has a shaved head with a black goatee beard and black-rimmed glasses. He has kind but unusual, silver-grey eyes and he is wearing dark jeans, which hug his hips, and a black shirt with the name of the bar embroidered on the left breast pocket. The sleeves of his shirt are rolled up to reveal vivid, colourful tattoos wrapped around both arms. He has his nose and his ear pierced.

Why are you always so attracted to tattooed bad boy Sam clones, Harper?

"Tell me to mind my own business, petal, but do you want to talk about whatever it is that's making those baby blues of yours look so sad?"

His voice is deep and rich as he smiles warmly, revealing perfectly straight, white teeth.

"A beautiful lady like you shouldn't be in a place like this alone."

His voice is filled with concern.

"I'm tougher than I look, honey, but thanks for your concern though. I appreciate it."

I smile, but I know it doesn't reach my eyes. He leans over the bar, and his muscles flex underneath his shirt, temporarily distracting me from my pity party.

"I'm Jack, by the way."

He introduces himself as I shoot back my drink and push the glass towards him, eyeing him warily.

"Peyton," I murmur.

He reaches for my hand and shakes it, gripping it gently while filling my glass with his other hand.

"So, do you want to talk about it? I've been watching you all night, petal, silently filling your glass. It's like watching a car crash that I can't seem to tear my eyes away from, but I can't watch anymore. You look like you could use a friend; you look so...lost."

He regards me intently, cocks his head to the side and pushes my now full glass across the bar.

"It's fucked up; *I* fucked up," I say quietly, but to the point.

Jack leans across the bar and softly brushes my hand reassuringly.

"We all fuck up at some point, petal; it's how we come back from it that counts. Like a Phoenix rising from the ashes, you come back stronger, you come back fighting. You look like a tough, beautiful, independent woman, who looks like she's hit a rough patch, and that's ok. It's ok to talk, it's ok to admit it and ask for help. You're only human."

His words are so wise and kind. I feel tears stinging my eyes from this stranger who knows nothing about me, but suddenly seems to know everything all at once.

"I hurt someone I loved; unintentionally. I made a bad choice, and I wish I could go back and change it, all of it."

He smiles kindly, and he cocks his head.

It seems the alcohol is making me want to wallow in my own self-pity. Great.

"Things have a habit of working themselves out, don't give up."

He leans closer to me, as if sharing a secret.

"I'll let you into a little secret, we men are extremely stubborn, and we don't realise what we've got until it's too late. It's in our DNA."

He winks, and I smile at his optimism. I shoot back my drink, and he refills my glass again.

"You should consider slowing down, petal."

I narrow my eyes at him and shoot back my drink insolently.

"I think you should consider minding your own fucking business," I snap, and he holds his hands up defensively.

"You're going to regret it in the morning; that's all I'm saying. No judgement here. You're going to wake up with one killer hangover."

I shrug. The truth is, I don't care. I'm way past caring. The constant nightmares are taking a toll on my sanity, and my finger is pressed firmly on the self-destruct button.

"Go and make it right."

I shake my head.

"I can't, I don't know how to anymore. It's over between us. I can't give him what he needs, Jack. I can't be the woman he fell in love with, it's not possible."

My voice is shaky, and I swallow past the lump in my throat, knocking back my drink. My head is spinning now, and I feel like I'm floating.

"I'm damaged, Jack, look at me! I'm a fucking mess! Don't you see?" I slur. "I'm broken, and I'm a selfish fucking bitch."

I let out a strangled sob, and the few people that are left in the bar are staring at me.

"Don't talk about yourself that way, petal."

I fumble with my purse and throw some money haphazardly onto the bar.

"I'm sorry, Jack, I have to go."

I climb from the bar stool and stumble as my feet touch the floor.

"*Shit!*" Jack curses and vaults over the bar.

He's at my side in seconds and steadies me. I balk as his muscular, corded arm wraps around my waist, and I push him away.

"I'm fine!" I snap, and he sighs.

"No, you're not fine. Please, at least give me your phone and let me call someone for you. It's not safe for you on your own out there."

I shake my head; the tears are falling freely now.

"No, please, I just need to go home," I sob.

I struggle from his strong grip, and I stumble again. I fall into his hard chest.

Fuck me, I'm so drunk. Who keeps moving the floor?

The room is starting to spin, and he steadies me. I just want to forget. I need to forget, just for a little while.

I look up at Jack, and before I know what I'm doing, I press my lips urgently to his. I expect him to push me away, but his hand snakes around my back, crushing me to him, and I rest my hand on his warm chest. His heart is beating erratically. His tongue feels like velvet against mine, and his lips are so soft. A soft moan escapes from my throat, and I need him to take it all away. I need him to make me forget. He sucks on my bottom lip, and his free hand wraps in my hair. I can feel his erection pressing into my stomach, and I reach down to stroke him through the material of his jeans. He growls and breaks our kiss.

"*Fuck.*"

We are both panting and breathless, all eyes of the bar patrons are on us.

"*Fuck! Fuck! Fuck!* We can't do this," he curses, and I shake my head.

"I want you, Jack."

His hand tangles in my hair and pulls me closer to him.

"Don't say things you don't mean, Peyton."

He rests his forehead on mine and looks in my eyes, as if he is waging an internal war with himself.

"I want you, please, Jack," I say more forcefully, and he closes his eyes.

"You don't know what you're asking for, petal. I only do one-night stands. I'm a complete prick, and I'm fucking selfish. I'll take your number, but I won't call. I'll break you. I'm not a good person."

I shake my head.

"Maybe I don't want you to call; maybe I want a one-night stand. I need you to take it away, Jack, please."

The truth is, it's what I need, what I've been craving. I need to forget Sam and move on, once and for all.

"*Christ alive,* what the fuck are you doing to me?"

Jack nods curtly and drags me across the room.

"Watch the bar, Nate," he calls out.

Jack pulls me into a back room with a pool table in it and closes the door behind us, flipping the lock. He stalks towards me and wraps his hand in my hair, tugging it gently. He crashes his lips against mine and kisses me deeply, his velvet tongue probing my mouth.

"I've been watching you all night. Fuck me, you are so fucking hot."

He breaks our kiss and lifts me up onto the pool table.

"Spread your legs wide for me, petal," he says sternly.

I do as he says, without question. He reaches down under my skirt and slides my knickers to the side. He sweeps his finger up my slit and growls.

"Christ on a bike, you are fucking soaking."

I reach for his erection and stroke him through his jeans. He moans softly and places his hand over mine on the bulge in his trousers.

"That's it, look how hard you've made me. You're such a bad girl."

I shiver at his words, and he pushes a large finger into my aching pussy.

"*Oh, Jesus!*"

He moves in and out, increasing his pace until I am practically riding his hand. He introduces another finger, and I lean back on my elbows, allowing him more access.

"Do you like me finger fucking your wet pussy?"

I bite my lip.

"Mmm," I moan, and it's all I can manage as he introduces a third finger.

He increases his pace, and I throw my head back as I feel my orgasm rippling to the surface.

"God, you're so fucking close, I can feel you throbbing against my fingers."

I moan loudly, as his thumb finds my sensitive swollen nub.

"*Oh, Jack!*"

He grins, like the cat that got the cream.

"That's it; give it up for me, Peyton."

He increases the motion, and I find myself panting for him.

"Look at me, petal; I want to watch you come."

His voice is demanding and authoritative. I open my eyes and my blue eyes lock on to his grey ones. His eyes are blazing and hooded with lust.

"Good girl, let go. Come for me now."

It's all it takes for my orgasm to tear through me like a lightning bolt. I scream loudly as Jack squeezes every last ounce of pleasure out of me.

"*Jesus,* that was the fucking sexiest thing I've ever seen, watching you come around my fingers like that."

His voice is low and seductive. I look at him, my eyes hooded with lust.

"I need you to fuck me now, Jack."

He smiles and starts to unbutton his shirt, revealing a large, muscular, tattooed chest. He takes off his glasses, and he looks so ruggedly handsome. He drops his shirt to the floor, slips off his biker boots and starts to unzip his jeans. He drops them to the floor, along with his Batman boxer shorts. My eyes widen as I catch sight of his impressive erection. He is huge and has a piercing on the end of his bell-shaped head.

"Do you want me to fuck you hard and fast, Peyton, or slow and gentle?"

I bite my lip.

"Hard and fast. Fuck, I need it hard, Jack," I pant desperately, and he nods.

"Nice choice, petal."

He winks as I take off my halter neck top and wriggle out of my leather skirt. Soon, I am laid on the pool table in just my black lacy French knickers. I am not wearing a bra.

"*Fuck*, you're so sexy."

I feel self-conscious of the scars that J.D left me with, but the dim lighting in the room conceals them, making them virtually unnoticeable. He steps closer to me and cups my breast in his large hand, flicking my nipple piercing.

"You have perfect tits, petal," he rasps.

Jack rolls my already erect nipple between his fingers, and I moan softly.

"Mmm, that feels so good."

He leans down and takes my nipple between his teeth, nipping gently. His other hand reaches down and tears my knickers off completely, the ripping echoes through the room. He shoves a finger into my pussy roughly and kneads my breast.

"I love how fucking wet and ready you are for me."

His voice is low and raspy.

"Are you ready for my big hard cock?"

I nod.

"*Answer me*," he orders.

"*Yes!* I'm ready for your cock, Oh God! Yes! Please fuck me, Jack!"

My voice is breathy and desperate as he removes his finger from inside me and reaches down into his jeans pocket. He tears a foil condom packet open with his teeth and sheathes himself.

"Look at me, petal. I need your eyes. Show me those eyes as I enter you."

My eyes lock with his smoky greys as the head of his thick cock finds my entrance. He shoves forward, entering me forcefully and causing me to cry out.

"Ahh!"

He stills, as a look of quiet concern washes over his rugged features.

"Are you ok, petal? Am I hurting you? Do you need me to take out my piercing?"

I shake my head no, and a look of satisfaction crosses his handsome face.

"OH GOD JACK! DON'T STOP! PLEASE DON'T STOP!"

I pant breathlessly. He nods and pushes himself deeper inside me.

"Harder! Oh, fuck me harder!" I scream.

"Do you like it hard and fast? You look like a hard and fast kind of girl."

I nod as he pistons in and out, filling me to the hilt as his piercing rubs against me in the most delicious way.

"Good answer, petal. Do you like it rough?"

I nod.

"Oh Jack! Give it to me, I need it hard and fast," I growl.

He pulls my hair and presses his lips to mine desperately. His rough goatee beard grazing my chin. I wrap my hands around his neck and pull myself up, riding his cock as his pace becomes frantic and urgent. He thrusts deep, and he moans.

"*Oh fuck!* You feel so good around my cock."

He lifts me up, so my whole body is laid on the pool table, and he climbs on top of me.

"Wrap those gorgeous legs around my waist and dig those fucking sexy heels into my arse."

I do as he asks and wrap my legs around his lean waist. I dig the points of my heels into his deliciously tight arse cheeks, and he throws his head back in ecstasy.

"*Jesus fucking Christ!*" he growls.

His thrusts become fast and hard. I writhe beneath him, panting and cupping my breasts in my hands.

"That's it, gorgeous, grab those beautiful tits."

He looks down at me with hooded eyes and his hand snakes down my flat stomach to find my swollen clit. He rubs my nub in lazy circles, and I can feel another orgasm rising. I arch my back up to create a delicious friction as his relentless rhythm becomes urgent.

"Let it go, that's it, fucking come all over my cock."

That's all it takes for my orgasm to ripple through my entire body.

"JACK!"

With one more thrust, Jack shouts his own release.

"FUCK, PEYTON!"

He collapses, spent on top of me. We are both left breathless and panting. After a few minutes, he pulls out of me, pulls the condom off, knots it, and throws it in the bin on the other side of the room. I watch him walk naked; his body is taut and athletic. His tanned legs are muscular, and he has full, vivid, colourful leg tattoos.

"Are you checking me out, petal?"

He chuckles throatily; I sit up and bite my lip.

"I might be. Do you have a problem with women shamelessly checking you out, Jack?" I say sassily, and he cocks his eyebrow.

"Not at all, especially if they're all as beautiful as you are."

I laugh.

"Flattery as well, wow and here's me thinking you were a bad boy."

He laughs too.

"I can be whatever you want me to be, petal," he says seductively, and I lick my lips.

He is extremely handsome, and he reminds me of a muscular, tattooed and pierced version of the male model, David Gandy. He starts to dress, pulling on his boxers, jeans and shrugging on his black shirt. I jump down from the pool table and start to dress too. We both dress in a relatively awkward silence. He finishes buttoning up his shirt, and there's a loud rap on the door, which makes me flinch. If he notices, he doesn't say anything.

"Jackers, I've closed up the bar for you, dude. All you need to do is cash up and lock up."

Jack clears his throat, avoiding my gaze.

"Cheers, Nate, I really appreciate it."

I hear a chuckle from the person outside.

"See you tomorrow, Casanova; I'll see you at the Green Parks at six a.m. sharp. Don't be late."

Jack laughs to himself.

"Yeah, no problem, man. I'll be there. See you tomorrow Nate, give Melody a kiss goodnight from me."

I hear the door close, and Jack opens the door. He walks out into the bar, and I awkwardly follow. Jack is behind the bar pouring us both shots of neat Sambuca. I perch on the same bar stool I was sitting at all night, and he pushes the glass across the bar. We both shoot it back at the same time, and I grimace at the burn at the back of my throat. He laughs.

"Can't keep up the pace, huh?"

I slam my glass down on the bar in challenge.

"Again."

He cocks his eyebrow and refills both our glasses.

"Let's play a game."

I smile as I am reminded of the game that Brody and I played on the tour bus in happier times, back when my life passed for normal. I nod.

"A girl after my own heart."

He smiles a dazzling smile.

"Right, we're going to play a truth game."

I laugh.

"After you take your turn you take a shot. I'll go first. I'm Jack Scott, I'm thirty-four, and this is my bar."

I cock my eyebrow. He takes a shot and smirks roguishly.

"I was keeping you on your toes, petal."

He winks, and I roll my eyes.

"I'm Peyton Harper, I'm twenty-eight, and I'm a tattoo artist. I work for Seb Henry, and I have a six-month-old son, called Freddie."

His eyes widen.

"You have a son?"

I nod.

"*Shit the bed,*" he curses, and I take a shot.

He refills our glasses.

"Are you...?"

He doesn't finish his sentence, but I can only imagine what's going through his head, so I finish for him.

"Am I still with his dad? No, I'm not with him currently. It's a long, complicated story. I won't bore you with it."

His mouth forms a perfect *'O'* shape, and he takes a shot.

"*Fuck*, you're...certainly full of surprises," he rasps and refills his glass.

"Ok, how can I follow on from that? Erm...I'm single, and when I'm not here, I'm a part-time male model. I'm also a travel writer and blogger. I have a brother, Nate, the guy who knocked on the door. He has a little girl, my niece. She's three years old. His wife, Hope, died of cancer just after Melody was born, and now it's just the two of them. We're extremely close...I'm relatively boring compared to you, petal."

He knocks back his drink.

"You're not boring, you're...*normal.*"

We both laugh.

"Normal I can cope with. So who's the mystery man who you hurt so badly?"

I take a deep breath, wondering if I can actually go through with telling Jack all about my complicated and sordid past with Sam. I knock back my drink for some Dutch courage, and he refills it immediately. It is as if he senses my reluctance to talk about my past.

"It can't be that bad? Who is he? Don't tell me he's some international mob boss who's embroiled in a conspiracy and on the run from the police."

He chuckles at his own joke, and we shoot back our drinks at the same time. *Here goes nothing.*

"Sam Newbolt."

He almost chokes on his drink.

"Sam Newbolt, as in Bolt from Rancid Vengeance, the rock band? *Fuck me.*"

I push my glass across the bar to him, and he refills both glasses.

"*Wow,* you're..."

I finish his sentence.

"...complicated, fucked up, broken, a complete disaster. Yep, all of the above, definitely."

I laugh bitterly, and he reaches for my hand.

"I was going to say brave, beautiful...complicated...yeah, but aren't we all to some extent?"

Something tells me that the game has ended, and we're not playing anymore.

"My life is a fucking car crash, Jack. You should run in the opposite direction."

I knock back my drink, and I feel tears stinging my eyes. He shoots back his drink and wipes his mouth with the back of his hand. He tops off both glasses in silence. I shoot back my drink and get up from the barstool. My head feels fuzzy, but I feel comfortably numb.

"I should leave."

I stumble as my feet hit the floor again, and Jack makes his way around the bar. *I need to get out of here.*

"Don't go, petal," he rasps, and he towers over me as he stands in front of me. "At least let me call you a taxi, please. It's not safe out there for a woman by herself; I would offer to drive you but looks like I'll have to call Nate to come and take my drunken arse home!"

He smirks, and a tear escapes from my eye. He wipes it away with the pad of his thumb.

"I'm so sorry. You don't need this, you said yourself you're not a good person."

My voice is small, and he lets out a breath.

"I didn't say I didn't want you, Peyton, I'm not a complete dick. All I'm saying is, I don't know *how* to do relationships. I leave the loo seat up, I leave my dirty underwear on the floor, I can't cook and I can just about work the microwave. I snore, and I'm terrible in the mornings until I've had at least three cups of strong black coffee."

I chuckle, and he smiles.

"There's that smile you've been hiding. Please sit down."

I sit back down on the barstool.

"I'll be right back."

He winks and strides across the bar to what I assume is an office. For the first time tonight, I check my phone. I have eight text messages and three missed calls. I close one eye to focus on the screen and scroll through my texts. Four are from Sam, and the rest are from Ruby and Brody.

Hey babe

How's it going?

Little man asleep

Jax and the boys sang him to sleep ☺

Reminded me of that scene in Three Men and a Baby! I recorded it, will send you the video, babe. We can keep him until tomorrow if you want?

Give you a break, you deserve it.

Let me know

R x

I scroll down.

Are you ok, babe?

Please call me

I'm starting to get worried

R x

I scroll to the next message.

Sam's was ready to tear the walls down

He's gone looking for you

Just giving you a heads up

Please call me, sweets

Let me know you're ok

Brody xxx

I open the next message.

Angel

Please call me

S x

As I gradually go through each text from Sam, they get more frantic.

Let me know you're ok, angel

I'm going out of my mind

Please

S x

I scroll down.

Call me, or I'm coming to find you

S x

I roll my eyes. *My possessive rocker, how I've missed you.*

FUCK this!

That was all the last message from him said.

Jack emerges from the office; he has changed out of his black shirt and into a tight white vest, which clings, to his muscles. His vest showcases his colourful, tattoo sleeves, and he looks delicious. I lick my lips at the sight of him.

"Is everything ok, petal?" Jack says, and I nod.

My phone starts ringing, and I really can't deal with Sam right now, so I reject the call. A few seconds later, it rings again, and I reject it again.

"Do you need to get that?"

I plaster a smile on my face and shake my head.

"No, everything's fine. It's not important," I say nonchalantly.

He narrows his eyes, and my phone starts ringing again. I roll my eyes and reluctantly answer it.

"*Jesus! Fuck!* Thank Christ you're alright, angel. Where are you?" he says, before I even get to say hello. His voice sounds hoarse and exasperated.

"Stop calling me, I'm not your fucking concern anymore," I snap, and he growls.

"Stop fucking saying that! You're the mother of my child, angel; you *are* my god damn concern," he roars.

"Please just leave me alone, Sam."

He breathes, and when he speaks again, his voice is softer.

"Look, where are you? You shouldn't be on your own, angel; it's not safe. I'm coming to get you."

I run my hand through my hair.

"I don't fucking need you! I'm fine!"

I raise my voice, and Jack regards me intently.

"Is everything ok, petal?" he says, and I nod.

I try to smile, but I know it doesn't reach my eyes.

"*Whoa!* Who the fuck was that? I'll ask again, angel, where are you?" he shouts, and a tear slips down my cheek.

I curse my emotions to hell for letting him get to me like that. I know I'm hurting him, but it's better this way. I have to let him go. Jack strides across the room and snatches the phone from my hand.

"Look, mate, you need to calm down, you're upsetting the lady...Yeah I know who you are...that's really none of your business...I'm just a concerned friend...you've made her cry...no, I don't give a fuck...I don't know what you've said to her, but I'm not standing by while you upset her...it doesn't sit well with me...I'll make sure she gets home...she's safe with me...no she doesn't want to fucking see you...no *you* fucking listen to me, mate...you're going to hang up the phone and I'm going to make sure she gets home safe...I know you don't know me, but I'll make sure she calls you in the morning...I'll take good care of her, you have my word...ok good...bye."

He hangs up the phone and hands it back to me.

"I can't believe you just fucking did that!" I shout, and he smirks.

"Man, that guy was pissed!"

He chuckles, and I narrow my eyes at him.

"You had no right to fucking do that!" I snap, and he holds his hands up defensively.

"Calm down, I'm sorry, ok? Look, come back to mine, it's not far from here. I'll take you home in the morning, I promise. I've got a spare room; you can even lock the door if it makes you feel safer. No funny business."

Should I really be jumping head first into another relationship, when I'm clearly not over the last one? The truth is, I'm still madly in love with Sam, but no matter how many times he says he forgives me, I'll always feel that distance between us. *If you love him enough, let him go.*

"Petal?"

Jacks voice cuts through my thoughts, and I start to panic.

"*Fuck!* I can't do this."

His face is filled with concern, and I feel a panic attack threatening. *Shit.*

"Just breathe."

He moves closer to me and cups my face in his hands.

"Breathe," he says softly.

"I-I."

I feel a panic attack rising, and my chest tightens. My breath comes in short bursts, and the tears are flowing freely now.

"*Jesus.*"

He moves me to a corner booth, sits me down, and drops to his knees in front of me.

"Deep breaths, yeah? It's going to be alright, I promise. I'm not going to hurt you, you're safe," he whispers softly and reassuringly.

He breathes with me and clasps my hand in his, stroking my knuckles gently. Soon my breathing returns to normal.

"I told you I'm damaged, Jack. I'm sorry," I choke out, and he shakes his head.

"You've got nothing to apologise for. Before tonight, I thought I could only do one-night stands, but something about you makes me want to try, Peyton. I know it's only been few hours, but there's a connection between us, I can feel it every time I'm near you. Give me a chance to show you that we can heal each other."

An overwhelming sense of fear and dread takes hold, I really can't do this. *Why would he pursue me when he knows I'm clearly hung up on Sam?*

I get to my feet and run, leaving Jack on his knees, stunned at my reaction. I have to get out of here. I push open the bar door and walk out onto the street. The cool air hits me, and suddenly, I feel drunker than I did when I was inside. As I step out onto the pavement, a photographer leaps out of the shadows and flashes a camera in my face. He continues the '*click, click, click*' of his shutter as an unfamiliar large black Chevy Warrior truck with tinted windows and two white racing stripes up the length of the bonnet comes to a stop at the kerb.

"Angel."

Sam's familiar rasp echoes through the open window.

Oh fuck.